PHIL TOMASSO III

THIRD RING

A Nicholas Tartaglia Thriller

Published By
Barclay Books, LLC

St. Petersburg Florida
www.barclaybooks.com
A Spectral Visions Imprint

PUBLISHED BY BARCLAY BOOKS, LLC
6161 51ST STREET SOUTH
ST. PETERSBURG, FLORIDA 33715
www.barclaybooks.com
A Spectral Visions Imprint

Printed and bound in the United States of America

ISBN: 1-931402-11-6

Other Books by Phillip Tomasso III:

TENTH HOUSE

MIND PLAY

And as Editor:

DRY BONES ANTHOLOGY

Special Thanks

It is sometimes hard for me to believe that already I am having my third novel published. Only a few years ago I thought about not writing anymore. The growing stack of rejection letters seemed to weigh more than I could have ever thought possible. I was still selling short stories—but I wanted to write novels. If not for the constant encouragement and support of family and friends . . . who knows? Luckily, I don't have to go there. So how can I sit back and take all the credit for this book? I can't. I would like to thank Corrine Chorney and Greg Palmer for their invaluable feedback. They, with unsurpassable enthusiasm, suffered through many drafts of this manuscript. Without them I do not think THIRD RING would be ready for printing. Also, I want to thank my new publisher, Becki McNeel.

So many of you read TENTH HOUSE, the first Nicholas Tartaglia thriller and wanted to see more. To all of you who asked for it—I give you Third Ring. I hope you enjoy!

TO
Maureen

Mom, Dad, with all my love,
This one is for you . . .

Hope you
enjoy!

Philip Tomarken
4/1/2002

"For we wrestle not against flesh and blood, but against principalities, against powers, against the rulers of the darkness of this world, against spiritual wickedness in high places."

Ephesians 6:12

PROLOGUE

October

The house stood alone at the end of a cul-de-sac and resembled a castle. Light poles lined both sides of the empty four-car driveway and led from the road up to the attached three-car garage. Several tall pine trees spaciously filled the front yard; a lone Chinese Maple stood amidst a rock garden in front of the bowed picture window.

In the basement of the large house, two black men used penlights to see in the darkness as they walked over sorted piles of dirty clothing strewn about the cement floor. The strong odor of bleach and laundry detergents filled the air.

They moved silently toward the intended target.

A card table stood in the back southwest corner of the basement with a plain white bed sheet draped over the top like a tablecloth. One of the men removed the sheet to reveal a safe bolted to the cement floor. A penlight was aimed at the face of the safe. The small circle of light highlighted the handle and spin dial on the safe. The second beam of light moved to display two large hinges on the side of the door on the safe.

The first beam of light left the face of the safe and moved to find the basement door at the top of the stairs. The door was closed.

"Did you hear that?"

"I ain't heard nothin'. Now shine that light over here on the safe."

Tension seemed to swirl around them. It grew inside both of them.

One of the men took a deep, anxious breath. They both knelt down beside the safe simultaneously. The larger of the two men set a black, leather medical bag down on the floor, unzipped it, pulled out a pair of black leather gloves, and put them on. Next, he removed and set on the floor a small black box.

"Anthony, man, I don't know about this," said the man holding a wavering beam of penlight on the medical bag and supplies. "I mean . . . hey man, what do you think?"

Anthony stopped unloading the items from the bag. He turned and faced his partner. In a deep and angry whisper he said, "What do I think, Whine? What do I think? We're here, aren't we? I'm on my stinking knees, aren't I? I'm about to blow open this safe door, right? So, take a guess, stupid, one guess. What do you think I think?"

"Okay. Okay. So we're going to do this. I get it. I got it. Just hurry up. I don't like this," said Whine.

"My God, when they told me I'd be working with Whine, I thought it was just a stupid nickname. I expected someone who didn't whine. You know how that goes, kinda like when they call a guy that's tall, shorty, you know?" Anthony seemed to be talking to himself. "Go wait in the car if you're that jumpy. I'll tell you, you're a pain in my . . ."

"Hey, Anthony, don't be like this, Anthony. Come on. I'm just a little nervous."

"No. I'm a little nervous. You . . . you're scared out of your mind," Anthony said.

"Don't I have a right to be? Huh? I mean, look at us."

Anthony ignored his partner. There was work to do and they did not have the large window of time Anthony would have liked to complete the task. "Hold that light steady. You're making the light shake so much, I'm getting dizzy."

"I'm sorry. I'm trying."

Although the beam of light continued to dance, Anthony pressed on. He placed putty in the palm of his hands, squeezed it, pulled it and stretched it over the top hinge on the safe door. He took a second piece of putty and worked it the same way, placing it over the bottom hinge.

"Is this going to be loud?" Whine asked. His voice cracked when he spoke.

Anthony grunted.

"I mean, is it going to hurt my ears?" With his free hand, Whine started to rub his ear.

"I brought ear plugs," Anthony said, choosing to ignore the baby-like characteristics of his assigned partner.

"Good thinking, Anthony. That's real good thinking. You thought of everything."

"I sure don't. If I did, I'd have put the damned plugs in my ears before I even picked you up tonight."

"Oh, you're funny. That was a good one," Whine said. He continued to rub his ear. His stomach felt upset, too. He could not kneel any longer. He stood up, then started shifting his weight from one foot to the other.

"Who's trying to be funny," Anthony mumbled while fitting explosives into the putty on the hinges. He connected wire leads to the heads of the combustible sticks and sliced the plastic wrap off the opposite end of the wires to expose copper. Anthony secured the bare ends of the wires into the detonator, the box he had set next to the bag. The beam of the penlight bounced all around on the floor while Anthony worked.

"Can you keep the light still here, huh? Steady?" Anthony spoke with his teeth clenched. His fingers fumbled over the instrument he held carefully in his hands. He did not want to risk dropping the device and having the small explosives detonate prematurely. He felt a sweat break out on his forehead, and used the back of his sleeve to wipe the perspiration away.

"Sorry, Anthony," Whine said, pointing the beam of light at what Anthony was working on. Whine breathed deeply, but quickly. To Anthony, Whine sounded on the verge of hyperventilating.

"That's it. We're all set. Are you ready?" Anthony asked. He stood up and wiped his gloved hands down the thighs of his pants.

"The ear plugs, Anthony. You said something about bringing earplugs. Where are they?" Whine wanted to know. He did not like sudden loud noises.

"I didn't forget anything. I have the earplugs. I wasn't going to forget to give you the plugs." Anthony reached into the bag and

pulled out two small, oblong, cardboard packets. Each packet held two yellow foam earplugs. Anthony and Whine inserted the plugs into their ears, backed away from the safe and moved toward the stairs leading out of
the basement.

"It shouldn't be too loud. It should be more of a compact-like explosion. We're far back enough, plenty enough out of the way to be safe, but let's duck behind this box," Anthony said. They knelt behind a box labeled in black marker as containing Halloween Stuff. "Here we go," he said. Anthony's thumb depressed the red button on the electronic control box; a red light began to flash. Anthony used a finger to lift the plastic safety cover away from the switch on the detonator. His thumb twitched over the switch. "One, two . . . three." Anthony flipped the switch.

A boom much louder than Anthony anticipated sounded and a flash of fire lit the basement. Billowing clouds of smoke rolled off the safe's hinges and filled the room. Anthony and his partner coughed and waved their hands through the air trying to thin out and get rid of the smoke.

The smoke lingered, rose, and dispersed some. Anthony and Whine ran back to the safe. Two penlights, like white lasers, cut through the smoke and were aimed at the safe door.

"Crap," Anthony said.

"What?" Whine looked around. He did not see anything amiss.

"The hinges are still in place." Anthony dropped to his knees and stared in disbelief at what the light revealed. The putty was gone, but the unscathed hinges remained. Anthony grabbed the safe's handle and yanked on it, trying to pull open the door. *Locked.* Frustrated, Anthony aimed his penlight at Whine's face and said, "*Now* what are we going to do?"

"Who in the Hell is in the basement?" A man yelled from upstairs, startling Anthony and Whine. The man's voice sounded muffled because it was coming from behind the closed basement door. The man began pounding on the door. He rattled and twisted the doorknob.

"I locked it when we came down here . . . wedged a screwdriver in the door jamb," Whine said. His big smile told Anthony that the idiot was proud of himself.

10

"Not as dumb as I thought you were." Anthony used the dim brilliance of his pen to look around the basement.

"I thought no one was supposed to be home," Whine asked. "No one was supposed to be home, Anthony, remember?"

"There wasn't supposed to be anyone home," Anthony whispered.

He reached into his black leather bag and pulled out a S&W revolver. "But believe it or not, Whine, sometimes things don't work out the way you had them planned."

"Ah man, Anthony. What are you doing with that?" Whine raised his hands in the air and took a hesitant step backwards. He felt his heart race, beating wildly behind his rib cage. He didn't like guns. He didn't like this situation to begin with, and a gun added into the equation could only make matters worse.

"Got to be prepared for such unexpected times." Anthony felt less than confident holding the gun. His hand shook. He found it difficult to breathe. The last thing he wanted to do was threaten someone with a weapon. It went against everything he believed. Sometimes, he knew, viable options were limited. He did not want to get caught thieving a basement.

"I said, who in the Hell is in the basement?" The angry voice yelled once again. "You're dead, you know! Dead!"

"Just because the book's in his safe, you don't think . . ."

Anthony's face, despite the dark basement, visibly paled. "We're in trouble, Whine. Forget about the book."

"I don't like hearing you say, 'we're in trouble.' I'm not as worried about getting the book as I am about this man knowing how to use it on us," Whine said in one breath. He stood in the center of the basement and pivoted back and forth to face the door and the safe. "Anthony, man, what if he uses the book on us?"

"What should I tell you, brother? That everything's fine? That you're not here, that you're really home asleep having a nightmare on the couch? Want to hear those comforting words?" Anthony checked his revolver, spinning the barrel to make sure it was properly loaded. He put his finger on the trigger.

"Do you have to be so mean? Here we are about to die, and you're making fun of me."

"I'm sorry. Yeah, we're in serious trouble," said Anthony. "But we ain't gonna die. Not if I can help it. How big is that basement window?" The window was a small rectangle over the washing machine. It would be a tight squeeze. They could get out of it if they needed too, Anthony figured. Would there be enough time for them to climb out, though? That screwdriver wedged in the basement door was not going to hold for long.

"This is bad. This is *so* bad. I didn't want to come tonight. No I did not. They made me you know . . . told me I had to," Whine explained. His story meant nothing. Anthony was in the same position. Although he hadn't been forced to steal the book, a tremendous amount of pressure had been placed on him. How can you say no to the church?

"Made me, too," Anthony said. He turned and looked at the safe. "We failed and a lot of people are going to be in more serious trouble than this . . . than the trouble we're in . . . just because we couldn't get that damned safe door opened."

"I don't . . ."

A gunshot exploded the knob off the basement door. It was too late to make a break for the window. Everything seemed to have been moving in slow motion for the last two minutes.

"Damn it!" Whine screamed. He threw his hands up to cover his ears. The gunshot sounded louder than the explosion only a moment ago.

Anthony kneeled, raised his weapon, and took aim.

Everyone started to yell at once. "Don't shoot!" Anthony yelled repeatedly.

"Don't shoot," the man at the top of the stairs continually answered. Smoke lingered. The room behind him was well lit. It made it hard for him to see down into his parents' dark basement. The penlights lay on the floor, casting dim beams of light at nothing in particular.

"No one's shooting!" Whine said, wanting to resolve this without anyone getting killed. "No one is shooting."

"Don't shoot, drop your gun," Anthony said, trying to sound calm, cool, collective.

"I can't do that," the man at the top of the stairs said. He sounded calm, cool and, more importantly, in control. "I won't set my gun down. You set your gun down and I won't blow the heads off either of you."

Whine knew something needed to be done. He felt like the peacemaker—the negotiator. No one really wanted to shoot anyone else, so he raised both his hands in the air while taking a single step forward. Anthony and the man on the stairs responded to Whine's movement by firing their guns. Anthony squeezed off two shots before a tiny flame erupted from the barrel of the man's weapon at the top of the stairs and the bang from his gun resounded. Someone cried out in pain.

Whine stood statue-still. His mind quickly assessed the situation. He feared he'd been injured, only not yet aware of any pain. His hands patted at his chest. "I'm okay," he whispered, thankfully. He looked and saw the young white man's body splayed upside down across the stairs with his head lying in a spreading pool of blood on the basement floor. Whine turned away and looked where Anthony had been kneeling, saying, "He's just a kid. He's dead. Anthony, you just killed . . . "

Anthony looked dead, too. A large crimson circle stained Anthony's shirt over the heart. Anthony's eyes were open and blood oozed from the corner of his lips. "Whine," Anthony whispered, then coughed.

Shaking his head, Whine knelt down next to his partner. He placed the palm of his hand on Anthony's wound. The blood was thick and sticky. There was a lot of it. "Oh man. Oh man, no. You've been shot." *How am I going to get him out of here?* He wondered. *What in the Hell am I supposed to do now?*

"My fingers are itchy, Whine. My fingers itch." Anthony was looking at Whine, but could not focus. He felt as if a cloudy film had grown over his eyeballs. His legs felt cold and he could not feel his feet at all. He shivered violently with teeth clattering.

Whine pulled off Anthony's leather gloves and stuffed them into his coat pocket. He held Anthony's hands. "Please Anthony, I need your help. Don't leave me here alone." Fear overwhelmed him.

Anthony coughed. "It really hurts to do that, you know." He closed his eyes.

"I can get you out of here, man. I'll get you to a hospital. We've got to get you to a hospital, man." Whine took Anthony by the hands, stood up, and attempted to pull his partner to his feet. "You've got to help me though, man. Anthony, try to stand up."

Anthony did not respond. Whine knew Anthony was dead.

Whine had never watched a person die. He never dreamt he'd be part of a scene as hideous as this. The church would be upset. The church would not be happy. This horrible twist of events changed everything.

Whine knew he needed to get out. He felt odd leaving Anthony's body in the basement, but could not risk carrying him out of the house, either. Someone would surely notice a black man running down a private residential street with a dead man slung over his shoulders.

"The gun," he said, picking up Anthony's revolver. Whine stuffed it into the waistband of his pants. As quickly as he could, Whine packed up Anthony's black medical bag.

Whine thought he could hear the sound of sirens. He felt panic stir inside him. He knew he was going to be caught. He did not want to be caught with a gun in his pants. He removed the weapon and placed it on the basement floor—but not near Anthony's body. He looked around the room. A red light flashed on a small plastic device mounted in the corner of the rectangular basement window. The kid came home, heard us in his house, and set off a silent alarm.

Whine stepped around the blood and body at the stairs. Once out of the basement, he ran toward the front door at the end of the foyer. He pulled open the door and ran out into the night.

CHAPTER 1

Thursday, May 17 (Seven months later)

When the brand new white Lincoln pulled into the driveway at a little after midnight, I had been halfway through editing the third chapter of the first novel I was writing. Whenever I went on stakeout, I brought my material to read beneath the narrow glow of a penlight. Hours could be spent waiting so I tried to use the time constructively.

There were many cars parked along the residential street. I sat in a car provided by the bank, and parked across the street from the house of the man I'd been observing. The man who got out of the car was Gregory Stiffner. He never looked my way. Stiffner went to his trunk and removed a department store bag. He stood at least six-five—a good six inches taller than me—and weighed well over two hundred and fifty pounds, sixty pounds more than what I weighed. His long shaggy hair looked dirty while, after a recent trim, my bristles stood slightly taller than brush cut length.

He held the bag by his side and walked into his house. Moments later, the lights in the house came on. Before I could do my job, I had to wait for the lights in the house to be turned off. And even after that, I would need to wait some more.

Setting the manuscript aside, I picked up a five-inch piece of plain plastic wrapped wire. Using a tool, I carefully stripped away an inch of plastic from each end and rolled the copper fibers in my fingers to keep them tightly wound. It only took seconds to complete the task. I set the wire onto the dashboard and, feeling anxious, continued to wait. I stared at the house and wondered how long it would be before those lights went out.

After another hour, I picked up the manuscript, removed the cap on my red pen and went back to line-editing the mystery with my penlight. Halfway down the page, the lights in Stiffner's house began to go out. I continued on with the editing. After some time, I noted with some satisfaction that I had finished editing an entire chapter. I flipped through the pages. There seemed to be large amounts of red ink everywhere. The manuscript looked like it was bleeding badly.

I set the chapter down and picked up the wire from off the dashboard, got out of the car, walked casually across the road and up Stiffner's driveway.

The key to unlock Stiffner's car door had been given to me. I tried it, first in the trunk and then in the driver's side door. It didn't work in either lock, but I didn't expect it to. Stiffner, a smart man, changed the locks and more than likely the ignition switch, too. A Slim-Jim would be out of the question. The car was armed with an alarm system. If I touched the glass, the alarm would trigger and sound. The alarm was armed and disarmed by a keypad on the door, located under the door handle. This was the feature I needed to bypass.

I removed the digital key the bank had given me from my pocket. It had a metal tip and a thin metal bar the size and length of a car key. The bar was between two pieces of magnetic tape. The grip of the key was large enough to have a small circuit board—like a mini computer—mounted inside the plastic. This would activate the tape. I inserted the tip of the key into the door lock; the bar helped push the magnetic tape along. On the grip of the key, I pressed a button. It searched for and found the electronic code necessary to digitally disarm the alarm and unlock the doors. Feeling successful, I slipped the magical key back into my pocket.

Kneeling by the car, I opened the door just a crack. I did not want the dome light to turn on. From another pocket I took out a small roll of black duct tape, peeled back and cut with my teeth, three two-inch pieces of the tape. I affixed the pieces over the switch in the side of the door. With the switch permanently depressed, it gave the impression that the door was still closed and the dome light in the car would not turn on. I opened the door all the way.

The wonderful smell of leather that can only be associated with the smell of a new automobile, filled my nostrils as I slid into the seat behind the steering wheel. The cushion of the seat puffed, blooming and forming to fit my body. The overall sensation felt amazing.

I tried to start the car using the key the bank had given me but, again, to no avail. The digital key would not work in this situation either.

I leaned over and opened the glove compartment, which provided just enough light to see under the steering wheel. I found and removed a small black panel cover that kept the vehicle fuses and wires safe.

I took out the wire I'd worked on in the car while waiting for Stiffner to go to bed and touched one end of the exposed fibers of the wire to the fuse associated with the glove compartment light. I touched the opposite end of the copper wire to the trunk's fuse. Immediately I heard a muffled pop sound.

When watching someone for a week, one can learn a-plenty. I dropped the wire, slid out of the car and went to the trunk. Magnetically affixed to the inside of the trunk lid I found a small black box, slid it open, and nothing. I was supposed to think Viola! Stiffner's spare ignition key. However, the box did not contain a spare key. The box was empty. I could not help but feel a little like Old Mother Hubbard. I tossed the box into the trunk and closed the lid quietly.

Back at the driver's door, on my knees on Stiffner's driveway, I reached under the steering column of the steering wheel. I removed a small light from my back pocket and switched it on. I aimed the tiny beam on the array of wires.

I fished around for my Swiss Army pocketknife, all the while feeling like MacGuyver. Using the minuscule pair of scissors, I clipped the plastic tie wraps that kept neatly bundled together all the wires and wire harnesses. With the tie wrap no longer in place, all the bundles of wires drooped toward the car floor mats.

Finding the two wires I needed, I clipped, stripped, and touched the ends together.

The car engine tried to turn, churned, made grinding noises, but did not start. "Come on," I mumbled, touching the wire ends together again. The engine turned over and the car started.

Satisfied, I sat up, and almost screamed. Standing at the hood of the car was Stiffner. He held a baseball bat in his large hands. He looked angry. His teeth were bared and his nostrils flared. He let out a stream of intimidating, huffing breaths.

I jumped into the car, pulled the door closed, and gripped the steering wheel. As I put the car into reverse, Stiffner swung the bat. The hood of the car dented inward. I watched for a quick moment as Stiffner continued to smash the front headlights. He moved with speed around to the side of the car and stood by my door. As I quickly began to back out of the driveway, he swung the bat like a sword; I swerved the car to avoid the whack. The bat connected, cracking the front windshield. The windshield now resembled a glass spider web. I hate spiders.

I glanced in the rear view mirror, shocked to find the rear of the Lincoln on a collision course with Stiffner's Maple. I had to stop the car and look behind me. I carefully avoided the tree and backed up into the road.

This gave Stiffner time to come at me from a different angle. He raised his weapon and whacked it against the passenger door window.

As I put the car into drive, Stiffner swung his bat again. This time it came through the glass. He threw the bat and reached into the car. His hands groped as he tried to grab me. I felt pretty sure he intended to strangle me.

"Where in the Hell do you think you're taking my car, buddy?"

"You haven't made any payments. The bank is reclaiming the vehicle," I said, wanting to speed away. With Stiffner in the window, I knew he might get hurt. He may want to kill me, but I was not here to injure the man. I was only here to repossess his automobile.

I let the car roll forward, then quickly put the car in reverse and backed up. This maneuver caught Stiffner off guard. He pulled his head out of the window. I sped backwards down the street. When Stiffner stopped chasing after the car, I stopped, put it in drive, turned around, and drove away.

Stiffner shouted obscenities, none seemingly necessary to mention—just use your imagination and anyone can figure out what was said, and you'll be, if not correct, at least close enough to understand the gist of Stiffner's vulgarity.

From somewhere behind me I heard the distinct sound of sirens and guessed a neighbor had called the police. This event did take place, after all, during the middle of the night.

I returned the car to the garage where repossessed vehicles were returned. My car, parked outside, sat in a small lot across the street. I started the engine, turned the radio on, kept the volume low, tuned it to Rochester's only country station and drove home. A long day, a long night, and my body and mind felt ready for sleep.

The bank would send someone to pick up the car I left parked across the street from Stiffner's house. And as always, they would hold onto my manuscript for me so I could pick it up in the morning.

I live in a small three-bedroom ranch house in the town of Greece, a suburb of the city of Rochester. I parked in the driveway, checked the mail, and went into the house. I took off my shirt. Affixed to my right shoulder, a flesh-colored patch attempted to curb my need for a cigarette. Though I have not had a cigarette in thirteen days, six hours and some odd minutes, the patch seemed to do little more than irritate the skin. I tore it off, went to the bathroom, and opened a fresh patch. I stuck it to the same arm, but under the location of where the last patch had been for the last fifteen hours.

I took a frosted mug out of my freezer and went out to the garage. My Uncle Tony had rigged an old refrigerator into a beer tap for me. I may have quit smoking, but I enjoyed my beer and having a half keg in the garage at all times cut down on the cost of buying bottled beer every week or so.

Once back in the house, I sat in the recliner in the living room, took the television remote off the end table, and sat back, getting comfortable in my favorite chair. I switched on the set and flipped through the channels until I found some local news, while sipping my drink. I lowered the volume to a whisper.

On the end table, beside the lamp, sat the answering machine. I pressed the play button and the first call was a hang-up. The second call came from Karis Bristol, my secretary and love of my life. We met in high school, dated, and parted prior to graduation. It is an odd and long—however adventurous—story as to how we wound up together again after ten years. Karis is a successful freelance-writer, but also works part time for me at the office, The Tartaglia Agency.

We have a wonderful working relationship: She can write all she wants when the phone isn't ringing or if the filing is up-to-date.

"Nick," her message said, "maybe we can meet for breakfast tomorrow morning before work? I'll be there. You know where. Love ya. Hey. If you don't get in too late, give me a call. All right? Good-night."

Without even glancing at the time displayed on the VCR, I knew it was far far too late to call her back, as much as I would have enjoyed talking with her. Tired tomorrow morning, or not, I planned to meet her for breakfast.

The third message came from Lynn, a public defense attorney and friend. When I had worked for a large private detective agency, we'd sometimes worked on a similar case, though from opposite ends of the playing field. "Nick? It's Lynn. Look, I need some help. Give me a call when you get in. I'll be at the office late. It's pretty important."

The fourth message—a second hang-up.

Dialing Lynn's office, I figured if she wasn't in, at least I could leave a message on her answering machine. To my surprise, she answered the phone on the second ring. "Lynn? Must be a big case if you're still at work."

"I was hoping you'd call back, Nick. Busy?" She sounded tired, her voice raspy.

"What? You mean now? Right now?"

"It's important."

"I guess I'm free until breakfast time," I said, setting my half-full mug of beer on the end table. "Meet you at the office?"

"I'll buzz you in." She hung up.

I went into the bathroom, splashed cold water on my face, and brushed my teeth and hair. "Who wanted to relax with a beer and fall asleep in a damned recliner, anyway?" I said to my reflection. My reflection remained silent. *Smart move.* I could tell from the reflected look though, that I was angry with me, and rightly so.

Lynn did not belong to a large firm, or even to a small one for that matter. She worked as a solo practitioner defending alleged criminals. From reading newspapers, I knew she handled more than her share of DWI cases. She represented shoplifters, people caught in possession of forged instruments, and the occasional violent criminal

—excuse me, the alleged violent criminal.

A relationship such as ours may seem odd to others because I worked to catch people doing things wrong while Lynn worked to help get them out of trouble. Even though she helped the underdog, she was still an attorney. Last I checked, lawyer jokes outnumbered private investigator jokes at least 10,000 to 1.

Her office sat sandwiched between floors of the Mercury Building downtown. I can honestly say at this time of night (or morning) there is literally no traffic. I parked in the vacant lot along side her building.

My mouth watered. I craved a cigarette.

In the front foyer, I found L. Scannella among a wall of names and doorbells. I pressed the button for her office. A moment later, a buzzing sound filled the room and I opened the door.

In the lobby, the first thing I noticed was the unattended security desk. There was a limp American flag draped around its pole in the west corner of the room. Dim lighting accented the darkness by creating even darker shadows. The only apparent light came from down the hall, past the main lobby. My shoes made loud cracking sounds on the floor as I walked toward the elevators. It was hard not to envision myself as the Norse god, Thor.

I took the elevator up and got off on Lynn's floor. Light shown into the hall from her wide-open office door. I stood at the threshold, saw her empty desk, and felt apprehensive. I kept a Glock on a shoulder holster under my sport coat. My hand reached reflexively for the butt. "Lynn?"

Inside the office was the receptionist's desk. There were two other doors in the office. The bathroom was on the right and the other was Lynn's office. Both doors were closed. The entire office remained silent. "Lynn?"

I pulled out the gun and held it firmly in both hands.

Someone came out of the bathroom drying their hands on a sheet of paper towel. I pivoted in that direction and aimed the gun directly at Lynn. She smiled, and said, "A little over dramatic, Nick. Don't you think?"

CHAPTER 2

Lynn Scannella was an attractive lady with hair so brown it looked black. Her large eyes matched that long dark hair. Full lips, capable of spreading into a heart-melting smile, gave her an edge most male attorneys lacked and could not resist. She stood a few inches taller than I did, tall and slim with long legs. She looked quite sensual.

"You just getting in, or been here all night?" I said, putting my gun away.

"All night. Want a drink?"

"What are you having?"

"Water."

"That would be fine." I moved into the office and closed her door. She went back into the bathroom. I heard the faucet run. "There's no guard in the lobby."

"Hasn't been for a while now. Rent's gone up and security down. I'm going to have to start thinking of a different location for my practice. I hear you got a new place a few months back."

"In Spencerport."

"Like it?" She handed me a cup of water. "Sorry, no ice."

I took a sip. "I love the place."

She led me into her office and motioned for me to sit down in the chair opposite her desk. She sat in her chair behind the desk. Paperwork cluttered the space in front of her. "All right, here's the problem. I'm in a bind. I had a wonderful paralegal. He had to quit. He's gone on to law school in Syracuse—a little too far away from

Rochester for him to make the commute. Not to mention, even before classes started, he was already receiving homework assignments."

"I'm sorry to hear that. And this has to do with me how?" I asked, moving around in the chair trying to get more comfortable. When I found I couldn't, I gave up. I leaned forward and placed my elbows on my thighs.

"I need help on a case."

"And?"

"And I'm asking for your help," said Lynn, sounding aggravated.

"Me?" I pointed a finger at my chest. "How can I help you? I don't know anything about legal research, or writing briefs. I'm a private investigator. Besides, I like what I do. I don't think I could just change jobs like that," I said, snapping my fingers.

"Are you done? Nick, I don't want you to become a paralegal, I want you to be my detective." She made an eyebrow arch. I loved when people did that—loved people who could do that. I couldn't do it, but have always wanted to ever since the late John Belushi made the facial expression famous.

"You want to hire me as your detective?"

"That's right."

"Lynn . . ."

"Nick, I have a big case. The man I'm representing is innocent . . . or partly so. He needs my help and I can't represent him effectively . . . at least not alone I can't. I'm going to need someone to help me with this. I need to prepare for trial, but also need to investigate his case. As efficient as I am, I can't be working on two tasks at the same time." She sounded desperate and came pretty close to begging.

I didn't want her to beg.

"And I can pay you, Nick."

I'm listening, I thought. "I'm listening."

"Not much. He has a trial in less than a month. He had an attorney . . . the attorney dropped him. Last Monday, the file's thrown on my desk, in a manner of speaking. If you work for me exclusively, I can give you . . ." She thought a moment, then gave me a price, and a generous one at that. She wasn't fooling me, though. She had a wage worked out before she had even called my house. "I'll even cover reasonable expenses."

She knew me well. "It's a generous offer Lynn, and I accept. When do you need me to start?"

"Now," she said, as if it were eight in the morning and we just arrived to work after a full night's sleep. She folded her arms over the papers clumped together on her desk and leaned toward me. "Our client's name is Gordon Birdie. He goes by the nickname, Whine."

"Cute."

"It won't be after you talk with him for more than five minutes," Lynn said. "He and a friend allegedly broke into a house in Pittsford. They were trying to burglarize the owner's safe when the owner's son came home early and unexpectedly. There were shots fired and Whine's partner and the owner's son died in the gunfight. Whine was caught near the house holding a medical bag filled with questionable materials."

"Questionable? Such as?"

"Such as dynamite, putty, wires . . ."

"Stuff to make bombs?" I said. The story had a familiar ring to it. It happened a while back. I remember at the time only paying vague attention to the news coverage. Much was happening in my life then.

"That's right. Police found a gun at the murder scene. Whine's prints match the prints on the gun believed to have fired the bullet that killed Philip Edwards, Jr."

"So this is the Edwards case, huh? I remember seeing some of it on the news."

"Everyone did. When the son of one of Rochester's most powerful CEO's gets murdered, you can guarantee the press is not going to let it go." She huffed. "There's a lot of political pressure coming down on this one, too."

"I can only imagine," I said.

"No. You can't."

Perhaps she was right and I couldn't understand the pressure. "Let me ask you this. You said his prints were found on the gun . . . Whine's prints . . . right?"

"That's right."

"They test his hand for residue?" I asked. When someone fires a gun, a residue can be lifted off the skin. The test results are admissible in court and prove whether or not an accused actually fired the weapon in question.

"The test done was inconclusive," Lynn said.

"Oh, and why is that?"

"Mr. Birdie's hand was covered in his partner's blood."

"Makes it a little hard to get an accurate test reading?"

"Apparently," Lynn said. "However, Whine was also found with leather gloves in his pocket. The gloves were tested, and the results came back positive. So if Whine had the gloves on when the gunfight took place and then took them off and stuffed them into his pockets . . ."

"Grand jury?" I asked.

"The police gathered evidence quickly and went right up to the district attorney's office. They compiled a compelling case and a grand jury found probable cause," Lynn said.

"Which means what exactly?"

"Which means, the grand jury is convinced the DAs office has enough evidence for a strong case against my client. They returned an indictment of first degree murder," Lynn said. "It was at this time the police actually arrested him for Philip Edwards, Jr.'s murder."

"For accidentally killing someone during a robbery?" I asked. "I'd think manslaughter at the most."

"It wasn't robbery," Lynn said. "It was a burglary. Robbery is stealing something off another person. Burglary is when you enter someone's home with the intent to commit larceny or any kind of a felony. Hell, you don't have to steal anything to be convicted of burglary. All you have to do is break into a house and commit any kind of a felony and the burglary charge will be added on."

"So you're going to let a first degree murder stick?" I asked.

"I am not going to let anything stick. I plan to talk with the DA tomorrow. I mean, I think the felony murder rule would clearly place Mr. Birdie in an Involuntary Manslaughter position," Lynn said.

"The felony murder rule?"

"Look, he and his partner enter a man's house, right? They plan to blow up the guy's safe and steal whatever the Hell could be in there. So the son gets home from wherever he is a little early. He catches the two men in his parents' basement and one of them accidentally kills the kid. . . . With me so far?" Lynn asked.

I nodded. Watching her lips move while she talked captivated me. "Grasshopper is with you so far, oh wise one."

Lynn smiled. "Okay, so the felony murder rule makes Mr. Birdie guilty of murder because he was burglarizing someone's home. The son was killed in the course of the felony. See? Simple."

"How about this," I said. "Does your client have any priors?"

"None. He's clean. So was the other guy with him, Anthony James . . . the other man that died."

"One more question," I said. "For right now, anyway."

"Shoot."

"Why isn't Whine out on bail?"

"It's not always as easy as the way they make it sound on television. The Monroe County Bail Schedule for murder is normally set at five hundred thousand dollars. In light of who it was that was murdered, the judge set bail at an even million."

"Gotcha." One million dollars. Even if someone went to see a bail bondsman for the money, the bondsman would still require a substantial percentage of that one million to cover the set bail amount.

"More questions?"

She talked a good talk, and she was going to pay me. "What do you need me to do?"

"For starters, before my appointment with the DA, I'd like for you to come with me tomorrow . . . today . . . so you can meet Whine. I want you to spend some time with him."

"Whine? I can't believe you call him that."

"You will, too. The name is more suiting than one might imagine."

"Didn't you already talk to him?" I asked.

"The minute I was handed the case. I knew I would need to protect his rights," she said.

"Those would be the rights found in the Constitution now wouldn't they?"

"You learn quick, my honorable Grasshopper," said Lynn. "Anyway, the first thing I told him was not to talk to anyone . . . not cellmates, not other people in the jail, not guards, not anyone . . . about the case," Lynn said.

"And he understood this?"

"Seems to have. At least, he told me he understood. He looked extremely scared. I mean, I understand he's in jail for allegedly committing some very criminal acts, but you want to know something? I really, truly, don't think he's guilty," she said, sounding lost in her own thoughts. "Anyway, Whine told me his previous attorney had told him the same thing . . . about not talking to anyone about his case," Lynn said.

"Well. Sounds like you and the previous attorney might have studied out of the same law text book."

"Ha. Ha. Then he wanted to tell me what happened, and I stopped him."

"You stopped him," I said. "Why?"

"I don't want to know what happened."

"You don't?" I asked.

"I don't."

"Why not?"

"I told him not to tell me what he did, but to only tell me what they say he did . . . they being the police."

"He understood this?" I asked. I wasn't sure if I understood it. I thought attorneys wanted to hear the truth, the whole truth, and nothing but the truth?

"He didn't understand, not at first. He kept trying to explain things to me, and I had to keep reminding him to stop explaining things to me. This definitely frustrated him," Lynn said. She was shaking her head.

I was not as dense as I looked. "And you want me to go meet Mr. Birdie, a.k.a. Whine, and get this explanation for you?"

"Not for me. I don't want to hear it," Lynn said.

"Then what do I want it for?"

"Because you have been hired to do the digging and I want you to have the right tools to do the job. As my employee, you will be canvassed under the attorney-client privilege. As just a P.I., the protection I could provide is a lot less encompassing. As my employee, I can keep matters between you and Whine a bit more confidential," Lynn explained.

"You should get yourself a full-time paralegal," I told her.

"I would, but lately with the caseload the way it has been, I don't have time to look for one," Lynn said.

"I know of one," I said. I thought of a woman I had rescued not too long ago. She had been out jogging and was attacked by three men. I fought the attackers off her, and when the police showed up all three were arrested. "When we're done here, I'll get you her number."

"Nick, you're like a jack-of-all-trades. Find me a good strong boyfriend and I'll owe you my life," Lynn said. She was looking at me when she said this and maybe stared a fraction of a moment longer than she should have. I looked away.

"See what I can do," I said. A thought of Karis entered my mind, as if a self-armed security shield dropped, stopping any incoming flirtatious missiles.

"Tomorrow? You said you had a breakfast date?" Lynn asked.

"I never said a date but, yes, Karis and I are meeting for breakfast."

"You should just go home and get some sleep."

I looked at a clock on the wall. "I will after breakfast. You heading home?"

"I'm whipped."

"Let me hang out, review your file, and familiarize myself some with the police reports and things," I said.

"Just make sure you don't take the file out of the office. And do me a favor. Lock the door when you leave."

"I will. I promise."

She gathered together the papers on her desk and stuffed them into a manila file folder. She then handed the file over to me.

CHAPTER 3

Friday, May 18

I was sitting in a corner booth of the restaurant, sipping coffee and staring out the window when Karis pulled into the parking lot. I waved to her as she walked toward the front entrance, but she didn't see me. She looked stunning. Today she wore that long, straight, auburn hair pulled back tight off her forehead and secured in a ponytail. Her dark eyes and full, pouty lips seemed to be her most attractive features, despite the long sexy legs that made her just as tall as I am.

Karis' light, flowery patterned sundress stopped at her ankles revealing white canvas sneakers on feet without socks. Over her arm she carried a white knit sweater. She entered the restaurant and looked for me. When our eyes met she smiled.

As she reached the booth, I stood up and we quickly kissed Hello. "Good morning," I said. We both sat down across from each other.

"Good morning, Nick. I waited up for you last night, hoping you would call," Karis said. "But I finally gave up and went to bed." The waitress came over. We both started with coffee and opened our menus.

"Something up?" I asked while trying to decide on eggs or pancakes.

"No, not really. I just felt like talking with you."

This woman is too sweet. "I worked late."

"For the bank?"

29

"Yeah. I don't know if I want to keep that repossessing job, though. Guy last night, he thought he was Babe Ruth or something. And, I know he wasn't making the payments on his car, but I can't help but feel like I'm working for them, instead of for the people." I emptied two packets of sugar into my coffee, then stirred in some cream. Karis drank hers black.

"Them?"

"You know," I said almost whispering, "not us. Them."

"I see who you mean by them. I get who them are, but them are paying you. And, I might add, them are paying you well."

"I got an assignment."

Karis looked up from her menu. Her head did this thing when she wanted more information. It cocked to one side. "When? This morning?" Karis sipped her coffee.

"Last night." Karis was a bright one. She was trying to figure out when the job might have come along. Her mind would be, at this very moment, working together a chronological time line. We saw each other last night, and I hadn't mentioned anything about a job. I worked until late last night, got up early (as far as she knew) to meet her for breakfast—so when would I have found more work?

"I thought you said you worked late for the bank."

"I did," I said. "When I got home there was a message on my machine from an attorney I know. It's a criminal case. A robbery . . . excuse me . . . burglary and murder case. They need a private eye, someone to do some research in preparation for an upcoming trial."

"Who is she?"

"Who is she, who?"

"The attorney," Karis said, holding her cup in both hands up to her lips, eyes never looking away from me.

"And how do you know this attorney is a woman?" I asked.

"Simple, Mr. Detective. You said, they need a detective. If it were a male lawyer, you would have said, he needs a detective. Since you used 'they' instead of 'he,' I believe the attorney is a female, and an attractive one, too."

"Her name is Lynn Scannella."

"And she's attractive?" Her tone was smug.

"She is."

"You dated her?" Karis asked. The smug tone was gone from her voice. She now sounded concerned.

"No. We just worked on a lot of cases back when I was with Safehouse. Usually on opposite sides," I said.

"So why are you going to help her now?" asked Karis. The waitress came back to our booth, topped our coffee and took our orders.

"Two reasons. One, she asked me. Two, she's not only going to pay me for my time, but pay me well . . . as you like to put it." I sipped some coffee. It tasted bitter. I dumped in two more packets of sugar and stirred it in. "Look, Lynn feels her client is innocent."

"And you?"

"I don't feel strongly one way or the other. I reviewed the file."

"You reviewed the file when?"

"All this morning."

"You haven't gone to bed yet? You've got to be exhausted." Karis sounded shocked.

"That goes without saying. I plan to sleep right after breakfast."

"We didn't have to meet this morning," she said.

I reached across the table. Her hand met mine. I gently squeezed her fingers. "I wouldn't miss having breakfast with you." She smiled. I loved that smile. She looked modest with her head cocked to one side and her eyelids batting at me. "Anyway, I read through most of the file."

"And?"

I said, "I told you. I haven't decided one way or . . ."

"Come on, Nick. I know you too well. You have an opinion. You've probably already cast your verdict." She stared at me with eyes silently demanding the truth.

Unable to look away from such a captivating stare, I sighed. "Okay, the guy looks guilty on paper. The police have plenty of evidence . . . more than just circumstantial evidence. But there is something about this guy that just makes me think he might be innocent. He was caught in the neighborhood . . . okay, that's circumstantial . . . but he had with him a black bag full of equipment used for making bombs, including dynamite. He's got leather gloves in his pockets. The gloves were tested and the police found residue consistent with firing a gun."

"Sounds bad."

"Looks bad."

"So what makes you feel like he's not guilty?"

"I don't know, instinct. Reading through the file I couldn't help but get this feeling. It's too simple. Two black men enter the house of a wealthy white man, get caught trying to rob him and wind up killing someone. The police catch the guy almost immediately after the murder, and they find all of their evidence contained in a bag and left at the scene. I mean, talk about having a case handed to you. The DAs got to be out of his mind with excitement. This is becoming a big and political case. I don't know. It bothers me."

"What? Are you saying it's a racial thing?"

"No. That's not it . . . I don't think."

"But you really think he might be innocent?"

"Innocent may be the wrong word, or too strong. Just like guilty isn't the right word. I just get this . . . I don't know . . . It's hard to explain. The point is, something is wrong with the case. It can't be that black and white," I said.

The waitress brought out our breakfast and set the wrong plates down in front of us. We thanked her. When she walked away, we traded plates. Eating a dainty forkful of scrambled eggs, Karis said, "So if you've taken the case, what's your first step? What do you need me to do?"

"Okay. Lynn wants me to take a ride out to the prison with her. The defendant is still behind bars, bail was set at a million and oddly enough," I said with sarcasm, "he couldn't post it. Lynn has an appointment with the DA after we meet with our client. This DA may have some important things to pass along. Afterwards, Lynn and I will compare notes and see where the next logical step might be." I noticed Karis had stopped paying attention. "Karis?"

"I'm sorry, I lost you there."

"I noticed," I said. "What's wrong."

"There's a funny feeling in me."

"You feel sick?" I asked.

"No."

I leaned as close to her as I could without resting my shirt in my plate of eggs. "Are you all right? Sure you're not sick?"

"I'm not sick, Nick. I feel jealous."

***

Once I arrived back home I undressed and went to sleep. The sleep felt fitful. Despite drawn curtains, the sunlight imposed itself and managed to light the bedroom enough to distract me. When I woke up, I found myself lying on my belly with the pillow pulled tight over my head.

The alarm clock on the nightstand read: 12:29.

I'd only slept three and a half-hours, but it didn't matter. My body felt ready to get up and rested enough to finish the day. I slid my legs out of bed, sat on the edge for a moment and rubbed the heels of my hands against my eyelids. Stumbling to the bathroom in anticipation of a long hot shower, I reached for a folded towel off the top of a laundry basket filled with clean clothing (that still needed to be put away).

I took a shower hot enough to begin to turn my skin red and it felt wonderful. As I towel dried my body back in the bedroom, the telephone rang. I looked at the phone on the nightstand and decided I'd just let the answering machine pick it up and heard an impatient sigh from the other end of the line, then, "Nick, if you're there, pick up. It's Lynn. It's almost one o'clock and I have to get to the . . ."

I picked up the phone. "Lynn? It's me. What's up?"

"It's getting late," she said with a definite bite in her bark. I imagined sharp teeth trying to gnaw at my ear. "I have to be at the jail to meet with Whine in less than two hours. Are you still planning to come with me?" she asked. "I was hoping we'd have more time to discuss his file before meeting with him."

"You never said when we planned to go up to the jail," I told her. "I would have set my alarm clock if we'd agreed on a time to meet."

"I'm sorry, Nick. You're right. Are you still up to going?" she asked again, only this time she spoke more calmly. I could hear the deep breaths she was taking. It seemed to help relax her.

"When? One?"

"One, one-thirty," Lynn said.

"Want to meet there, or at your office?" I asked.

"Come by the office as soon as you can, we'll quickly review your thoughts on the file, and then we can drive up to the prison together . . . talk some more if we need to. How's that sound?"

"Like a plan. I just stepped out of the shower. Let me get dressed and I'll be right there." With the telephone cradled between my ear and neck, I tossed the towel onto the bed, and put on my boxer shorts and socks.

Lynn said, "Okay. Hey Nick, I'm sorry if I sounded angry. I'm not. I mean, I am . . . but not at you. You just can't imagine the heat I'm getting. Half the messages on my machine concern this case. I truly believe it's going to be very difficult to find an unbiased jury on this one. I need to work on a motion to change venue. Hell, I need to work on plenty of motions. I might need to call an agency and see if I can rent a paralegal, too. It's not as if Whine is my only case. Idealistically, I'd love to work only on one client at a time. That's just . . . look at me going on here. I'm sorry, again."

"Don't worry about it. I wish I could help more."

"Oh, you will. I have plenty of work to keep you busy," she said.

"I'm sure you do. Okay, I'll see you in a little while. Hey, you want me to see about that paralegal I know?"

"I do Nick, but not now, not this morning," Lynn said anxiously.

***

I showered, dressed and drove toward Lynn's office, stopping only long enough to place an order at the McDonald's drive-through. I ate two burgers and an order of fries while I drove and kept a large cup of ice-cold soda between my thighs.

I finished eating just as I parked in the rear of the Mercury Building. I rolled up the window and placed the food wrappers and napkins into the take-out bag and tossed the bag into the back seat. (I was born a slob. I'm not proud of it, but flexible enough to accept and adapt to the personal flaw. This seemingly unchangeable characteristic drives Karis crazy).

Unlike last night, the foyer bustled with people and activity. I still noticed the empty security guard station, and felt bothered by the sight of such a vacancy. I walked down the hall, took the elevator to Lynn's floor and went to her office. This time a secretary sat behind the front desk ready to great me. A gold nameplate read: Heather Slimms.

"Mr. Tartaglia?" the secretary asked. I nodded. She pressed a button on her telephone.

"Yes?" I heard Lynn say from a speaker on Heather's phone.

"Mr. Tartaglia is here," Heather Slimms told the attorney.

"Send him in, please."

"Miss Scannella is waiting for you in her office," Heather told me. She looked toward Lynn's closed office door and pointed with the eraser on the end of her pencil.

"Thank you," I said.

"Can I get you a cup of coffee?" Heather asked as she stood up. She looked to be in her late thirties. She was heavy, but also—and I have never used this word to describe a woman before— handsome. She looked professional with short cropped, dark brown hair, and gold, round-rimmed glasses. She wore a slate gray business suit with a knee length skirt.

"I would appreciate that, but I'll get it."

"It's nothing, and besides Miss Scannella's waiting for you. I'll bring it right in. How do you like it?" She moved from behind the desk to where a coffeepot sat on top of a cart on wheels.

"Two sugars, two creams. Thank you."

Heather smiled. "You're welcome."

I felt funny just walking into Lynn's office, so I knocked. "Come in," I heard Lynn say. I opened the door, stepped into the office and closed the door behind me. The blinds were open allowing for bright sunlight to fill the room. "Have a seat," she said. With a wave of her hand, she motioned for me to sit in the chair across from her at the desk. She continued to busily scribble something down on a piece of paper inside a file.

I sat down and said, "Sorry to keep you waiting."

She finished writing, set her pen down, and closed the file. "It's understandable with how late you were up. I'm surprised to see you here now. I thought for sure you'd take longer getting here." She tossed the file onto the top of a two-tier tray that was positioned on the corner of her desk. "You read Gordon Birdie's file?"

"Yes."

"And?"

"I'm not sure how I feel. I have questions."

"Good. So does the prosecution. Hopefully the questions you have and my questions combined will help us build a strong defense.

See, we need to work both sides of the case. We need to ask the right questions and be prepared for any questions the prosecution asks."

"So what you're saying is—we have to develop the DAs line of questioning, as well as our own?" I asked.

"Exactly. We need to be ready and prepared for anything that comes up. In short, we need to anticipate everything . . . every angle possible." She stood up. "Ready?"

"Thought you'd never ask."

As we left the office, Heather stood at Lynn's door just about ready to come in. She had my cup of coffee in her hand. "I'm sorry," I said.

"That's all right. I have a lid to put on the cup, if you'd like to take it to go?" Heather said. "Miss Scannella . . . I can pour you a cup, too?"

"Wonderful." Lynn said. We took our cups of coffee to go and left.

CHAPTER 4

The Monroe County Prison was located in Henrietta. Lynn drove quickly, consistently going ten miles over the posted speed limit. We talked the entire away, but not once did our conversation drift toward Whine and his case. She wanted to know what happened to my position with Safehouse, the large private investigative firm. Rumors had circulated. She wanted me to confirm or deny. I pleaded no contest; I neither confirmed, nor denied the rumors. "The boss and I had a falling out. Karis and I found a place to operate the new agency out of, and so far things have been going well."

I asked Lynn how she wound up, one, being a lawyer, and two, how did she wind up as a defense attorney.

"My father worked as an assembly operator for a factory," she said. "He worked ten- and twelve-hour days, five, sometimes six, days a week."

"Long hours."

"Tell me about it. The company paid him well, but he hated the job. The place was literally a sweat shop."

"Air conditioned in the summer?"

"He wished. Place would get so hot, when they handed out paychecks each week and he'd stick his in his back pocket, the ink would run off the check," she said. "And that's not a joke."

"I worked in an auto plant once, part of a college summer help program. That's the thing I remember most, the sweltering heat," I said. "One time I saw a guy step away from the assembly line and just collapse. Heat stroke."

"He worked B-shift then, my father, something like three in the afternoon until some time in the middle of the night. I remember during the summer, when I was young and off from school for summer vacations, I would spend the mornings and early afternoons with him," Lynn said.

"That's nice, at least."

"It was. He would cut the grass and I would use hand trimmers and go around the trees and the mailbox post doing the trim work. Then we'd sit in folding chairs in the backyard and drink lemonade together. When he was home, we did a lot together."

Lynn was into her story, it showed on her face, and I was into her rendition, though I thought I could guess where she was headed with the tale.

"Then it would be time for him to leave for work. He would kiss me good-bye, and give my mother a kiss good-bye," Lynn said. "And the expression on his face would change drastically. I'd watch him get in his car, back out of the driveway and through his windshield I'd see his eyes. He looked nothing like my father anymore. He was just a man heading to work, in a job he hated. He looked like an angry, bitter, stranger."

"I can't say I blame him," I said.

"I remember asking my mother once about the way he looked and she told me what I already knew . . . it was because he hated his job. It bored him. I asked her, why doesn't my father just quit then? And my mother, she told me, she said that for a man with little more than a high school education, the job paid him enough money to take care of his family. How could he walk away from a job like that, like it or not. My father made enough money to take care of his family and to him nothing else truly mattered. So when I got older, my father would tell me to do well in school and to go to college. He told me college would let me find a job doing something I wanted, a job where I could use my head and challenge my brain, and I believed him."

"But why law school?" I had to ask.

"My father went in to work one day. He worked on this big machine that had this mechanical arm with a blade that dropped down and chopped metal in two. One day a chunk of metal shifted on the conveyer belt and the flow jammed. My father switched the machine off, reached in, and his movement along the belt activated the sensor. The large blade on the mechanical arm came down on my father's back . . ."

She was crying, perhaps had been, but I only just noticed. We were stopped for a red light. "Lynn, why don't you pull the car over."

"I'm all right. I'm okay," she said. The light turned green.

"You didn't have to tell me this, you know. Especially if you knew it was going to upset you like this."

"I know. I wanted to."

I waited.

She sighed, used the back of her wrist to wipe tears away. "The stupid company he worked for . . . gave his life for . . . said that he by-passed the machine's safety feature. Of course the insurance company backed what the factory people were saying. They wanted to try and make my father look negligent for his own death. The Workers' Compensation attorney was good though. He had a small office near the factory. The union my father was a part of kept him on a yearly retainer. It took two and a half years, my mother and I stopping in to talk with the attorney every month, and several hearings at the compensation board, but that attorney won my father's case."

"And this attorney was your inspiration?"

"My father was my inspiration. His attorney helped me decided just what I wanted to do with my life." She pulled into a parking lot, a visitors sign posted by the entrance. She parked as close to the facility as possible.

"It's a good story," I told her.

"It's a painful one."

***

Of the lock-ups in the city, the newest was the Monroe County Prison. If it weren't for the electrified, barb wired fence around the perimeter, the architectural design might lead non-Rochesterians to believe they were seeing a junior college instead of a minimum-security facility. Several brick buildings with bars in the windows stood clustered together. Well-manicured lawns, maturing maple trees and island rock gardens planted on a bed of large cedar chips

39

made up the landscape on either side of a winding cobblestone walkway. The walkway led from building to building and to the parking lot. Along the north side of the most northern building of the prison, I could see a baseball diamond, basketball courts and picnic tables.

We got out of the car. Lynn started walking toward the entrance carrying a leather briefcase in her left hand. She looked very professional and in looking professional, I realized how sexy professional could look.

Lynn and I entered the center building. She walked up to a desk in the main lobby. I followed. The police officer smiled when he saw Lynn approach. He produced a clipboard and held it out for her to sign in on the registration form.

"How are you, Lynn?" The police officer asked.

"Busy." After signing her name she passed the pen and clipboard over to me. "This is Nicholas Tartaglia, a private detective working for me on Gordon Birdie's case."

"Sign in please, Mr. Tartaglia."

I did as I was told.

The police officer took the clipboard, slid it under his counter. He turned to his computer. His fingers slapped at the keys. "Gordon Birdie. He's in his cell, building Three-R. I'll phone ahead, tell the guard you're coming down. You want Mr. Birdie waiting in an interview cell?"

"I'd appreciate that, save time," Lynn said. She looked at her watch. I knew she was thinking about her appointment with the DA.

"No problem, Lynn. If you need anything else, let me know."

We walked down a wide hallway. The walls were mauve and gray. The colors had a calming effect on me. We rounded the corner and came face-to-face with a closed steel double door. Each door had a narrow rectangular windowpane. A sign hung centered over the doors reading: 3-R. Lynn pressed a doorbell on the wall by the right door. A female prison guard appeared on the other side of the glass window and smiled. She unlocked the door and pushed it open.

"How are you, Lynn?" The guard asked.

"Fine," Lynn said. She and I stepped through the doorway. The guard closed the door and locked it again. I immediately noticed the difference in decor. The walls were cinder block, painted a dull shade of battleship gray; here I felt more confined rather than calmed. I heard Lynn say, "This is Nicholas Tartaglia."

"How are you, Mr. Tartaglia?"

"Nick. I'm fine, and you?" I said.

The guard smiled. "Busy." She looked from me to Lynn. "I can take you down to the interview room if you'd like? Gunther is rounding up Mr. Birdie now," the guard said.

"That's okay. Which room is he going to be in?"

"C-two."

"We'll stop at the machine, grab some sodas and head to the room," Lynn said. "Okay if I bring him a can?"

"You just make sure he drinks it, and you bring the empty back out with you."

"Of course," Lynn said.

"Sure you don't want me to take the two of you down, Lynn?" The guard asked. Lynn nodded. "Okay, then Gunther should be there to let you in." She sat back down in her chair behind the desk by the door. She started typing on the keyboard while her eyes watched the results of her work displayed on the monitor. She indeed looked very busy.

Lynn and I walked to an employee break-room area and she bought three soda pops and a couple of different candy bars. "Have a preference?"

"None for me. Thanks," I said.

Lynn stuffed the goodies into her purse and we went and waited for Gunther by the door to the interview room. I glanced through the one-way glass and decided the room better resembled a police interrogation room.

Through the glass window on the door, I watched as Gunther entered the interview room from a second door at the opposite end of the room. He had a prisoner with him. The prisoner was a young black man dressed in an orange jump suit. "Gordon Birdie, I presume."

"That's him," Lynn confirmed.

The prison guard, Gunther, sat Gordon Birdie at one of the three chairs around the lone metal table in the box shaped room. He removed Birdie's handcuffs and clipped them onto his belt. He held up a finger as if he might be instructing the man to sit and wait for us.

Gunther came to our door and used his key to unlock it. He stepped out into the hall, then closed and locked the door behind him.

I watched Birdie through the window. The accused man sat with his hands folded on the tabletop, one knee bounced up and down anxiously, all the while staring straight ahead at the boring gray wall.

Gunther smiled, looking past Lynn at me, and shook my hand. "I'm Gunther. You must be Whine's attorney?"

Lynn snorted as she forced herself to smile. "Actually, I am Lynn Scannella, Mr. Birdie's attorney. Mr. Tartaglia, here, is a private investigator helping me with the case."

"You can call me Nick," I said.

The guard's complexion turned a bright shade of red. "I apologize, Miss Scannella."

"Lynn," Lynn said. "It's all right."

Eager to move on and to put his blunder behind him, Gunther said, "Under the center of the table, where the both of you will be seated, is an emergency call button. I'll be right outside the door anyway, but if you need me to respond more quickly, just press that button." Gunther smiled. "You know, in case of an emergency."

"Thank you. May we go in?" Lynn asked.

"Of course," said Gunther as he unlocked the door.

Lynn walked in first, leaned her briefcase against the table leg and sat down across from Birdie. I saw her finger casually glide along the bottom side of the tabletop. I could tell she'd found the emergency button when she shifted around in her seat and cleared her throat.

"How are you today, Mr. Birdie?" Lynn asked.

I studied Birdie. He was not a big man, nor did he appear intimidating in any way. His hair was cropped down close to his head. He needed a shave; he looked to have a couple days worth of stubble covering his face. In the file I had read that he was in his early thirties. He looked younger. He couldn't weigh more than one hundred and eighty pounds. He couldn't be more than six feet tall. He looked nervous with his eyes darting around the room, or maybe it could have been that he looked scared, genuinely scared.

"I'm fine. Who's this?" Gordon Birdie looked at me while he spoke.

"This is Nicholas Tartaglia. He's going to help us sort through the mess you're in. Mr. Tartaglia is a private investigator and has been retained by my office to investigate your case. Do you have a problem with that, Mr. Birdie?"

"He's going to help you to help me?"

"That's right," I said.

"Then I'm glad to have you on our side. Cause, I gotta tell you Mr. Tartaglia . . ."

"Nick."

"Okay, Nick," Gordon Birdie said and smiled. He looked like he might be waiting for something. His eyes looked hungry, and his mouth was open as if in anticipation.

Lynn removed the soda pop and candy from her purse. For the next few, and revolting, minutes we all sat silently while Gordon Birdie devoured the chocolate and gulped down his drink.

When he was through with his snack break, Gordon looked from me to Lynn to me again. "I gotta tell you, Nick, I didn't kill that man, that boy."

"But you were in his house?" I said.

"Yes."

"Robbing him?"

Birdie lowered his eyes. He no longer seemed interested in making eye contact with me. "Not exactly. That's not exactly true, sir."

"Mr. Birdie," Lynn said. "Nick needs to ask you some questions. And you have to answer them. The only way he can help you is if you give him the truth. The last thing we want is to go to court unprepared. If we don't have the truth, then we are doing little more than wasting precious time." Lynn stood up. She glanced toward the door.

Gordon Birdie stood up. I stood up ready to take action, but then it dawned on me. Birdie wasn't standing up so he could attack Lynn. He stood up because she stood up to leave—the perfect gentleman. Some murderer, I couldn't help but think.

When Lynn left the interviewing room, both Birdie and I sat back down. He looked at me for a long time, but his eyes did not meet mine. He was looking at my chest and my arms. He seemed to be studying my shoulders for the longest time. Then, braking the silence, he said, "We . . ."

"I'm sorry. We?" I said.

"His name was Anthony James," Birdie said. "Everyone calls me Whine. Anyway, we . . . Anthony and I . . . were the two who broke into Edwards' home."

"And Mr. James was the one who died?" I asked, drumming my fingers on the table.

"Yes. The kid shot him. Ah man," Birdie moaned. "This ain't no good."

"What, Gordon?" I said. I chewed on my lip and continued to drum my fingers on the table.

"Call me Whine, please. Gordon and Mr. Birdie, those are names that just don't sound right to me. I mean, my dad, he was always Mr. Birdie . . . and I have a hard time ever remembering anyone ever calling me Gordon." He smiled at me. His teeth were straight and white. His smile was nothing but friendly.

I smiled back. "Fine, Whine. What's the moaning for?"

"Guilt." Whine made eye contact with me for a moment, then looked back at the tabletop. "How am I supposed to speak badly of the dead?"

"Philip Edwards, Jr.?" My fingers drummed.

"Man, what's up with you . . . shaking, and tapping your fingers like that? Damn. I'm the one in prison waiting to go to a trial where I might be found guilty and given the death penalty . . . or worse . . . life without parole. Why are you so jumpy? Man, why can't you sit still?"

"I quit smoking," I said.

Whine shook his head and gave me a look clearly calling me pitiful. "Today?"

"Two weeks ago," I said. I needed to get him back on track. "Listen, you were talking about speaking ill of the dead . . ."

"Shit, no. I'm talking about Anthony. I mean . . ." Whine stood up quickly. His actions surprised me. I pushed my chair back quickly and got into a defensive stance. I looked to the one-way mirror sure that Whine was making security guard Gunther and Lynn just as uneasy as I appeared to be, that is, if they were watching.

"Can we sit back down?" I asked.

Whine paced back and forth. He stopped and stared at me with his hands balled into fists planted firmly on his hips. After a moment his fingers relaxed and unrolled. He rubbed the palms of his hands up and down the sides of his orange jump suit.

"I didn't kill Philip Edwards, Jr.," Whine said.

I cleared my throat and nodded. I waved my palm over the table, indicating the empty chair. Whine sighed and sat. I said, "Your prints, Whine, they were on the gun that is believed to have . . ."

"But Nick, I didn't kill him. Anthony did. I just tossed all of Anthony's stuff into his bag . . . I left the gun at the scene. I mean, I touched the gun—and I tossed it away from Anthony's body. I didn't want the gun, I don't even like guns. I guess I didn't want the police finding the gun anywhere near Anthony is all. But let me tell you this . . . after the shooting, after Anthony died . . . I got the Hell out of the house. And let me tell you, it all happened fast, lightening fast."

"Why were you in the basement? What were you going to steal out of the basement?" I asked.

Whine stood up again, but more slowly this time. He paced around his half of the room and stopped in front of the one-way mirror. He had his back to me when he said, "A book."

I did not know if Lynn was listening to this. I had the distinct feeling that she was not. She did not want to know these particulars of the case. She wanted me to find them out and research them. I said, "A book? You broke into this man's house for what kind of book?"

"It's a long story," Whine said.

"You're in here, in prison, Whine, on murder charges. If you don't tell me your story you may wind up spending the rest of your life in here. Now, I've never been to prison, Whine, I've never done time but I'll bet it's safe to guess that being in prison kind of sucks. Wouldn't you agree?" I asked. I know I sounded harsh, but I wanted to find out all I could as quickly as possible. Lynn had stressed the fact that all of this would be going to trial soon. That meant I needed to find answers as soon as possible.

"See, Mr. Edwards? He's not a good man . . ."

"Wait a minute. Philip Edwards the father or the son?"

"The father. I suppose the son wasn't any good neither . . . the apple never falls too far from the tree, see what I'm saying. But that's just speculating on my part. I don't know shit about the son. No, what I'm talking about is the father. Philip Edwards was not a good man," Whine said.

"Edwards is noted for his charitable contributions. United Way saluted him annually for his sponsored drives and employee incentive community volunteer work," I said, not bothering to tell Whine the malicious death of junior only made Edwards more loved by the people of Rochester.

Whine looked at me. "I know about that Mr. Edwards, but he has another side," Whine said.

"Don't we all," I said.

"The side of Mr. Edwards I am talking about is darker than the second sides of most of us." Whine sat down again. He folded his arms on the table and leaned in close.

"Darker?" I said. "How dark?"

"Pitch," Whine said.

"Okay. Sounds pretty dark. Tell me why or how you know this."

"Man, I can't tell you that," Whine said. He pushed away from the table and leaned back in his chair, folding his arms across his chest. "Why do you think I'm in here?"

"Because you couldn't post bail," I retorted.

"Wrong. I mean, you're right, but you're also wrong," Whine said.

"Look Whine, I'm trying to help you. I want to help you. What I won't do is sit here and play word games with you. Either you want to tell me what was going on that night, or you don't. One thing's for sure, after your court date, I won't be the one doing life in prison," I said. I wanted to stand up and make like I was leaving, but I just got here and didn't want Whine to think I quit things that easily.

"Look man, look Nick, there is so much going on here . . . I don't expect you to understand it. Man, I don't understand it. One thing I know for sure, and you can ask anyone at my church, I'm safer here than anywhere else right now," Whine said. He rested his elbows on his knees, lowered his head and appeared to be staring at the ground.

"Safer here than where? On the outside?" I asked.

"That's right."

"You think you're safer here, than on the outside of a prison. Why?"

"Look man," Whine said. "Look, I can't be telling you all that goes on."

"Whine, I don't think you're getting it . . ."

"No Nick, you seem like a nice guy, but I don't think you're getting it. I could sit here and tell you about how it went down that night, and I will if you want me to, but that has nothing to do with what's going on. It don't have nothing to do with it," Whine said.

"Do me a favor then. Start by telling me what happened that night, the night of the burglary and murders," I said. "After that you can try to tell me about the bigger picture. For now . . . all I'm looking for are the facts of what happened that night."

I leaned back in my chair as Whine's story got underway. It took nearly twenty minutes to recite. "Man, Nick, and that's what happened. I swear. I didn't shoot nobody. Hell Nick, I never even fired a gun before."

"The gun they found in the basement had your prints on it. You had gloves with residue on them . . . consistent with residue found after someone fires a gun. You were caught by the police with a bag filled with materials used to make explosives," I said.

"Damn Nick, I just got done telling you how that all happened. I took the bag, yeah. I panicked. The gun, I tossed it away from Anthony's body . . . the gun, the bag, they weren't mine." He let out a loud, long sigh and ran the palms of his hands over his face, rubbing his eyes. "We done?"

"Almost. Let me ask you two more questions, all right?"

"I need to hear them first before I agree to them," Whine said.

Whine wasn't whining too much in my opinion. If I had to give him a nickname at this point it wouldn't be Whine, it would be something like, You-stubborn-bastard-you. "Look Whine . . ."

"Just ask your questions, all right?"

I smiled. "Sure, Whine. How come you aren't out on bail?"

"Man, you ever listen to yourself talk? Didn't we go over this one before? Did you hear what the judge set bail at!" He wasn't asking me a question. He was enraged. He slammed his hands down on the table to illustrate his point. "One million dollars. Who the Hell does he think I am? I ain't got any family. It's just me and my girl—where is she supposed to come up with one million dollars? Even the bondsman wants something like one tenth of that amount. That's like one hundred thousand bucks. One hundred thousand bucks, Nick. I have an apartment, I don't own any home. I can't mortgage what I don't have."

"And no family?"

"Told you. None."

I sighed. I waited. "You said there was another reason."

"I told you Nick. I told you. I'm safer in here. That's it."

"Whine, what was in the book?"

While leaning back in his chair and folding his arms across his chest, Whine said, "Ah man, here we go again."

"Whine," I prompted.

"I can tell you, all right . . . but remember no matter what, I will always deny that I told you this. Hell, you ain't going to believe me anyway. Still, someone asks me where you found this out, I'm gonna say I don't know, and will swear it to my dying day that I didn't tell you."

"This better be good," I said.

"No Nick. This is not good. This is so far from good that you'll find yourself at the opposite end of the rainbow, if you know what I mean."

"Well?" He had my attention, my curiosity piqued.

"The name of the book, it's called The Talisman."

"The Talisman. I know what that is. I know what it means, but Whine tell me, what does it mean to you?" I asked.

"That's it Nick. That's all you get from me about the book. That . . . and the fact that Philip Edwards is a sick, sick crazy man."

"Philip Edwards. CEO of Rochester's largest company is sick and crazy. Okay. Got it."

"Hey, you don't have to believe me. I ain't askin' you to believe me. I told you, you weren't going to believe me. I can give two shits what you think. You wanted some information, and against my better judgment, I gave it to you. Do with it whatever you want," Whine said.

"You're gonna have to tell me why he's crazy and sick, Whine. You really gave me nothing. I'll bet most of Rochester thinks that you're sick and crazy, but if I asked them why they thought this I bet they'd tell me why . . . they could explain in great detail to me why they think you are sick and crazy," I said. I wanted to push buttons that would deliver answers.

"I'm done Nick."

"Says who, Whine? Who?"

Whine jumped up and yelled, "Guard!"

CHAPTER 5

Lynn drove us back to her office building all the while asking how things had gone between Whine and myself. I kept telling her, Good. I told her I would be in touch as soon as I had something worth reporting. In the parking lot we said a quick good-bye then I watched her walk into the lobby of her building. I walked to my car, lost in thought.

I knew where to begin my investigation and so I drove toward Brockport, a small college town on the western edge of Rochester. I had a friend out that way who I believed might be able help.

Whine had said things I'd heard, but neglected to pick up on during the interview. I listened closely to every word said and though my memory is far from great, I did not want to take notes during the talk. I thought it might offend him and did not want to offend the client. However, if I'd done some deciphering while he talked, I would not have missed a prime opportunity to redirect my line of questioning. Having this time to reflect back on the conversation— the points I'd missed now stared me directly in the face. I'd like to call those points . . . a lead.

Quickly, I called Lynn's office. Heather Slimms answered the telephone. "Heather? This is Nicholas Tartaglia."

"Mr. Tartaglia, I'm sorry. She came and she left. She has a meeting with the DA."

"I know all about that," I said. "I just have a question that maybe you could leave in a message for her?"

"Sure. What is it?"

"What church does Gordon Birdie belong too? That's the question. If she can find that out . . . maybe it's in his file. I don't remember seeing anything about a church, or religion in there, but then again, I wasn't looking for one."

"Okay, I'll ask her. Anything else?"

"Not that I can think of at the moment. Thanks, Heather." I hung up.

At a red light, I connected the PC modem card to the cellular phone and switched on the computer, taking me on-line.

The light turned green. With one eye on the road, one on the computer screen, I typed in yahoo.com. At the next red light I choose to look in the cyber jungle under books. At the search prompt, I typed: talisman, the . . .

When the light turned green I had just enough time to glance at the monitor. Over five hundred sites had been found. I had my work cut out for me.

***

St. Anthony's had been a small church with no parking lot to speak off. The church had sat across the street from the college campus, just a short walk away from the faculty parking lot—which was where I parked. The visitor's lot was at the opposite end of the campus, on the other side of the railroad tracks and I didn't feel like walking that far—I'd risk the ticket.

I knew the priest of the church pretty well. Father Paul and I had worked together on a big case last year. Undetected and for decades, a religious cult had held midnight mass once a month in the basement of St. Anthony's. The cult, known as the Tenth House, sacrificed animals and people. The cult was gone now, burned down in a fire; the entire church was in the process of being rebuilt. The community had rallied after the fire—long story—and rather than go without a church, demanded that it be rebuilt. The memories of that basement were too strong for me; the horrors I'd witnessed were unspeakable. I could not imagine going back there—even after rebuilding.

However, still standing was the rectory, which used to be around in back of the church. The debris from the fire had been cleared away and the reconstruction of the basement had begun, but little else. Father Paul still lived in the rectory. It was a small, white vinyl-sided house with an unattached garage on the side. I went to the front door and knocked.

Father Paul answered. He smiled immediately and pushed open the screen door. "Nick, it's good to see you. Come on in, come in."

I stepped into my friend's home and felt immediately comfortable. I've been visiting with Father Paul regularly since the downfall of the cult. The priest stood five-eight with dark, slicked back hair. He had stunning twilight-blue eyes, always looked clean-shaven, and seemed to always be dressed in a traditional black shirt, white collar, black slacks and shoes. A little out of shape, Father Paul's belly silently begged for the priest to do sit-ups.

"What did you think of the sermon Sunday?" Church was being held at an empty building along Main Street, by the canal. The parishioners showed up early and set out folding chairs and candles.

I shrugged. "Good."

"Good? You sure you're a writer? Good is not much of an adjective and won't help me self-evaluate the message." Father Paul stood with his fists on his hips.

"I'm sorry, Father. Okay, how about: The sermon felt, I don't know, forced. I would have liked to hear a related story to the message. Maybe something humorous."

"Open with a joke?"

"No," I said. "But between breaths, compare the message to a story of something that might have happened to you, or to your friend, even if it's contrived. I guess I have a hard time understanding Bible passages. I think for me . . . personally now I'm talking about . . . I have a hard time getting the gist and I need it explained to me in a way I can relate. Know what I mean?"

"In a blasphemous kind of way, yes, I do." Father Paul snickered. "How about something cold to drink? Or coffee?"

"Cold sounds good. Anything, really."

"This a social call?"

"For the most part."

"Business, huh?" Father Paul nodded at me as he walked me into his den. "Here, have a seat. I'll be back with the drinks."

When he came back from the kitchen he handed me a large glass filled with ice tea. We sat down across from each other, him in his leather recliner, me on the comfortable sofa. The first time we did this—last year—I had come to ask the priest questions about the supernatural and paranormal and to see if he knew anything about the Tenth House.

"Once again, I'm here to ask for your help."

"Inner religious turmoil?"

"Not quite."

"Confident in that department, huh? Okay, then sure, Nick. Shoot," he said, taking a sip of iced-tea. He leaned forward to show his devoted attention and rested his elbows on his knees.

"Have you ever heard of a book called, The Talisman?"

"My goodness, Nick, where do you come up with all of this stuff?" Father Paul asked. He no longer looked comfortable. He leaned back in his chair and crossed one leg over the other. "Don't you ever just follow around husbands cheating on wives? Isn't that what P.I.'s mostly do? Spy?"

"Not always that simple. If I'm bothering you . . ."

"You're not bothering me, not at all. In fact, I don't know if this is good or not, but in a way you bring excitement around with you. It feels good to get excited," the priest said. "So you must know something about the word, the title of this book, or you wouldn't be here. Nick, do you know what a talisman is?"

"I do."

"Explain it to me," Father Paul said.

"It's a magical charm, a medallion," I said.

"A medallion, maybe. Doesn't have to be. It could be a coin, a statue. It's something tangible, something you can hold or touch. It can either be meant to protect you from harm, or it can be meant to harm you."

"Okay, what does this have to do with the book?"

"I'm not sure. Can't say as I've ever heard of a talisman in book form. That's not to say one does not exist. It is just that I have never heard of one," Father Paul said. I could tell by his contorted facial expression that he was thinking, trying to conjure up an answer. His brow furrowed and his lips were pursed tightly together. His thumb and middle finger rubbed at his temples.

Discouraged, I sat back and set my glass of ice tea on the end table by the arm of the sofa.

Father Paul asked, "Have you checked the Web?"

"On my way here. I scanned it. Nothing seemed to jump out at me though . . . but there is a lot there to look through."

Father Paul smiled. "I don't doubt that there is. I'd have to wager a guess that aside from pornographic material on the web, religious and cult related material sites would have to be one of the biggest. Have you posted your question on a message board?"

"Actually, I just started working on the case this morning. Aside from the book search in Amazon, this is my first stop. But I like your thinking." Father Paul went on-line this past autumn. He and I had gone computer shopping together. I had told him to wear the white collar, believing it would discourage salespersons from trying to take us for a financial ride. "Mind if I go online?" I asked pointing at his roll top desk. The computer was behind the closed roll.

"I'd love for you to stay and work your case, but I've got a couple coming over soon, should be here any minute. Marriage counseling," the priest said.

"No. Don't worry about it. You gave me a path, and that is more than I can ask."

"If you don't mind, I'll look into it for you . . . I guess you might say I've become secretly fascinated by the supernatural, not to mention I find playing on the Internet to be addicting."

"I wouldn't mind at all, Father. I'm looking for anything that you might think could be important. Since I know nothing at all about it . . . pretty much anything you find will be useful. Find out, if you can, who published it. I'd love to know how many copies were printed. Maybe see if the book is still in print. I can't say for sure if we're dealing with any kind of a cult . . ."

"Let's hope not."

"Still, you might be able to see if there are any cults, or religious fanatics who locally follow the word of this book. If not locally, try to find which might be the closest church . . . and I use the word church in quotes . . . that believes the crap printed in this talisman dime novel. Should I write these questions down?" I asked. It had been a mouthful. Once I start a line of thinking my train of thought becomes a web of paths. I realized I needed to write everything down—for myself. The thoughts needed to become more organized.

Working off an outline might be the best way to proceed.

"No need. I understand where you're headed. I may not remember what you said word-for-word, but I'll be close enough so that the answers should satisfy your needs."

Before leaving, I thanked my friend for the drink and his time. Father Paul said, "Anytime, Nick. God bless."

CHAPTER 6

It was nearly five o'clock when I pulled into the rear lot of my office building. I parked next to Karis' car. I locked the doors and walked around to the front entrance, which was on the south side of the building. I liked the people in Spencerport. They smiled, waved, and said things like "Hello" when you passed by one another. They also seemed to walk everywhere. Maybe because nearly everything seemed in walking distance. The library, post office, a grocery store and a small shopping plaza sat across the street from my office; a gas station and pizza place, sat kiddy-corner to it on the south, and to the north were a small movie theater and dry cleaners. Up and down Main Street, small businesses occupied the buildings on either side of the road. There was a sports bar, hair and nail salon, used bookstore, small Italian restaurant, and a knick-knack venture that sold crafts by local artists on consignment.

My agency and Reliquus, the antique store beneath the agency shared the outer front door. Once through that door, there were two more doors. The one on the right led to Reliquus. The door on the left led to the staircase to my office. I climbed the stairs two at a time. The frosted glass on my door had printed in bold black letters: The Tartaglia Agency and, underneath it, my name. I walked through the unlocked door into the reception area.

The hardwood floors had a thick coat of polyurethane applied two months ago, and though they looked wonderful, the strong chemical smell persisted to linger. Karis, who sat behind her desk in the center of the main room, and who looked up from her computer as a I walked in, had spent the first few weeks back in November beautifying the place. And since I loved and collected artwork on lighthouses, Karis strategically used some of my personal collection to decorate the reception area and my office.

"Hey, hon." I smiled.

"I wondered if you'd be coming back to the office," she said, leaning back in her chair.

"Writing?"

"I was," she said. "Editing, really."

"Don't let me disturb you. I've got to get on the net. I have some research to conduct," I said.

"The murder case."

"Yep."

"Gonna work long?" she asked.

I continued to smile. "I might. Why?"

Karis stood up, walked around to the front of the desk and leaned against it. She rubbed her legs together and twisted her waist some. Her eyelids batted. "I thought I'd stop at the video store, rent a movie and pick up some Chinese. We could go back to my place?"

I contorted my facial expression so I could look Jerry-Lewis-confused. "You want to do that tonight?"

"Nick . . ."

"I'm just kidding. Actually, that sounds wonderful. I'll give you a half-hour head start. I'll get some things going on the web, giving you time to get the video and chow and get home." I walked closer to her, took her in my arms and held her close. She smelled like Lilacs. "I love you."

"I love you." She kissed me. "Don't be too long."

"If I am, just eat without me, and wait for me in bed . . . naked, of course."

"Of course." She bit my lower lip; held it tight between clenched teeth. After a slow, rolling growl, she released the lip. "Nick?"

"Yes, dear."

"Don't be late."

"You know what dear? I love when you bite me."

"I'll say it one more time. Don't be late, or I won't ever bite you again."

With plans made for the night, I found myself agitated with how slow the computer operated. While it took its time connecting to the net, I fished a notepad and pen out of my desk. At the search prompt displayed on the monitor, I typed: Talisman message board, and waited. I found nearly as many messages boards as I had web sites. I liked message boards. You post a question at the site and sometimes within hours people reply to your message.

At the message board prompt, I typed in my message:

> I have some questions about a book
> called The Talisman. Anyone heard of it? And
> I don't mean the novel by Stephen King and Peter Straub!

I figured a direct approach would be best. I book-marked the message board so I could check it easily in a day or so.

I went back and searched for more talisman web sites. When the five hundred sites came up, I clicked on the first link and waited patiently for it to open. It appeared to be a church's web site with quotes from the Bible posted on the home page. I quickly scanned the document looking for the word talisman but did not see it. I backed out of the site and went to the next link. Again I was confronted with pages of quotes and passages from the Bible, and I again scanned the document to no avail.

I continued on with the process, but as I continued, instead of just scanning, I began to read the passages. I also printed pages that I thought sounded interesting and possibly important. I nearly jumped when the telephone rang.

"Tartaglia Agency," I said. My eyes continued to read the passages displayed on the screen in front of me. "Nicholas Tartaglia speaking."

"Nick? It's Lynn."

I sat back in the chair and spun away from the monitor. "How'd it go with the DA?"

"He's an asshole."

"Went that well, huh?"

"We can talk about it later. I got your message asking about where Whine goes to church. How is that relevant?" Lynn asked. She was dying to know what had been discussed. It seemed to be killing her that she was out of the loop.

"Trust me. It is."

"Well, I don't know the answer to that. I'll have to call the prison . . . but it won't be until the morning. Can you wait that long?" Lynn asked.

"I can. I've got enough reading to hold me over until then."

"What are you reading?"

"I told you, when I have enough information, I'll fill you in," I said. I spun back around in the chair. I noticed on the monitor a web site that did not appear to be from a church, or I might edit that by saying, a traditional church. The link read: http://magicaltalisman.com, so I clicked on the link. The monitor displayed a black screen. Then stars appeared and began to twinkle. Slowly the screen looked as if it were moving down, and words appeared announcing the name of the site in gold-bronze letters. "I'm sorry, Lynn, did you say something?"

"Yes, I said something. I asked you to try and write a report each day so we can keep it all straight. All right?"

"That sounds fine. I can do that."

"You're not really paying attention to me, are you?"

"Not right now Lynn. I'm working."

"I'll expect reports," said Lynn.

"I'll write them. Anything else?"

"No. I'll have the name of the church for you tomorrow. If I get a minute, I'll try to get a hold of someone at the jail this evening before I head for home. Nick . . . have a good night," Lynn said.

"You too," I said and hung up the telephone.

The web site was decorated with pixies and moons. I clicked on the link that read, About the site.

The telephone rang again. "What else do you need Lynn?"

"It's not Lynn. It's Karis, and where in the Hell are you?"

"I said I'd be along," I said. I wanted to stick my foot in my mouth.

"Nick, it's almost seven o'clock."

I looked at my wristwatch and gasped. "Oh my God, Karis . . ."

"Yeah, Oh my God, Nick."

"Karis . . ."

"I'm going to call it an early night, Nick."

"Wait, Karis. I'm packing it up right now. I'm on my way."

"I've already eaten. I'm going into my room and watch the movie in there, there's no point . . ."

"Karis, Wait. Just hold it. I'll eat in the kitchen by myself. You can start the movie and when I come into the room . . . I won't ask any plot related questions . . ."

Silence filled the distance between us for a long few moments. "Karis?"

"I'm thinking," she said. "If you come right now . . . you'll still have to heat the food up on your own."

"I'm a bachelor. I know how to use a microwave."

"I suppose if you eat quickly enough the most you might miss is the coming attractions."

"I won't even chew," I said.

"You don't have to be a pig about eating," she said, laughing.

"Not while I eat Chinese, no I don't."

"And what's that supposed to mean?" She asked. I could clearly hear a flirtatious tone in her voice.

"What? I said nothing."

"It's what you didn't say that intrigued me."

"Oh? Intrigued?" I asked.

"That computer off?"

I told her that it was—a small white lie on my part. "I'm on my way."

We hung up. I looked at the computer screen and decided to bookmark the web page. I logged off the computer and switched off the equipment in the office. I locked up and left.

I was hungry and didn't have Chinese on my mind.

CHAPTER 7

Saturday, May 19

I woke up alone around ten on Saturday. I could hear Karis making noise from somewhere else in her house. We made up last night, all night, and so now I did not feel rested at all. While yawning, I stretched, reaching my arms up over my head and arching my back. I slid out of bed and gathered up my clothes from around the room. I went right into the bathroom and took a shower. I had a couple of drawers at Karis' house, one in her room for clothing, and one in the bathroom for my toothbrush, deodorant and razor. She had similar drawers at my place.

When I went into the kitchen Karis was sitting at the table sipping coffee and leafing through the morning paper. I said, "Why didn't you wake me?"

"You looked tired, besides, I kept you up all night. I thought I'd let you get some sleep." She flashed me a warm smile. It felt good when things were right between us. We locked lips in a long passionate good morning kiss.

I poured myself a cup of coffee, added cream and sugar and sat at the table next to the love of my life. "Plan on sharing that?"

"The paper?"

"The sports, anyway."

"Have it," she said. She shuffled around the sections, found the one I wanted, and gave it to me. "Plans for today?"

"Depends. I want to check my messages at the office. Why? Have something in mind."

"It's raining out, I thought we'd just go window shopping at the mall, or take in a movie?" She asked.

"Sounds promising to me."

"Sounds like nothing to me. Call your office and check your voice mail before we make any plans," Karis said. She shook open the paper and buried herself into her reading.

I picked up the telephone and called the office. I waited for the prompt and then entered a security I.D. number. One new message and it was from Lynn. She told me that Whine's church was the First Bible Baptist Church on the corner of Stutson Street and Lake Avenue. She also told me that they have a Saturday morning service at noon.

I hung up and looked at the time. It was not quite eleven. "Karis . . ." I said humbly.

"Where are you off to?" Karis asked.

"Church."

"Father Paul?" Karis asked. She continued to read the paper. I knew she was disappointed our plans would be broken, but she didn't let it show.

I sat back down next to her. "No. I have to go to where Gordon Birdie went to church. When I was talking with him yesterday he said something to me like; 'you can ask anyone at my church.' Only, he didn't stop there. He kept on talking, and I never got back around to asking what he meant by that."

"Family?"

"Doesn't have any, but he did mention one other thing I wanted to check up on," I said, taking a sip of coffee. "Mind if I top this off and bring it with me?"

"Are you going to leave the cup in the car when it's empty?"

"Probably . . ."

"Nick," she said, laughing.

"What . . . you want me to lie to you?"

"Never. Take it, take it," Karis said. She set down the paper. "Just don't forget me tonight. Okay. Let's do something."

"I'll do my best."

"Do me one favor then, all right?" Karis asked.

"Anything. What?"

"At some point during the day, call me."

CHAPTER 8

The rain was coming down hard. I drove ten miles under the speed limit with my windshield wipers slapping back and forth on high. The sky resembled this evil and contorted looking face, the color of charcoal with a battleship gray lining, and its mouth was opened and it was vomiting rain as if the world were one big toilet bowl.

I had taken I-490 East to I-390 North. My mind began to spin, sifting through details relating to Whine's case. More and more questions kept popping up in my head. Most of the questions I felt might be satisfied once I learned the deal on the book.

At the last exit on the expressway, I took the ramp onto the New York State Parkway and headed east. It was a short stretch of road from the expressway to the eastern end of the parkway—while going west could have taken me all the way to Niagara Falls. When I reached the end, I made a left onto Lake Avenue. The church sat at the next light on the right in a corner lot. Parking was in the rear and only a few cars were back there. Then again, I was nearly an hour early for service. I parked up close to the white clapboard chapel and waited in my car for a moment, hoping the rain would let up some, or—better yet—stop all together.

The rain did not look like it was going to slow so I shut off the car and pocketed the keys. I stared at the entrance to the church in an attempt to gage my break-for-the-door maneuver. The plan sounded simple, run with all my might and I shouldn't get too wet.

I opened the door and slammed it shut while already beginning my mad dash for the few stairs that lead up to the church doorway. My feet came down in a large, deep puddle that I had not noticed. I took the four stairs two at a time and went to pull open the door on the right. It was locked. I pulled open the door on the left and practically jumped into the church vestibule.

I was soaked. Water was in my shoes and my socks did everything they could to absorb every last bit of water. I gave my head a shake, then finger brushed my hair.

"Good day for ducks, wouldn't you agree," a man's voice said from behind me.

I turned around. A tall and handsome looking older man stood in front of me. He held out a towel for me to use. He was an African-American with light brown skin, big brown eyes, and, aside from Karis, he had one of the warmest smiles I have ever seen.

Taking the towel I said, "Thank you, and I disagree."

"You disagree?"

"I do. I saw some ducks on my way here and let me tell you, even they didn't look too happy with this weather." I smiled.

The man laughed and held out his hand. "I'm Jacob Brown, the Pastor of this church."

While shaking his hand, I said, "It's a pleasure to meet you. My name is Nicholas Tartaglia. You can just call me Nick."

"Nick, what brings you to this church? I mean, it's a small church and I know pretty much everyone. Occasionally though, and I love when this happens, some new faces show up . . . like yours. When this happens I try as best I can to introduce myself and to make myself available to answer any questions you might have," Pastor Brown said. "Regular service isn't until tomorrow, but today . . . as you've guessed, and in another hour . . . we have a special prayer service."

"Thank you for making me feel welcome. I appreciate that," I said. I wondered if he would continue to be as willing to talk when he found out I was here to ask questions concerning Gordon Birdie. "I do have some questions, Pastor."

Pastor Brown regarded me thoughtfully. He motioned with his hand for us to walk into church. The room appeared to be shaped like an inverted triangle. The altar and the pulpit were at the point of triangle. The rows of pews from the back of the church to the altar became shorter in length with each new row. To the left of the altar was a choir pit. In front of the pit sat three elderly looking people. One young and very attractive lady stood in the choir pit wearing a Windex blue choir robe. She had a chorus book in her hand, but appeared to be holding it funny. I didn't want to be rude and stare, so I turned my attention back to the Pastor. We continued to walk slowly down the center aisle.

"I don't want to be misleading here," I said tentatively. "I am a Catholic . . ."

"We're Baptists here, not all that different a practice from Catholicism, really. In fact, we have many devout Catholics who come to church here, but that is beside the point, really, and I did not mean to interrupt you. I'm sorry, Nick."

"No need to be sorry," I said. "In fact I think I am giving you the wrong impression. You see, I'm a private investigator."

Pastor Brown stopped walking. He stared at me with an odd and intense look. I could find no trace of that warm, loving smile—and believe me, I was looking for it. "I've been hired by Gordon Birdie's attorney to find out all I can about why he and a Mr. Anthony James decided to burglarize Philip Edwards' home."

"I have nothing to say about that . . . nothing, except that both Gordon, and Anthony were outstanding members of this church. Outstanding members. Now I understand full and well what you have told me. You are on the same side as Gordon, trying to help him, don't think I don't understand that, because I do. Just the same, I have nothing further to say." Pastor Jacob turned to face the altar ready to walk away from me.

"Pastor Brown, look, I need some questions answered," I said, raising my voice. I did not want to cause a scene, but I needed to get back the Pastor's attention. The old people in the pews stared at me. One old lady appeared to be adjusting her hearing aid so she could hear everything more clearly. The girl in the choir box was looking in my direction, but did not seem focused on anything in particular. "Pastor Brown, please . . ."

My body went rigid as something powerful gripped my neck and shoulder. I was forcibly turned around, and now stood facing a giant looking black man. This man, holding my neck and shoulder in a vise one might refer to as his hand, had shaved his head. He, too, had large brown eyes. At this moment they did not look warm and caring, but I suppose given the right circumstances, like at my funeral, they could. "I think Pastor Brown said he wanted for you to leave," the giant said, while needlessly tightening an already painfully tight grip on my neck.

"Actually, he said that he had nothing further to say," I managed to point out.

The grip got even tighter.

"Look, Lurch, I just quit smoking . . . and this thing, this . . . what you're doing? That ain't helping any."

"Pastor Brown would like for you to leave now." The giant man, who I so fondly nicknamed Lurch because of his Addams Family qualities, walked me down the center aisle toward the vestibule.

As he was doing so, I noticed a look on the choirgirl's face that I clearly recognized as concern.

"Ever do any professional wrestling," I asked once Lurch and I were in the vestibule, and only after he let go of my neck. I rolled my shoulder and head, trying to ease the discomfort.

"Look buddy, since we're in church . . . I won't be kicking your ass this time. Leave the Pastor alone, got it? Don't come back here, all right? If there's a next time, church or no church, I'll kick your ass."

"Lurch . . ."

"Name's not Lurch," said the giant.

"Okay. Listen, all I'm looking for are some answers. I'll bet you know Gordon Birdie," I said. Lurch reached around me. I nearly flinched. He pushed open the door. I ignored his insinuation. "I'll bet you knew Anthony James, too. You guys are all around the same age. Right?"

Lurch raised his hands, ready to push me out the door. I took two steps back toward the door. "Were they friends of your? Don't you want to try to help Gordon?"

"If Whine killed a man, then the only one who can help him now is God," Lurch said.

"But what if there is more to it than that?"

"God will sort through the facts regardless of what this country's justice system decides."

I was out the door, on the step, in the rain, and people were coming up the stairs quickly. Lurch turned and walked away.

"Excuse me," I mumbled to everyone as I tried to get down the four steps and back to my car.

I stood at my car and reached into my pocket. I was being watched. I could feel it. As I went to open the door I looked up. Standing on the side of the church, holding an umbrella, was the choirgirl. She stood silently. She did not call out to me. I decided to call out to her. "Miss?"

"Sir?" Her voice was soft and frail sounding.

I approached her tentatively, not wanting to frighten her. I was soaked, but at this point, I could care less. "Miss?"

"You said you are working to help Gordon?"

I knew something instantly, something I should have realized the minute I had first seen her. She was blind. "Yes," I said. "I'm a private investigator helping the attorney who represents Mr. Birdie."

"Do you ever get to see him? Do you go and visit with Gordon?"

"I have, I will again, yes." My mind clicked. When I met and talked with Whine the first time, he said two things to me that I did not follow up with further questions. The first had been about his church. The second had been about his girl. "Are you, were you . . . was Mr. Birdie your . . ."

"We were seeing each other. I can't believe I just told you that. No one knows. My brother, you just met him?" she said.

"Lurch?"

She laughed. "His name's Marlow. He wouldn't understand . . . especially now." She closed her eyes. "I'm sure you've noticed that I'm blind. Well, Marlow, he's very protective of me."

"I can appreciate that," I said. "I have two sisters. I'm the same way . . . or I was. They're a lot older now. He'll grow out of it." I worried about one sister more than the other. I didn't worry as much about the one married to a homicide detective.

"Maybe. I mean sometimes it's nice, him looking out for me." She smiled and opened her eyes. They were hazel and quite lovely. Her skin looked smooth and soft. "I have to get back inside or my brother will come out looking for me. If you see Gordon, will you tell him . . . can you tell him . . ."

"Do you want me to tell him that you love him?" I asked. My heart felt as if it might melt. This young woman seemed so sweet and innocent. Marlow may be a big mean bully, but if he spent his days looking out for his kid sister, I had to give the man due respect.

"Would you?" She was blushing.

"I will. What's your name?"

"Lydia Henson," she said, putting out a hand.

I shook hands with her. "My pleasure, Lydia. My name is Nicholas Tartaglia. Call me Nick, though. Okay?"

"Okay."

"Lydia, I might have some questions for you. Is there a way to get a hold of you?"

"On Monday nights we have a woman's Bible study."

"Here?"

"No. We meet at, you're gonna laugh," she said.

"I won't laugh. I promise."

"Marlow bowls on a league at Greece Bowl and because he wants me with him, we meet at the bowling alley. We get a table in the bar, order soda and popcorn, and talk about the Bible."

"In the bar," I said, laughing. I know I promised . . . but it was hard not to.

"You promised," she said.

"I'm not laughing. I was clearing my throat," I said.

"I'll just bet you were."

"So if I show up Monday . . . how can we work this?"

"We get there around seven. Marlow likes to bowl a couple of games before the league starts, to warm up. If you come into the bar and say something . . ."

"A code word?"

"Exactly. Say something like . . ."

"John-Jacob-Jingle-Hymer-Schmidt?"

Lydia laughed. "I'm being serious. You should be too. This isn't funny."

She was right. "I'm sorry. I could say . . . I don't know, how about anything I say is going to sound stupid because I'll be there alone. So I'll be this pathetic looking guy walking into a bar and talking to myself. I'll whistle the nursery rhyme. How's that?"

She smiled. "Fine. Fine. Then you can go and wait outside, give me a few minutes and I'll join you. I'll tell the others I need to use the little girl's room."

"Sounds good. I'll see you Monday."

"Monday. And Nick, you won't forget to tell Gordon?"

"I'll tell him Lydia. Don't worry."

"Nick, how's he doing, when you saw him? How was he?"

"He was all right, and I'm not just saying that."

She reached out to touch me. I thought she was looking for my hand, but when I gave it to her, her fingers stepped across my arm, up my shoulder and found my face. She rested her palm on my cheek. "I really do love him. You're going to help him, right?"

"I am really going to do my best," I said. We said good-bye and I watched her as she slowly turned around. She held out her right arm so her hand could skim the church to guide her back to the side door. She walked slowly to the door. Only when the door closed did I turn and go back to my car, completely drenched and soaking wet.

She was an intriguing young lady. Whine seemed like a lucky man—even if his romantic life could oddly be paralleled to the story of Romeo and Juliet.

And with that thought, an idea came to me. I drove back toward Spencerport thinking of the antique shop under my office. They specialized in odd relics. What could be more odd than a secret book written who knows how long ago? More than anything at this point, it was worth a shot.

CHAPTER 9

Reliquus. It was an odd name and when I first asked the owner, Mrs. VanValkenschmidt, what it meant she explained to me the name was Latin for remaining. It is also where the word relic derived from.

I pushed opened the door to the antique shop. A small bell jingled, signaling my arrival. The door closed silently behind me.

Frieda VanValkenschmidt bought the building nearly thirty years ago. She and her husband were well off and worldly. They traveled and collected antiques together. Mr. VanValkenschmidt had been twenty years older than his bride, and when he died at the young age of fifty of bone cancer, he left his widow—as she had chosen to put it—well to do.

Karis and I first met Frieda when we signed the lease for the upstairs office space. The following day, Frieda had baked us a plate of chocolate chip cookies (a personal favorite). Oddly enough, Karis had baked Frieda one of her famous apple pies. I bought milk at the gas station and convenient store across the street and we all sat and ate and talked.

Looking around the store, where one would expect to see rows of neatly placed items and relics out on display under a stand-alone spotlight, I always felt amazed to see such clutter. I wouldn't know a valuable object from a worthless one. However, despite the disarray, something in the gut told me I was standing in the middle of a good-sized fortune of merchandise.

I made my way to the glass counter at the back end of the store.

On display and locked under the glass counter were small, I'd imagine, easily shoplift-able items. I saw flashy looking jewelry. Most of the diamonds, rubies and emeralds were so large I could not imagine them to be real, though Frieda had assured me they were genuine gems. Sharing space with the stones, I saw pens, brooches and three Mickey Mouse wristwatches.

"I'll be out in a minute," a woman's voice called to me.

"Take your time. That's fine," I hollered toward the doorway behind the counter. It led to a back room. On the wall above the counter was a two-way mirror. I knew if I owned a store with valuable items like this I would want to watch everyone at all times, too. Frieda also pointed out the entire store was canvassed in the lenses of strategically placed surveillance cameras.

Hanging on the walls I noted some paintings looked old, while some looked newer. I recognized not-a-one and wouldn't be able to tell you if the artist used oil, or finger paint. There were many places where a variety of vases (pronounced either with a long or short sounding "a") sat on display. In the corner, sitting in a stand near the cash register was an autographed white Fender guitar, the strings strung incorrectly. Frieda assured me it, at one time, belonged to the late and great Jimmy Hendrix.

The door behind the counter opened and a woman in her mid sixties entered the room. She had silver hair and wore it long, showing off the natural curls and ringlets. As always, I clearly saw dark brown eyes sparkling brilliantly with excitement and anticipation—but in anticipation of what, I have no idea. She was tall, a few inches smaller than I, and thin with an apparent and shapely figure. She gave me a warm smile, but then burst out laughing. "Well, how are you Nicholas?"

"What's so funny?" I asked.

"You. You look like you took a shower with your clothes on!" Which, in this case, would explain those sparkling brown eyes.

"Fine, Frieda, fine. Laugh at a man about to catch pneumonia," I said sliding my hands into my pockets.

"I'm sorry. You're right. That's not funny. Can I get you a towel or something?"

"No. I'm fine. I have a change of clothes upstairs, but thank you. That was much nicer than laughing at me," I said, smiling. I was sure

I looked a sight. I felt, well, icky. There was nothing like wearing wet clothing, it clinging to the skin in an awful, cold way.

"So what's on your mind? You must be here on business, or you'd have changed first," Frieda said, insightfully.

"Such a smart woman," I said. "I do have a question for you. It's about a book . . . possibly an antique book."

"I have some books here, first editions, some signed by the authors," said Frieda, turning and pointing to a small bookcase along the right wall. "Do you know the author and title?"

"I know the title," I said. "It's a book about magic. It's called *The Talisman.*"

Frieda stared at me for a few seconds. She looked like a woman concentrating. Perhaps in her mind she was running through a mental card catalog; her own inner Dewey Decimal System. "Black or white?"

"Black or white, what?"

"Magic?"

"Magic comes in colors?" I said, smiling. I had to be on the right track. Even Frieda had an idea of what I was looking for. "What, like good magic is white and bad magic is black?"

"That's it exactly. It even has different spellings. White magick ends in a C.K. Now, I don't have any books on magic, or magick with a C.K. in my store. I have more of the classics. I can do one of two things for you, however. I know of a small bookstore down near High Falls, along the river? It's a bookstore on the occult and supernatural. I can't remember the name, but," Frieda said, pausing. She used her thumb and finger to rub the bottom of her chin. "Hold on one second."

Frieda spun around and exited through the door leading to the back room. She returned almost immediately with the Rochester Yellow Pages. She flipped through the book and stopped on bookstores. She used the tip of her finger as a guide to scan the names on the page. "Here it is, Magic Circle. You know where it is? You go down State Street heading south, and just as you pass Kodak Office, on the left, is Platt Street. You turn down there, and then make a left onto Mill Street. It's one of the shops along there."

"Right by the High Falls Bridge?"

"That's right." Frieda selected a pen from a cup of pens and pencils, and on a small square of paper, copied down the bookstore's telephone number and address. She handed me the paper.

"Frieda . . . thank you."

"You kidding me? This was fun, playing detective. You can ask me for help whenever you need it." She waved to me as I was leaving.

"You can count on it," I said, pulling open the door. The little bell jingled. I said, "Hey, how'd you know about this place?"

"Just because I don't carry any vintage books on magic doesn't mean I never studied the religion," she said flashing me a curious smile.

CHAPTER 10

Later Saturday night, and once the rain stopped, Karis and I went out for dinner to one of my favorite burger places down by Lake Ontario. Regardless of the time of day, the parking lot always looked at least three-quarters full.

Inside, orange booths with brown tables lined the walls and window-front, while a grouping of tables with orange chairs filled the center area. When people walked in they stood in front of and along the orange counter and waited to order. Orders for food were given to employees who, for the most part, all appeared to be under the age of twelve. However, when these minors took an order they did not write it down regardless of how long or complicated, and then proceeded to fill the order precisely.

Karis and I ordered the same, a burger with everything, fries with heavy hot sauce, and a large soda. We found a booth in a corner. I sat with my back to the wall. I liked to watch people, and I felt safer this way. Can't sneak up on someone if they sit with their back to the wall. While we ate, I told Karis about my day.

"You know what's weird about this?" Karis asked.

"Everything?"

"Aside from that. What bothers me is that some of it rings true," she said dipping a hot-sauce dripping fry into a pool of ketchup. "I'm thinking specifically about that Pastor."

"Brown? Jacob Brown? Yeah. I've been thinking about him, too. And Lydia's brother Marlow."

"Odd behavior," said Karis. She ate that fry and managed to look lovely doing so.

"Think they're merely concerned about the reputation of the church?" I asked, picking up my hamburger with relish.

"Could be. They'd have reason to be. Don't you think it's got to be more than that, though?"

"I do. That's why I'm meeting with Lydia." I took a bite, savoring the flavor.

"And what about this book, The Talisman?"

"Nothing solid yet. I thought maybe after we eat we could take a ride downtown."

"Check out the bookstore?" Karis asked.

"I called after changing into dry clothing and the place wasn't even open yet. It has like B-shift hours. Magic Circle opens at dusk and closes at three in the morning," I explained.

"Dusk?"

"Yep." I swirled my soda cup around before taking a long sip on the straw. "Wanna go?"

"Are you making a date with me?"

"I bought you dinner already, didn't I?" I asked.

"But what do you expect in return for this luxurious dinner and a trip to the bookstore?" She asked. She winked, waiting for an answer.

"Nothing. Just sex."

Karis shrugged. "Oh. Well, if that's all then . . . I will go with you to the Magic Circle tonight."

I enjoyed driving south down Lake Avenue. The area possessed a strong sense of negative-atmosphere. The homes were large, but run down with prostitute littered corners and drug deals made in the open, while others walked with bottles concealed in brown paper bags. I know this all sounds so stereotypical of a big city street, but unfortunately in this case—as in most cases concerning big cities— the description was true.

"Talk with Lynn at all?" Karis asked. The Kodak tower loomed in the sky, bright red lights glowing in the still soft, though quickly darkening, blue sky. "Nick?"

"What?" I said.

"You heard what I said," she said, poignantly.

"You were nagging, not asking," I answered.

"I was not nagging. I asked a question."

"About my boss."

"Yeah well . . . you're my boss, and I sleep with you," Karis said, grinning.

As I brought the car to a stop at a red light, I turned and gave her a stern and serious look. "Not all of us have your loose sense of morals."

The comment earned me a slap on the arm. "I deserved that."

"Yes you did," Karis said. "And for your information, when I first brought up the question, I was only asking in a work-related way," Karis said. She used a matter-of-fact tone of voice.

"Is that so?"

"It is."

"Well then, no. I have not seen or talked to her since yesterday. I will need to get a hold of her though. I want to go back up and talk with Whine on Monday. I don't know if I need her with me, or if I can get in to see him without her," I said. I had two reasons for wanting to see Gordon Birdie. One, I had a few questions to ask him about his church and the church's Pastor, and two, I needed to let him know I'd met and talked with Lydia Henson and to tell him that she loved him.

The red and white striped electronic arms to Kodak's visitor parking lot stood raised in the air as if welcoming us to park on its hollowed ground. So we did. We locked the doors and walked toward the sound of a large and powerful waterfall. Glancing south, down Mill Street, I saw a Magic Circle sign hanging over the sidewalk.

"Closed," Karis said. "I can see a sign in the window. I guess it's not dusk yet."

"I guess not." I reached for her hand. "Want to take a walk?"

Holding hands we strolled out onto the High Falls Bridge. The Genesee River raged as it flowed ravenously over a large waterfall providing power for much of the city. Rochester Gas and Electric sat on the banks of the river, sucking as much energy as could be sucked from the powerful body of rapid moving water. Across the river, on the eastern bank, sat the Genesee Brewing Company—making the finest local beer around.

"Ever hear of John Cougar Meloncamp?"

Karis shook her head. "The singer?"

"Yep. He shot a movie here, down there," I said pointing to a small island where the river forked, a hundred and fifty yards or so from the bottom of the falls. "I mean the entire movie wasn't filmed there, but some of it was. The film was called . . ."

"After Image. I remember that. They filmed most the movie in Rochester, at different locations." Karis looked proud of herself. Movies were not her thing. She watched them with me . . . mainly because I enjoyed them almost as much as reading . . . but she could take them or leave them.

We stopped halfway across the bridge, leaned on the sea-foam green railing and stared down and out at the dark brown water. The noise from the waterfall sounded thunderous and yet it relaxed me. I watched the mist and spray rise into the sky and actually felt some of the spray on my face. Then, for some reason, I thought of fire trucks and fire hoses. I closed my eyes.

"What are you thinking about?" Karis asked.

"The water."

"You were not," she said.

She knew me too well, perhaps better than I knew myself. She was right. Though I was staring at the water, my mind was lost on a day in the past.

"The kids?" Karis inquired.

"I guess." I leaned my forehead on the railing. "So many of them died. I can't help feeling like I failed."

"None of it was your fault, Nick. None of it."

"You know a lot of times at night when I can't sleep and I spend hours in front of the computer . . . planning on writing . . . I don't. I just sit there, stare at the monitor and think about all of those kids and the way they died."

The cult was known as the Tenth House. Karis' daughter had hired me to stop a human sacrifice. I saved the girl the cult had chosen to sacrifice—but in the process, many lives were lost. There is a lot more to the story—but it's just that—another story.

"It's not going to be easy to forget," Karis said.

"I'll never forget it."

"That's not what I meant," Karis said. "What I mean is, it happened less than a year ago. The memory and your pain are all fresh. But let me tell you something, Nick, you did everything in your power to save those people."

"You know what it is . . . what's bothering me?" I asked, lifting my head and taking in a deep breath. I looked into Karis' eyes. "It scares me that, in a way, I'm responsible for someone's life again."

"No one said Gordon Birdie, even if found guilty, is going to get the death penalty. That doesn't even look like an option for the DA," Karis said. She was smart.

"Life in prison, death penalty . . . is there a real difference?"

"Nick, if Gordon is sentenced to life in prison that would not be your fault. You've been on the case for a short time and look at all you've accomplished." Karis turned me around to face her. She stood in front of me, demanding eye contact and firmly held me by the arms.

"It's going slow. He doesn't have much time before his trial."

"Regardless, you are doing everything you can. I guess it's normal to doubt yourself every once in a while, but don't let doubt stop you. You're a bright man, creative and I love you. And you know what else, Nick?" Karis asked.

"What?"

"It's dusk."

"And do you know what else, Karis?"

"What?"

"I love you."

CHAPTER 11

Walking into Magic Circle, my nostrils felt immediately assaulted by the pungent aroma of flavored burning incense. Unfortunately, the flavor resembled body odor. The square-shaped room illuminated by lit candles burning everywhere, had black walls with stars and moons and suns and planets painted on them. In a corner near the front counter was a coffee bar with two coffee carafes, a cream and sugar bowl. Under the counter was a can of interior paint and used brush.

"Umm," Karis said. "Incense."

I had to see her face because I could not tell if she enjoyed the scent, or was pulling my leg. She wrinkled her nose at me. Good. The place stunk to her as well. "A lot of books here," I pointed out. "A lot of stuff too."

"This must be like a witch's grocery store," Karis said, whispering.

"Sacrificial lambs must be in the meat aisle." We chuckled softly.

"Can I help you?"

Startled, Karis and I spun around. On the floor filling a rack with books knelt a young woman with straight, long, black hair. She wore glasses, and though she must have been annoyed with us, she offered a friendly smile. She wore a silk, purple blouse, black slacks and black boots that resembled those worn by Mary Poppins.

"Didn't see you there," I said.

"Apparently not," the woman said as she stood up. "What can I help you with?"

"How much do you know about magic?"

"Want to see my WICCA card?"

"What's that?" Karis asked.

"Never mind. Obviously the two of you are novices in this area," the young woman said. She was not asking. She simply stated a fact. "Is it something specific you are looking for?"

"Two things," I said, extracting a business card out of my wallet. "Are you the owner?" I asked. I couldn't be sure. I guessed the young woman to be around eighteen. While accepting my card, she nodded. "My name is Jasmine."

We all shook hands and introduced ourselves. "A pleasure," I said. "This is an interesting place. Get a lot of customers?"

"I do all right. Most of my regulars show up closer to midnight," Jasmine said. I could only imagine.

"Look, I see you're a private investigator, so you're not with the police, right?" Jasmine asked. She stood comfortably with her hands on her hips so that her thumbs were in front and her fingers rested on the small of her back.

"Right."

"You gave me your card to let me know you are not interested in magic, and that you are here on business, right?" Jasmine asked.

"Right."

"Can you get to the point of this visit then Mr. Tartaglia? I have work to finish up before the place gets busy." She spoke in a calm and pleasant voice. She was serious about her request. For a young woman, she knew how to handle herself well.

The store's door opened. A young man in a tan overcoat, slacks, white shirt and tie walked in. "Can I help you with something?" Jasmine asked.

"Just looking, I'll let you know," the man said, walking toward a shelf of books.

I smiled. She smiled. Out of the corner of my eye I saw Karis' expression. Karis was not smiling. After a moment of silence, I said, "I'm looking for a book. I guess first I want to know if you have a copy, and then second, whether you do or don't, I'd like to know what you might or might not know about the book."

"A book. What's it called?"

"The Talisman."

Jasmine laughed softly while shaking her head. "Mr. Tartaglia, I hate to tell you this, but there isn't any such thing."

"Yeah? And why do you say that?"

"There are a couple of reasons. First . . . if there were an actual book, we'd have bootleg editions all over the place. People have written books about the book, sure. I've read some of them. Each one is completely different, and do you want to know why? Because no one knows what The Talisman . . . if it ever existed . . . contained by way of content," Jasmine said. As an almost afterthought, she added, "There was one thing consistent in each book that I have read, though."

"And what was that?" I prodded.

"The three rings," Jasmine said, reaching under her counter. She pulled out a spiral notebook and pencil. "Apparently, The Talisman is a collection of three books. You know the Olympic Games symbol? How all the rings loop into one another? Well, picture just three rings, standing on top of each other . . . like a figure eight, with and extra 'O.' The top ring loops into the middle ring and the middle ring loops into the bottom ring." She drew us a diagram. She pointed to the top ring with the tip of her pencil. "This one is symbolic of Heaven, the middle one earth and the third ring is Hell."

I thought for a moment about what Jasmine was saying. "Three rings. Heaven, earth and Hell?"

"Right. Now, that was the consistent thing in each of those books," Jasmine stated. "And for the most part, they all gave similar explanations around the three rings. You see, the first ring, Heaven, is supposedly Book One in The Talisman and the second ring is Book Two . . . a book about earth . . ."

"I get it," I said. "The last ring is Book Three."

"Yeah, you've got it, but only part of it. See, here's how it was supposed to work. None of the books would work . . ."

"Work?" Karis asked.

"Yeah, work. See it's a magic book . . . a book of spells and insightful philosophy about Heaven and Earth and Hell," Jasmine explained.

"Go on," I said.

"Okay, some magic from each of the books might work if you only are in possession of one book but the magic would be weak. If you are in possession of two books, then the magic spells are stronger. And ultimately, if you have all three rings, then your powers are limitless," Jasmine said with genuine enthusiasm and animation. "That's the theory, anyway. And the three books together supposedly make up The Talisman."

"When you say spells, what are you talking about, actually?" I asked.

"See, that's just it. No one knows. Not for sure, because there is no proof that any of the three books actually exist," Jasmine said. She put away her notebook and pencil. She seemed ready to wrap up this conversation. "But, the bottom line for the purpose of The Talisman is simple, at least I think."

"Enlighten us," I said.

"Well, if the books are in the hands of someone good, then the white magic produced could be wonderful . . . clean the oceans, stop hunger, that kind of thing," Jasmine said. "So if that's true, then the opposite would be true, right? If the books were in the hands of the wrong people, then the black magic produced could be devastating. Ever hear of the Gates of Hell? Well, if the Ninth Gate is ever opened, then the devil will walk the earth. Can't even imagine what that would be like."

Mumbo jumbo is all I kept thinking. I believed in ghosts and the supernatural. I believed in Heaven and in Hell. But I don't think I believed enough in the devil to actual imagine him walking around on earth. To me, that conjured up a comical image in my mind.

"You don't have to believe me if you don't want to. You were the one who asked all the questions. I just gave you my opinion that's all. It does not mean that any of it is true," Jasmine said.

A loud noise came from behind us. The man that had entered the store some time ago had knocked over a rack of bottles filled with colored fluids. Many of the bottles had shattered. "Hey," Jasmine said, "you know you're gonna have to pay for those."

The man was not looking at Jasmine. He was looking at me. He did not look concerned about the broken bottles and the spilled potions, but still managed to say, "Sorry about that." He took some steps backwards.

I cocked my head to the side, trying to figure out what was going on. It came to me like a punch in the stomach. I said to the man, "You know something about this?"

My voice seemed to have the effect a police siren might have on a criminal caught in the act; the man turned and ran out of the store.

CHAPTER 12

I chased the man leaving the Magic Circle, turning right on Mill Street and just caught a glimpse of the man's leg as he rounded the corner heading for the bridge.

When I rounded the same corner, I saw his figure under the streetlights standing on the bridge. "Hey," I yelled again. "Wait!"

Even from a distance I could tell the man appeared surprised to see that I'd chased after him. He began to run again. Believe it or not, I gained on him. As he approached the halfway portion of the bridge I realized I could lunge and wrap my arms around his legs. So I tackled him.

We both came down hard. The heels of his feet crashed into my chest, nearly knocking the wind from my lungs. We both grunted. He wriggled and twisted, trying to kick free. "Hey, wait. I just want to talk to you," I managed to say while twisting with each wriggle, and wriggling with each twist to keep from letting his legs get free.

The man spun onto his back and sat up in what seemed like one swift motion. I felt his fist slam down on my back before I could even react to his spin. Caught by surprise and now in pain, I let go of him.

As the man scrambled to stand up, I grabbed onto his leg and brought him down again. This time I made a fist and slammed it like a hammer onto his leg three times. "You should never have hit me. All I have is a couple of questions," I said again, but this time noted that I had a larger percentage of his attention. I stayed on top of his leg. He did not try to kick me, or to move.

"Yeah? Like what?" The man's eyes were opened wide. He was staring at me like I might be crazy. Given the circumstances, I can't say I blame him.

"Like, why did you run out of the Magic Circle the way you did?"

The guy kicked free. We both jumped to our feet. He wasn't going anywhere.

"What way?" he asked.

"What way?" I mocked. "Like a bat out of Hell-way. You knocked over a display rack . . . look, you know exactly what way I mean."

"I do not," he said.

"You were listening in on our conversation, weren't you? You heard what we were talking about, and for some reason you thought you should go tell somebody what you heard. Am I close?"

"No. So?"

"No or so? Who were you going to tell?"

The young man looked over his shoulder toward the waterfall. Something in his eyes, in the way they looked, told me I was close. Close to what, I had no idea, but close to something. "Who were you going to tell?"

Once the young man felt certain I was not going to beat him up, the look of fear in his expression changed transforming into unsubstantiated confidence. "I wasn't going to tell anyone anything. I was in there, just browsing, you know? I was just browsing. I decided to leave and you, you freak, came running after me like a mad man. You can't just chase people and tackle them. You ever heard of laws against assault and battery?" He asked me.

"Heard of 'em, never read any of 'em. I'll just take your word that they exist," I said. I pulled out a business card. "I'll tell you what, here's my card. Maybe you were telling the truth, and maybe you weren't just now going to run off and tell someone what you had overheard in the store. But just in case I'm right . . . take this. It might come in handy."

The guy took the card and without looking at it, tucked it into his breast pocket. To me—his stuffing my card away confirmed my hunch. He was going to tell someone what he had heard. As the young man turned and walked down the bridge toward the brewery, I began to wonder what the piece of information might mean? One way or another, I knew I'd find out. Someone was going to get my business card. I guess the best thing to do would be to expect a calling in some shape or form.

"So you gave him a business card?" Karis asked.

"Well, yeah."

"But you have no idea why he ran?"

"He was listening in our conversation. He heard something important that he thought someone else should hear," I said.

"Someone connected to Gordon Birdie's case?"

"Maybe. I doubt it. More than likely he knows someone connected with the book, or books. What do you make of all of that?"

"The Talisman? The three books? I don't know. It's weird. I mean, I'm not saying it's not true . . . or that it couldn't be true . . . but I'm having trouble here accepting it all at face value. Maybe if I saw one of the books . . ."

"That's exactly what I'm thinking," I said. I thought I might know where to look next for a, as we P.I.'s liked to call it, clue.

I took Karis home. It had been a long and intriguing night and besides, she looked tired. She invited me in, and as tempting an offer as it might have been, I declined, settling for a long and passionate kiss on her front step.

"Does that change your mind?" She asked. She held my face cupped in her palms.

"Oh, a part of me wants to stay," I said, "a big part of me. But I have a few more things to do before I can call it a night."

"You are dedicated, Nick. Be careful, all right?"

"I will. Sleep well and I'll talk to you some time tomorrow."

I did not have a definite plan in mind, but as I got back in the car, I thought I might know where to start this midnight-search. I started the engine and backed out of Karis' driveway.

CHAPTER 13

I drove north up Lake Avenue toward Stutson Street and pulled into a gas station across the way from the First Baptist Church. I got out of the car and walked across Lake at the light. I kept my hands in my pockets and attempted to look nonchalant as I strolled down the sidewalk. The church looked peaceful, empty. I ventured off the sidewalk up the small grassy embankment into the church's gravel parking lot. Two cars sat parked side-by-side.

I saw light through the thick privacy basement windows, but was unable to see anything else. The glass obscured the view. I quickly jotted down the license plate numbers. I went up the stairs to the door and pulled on it. Locked. I remembered a time when churches kept their doors unlocked all night long. They were, after all, still considered a place of sanctuary, weren't they?

Walking down the stairs, I heard tires crunching gravel and saw headlights brighten the darkened lot. Then I saw a third beam of light search the trees and bushes at the back of the lot.

It was a police cruiser I had no doubt. I also did not doubt that the officers were looking for me. They must have seen me cross the road and come up to the lot. Great.

Deciding to make a break for it, I ran back down the embankment, down the sidewalk and across the street to where my car sat. I climbed in, started the engine and pulled out just as I saw a police officer standing on the embankment, a flashlight in hand, its beam playing up and down the road.

Enough was enough. For a brief moment I entertained the thought of heading over to Karis' house. My body told me to go home and get some sleep instead. I agreed with my body and went home.

When I arrived at the house, I was only partly surprised to see a police car parked in my driveway. I thought I had a pretty good idea why the police might be visiting. I pulled in along side of the cruiser and got out of the car. The police officer, who had been perched on my front step, stepped down and walked toward me.

The cruiser door opened and I felt completely surprised to see my brother-in-law, homicide detective, Tommy Cerio. He worked for the Rochester Police Department and was married to my sister, Arline. They'd just had a young baby girl together, Madaline. What could Cerio be doing at my house at this time of night?

"Hey Tommy," I said. "What's up?"

"I was about to ask you the same thing. Been out all night?" He asked, walking around to the front of the car. We stood in front of the cruiser's headlight beams. The policeman in uniform joined us, but kept quiet.

"Feels like it," I said. "Why aren't you at home with my sister and the baby?"

Tommy smiled and ran his hand through his hair, using his fingers like the teeth on a comb. "That's a real good question, Nick. Real good. What happened tonight?"

Trick question. "What do you mean?"

"I remember back a while ago there was a hit and run accident, happened out by a night club. We caught the guy that killed a young college girl within the hour—and there wasn't one witness at the scene of the crime. Know how?"

I wagered a guess. "Psychic hotline?"

"Nick!"

"Okay, how?" I asked.

"The license plate just happened to fall off the car. The screws were rusty and the plate fell off the car right next to the body. How's that for luck?" Tommy asked. He leaned against the hood of the police car. "Something like that happened tonight, Nick."

"Hit and run?" I asked. I knew what was coming. It was hard not to be a wise guy. I had been up all day. It was late and I felt extremely worn out.

"Someone filed an assault and battery charge against you Nick." Tommy sighed. "Nick, did you chase someone out of a store and punch them three times?"

"What if I told you he hit me first?"

"Did he?"

This time I sighed. "After I tackled him."

"Nick, what the Hell were you doing? What were you thinking?"

"I'm on a case. I'm working for a public defender in the Philip Edwards, Jr.'s murder," I explained.

"And the public defender asked you to rough up a witness . . . Nick, you can't beat up on people. You might be a private investigator, but you are not Mike Hammer and this isn't a Mickey Spillane novel," Tommy said. "Best I can tell, this guy has only filed a complaint with the police and planned to file a restraining order first thing Monday morning. Tomorrow morning he could very well file a civil suit against you, as well. I really don't have much more on it. Some of the form the guy filled out is blank."

"I know the deal." With a civil suit, the creep could take me to the financial cleaners. "So what, am I under arrest?"

"Afraid so," Tommy said. "We'll take you down to the station and do the paperwork. You have an attorney?"

"I know a public defender I might be able to call," I said.

"I'll keep you out of any cell until he comes."

"She."

"She, what?"

"Until she comes. Lynn Scannella is the attorney I'm working for," I said.

"If you know her number, you might want to call her now, have her meet you down at the station." He unclipped a cell phone from his belt and handed it to me.

It was nearly eleven o'clock. I dialed and waited for her to answer, when she did I said, "Lynn? It's Nick. What were you doing? Sleeping?"

After I disconnected the call and gave the phone back to Tommy I asked, "Why are you out this late at night, Tommy?"

The silent police officer opened the back door to the police cruiser and I climbed in. Then he and Tommy got into the front seats. The police officer backed carefully out of my driveway.

"Well, seems like since that . . . fiasco seven, eight months back, everyone on the force now knows that we're related. There's a special note in your file that anytime your name comes up . . . anywhere . . . that I should be contacted," Tommy said, though he did not sound happy about it. "Chief Delski wanted it that way. I've been appointed to watch over you."

"So you've become like my big brother?" I asked, smiling.

"More like your father, Nick . . . and I don't want the role," Tommy said. He sounded angry. I could tell he was holding back. He wanted to yell, but was keeping his control. "I work hard enough during the day and don't appreciate being called out during the night to come find you."

I sat back and looked out the window. "If it's any consolation Tommy, I am sorry. But if you have to be mad at anyone, I'd be mad at the guy who filed the charge. I mean, I barely hit him. What's the big deal?"

"Please, Nick. Please. I don't want to talk about any of this anymore tonight."

One good thing had come out of this. The secret identity of the man from the Magic Circle would be revealed. If he had planned to file a restraining order, then I would be given his name, address and place of business. How else would I be able to avoid him?

As we drove toward the police station I began to wonder what Lynn might have to say about my particular situation. If word of my arrest were leaked and linked to Lynn and Gordon "Whine" Birdie . . . bad press would not help her case any.

***

My attorney showed up wearing an expression quite similar to the one worn by my brother-in-law. She was swift and efficient getting things squared away, but more importantly, she was silent. Only after we gathered my personal belongings and got outside did Lynn decide to speak to me.

"Nick . . . what the Hell did you think you were doing tonight?" We were in the back parking lot standing near her car. She had her hands rolled up into fists and those fists planted firmly on those shapely hips. She looked cute when she was angry. If I had smiled, it would only have made her more mad, so I controlled the urge.

"I was doing my job, Lynn."

"Your job? Tackling a man on the bridge and beating up his leg . . . That's part of your job?" She yelled at me through clenched teeth—a good way to manipulate voice volume control. I did not think she expected an answer, so I remained quiet. "Nick?"

"What?"

"Answer me, damn it! You think I'm standing here talking to you because you're a good listener?" She looked very, very angry. Her fisted hands slid off her hips and her arms went straight and rigid at her sides—I don't think I could have bent them at the elbows if I'd tried.

"I was looking for answers," I said and told her about the Magic Circle and the events that unfolded. "So you see, he knew something or someone. He was on his way to tell someone that I was looking into the book . . . or books. You want to know something good, well, interesting?"

Lynn stared at me for a moment. She took a deep breath and relaxed her stance. With a sigh, she said, "What?"

"Except for being in jail that last hour, I haven't thought about smoking a cigarette for nearly the entire day," I said and flashed Lynn a large smile.

I could tell by her expression that she didn't know whether to punch me in the head or laugh. Finally she did the latter, and I felt relieved. "Go home, Nick. Get some rest."

"Think I could bum a ride?"

The silent night was shattered when Lynn released a loud, frustrated sounding growl. "Was hiring you a good idea?" Lynn opened her door. "Hop in, Nick."

By the time she pulled into my driveway, her mood had changed. "You are interesting, you know that?"

"Not on purpose," I told her.

"Let me ask you, for this investigation, are you getting anywhere?" She asked while running her fingers through her hair. She spoke in a soft, tender voice. "I mean, are you finding out anything that's going to help my case, my client?"

"I'm looking," I told her. "I haven't got answers yet and if anything, all I've come up with are more questions, but we've got some time."

"Not much, Nick. The clock is counting down fast." She wet her lips with her tongue. "I guess you better get going."

I sensed something more going on here. "Something else bothering you, Lynn?"

"Why do you ask?" She had both hands on the steering wheel.

"No reason. It's just all of a sudden you sound down."

"Nick . . . it's nearly two o'clock in the morning. It may be Sunday for you tomorrow . . . or today, but I planned on getting up at seven and going in to the office. I feel pretty un-rested right now, can you imagine why?" Lynn asked.

"Sorry. I'm going," I said while opening the car door.

She grabbed onto my arm. "Nick wait."

I turned back to face her with one leg out the door.

"I'm sorry. I'm not really upset with you. I mean, I am mad that you got arrested tonight and that I had to come and get you out. I mean, I'm glad you thought to call me and I could help, but the circumstances around your call . . . well, they weren't what I'd have anticipated," Lynn said.

"Anticipated?" I felt confused.

She looked away from me and out the front window. "When the phone rang and I answered it, I was . . . happy to hear your voice. But then when I found out why you were calling, I guess you could say I was disappointed."

Disappointed. Uh-huh. "Lynn, I'm . . . me and Karis . . ."

"I know, Nick. I know. You asked me what was bothering me and I told you. Please get out of the car, aside from being tired and not mentally lucid, I am also extremely embarrassed. Good-night, Nicholas." She would not look at me.

I climbed out of the car. Before shutting the door, I said, "Lynn . . ."

"Good-night," she said.

I closed the door. She backed out of the driveway and drove away. While I walked toward the house, fumbling around in my pocket for the keys, I mumbled, "What an interesting night."

Before I could react to the shadow I saw, the figure owning the shadow struck my shadow on the back of the head. I remember hearing the sound of my keys falling with a jingle as I hit the ground. Someone jumped onto my back and something like a pillowcase was pulled over my head. I was hauled to my feet. Two quick punches were thrown into my gut and the breath was knocked from my lungs. Gasping I braced myself for the next blow, all the while trying to hear what was going on around me. There had to be at least two of them. One was holding me tightly and one threw punches.

I heard the heavy breathing of a man next to my ear before his threatening words were whispered, "Leave Whine in jail and quit your investigation. Got it?"

They didn't want me to respond, or they would not have punched me in the stomach again. As I went to double over, the person holding my arms let go, and I fell once more to the ground. My hands reached for my head, to pull the bag off, and in that instant I felt a striking blow on the neck and lost consciousness before I had time to realize anything else.

CHAPTER 14

Sunday, May 20

"Hey Mr. Tartaglia? Mr. Tartaglia, you awake?"

It was the voice of a boy. I heard him loud and clear, in fact his voice sounded amplified, as if speakers had been placed up to my ears. I could not open my eyes. I tried and tried, but they would not open.

"Let me roll you onto your back," the boy's voice said. Brilliant sunlight nearly blinded me and did nothing for the painful throbbing behind my eyes. I shut my eyes tightly against the morning rays.

"Billy?" I asked, knowing the paperboy's voice. "Where am I?"

"Your front lawn. Looks like you stumbled home, but couldn't make it all the way in. When my dad does that, I usually find him at the bottom of the stairs. At least he makes it into the house. You should hear my mom," Billy said, rambling.

"Can you help me up?" I asked.

He set down his orange bag filled with copies of the Sunday paper. He took hold of one of my arms and helped to pull me up onto my feet. Standing up, I felt dizzy and leaned on the boy for balance.

"My mom, she always tells my dad that that was his last chance. She always threatens to kick him out. She hasn't done it yet, so why should he ever expect her to keep her promise, right? I wish she would do that with me. But oh no, when I get punished, the punishment always sticks," Billy said.

I felt for my wallet. It was there, but in the wrong pocket. I removed the billfold and opened it. Inside I found a note. It read simply: Leave it alone!

The words on the card were not particularly frightening. The whacks on the head were meant for punctuation and intimidation. For the most part whoever wanted to make a lasting impression had succeeded.

The letters in the note were made in generic letters with a little personal slant.

"I remember one time when my dad came home, and he didn't pass out, and I met him at the door and I said, dad didn't you say you were going to give me some money? And you know what he did?" Billy asked. He was walking me to my front door.

"Oh, my keys," I said.

Running back to the spot where I had laid unconscious, Billy picked up my keys and said, "My father? He pulled out his wallet and he gave me a ten-dollar bill. Then he told me that we were even. I had to do everything I could not to start laughing," Billy said.

I unlocked my front door. "I get a paper, Billy?"

Billy ran back to get his bag of papers. He handed me one and I gave him a ten-dollar bill. "Thanks for helping me, Billy. You're a good kid, and a hard worker."

Billy stood statute-still and stared at me. "You mean that Mr. Tartaglia?"

"I sure do. I hope your parents are proud of you and all that you've accomplished," I said, knowing full well that both of Billy's parents ignored him. His father was a well-known alcoholic. The mother spent far more money than was brought in. If I had to take a guess, I'd wager that most, if not all, of Billy's paychecks from delivering papers seven days a week went to one or both of his parents to support their selfish habits. "That ten Billy, it's a tip. Don't tell anyone I gave it to you. All right?"

"I better go now," Billy said. "I got a lot of papers left to deliver. And Mr. Tartaglia . . . thank you."

I went into the house, closed and locked the door. I felt dizzy. My legs were unsteady. My head ached. I tried to run my hand over the spot where I had been hit, but the area on my skull was sensitive and caused a sharp throbbing pain when I touched it. There seemed little else to do except call for a ride to the hospital.

***

Karis and I walked out of the hospital. She held tightly onto my arm. "Look Nick," she said, "the doctor told you it was a concussion and he suggested you go home and rest. I know you . . . and I don't believe for a minute that you have any intention of going home and resting like he's suggested. But I must insist . . ."

"Karis . . ."

"No, let me finish," Karis said, fishing car keys out of her purse. "You're going to come back with me to my house. I'll fix you up on the sofa. You can just watch television and relax. How does that sound?"

"It sounds fine. I was going to tell you, my head is killing me. I want nothing more than to go and rest."

Karis gave me a quizzical look. "Really?"

"Honest."

"Well, good then" she said, sounding uncertain. "Then you'll come to my house?"

"Perfect."

"But Nick, when I get you home and settled, you are going to explain to me everything that happened last night. None of this crap you told me earlier. The doctor might have bought your story of tripping on your front step and whacking the back of your head on the sidewalk, but I don't." She gave me a look that said it all. Either I tell her what she wants to hear, or she'd beat it out of me. I decided—depending on the intensity of the headache—that it might be fun to let her try and beat it out of me first.

CHAPTER 15

Monday, May 21

I had upgraded my stay on Karis' sofa to the bedroom. We spent a good part of the night talking. Karis' concern grew considerably as I described for her the events of the previous night. We talked at great length about who might have hit me over the head. (I did not tell her about the note in my wallet). Knowing today would be busy, I woke up extra early and crept quietly out of bed. I showered and dressed. In the kitchen I made scrambled eggs, toast and coffee. I set the table. When the coffee finished brewing, I woke up Karis.

We ate and she gave me a ride home, but not before asking me ten thousand times how I felt. Once I convinced her I was not going to die, she let me out of the car in my driveway. "I'll see you at the office a little later?" I asked.

"I'll be there. I plan to finish designing the web page for your agency."

"So glad you know how to do that stuff. Can't wait to see it."

"I hope I can finish it up today . . . maybe even before lunch," she said while smiling proudly.

"Tell you what, even if it's not done . . . I'll still love you," I said, kneeling back into the car.

"Promise?" She asked.

"I promise," I said, leaning in close for a juicy kiss good-bye. I could see it in her eyes. She wanted to warn me, to tell me to be careful. I'll bet it took a lot of reserve not to say those words. So I said, "Hey, I'll be careful, too."

"I love you, Nick," she said. I watched her drive away.

Inside I changed into fresh clothing. I affixed a fresh cigarette patch onto my arm while dialing Lynn's number at the office. An answering machine kicked on. I looked at the time. It wasn't even nine yet. I left a message. "Lynn, it's Nick. Look, I need to run up to the jail this morning and see Gordon Birdie. I have a few questions for him. I hope it's all right. I plan to go up there, well, now."

I drove slowly trying to concentrate on the road. My mind was loaded with questions. Someone wanted me off the investigation bad enough to whack me on the back of the head with a blunt object, but not enough to kill me. Instead of tracking down just one book, I now had to be on the lookout for three. And to top off my ice cream Sunday would be the restraining order filed, with possible civil charges to boot.

I parked at the prison and made my way to the first officer on post. I explained to him who I was and gave him a business card. I suspect Lynn received my message and called ahead to make sure I could get in with no trouble. Gunther, the officer I'd met last time, led me down a series of halls. He had me wait while he went to retrieve Gordon Birdie.

I went to the break area and bought a Coke and candy bar. I watched Gunther lead Gordon Birdie into a conference room. Gunther left him cuffed, came to the door at my end of the room and let me in. "Hey Gunther, you think we could lose the cuffs?" I asked.

Gunther eyed me for a moment, then while nodding and shaking his head, he walked over to Gordon Birdie and removed the restraints. "I'll be right outside the door, Mr. Tartaglia."

"Thank you, Gunther," I said and waited for the guard to leave to room. Only when the door closed and locked did I go and sit across from Gordon Birdie. "How you been?" I gave him the candy bar and set the drink on the table.

"Survivin.' You?"

"Working."

"Man, I thought I told you to let it alone. Gettin' outta here might be the worst thing could happen to me," Gordon said.

"I know a little bit about the book that you thought was in the safe," I said.

"Yeah? So?"

"So . . . I think I need to know a bit more. I think I need to know what you know."

"Damn, Tartaglia . . . are you listening to me, or what, man? I just told you I don't want to get out of here. It's bad in here, yeah. It's real bad. Last night, some rapist . . . while he was sleeping . . . had boiling water thrown through the bars onto his face. While he was sleeping, man," Gordon said.

"He's a rapist," I reminded him.

"But while he was sleeping."

"Asleep, awake, for a piece of shit like that, I don't see much difference," I said. I had no sympathy for rapists, or child molesters. It felt somewhat good to know that even criminals can't stomach those kinds of cowardly and sick, sick acts of sexual violence. "Why, you want out? Think you might be safer on the outside?"

"I still ain't got the money for bail," he said.

"Let's say you had it . . . the church raised it . . . would you want out?"

"Man, all I'm sayin' is, no matter what, I feel safer in here." Whine nodded his head up and down. He appeared to be agreeing with himself. Then he looked at me. "Man, you look like shit, though."

"I spent some time in the hospital yesterday. Got home late and someone came up from behind me. They clobbered me pretty good. Wound up spending the night on my front lawn," I said while gently massaging the wound.

Gordon looked real serious. "Know who did it?"

"No. Not a clue, yet."

"Know why?"

"I have an idea."

"Me too. It has to do with what you've been sticking your nose into," Gordon said. He ripped open his candy bar and took a big satisfying bite.

"And how do you know that?"

"'Cause. Why else you be tellin' me? You wouldn't be. You got thumped on the head because you got involved with this case. Nick, man, don't do me any favors. Tell that pretty lawyer of mine, too.

Let me stay in prison," Gordon said while peeling the bar out of the bottom half of its wrapper. He finished it in a second bite.

While Gordon chewed I said, "So that's it?"

"That's it."

"You got nothing else? You don't want to talk about the books."

"Books?"

"Yeah. The three books." I stood up and pushed in my chair.

"Man, what three books. The Talisman. One book. That's all there is," Gordon said quickly. He snapped open the soda.

"Actually, there are three books that make up The Talisman, but, well, you're not interested in talking about it." I walked away from the table toward the door. It was killing me. He knew more but would not let on.

"No sir, I am not. Thank you for the candy and the drink," he said. "Hey, ask Gunther if he can let me sit in here a minute and relax and finish this drink 'fore he has to be takin' me back, all right?" Gordon asked.

I made a fist as if ready to knock on the door. "Sure, sure I will. Oh, I almost forgot," I said, feeling a little like Columbo. "Lydia wanted me to say Hello and for me to tell you that she loves you."

"How did you find out about Lydia, man?" Gordon said, getting to his feet and snarling, revealing chocolate smeared on those brilliant white teeth. "I don't want you messing around with this do you understand me? I want you to stay the Hell away from her. Stay as far the Hell away from her as you can possibly stay!" Gordon's voice volume had continued to rise, but he was not at the point of yelling. Gordon was closer to telling me what I needed to know.

"I won't let anything happen to her," I said.

"You can't even protect your own sorry ass; don't be tellin' me you're gonna watch out for her, too."

"I don't want anything to happen to her. She seems like a sweet girl," I said.

"Ah, man. She's the best, you know? She's that girl that you just know you've got to marry."

"Gordon . . . Whine . . . if you're in here, how can that happen? How can the two of you ever get married."

"Hell. Me being in here isn't the biggest barrier that would stop Lydia and me from getting married," Gordon said.

"Lurch?"

"Her brother, you mean? Yeah. Lurch. Oaf. Big fat oaf. But I respect the man, oddly enough. He takes care of his little sister . . . maybe too much, but he's just lookin' out for her, same as I'd do if I had a sister," Gordon said.

"And a blind sister, at that."

"You got it, man. You know exactly what I'm saying," Gordon said, losing the fight in him. He sat back down. However, I had him.

"Come on. What's going on here, huh? What is going on?"

"You do me a favor, Tartaglia?"

"Depends. What is it?"

"As much as I don't want you anywhere near Lydia, I got this sinking feeling that you are going to see her again . . . and man you don't even need to answer that one. I already know the truth. It's like heartburn in my chest. Tartaglia, I want you to promise me that you'll tell Lydia that I'm safe, you know, for the most part. And Tartaglia, please tell her that I love her too. You'll do that? You'll do me that favor?"

"I can do that."

"You promise?"

"I promise."

"Next time you see her, you'll tell her?"

"First thing."

"Swear?"

"Damn it, I gave you my word!" I walked back to the table and sat down.

"All right, all right. I believe you, man. I trust you." Gordon Birdie lifted the soda can and drank what was left. He yelled, "Gunther! Guard!"

"What the Hell do you think you're doing?" I asked.

Gunther entered the room.

"I want to go back to my cell," said Gordon.

"Wait," I said. "Whine . . . I thought we were going to talk, the books. What about the books?"

"Man, I never said that. I just asked you to do a favor for me and you promised me you would do it," Gordon said. He was smiling as he held up his wrists. Gunther locked the cuffs in place.

"Quid pro quo. This for that."

102

"Quid pro quo . . . man, I don't know nothing about any Quid whoever whatever."

"I'll be back," I told Gordon. "Be ready."

While Gunther led a smiling Whine toward the opposite doorway, he answered, "I'll be waiting."

"Yeah and next time I come to visit see if I bring you any junk food," I said.

Before the door closed I saw the smile on Gordon's face vanish.

CHAPTER 16

I called the police.

When Detective O'Mara answered, I said coolly, "Well Hello, detective. Is Detective Cerio in?" Deanna O'Mara was my brother-in-law's partner. She looked like she might be eighteen. She wasn't, she was closer to thirty. She was cute with blond hair and blue eyes, but for some reason we did not get along. Our personalities clashed. The funny thing—they seemed to clash for no apparent reason.

"He is, Mr. Tartaglia. Hold on," O'Mara said. She called me by my last name out of disrespect. I always asked people to call me Nick. The tension I felt between us was strong. Tommy once told me it had to be a physical attraction, but he's nuts and so are his theories.

When Tommy Cerio came on the phone he wasted little time. "Nick . . . what do you need?"

"Need? Tommy, bro . . . how about something more cordial? A lot of people when they get on the phone say 'Hello.' A little old fashioned, but it does work and is still widely used and accepted . . ."

"Cut the crap, Nick. What's up? Where are you?"

"I'm just now leaving the jail. I had a visit with Gordon Birdie. Why?"

"Why? Why are you calling?"

"I wanted to find out if you had anything more on that restraining order," I said. "Do you?"

"You sound almost excited about it. Nick, I'm a homicide detective . . ."

104

"And?"

"And. And that is not a part of my job. Look Nick, I'm busy. Maybe you don't read the papers . . ."

"The funnies and the television listings. Once in a while I read the horoscopes but they always seem to be right and I find that just a little too spooky . . ."

"Nick, we're now in the middle of a serial killer investigation. We've got three bodies . . . and there is no mistaking the fact that the murders were committed by the same person or persons," Detective Cerio said.

"The two women from a few weeks back?" I asked. My brother-in-law sounded a little stressed out. He was being serious. His work was serious. I respected that. He was now telling me information . . . that maybe he shouldn't be telling me . . . and that told me that I was respected as a professional.

"The first woman was about a month ago. Two weeks ago the second body turned up."

"Seems like every two weeks then?" I asked.

"Well . . . you'd hope. The thing with serial killers, once they get started, the killings will eventually become more frequent and then they tend to become more violent and gruesome," said Tommy Cerio.

"Any leads?"

"Some. Not much. Grab a copy of this morning's paper. Reporters know nearly as much as we do. Some of the specifics of the case have been kept confidential of course, but the article's pretty accurate."

"So what, this last victim was found last night?"

"After I brought you in. A man this time. The MO without a doubt is exactly the same . . . I can't get into it, and you won't read about it in the paper . . . and all of the victims were black."

Cerio sounded, aside from stressed out, tired, too. I could tell he was putting everything he had into the case. Rochester, a seemingly quiet city, had become notorious for its bred serial killers. "Never went home, did you?"

Cerio remained silent for a moment. I think he was ignoring my question. "Here's the information you wanted, Nick. Thanks O'Mara," he said to his partner. "Nick, you there?"

"Here. But look, you're busy and I understand . . ."

"Too late, Nick, I got the damned information in my hand. I'm sure an officer will be by to serve you. For now, the name of the man you battered and assaulted is Michael David Anthony," Cerio said.

"What the Hell?" I said. "Is that directory style, right-side-up, upside-down?"

"Michael is his first name. Anthony is his last name." Cerio gave me the young man's address. He lived in Hilton. "He did not fill out his place of employment on the form."

"Thanks Tommy. Look, anything I can do to help let me know. All right? Even if it is nothing more than some menial leg work."

"Thanks, Nick. I appreciate the offer and who knows, I might just take you up on it at some point."

I had planned to tell my brother-in-law about my trip to the hospital. At this point and with his current workload it didn't seem important. Besides, I now had a name—and quite possibly the same name of the person responsible for clubbing me on the back of the head.

I graciously thanked my brother-in-law. We hung up. My telephone rang. I answered it. "Hello?"

"Nicholas? It's Father Paul."

"How are you, Padre?" I began the drive back to the office.

"Fine, just fine. Look, I've been searching . . . up all night on that blasted computer . . . and I've turned up a lot of this and that, but not much of anything."

"I understand." At this point I thought I might know more about the books than my good friend.

"I don't want to give up, but I wanted to let you know that I feel like I am moving at a race horse's speed, but have nothing to show for it," Father Paul said.

"I've been doing some checking around myself. I think I might have found some interesting pieces of information. I think we should still get together and compare notes. Hey, and one more thing. Do you know anything about The First Bible Baptist Church on Lake and Stutson?"

"I know of them. I don't know the Pastor, if that's what you mean."

"When we get together we'll talk. I'm headed back to the office right now, but I'll be in touch."

"Nick, let me just say, of all the information I did gather from the Internet, I have been able to put one thing together about this book," Father Paul said.

"That there are three?" I said.

"Three what?"

"Books."

"Really?"

"Really. I'm sorry. I thought that's what you were going to say. I didn't mean to interrupt. You were saying?"

"I think what you are looking into has potential danger connected with it. A lot of people do not believe in the supernatural. I know you do and you know I do. The paranormal and things like that . . . well, you know my story," he said. When we had first met he shared a personal ghost story. It had been quite chilling. The event had strengthened the then young priest's faith. "I just think we both need to keep in mind that, well, evil is real . . . real and very, very powerful."

CHAPTER 17

After talking with Father Paul I finally arrived at the office. Karis was there and diligently working on the new web site for The Tartaglia Agency. So far the site looked great. I spent a good part of the day locked up in my office searching the Internet for information on my elusive, perhaps non-existent books. Jasmine at the Magic Circle seemed the most insightful, even though she had explained that she had been speculating on most of it.

After becoming completely frustrated with the computer I pulled out my log journal and read over the information entered. I kept the journal accurate and up to date. There would be no way for me to remember every detail of every conversation without making note of each instance as soon as possible. If any case I worked on went to court, my notes would be very important and could be used as evidence.

Once I finished reading through the logbook, I added to it my conversation from earlier in the morning with Gordon Birdie, and with Tommy. At this point I realized something. Up until now I have only been doing one thing for the case. I have only been looking for the book or books. I have not been looking into Philip Edwards' role in all of this. The answers might be far clearer coming directly from the source.

I jotted down my thought into the log and put the book away. I went out into the office—Karis was gone, a note on the PC told me she'd be back later and was signed with X's and O's. In the left corner drawer of the desk I found the morning newspaper. I took it back into my office and read all about Cerio's serial killer.

There was one item in the article that I found interesting. I would need to call my brother-in-law back at the police department. The article was vague about the stab wounds, but clear enough to express that each of the three victims had the same design cut into their abdomen region.

***

At exactly seven o'clock Monday night I pulled into the Greece Bowl parking lot. I stayed in the car for a while, the engine running, the wipers rhythmically swinging, tick-tock, back and forth across the windshield. April Showers were supposed to bring May Flowers, not April Showers bring May Showers.

The parking lot was not very full. Most winter leagues would be finishing up soon. Most of the bowling centers in Rochester did not have summer teams. Bowling during the winter is fine; it keeps you busy and gets you out of the house during the five and a half months of snow and bitter cold temperatures. It seemed unlikely that people would want to be stuck inside bowling when the weather outside finally became enjoyable.

After fifteen minutes I went in.

The place was loud. I don't just mean loud to my ears; the bowling balls being thrown and rolling and crashing into pins; people screaming and talking loud and shouting; music playing and interrupted by the announcements made over the P.A. system. I mean loud to my eyes. The carpets resembled something out of Disney's Fantasia; bright blue- and red-swirled tweed carpeting with what could be shooting stars, or comets with long white-hot fiery tails mixed with abrupt splatters of fluorescent green. Wow, I mean, where are my shades?

To my immediate left was an alcove-area filled with video games and people manning them. On the right sat the front counter. The girl working the counter handed out bowling shoes and ran the cash register. Along the walls stood racks filled with bowling balls.

Moving in to the place some more and just past the video games on the left, I found an entranceway to the bar. I saw through the bar at the opposite end was another entranceway and just beyond that a diner. I could smell burgers and French fries. I felt suddenly hungry.

Nearer the second entranceway I saw a table of young women. On the center of their table sat a large bowl of popcorn. Each of the ladies had a drink and a copy of the Good Book open in front of them. One lady had her back to me and since I could not see Lydia—I assumed this person to be her.

I walked past the entranceway and rounded the corner. To my right, people were bowling. Casually my eyes roamed over the bowlers. When I saw Marlow Henson (a.k.a. Lurch), I did my best to stand back and watch him without being observed. He rolled a pin smashing strike—which was, in and of its self, impressive. What impressed me more was the size of his biceps muscle when he made his approach with the ball curled up to his chin.

I went down to the second entranceway and ignored all the people enjoying their meals seated at the diner's counter and entered the bar whistling the John-Jacob-Jingle-Hymer-Schmidt song. The young woman that had had her back to me was indeed Lydia, Gordon Birdie's girlfriend. I watched her face as I whistled and her expression did not change. She was taking a sip of soda as I walked by with my hands stuffed in my pockets.

I left the bowling center and stood outside under an awning. I checked my watch. It was twenty minutes after seven. The next time I checked my watch it was thirty-five minutes after seven. I wondered if something went wrong. Perhaps Lydia had second thoughts about talking to me. Maybe Lurch somehow found out about our appointment and was preventing her from coming out tonight.

Just as I was about to go back in, ready to sing John-Jacob-Jingle-Hymer-Schmidt this time, one of the doors opened and Lydia came out.

CHAPTER 18

"Nicholas?" Lydia said. She had a walking stick out in front of her. Her free hand was outstretched, tentatively reaching for security.

"Here I am," I said. I reached for her hand and for a brief moment felt the muscles in her hand and arm tighten.

"It's raining."

"I know. I'm sorry."

"It's going to be hard to explain why I'm wet when I get back from the ladies room," said Lydia. She smiled.

"Would you prefer I leave . . . and we try this again some other time?"

"No." She backed up to the wall. The small awning overhang protected us mostly from the rain. "Did you see him?"

"This morning. And I told him that you loved him," I said.

"How was he?"

"He looks good. He made me promise before I left to tell you that he was safe and that he loved you."

Lydia started crying. I touched her shoulder and she fell into my arms. Her sobs came out strong and her body trembled. I hugged her tight; my hands rubbed circles on her back.

"I'm sorry," she kept saying. "I'm trying to be strong. I just can't stand thinking of him in there. Night after night I lie awake in bed, worried sick. It's eating me up inside. My stomach hurts so badly . . . and my heart, my heart is breaking apart! I want him to come home. I want this, this stupid nightmare to be over—to have never have happened, and I just want Gordon to come home!"

I let her get it out—as much as she could, or was willing to release. When she regained some emotional control, she pulled slowly away. "I'm sorry," she said again.

"There's no need to say you're sorry. I can't even imagine what you must be going through," I said.

"I don't have that long. You have questions, right? Best start asking them now."

I felt funny rushing right into the red meat of the matter, but she was right. She didn't have long. Sooner or later her Bible study friends would come looking for her or worse, Lurch might do the searching himself. "Gordon and an Anthony James . . . members of your church . . . broke into a man's house. They weren't planning on robbing his possessions, and they weren't planning on killing him. They were after something. Do you know what they were after?" Of course I knew the answer. I needed to hear it from her. Confirmation that Gordon Birdie was telling the truth.

"A book."

Bingo. "Why?"

She hesitated. "People tend to talk in front of me. Sometimes I think they believe I am not just blind, but deaf, too." She collapsed her walking stick and stuck it in her pocket. "There is a, oh, I don't know what you'd call it, a movement? Does that make sense? A group of people in the church dedicated to serving God."

"Isn't that what religion is all about in the first place?"

"Religion? I suppose. But I mean more than showing up for church every Sunday . . . or having a Bible study one night a week in a bar at a bowling alley. I'm not even talking about volunteering to do missionary assignments," Lydia said. She could not see me, but her face was turned, and her eyes looked directly into mine while she spoke. Her soft looking chocolate skin was streaked with wide tear stripes—the only temporary imperfection visible. "A lot of it has to do with the book that Gordon and Anthony were trying to retrieve. See, both Gordon and Anthony, they don't have any family and that's why they were chosen. They're like the orphans that used to run the mail back during the time of cowboys and Indians?" said Lydia. "You know . . . orphans were sent because there was a good chance they'd get killed," she managed to explain. Crying again, she shrugged my hand off her shoulder. "I'm all right. I just remember him telling me that he volunteered for this . . . that stupid assignment. He wasn't supposed to tell anyone, you know. He told me though. I begged him not to do it. He knew how dangerous it was. He knew by doing this thing that he'd be risking our future together."

"So why did he do it?" I had to ask.

"You a religious man, Nicholas?"

"Somewhat. I guess so," I said.

"Gordon did it for God."

I understood what she was saying, but hearing her say it had a tremendous impact on me as if the weight of understanding had suddenly become too heavy to bare. Gordon's love for Christ was more powerful than his love for Lydia, and he loved Lydia. He did. I knew this to be a fact but Gordon loved God more.

"So Gordon and Anthony were to break into the home of Philip Edwards. They were supposed to steal a book."

"That's right."

"Did they get the book?"

"No."

"How did your church know that Edwards had the book?"

"I don't know."

"Do you know what the book is?"

"Yes."

"Have you ever seen the book?"

Lydia shook her head with a broad smile.

I said, "I guess that was a dumb thing to ask."

"It wasn't dumb. I know what you meant. No, I have not seen the church's book, or the one Edwards is supposed to have . . . there are three . . ."

More confirmation. That Jasmine girl seemed to know what she was talking about. I would definitely need to see her again. "Lydia, if the church has one, and the church believes that Philip Edwards has one . . . where is the third book and what can you tell me about the books?"

Before she could answer, the door from the bowling center opened. I had to shake my head back and forth because I could not believe what I was seeing.

CHAPTER 19

"What in God's name is going on out here? Huh? Lydia . . . get back inside," Marlow Henson said. He may have been talking to his little sister, but his eyes, burning like fire, never looked away from me. His bowling shirt fit him too tightly and those muscles rippled beneath the stretched fabric.

"But Marlow," Lydia pleaded, shaking open her walking stick. Marlow used a protective arm to guide her back through the doorway.

I thought fleetingly about running. When the door shut and we were alone under the awning, I said, "Marlow . . . "

"You shut up!" His finger was in my face. I slapped his hand out of the way.

"The Hell I will," I said.

"Oh, the Hell you will, huh?" Marlow curled his fingers into a fist.

He was being dramatic. His bulking size more than likely kept him out of a lot of fights. This obvious inexperience gave me the advantage. I didn't want to hurt the ox, but the man was leaving me with little choice. While he performed a slow intimidating show, I threw a quick strong punch into his solar plexus, an area tightly guarded by brick-solid muscle. The punch did the job, knocking the wind out of Marlow's lungs. I moved fast and used my left-hand to jab his right fist out of the way, then threw a punch square into his nose. The bone did not break, but both nostrils bled.

Marlow landed a punch that made the side of my head feel as if it had been flattened. My ears rang while my eyes fought to focus.

I kicked out my right foot and brought it back behind his left knee knocking him off balance, and shoved him back using both hands. He fell backwards onto the pavement into a puddle of rainwater. I stood still, both hands up and ready to dish out more if he still felt like fighting.

Staying in the puddle, Marlow stared up at me looking slightly dazed and disoriented. "You are a tough little guy, huh?"

"Not really. I've just been in a few more fights than you, is all."

"Believe it or not," he said, talking calmly, "I've been in very few real fights before."

"I figured as much. We done here?"

"You mean fighting?" He asked while wiping the blood away from his nose. "Yeah, man, we're done."

I held out my hand and helped him to his feet.

"But that don't mean I want you around no more! And another thing I don't want you involving my sister in any of this. Man, why have you got to be talking to her? There's nearly a hundred people in our church and you pick the little, innocent blind girl to gouge information out of?" He was mad still, even looked ready to try taking another swing. I remained defensive, ready for any attack.

"Marlow . . . I tried coming and talking to your Pastor first, if you don't remember, but I was thrown out. I know more than you might think . . . or might expect. Don't you care about Gordon Birdie? The man is in jail. He's in jail for something your church involved him in," I said.

"Boy you got it all wrong, and I don't care to be discussing this with you," Marlow said. He turned around. He looked ready to go back inside, but stopped. Without looking back at me he said, "If I catch you near my sister again I'm going to have to kill you."

"Now is that a nice thing to say?"

As he pulled open the door, I grabbed his shoulder. "I'm going to keep digging, Marlow. If your sister is the only person brave enough to talk to me, then I will be back to see her."

I let go of him and he went inside. I didn't have to worry about Lydia. I did not think Marlow yell at her, though he might verbally reprimand her for talking to me. He might yell, he might scream and he might punch a wall—but he loved Lydia too much to hurt her.

Walking back to my car I shook my hand. Damn, punching the man felt like slamming your fist into a concrete wall. My knuckles already felt sore and achy—and my head was spinning. If he ever trained to become a fighter, I'd bet on him; with one punch I knew my head was going to ache and throb the rest of the night.

CHAPTER 20

Kodak's visitor lot was closed this time. I had to make a left onto Mill Street and then do a U-turn to park alongside a meter. The sky looked black, obscured by full clouds with rain that just kept falling. I fed the meter and walked toward the shingle hanging over the Magic Circle doorway.

As I walked by the bridge, I clearly saw a figure dressed in dark clothing standing under one of the lights about halfway across. The figure, as best I could tell, was staring back at me.

I walked on and reached the door to the Magic Circle. A sign hung inside the door. Closed. I looked at my watch. It was after eight. The sky was bleak, clearly signifying dusk. Jasmine could be running late.

Getting soaked, I crossed the street and went for protection from the rain standing in the entrance to a parking garage. I crossed my arms over my chest, began to wait, and found the wait not to be long at all. Of course it was not Jasmine who showed up.

The man from the bridge was making his way down the cobblestone sidewalk. He appeared nervous; kept looking over his shoulder. The man looked a to be a little shorter than me and was dressed in all black, but unlike me, was wearing a rain slicker. I felt envious.

He stopped in front of the Magic Circle. I stepped back in the garage, hoping to hide in the shadows. I watched as the man used a key to open the door. At this moment I ran at the store and walked in on the man's heels. Once inside I shoved him forward even before he could turn around. I shut the door.

"Who are you and where is Jasmine?"

When the man remained silent on the floor, I kicked his feet. "Answer me!"

"I don't know anything. Nothing. I swear."

I didn't believe him. I kicked his feet harder this time.

"Look, I don't know you. I have no idea who you are," the man on the floor said. He sounded scared—no, terrified.

"Who are you afraid I might be?"

He paused because I'd stumped him. "Look, I have no idea what's going on. All right? I'm Jasmine's brother. That's all there is. Okay? I don't want any trouble."

"I'm Nicholas Tartaglia. I'm a private investigator," I said, holding out my hand. I helped Jasmine's brother to his feet. "I was here last night and I talked with your sister. She was very helpful, but unfortunately our talk got interrupted. I have a few more questions for her. If you know where she is . . . it's important that I see her?"

"You're a P.I.?"

"That's right." I pulled out and handed him a business card.

"So you're not one of them?"

"One of who?"

"I don't know. Honestly I don't. Jasmine called me early this morning. She sounded all shaken up. She said she wasn't in Rochester, that she'd closed up the store and wasn't sure when she'd be back . . . if she'd ever be back."

"Jasmine tell you where she was?"

"No. I asked, too. She wouldn't tell me." I could tell he was lying.

"So what are you doing here?"

"That's just it. When she called, she told me she left something behind. A book. She wanted me to get it and . . ."

"And what? She wanted you to send the book to her, right?"

"Yeah," the man said, cowering.

"I'm not going to hit you . . . just be straight with me," I assured him. "Where's the book?"

"In a lock box in a safe in the back room."

I said, "Let's go get that book, and then we can discuss where your sister is, all right?"

***

Lynn Scannella answered the telephone on the fourth ring. She sounded like she'd been fast asleep. "Hello?"

"Lynn? Nick."

There was a moment of silence. "Hell, Nick. You gonna make a habit out of calling me in the middle of the night? You aren't in jail again, are you?"

"Not as far as you know," I teased. "Look . . . you said you'd cover expenses?"

"Reasonable ones."

"I need to go to Florida."

"Nick . . . reasonable expenses. Can you hear yourself . . . Florida? When do you want to go?" She did not sound one bit drowsy anymore.

"Tomorrow?"

"Tomorrow? Nick, have you got any idea how much that will cost booking a flight last minute like that?" I could picture her in her bedroom sitting on the edge of her bed ready to strangle the phone. "Do I want to know what's in Florida?"

"A bookstore owner."

"Let me ask you something, Nick. Do you see some truth in Whine's story? I mean, do you really see something there that is going to help me with his trial?" Lynn sounded doubtful.

"Something's going on," I said. I told Lynn about being clubbed in the back of the head.

"My goodness. And you're all right?"

"Fine. There's a little bump and aspirin did the trick. But you see where I'm going? I'm close to something and I'm making people uncomfortable. They want me away from this investigation. Most of my probing, so far, has been centered on the book . . . or books, really."

"Books?"

I told Lynn about Jasmine and the Magic Circle. I finished by explaining to her Jasmine had closed up shop and gone south, you might say, to Florida for an unscheduled, perhaps, permanent vacation.

"And you talked with her brother?" asked Lynn. "You found out where she's staying in Florida?"

"Kissimmee . . . and that's not an Italian offer," I said, sure to pronounce the city as kiss-a-me. It was incorrect, but I could not, for the life of me, remember how to say the name properly.

CHAPTER 21

Tuesday, May 22

I arrived at the office early Tuesday morning. I went on-line and booked a mid-afternoon flight to Florida. There would be a one-hour layover in Washington, D.C. on the way down, and a one-hour layover in Georgia on the way back. I finished the travel arrangements using my AAA membership, receiving a nice discount for a car rental once down in Orlando and was guaranteed a mid-sized vehicle would be waiting for me upon my arrival. From Orlando I could then drive to Kissimmee.

Next to my desk was my packed suitcase. In it I had the locked box from the Magic Circle. All night long I'd been tempted to open it. Opening it was not my place. I had my ideas about what might be inside—when I saw Jasmine in Florida, I'd let her open it and either confirm or shatter my speculations.

I heard Karis enter the building. She was talking to someone—another woman it sounded like—and thought it might be Frieda VanVelkenschmidt, from Reliquus, from downstairs. The two were laughing.

The telephone rang. "Tartaglia Agency."

"Nicholas? This is Lydia."

"Yes, Lydia. What's wrong?" She sounded upset and apprehensive. I could clearly hear a tremble in her tone of voice. "Lydia, is something wrong?"

"I just got something in the mail . . . it's a letter in Braille."

"What's it say?"

"It tells me to stop talking to people, or else. That's all it says. Stop talking to people, or else."

"Does it say anything about Whine . . . Gordon?" I could not imagine who in their right mind would dare threaten this young woman. I knew she felt frightened.

"No. Nothing."

"So somebody knows that you have been talking to me . . . and maybe about the books, but maybe they don't know that you and Gordon are an item," I said. I wasn't sure what that meant, if it meant anything. I thought back to the warning I'd found in my wallet on Sunday morning. The two warnings sounded similar, except for mine being written and not in Braille.

I did not like the warning tone of Lydia's message, despite the vagueness of any threat. The message was so vague that calling the police might prove completely useless—except for the fact that the letter was in Braille. I wondered how hard it would be to find an instrument to construct a letter in Braille?

"Did you show this to your brother?"

"No. I didn't show my brother."

"Did the letter come with the rest of the mail?" I asked.

"No. Well, it was the only thing in the box. I got the mail yesterday," she said.

I looked at my watch. It was barely after eight in the morning. "Well, I think it is safe to say that today's mail could not have been delivered yet. Where do you live? You want me to come over?"

"I'm kind of scared and Marlow's at work."

"What's he do for a living?"

"He's a factory worker," she said, and told me the company he worked for.

"Did you want me to stop by?"

"I think so, Nicholas . . . if you don't mind. I guess I am a little more frightened than I just admitted."

She gave me her address. My flight did not leave until a little after noon. There was plenty of time. I went out into the lobby and was taken immediately aback by who I saw standing in front of, and talking to Karis.

***

Seven months had passed and I don't think a day has gone by where I didn't at least once think about Eleanor Kasap. When we first met though, she did not introduce herself as Eleanor. Neither did she look at all like the way she looked today. Her hair was wrapped in a bun, with curly strands that dangled near her ears. She wore a lacey white blouse with a knee-length skirt, stockings and high heels. When I first met her she'd gone by the name of Scar, had been dressed in black with dark lipstick and earrings that pierced more than the ears.

"Eleanor?" I felt stunned. "My goodness . . . you look beautiful!"

She rushed into my arms and we hugged each other tightly. We'd gone through a lot together.

"School's out," she said. "I finished my last exam yesterday."

"Gee, Nick . . . you look handsome as ever," I said, complimenting myself.

Eleanor slapped my stomach playfully. "I'm sorry, Nick. Gee, you look handsome as ever."

I shook my head. "Doesn't quite mean as much when I have to remind you."

We laughed. "Miss me?"

"You know I did," I said. "How'd you finish out this year?" She just completed her sophomore year as a criminal justice major, with a minor in English. Eleanor also had known Karis' daughter—who had died during her freshman year of college at the hands of the Tenth House cult.

"It wasn't easy. I managed to hold onto a three-point-oh average."

"That's great, nothing to be upset about," I said. We small talked for a while longer. In the back of my mind I knew I had to leave. Lydia Henson would be waiting for me, but I did not want to cut this meeting with Eleanor short. It felt wonderful seeing her.

After a few more minutes of catching up, Karis said, "Nick . . . Eleanor has a question to ask you."

I caught Eleanor flashing Karis a sheepish grin. "Well?" I asked.

"I need an internship. The school was going to set me up as a co-op at Kodak as a security guard, but I didn't really want that. I told them I knew someone who might have a position for me for the summer."

"Yeah, and who's that?" I asked.

Karis grinned at me from behind Eleanor.

"Nick," said Eleanor, only it came out sounding like a skipping CD. Ni-i-i-i-ck.

My mind shifted into gear. "Actually, Eleanor, I don't know about this other offer you were hoping for . . . but if you are at all interested, I might be able to find some work around here to keep you busy."

"You mean it?" Eleanor's face lit up with a wide smile.

"Sure. Hell, these hardwood floors haven't been swept or polished since I-don't-know-when. And the bathroom . . . "

Eleanor slapped my stomach again. "Always a wise guy, aren't you?"

"You might say. Okay, seriously. I can use your help. In fact, I've got an assignment for you. I have to leave for Florida this afternoon," I said.

"You do?" Karis asked. "You didn't mention that?"

"Just came up. Last night. I didn't get a chance to tell you about it. I called Lynn and she approved the cost of an airline ticket," I said. I could tell Karis was grinding her teeth by the way her jaw muscles moved behind her cheeks. "I'm going alone," I added.

"So what do you want me to do?" Eleanor asked.

"Take a ride with me. I'm on my way right now to talk with a lady who has received a threatening letter. Lydia," I said.

"The blind woman?" Karis asked. "Who would do that?"

"I don't know . . . but I can't wait to find the person," I said, and though I'd made no mention of beating the person senseless, everyone knew what I meant.

CHAPTER 22

While I drove, I filled Eleanor in, telling her about the case.

"My goodness, Nick . . . I thought we'd be like, I don't know, following husbands that cheat on their wives," Eleanor said, sounding exasperated.

I started laughing. She just looked over at me as if silently asking, what on earth is so funny? "Father Paul said the same thing."

"Father Paul? He's working on this too?" Now she laughed. "Just like old times, huh?" There was nothing good about "old times" so our laughter died quickly away. Perhaps the only thing good to come out of that estranged course of events was the friendships formed.

"As far as I'm concerned, these books have something to do with the supernatural. And even though I hate thinking about having to deal with anymore cults, or cult fanatics . . . I've got a job to do, we've got a job to do." I hopped onto I-490 East and headed toward Downtown. "Let me tell you something, being smart isn't knowing all the answers; it's knowing where to find the answers."

"Yeah, yeah, yeah. So you get yourself into another obscure situation and you go and drag Father Paul into the mess with you," she said. She was teasing, but what she was saying couldn't be closer to the truth.

"And now you," I added.

"And now me."

"Father Paul is only doing some on-line research," I said,

defending my position.

"However you chose to justify it," she said, smirking. "Hey, got a cigarette?"

"Quit." I did not sound happy about it.

"You quit?" She sounded shocked. "Get out of here."

"No. I'm serious. It's been like three weeks. I'm wearing one of those nicotine patches," I said. "You know, it releases nicotine in your system periodically throughout the day."

"And it works?"

"I haven't had a cigarette yet," I said, neglecting to add that I thought about having a cigarette nearly every minute of the day.

"So no cigarettes?" Eleanor asked.

"None."

She fidgeted in the seat. "How about, got an extra patch?"

***

Lydia Henson lived in a rent-controlled high-rise apartment building located in the heart of Rochester's inner city. Parking was limited so I was amazed to see a spot directly in front of the building and pulled into it. Before I could shut the engine, an armed security guard came outside to confront me.

"Can't park there," he said, pleasantly. "Afraid that's just for emergency vehicles. There's a lot about a block and half down. You can park there."

I saw no point in arguing. I drove a block and a half and parked in a lot between two buildings heavily illustrated with spray paint graffiti. In all actuality, the work was quite impressive. The artist, or artists, work showed—at least I thought—promising talent. One wall displayed a black Jesus depicted on the Cross. Behind him, modern black people with radios and skateboards in their hands, stood with heads bowed. The second wall revealed a rendition of the city's skyline on a bright sunny day. Both paintings told me one thing, and it felt comforting. Despite the madness and despite the chaos in the world, hope still existed. Maybe there wasn't time left to fix all that was wrong in this life, perhaps there would be an eternity in the next.

When we reached the apartment building, we entered the first set of doors and stood in a vestibule. The next set of doors was locked.

We could see the security guard in an enclosed box only a few feet from the entrance. He had a newspaper spread out in front of him and looked engrossed in an article.

To our right stood a directory of tenants listed in alphabetical order. Next to each name I saw a three-digit number. I found Henson's number, picked up the telephone mounted to the wall by the directory and waited for Lydia to answer. She buzzed us in.

The guard looked up from his paper and smiled at Eleanor as we walked by toward the elevators. Lydia lived on the seventeenth floor.

When we got off the elevator the first thing I noticed was the pungent odor of urine.

"Smells like a hospital," Eleanor said.

"Worse," I added. We went down to Lydia's door and knocked.

Lydia let us in. "Lydia, this is an associate of mine. Her name is Eleanor."

Lydia and Eleanor shook hands and exchanged Hellos. "I just made a pot of coffee and I have cookies in the oven. Chocolate chip. Does that sound all right?"

"Wonderful," I said. "But you didn't have to go to any trouble."

"It wasn't," Lydia said as she turned and led us toward the smell of cookies baking—an aroma in thankful and direct contrast to that of the assaulting odor contained in the hall. She walked through her apartment effortlessly. I noted a sofa, love seat and recliner. There was no coffee table. There was an impressive stereo system in the corner and beside that stood a rack filled with an impressive collection of compact discs. In the opposite corner was a palm tree. The walls were bare.

The apartment was not as small as I'd have imagined. There was the living room, the kitchenette, a small dining area, bedroom and a bathroom. Lydia asked us to sit at the table in the dining room. "That's the letter there on the table," she told me.

I knew that for Lydia to have read the letter, she would have touched it and ran her prints all over it. Preserving the paper to check for prints would be futile. I picked it up. It resembled a blank piece of paper. I ran my fingers over it. In the center of the page the tips of my fingers felt tiny bumps. It meant nothing to me. I handed the letter to Eleanor. "Lydia, how hard would it be for someone to type out a letter using a Braille machine?"

"They have them at the libraries and museums."

"Braille machines?"

"Yep."

Eleanor set the letter down and went into the kitchenette. "What can I do to help?"

Lydia handed Eleanor three coffee cups, saucers, spoons and napkins. "If you don't mind setting those on the table, I think the cookies should be about ready." Lydia slid a potholder mitten onto her hand and pulled out a tray of cookies. She set the tray on the stove. "We'll just let those cool a minute." She brought over the pot of coffee, placed her finger into her cup and poured. She stopped when the hot coffee touched her fingertip. "You might want to each pour your own coffee," she said, setting the pot down.

"You know, I'm sorry about the other night . . . with everything that happened between your brother and I." I bit into a cookie filled with chocolate chips. "Man this is good."

"You know, my brother might look big and mean, but he's not. I don't think he's ever really been in a fight before," Lydia said. She began to laugh. "I wish I could have seen the way he looked, though. I felt bad for him, really I did, because I guess he came back in soaking wet."

"I am sorry." He was bloodied up too, but maybe he didn't want his sister to know that much.

"In a way, he asked for it," Lydia said, thoughtfully.

"He's just trying to look out for you," I said.

"I know that. Trust me. I know."

"Before he interrupted I had asked you a question." I thought I knew where the third book was. I was pretty sure it was in a box in my suitcase ready to fly with me to Florida, but I asked, "Do you know who has the third book? If your church has one, and you believe that Edwards has one . . ."

"I have no idea Nick. And I have no idea what is in the book, or any of the books. Other than what I told you, I really know nothing about any of this." She sounded upset. "More coffee, Eleanor?"

"No thank you. I'm all set."

"Nick?"

"No. I'm good. Lydia, I have to take a trip . . . I'm not going to be gone long, but if you need to get a hold of me . . . how did you get a hold of me today?"

"I called information."

"Remember the number?"

"I programmed it into my speed dial," Lydia said.

"Okay, good. If you need anything, you can use that number and talk to either Karis or Eleanor," I said, flashing Eleanor a wink. "They both know what's going on for the most part. When I get back, we'll talk again."

"Nick, do I have anything to worry about . . . I mean this letter, is that something I should worry about?"

"I honestly do not think so. At the same time, I do not want to take this letter too lightly. You can call the police, in fact, that might be an excellent idea," I suggested.

"I don't want to do that," Lydia said.

"Why not?"

"What will they do?"

She had a point. "We're going to figure this out Lydia," I assured her.

"So you want me to follow her," Eleanor asked when we were back in my car.

"Like a shadow. At least while I'm gone."

"So the letter bothers you?"

At the next red light I pulled out my wallet and showed her the warning I'd received. "Got to think the same person is behind this. So it shows some persistence. I've got no choice but to feel bothered."

"I don't have a car."

"You can use mine. Drop me off at the airport . . . just don't forget to pick me up tomorrow evening."

"Money for gas?" Eleanor asked sheepishly.

"I'll spot you an advance. Don't worry about it," I said.

"You know what was unnerving about Lydia's apartment?" Eleanor asked.

"No. What?"

"No lamps."

CHAPTER 23

"You got a phone call while you were out," Karis said when Eleanor and I returned to the office.

"A police officer stopped by?" I asked in anticipation of the restraining order.

"No. That's not what I said."

"One will," I said. "I'm sorry. Who called?"

"Your old boss."

"Ned?"

"Yeah. Wants to know if you can come out to his office. I told him you had to catch a flight at noon, he said he'd even give you a lift to the airport. He swore it was urgent and that he needed to talk with you as soon as possible."

After getting my suitcase and giving Karis a long and heated kiss good-bye, Eleanor and I went back to the car. She drove me out to Brighton where Safehouse Investigations was located and stopped in front of a red, brick-faced building.

"Okay, you know my cell number. You run into any problems, you call the police first and me second. Understand?"

"I got it, boss," she said and smiled. "I'll keep a close eye on her. I promise."

I trusted Eleanor. The young lady possessed an air of extreme intensity. "Okay. Careful with the car," I said while getting out of the car. I pulled open the back door and removed my suitcase.

Eleanor pulled away and I made a quick call on my cell phone before going inside.

Once inside I took the elevator up to the sixth floor. Overwhelmed by an uncomfortable sense of déjà vu, I forced myself to walk down to the suite that housed the agency. The doors to the agency were frosted with the Safehouse in bold black letters across both doors. I entered.

The receptionist, Betty, had not changed. She sat behind her desk with a mystery novel open in front of her. She looked up when I entered. She—with her large brown eyes and curly brown hair—had to be in her early forties. I noticed when she smiled at me some of the dark lipstick she wore had smeared on her front tooth. "My God, Nick. How have you been? Ned said you'd be coming in," she said while getting up from her chair. She came around to the front of the desk and wrapped her arms around me and hugged me tight. "I've missed you. Really, how've you been?"

"Good Betty. I've been doing very well." I said, setting down my bag. I wondered how exactly Betty meant her question. Both she and Ned had been convinced I'd lost my marbles. I couldn't work in an office where people thought I might be off my rocker. There would be no trust. To do my kind of work, I needed my fellow employees to trust me.

I asked, "How have you been?"

"You know. Same old, same old," she said. She whispered, "Place ain't the same without you. I think Ned's upset with himself for letting you go."

When I had been working on the Tenth House case, Ned caught wind of some of the rumors floating around. He was afraid I'd cracked up under pressure. He presented to me an ultimatum, so I walked. "That's not what this is about, is it? He's not going to offer me a job?"

"I don't think so, Nick," Betty said. "He's in his office. You can go on ahead and knock. But don't leave without saying good-bye to me!"

"I wouldn't dream of it," I said. I leaned forward and kissed her cheek. "Can I leave the bag here?"

"Sure," she said.

"For what it's worth, I've missed you, too." Which wasn't entirely true. I've been busy with my investigative agency, and hadn't even thought of Betty until just now when I entered the agency and saw her sitting behind her desk.

As I walked over to Ned's closed office door, I reflected. Ned's an all right guy. He was a cop down in Florida working vice and had been shot during a drug raid. The bullet came pretty close to his heart. That day had been like a sign from God for Ned. He retired early from the force, took his pension and moved up to western New York. He wanted to get far away from Florida, and thought a city where the seasons changed quarterly would be a pleasant experience. Little did he know winters in Rochester dominated, while spring and fall only lasted a total of two weeks a piece . . . and summers, forget about it.

Unfortunately, once a cop, always a cop; it wasn't long after Ned arrived in Rochester that cabin fever set in and he became stir crazy. Ned took a job working as a PI for a small company. Once he learned the ropes he quit and opened Safehouse.

I knocked.

"Come in," I heard Ned's voice say. Ned had a rough and gravely tone of voice that always sounded like he might be talking in a loud whisper.

I opened the door. Ned sat behind his desk. Ned, you might say, is eccentric. He had black carpets, black curtains and a black desk. The walls were painted a brilliant shade of white. On the walls were framed paintings of, what I liked to call blob-art. It looked as if the artist dipped his brush in black paint and sprayed the paint onto the canvas by pitching the paint, without letting go of the brush.

Someone sat in one of the two chairs in front of Ned's desk. "I didn't realize you were busy," I said. "Betty told me you were expecting me. I can wait . . . "

"No Nicholas, come on in," Ned said. He stood up. "Man you look great. It's good to see you." He came around from his desk and hugged me, though not nearly as tight a hug as Betty had given me. Close, but—as former President Clinton would never say—no cigar.

"You look good, too," I said. What else could I say, especially because since he did look good. Ned possessed a full head of wavy silver hair. His eyebrows were thick and silver and were set over deep-blue eyes. His face's center point was a small nose, but his rugged chin enhanced the features. Ned, as always, looked fit managing to hang on to his solid, muscular build.

I saw the face of the man sitting in the chair. "What's this about?" I asked. "If my sources are correct then, I'm not supposed to be within one hundred yards of him," I told Ned, pointing at Michael David Anthony, the man from the Magic Circle.

"There is no restraining order," Ned said. I did not look away from Mr. Anthony, who sat with his hands folded in his lap and his eyes studying his fingers. "We took care of that, called the police and canceled those charges."

"Care to tell me what's going on here Ned?"

"Michael works for me."

"For you?" I asked. I was suddenly dumbfounded. Instinctively, and perhaps defensively, my hands went to my hips. "What's he doing following me around, Ned?"

"You got it all wrong," Michael Anthony said. He had hair like Tom Cruise, fine and dark brown with matching dark eyes. His jaw looked square and strong. The most comparable feature was the big, bowed nose. He couldn't be more than twenty-one.

"I am not talking to you, ass-face," I said.

"Hey, hey, hey, Nick. Is that called for?"

"I'm sorry. You're right. That was uncalled for," I said. I felt hot inside.

"Don't say you're sorry to me," Ned said. He sounded very much like a father. I ignored him.

"Why was he following me?" I asked.

"He wasn't. He's working a case."

"For who," I asked.

"You know I can't tell you that." Ned went back to his chair and sat. He motioned for me to sit. I began to grind my teeth as I sat next to Anthony. "I called you in, not to talk about cases, but to take the opportunity to introduce the two of you . . . and so we can put the past behind us and let bygones be bygones. What do you say, Nick?"

"About what?" I asked.

"Come on Nick. Anthony has dropped all charges against you. He did it as a personal favor to me," Ned said.

He had me. He made his point. Ned was not the enemy, and for that matter, neither was Anthony. I knew nothing about this man. Well, I knew one thing. He was somehow involved with my case—or close enough that I wanted answers.

"I'm sorry Ned, and I am sorry Anthony." I reached out a hand.

Anthony looked at it. He let me hang a good six seconds before he accepted my hand. I felt his grip tighten more than necessary when we shook hands. I did my best to pretend it did not bother me, but the little jerk was strong.

I stood up. "We done here?"

"Nick . . ."

"Look Ned, I appreciate you looking out for me. I'm on a case, and need to catch a plane. When I get back, I'll give you a ring," I said.

"You mean that, Nick?" Ned asked.

"Course I do. What do you say?"

"Wonderful. Michael's going to give you a lift to the airport," Ned said.

"Thanks," I said as Michael stood up. "I got a ride."

I reached over the desk and shook hands with Ned, and then, reluctantly, with Anthony—except this time I gave him the squeeze. I stared at his face when I did it, and caught the wince cleverly disguised as a twitch. Ah, satisfaction.

I gave Betty a hug and a kiss and told her to take care. Outside sat a white taxicab waiting for me and I was immediately thankful that I'd called for the ride before going into Safehouse. The driver got out of the car and tossed my bag into his trunk. I climbed in and told him, "Rochester International, please."

***

I didn't spot the tail from Safehouse to the airport, but Michael David Anthony had a lot to learn about following people. Had I of been driving, I would have picked him out sooner. Still, when I went to my gate and waited to board the plane, Anthony might as well have completed his stakeout sitting next to me. I could not figure out why he was following me. It bothered me having my privacy invaded this way, but it piqued my curiosity, too. I doubted the little twerp was going to fly all the way to Florida to keep an eye on me, but I would wait to board the plane, just to see if he had a ticket.

After ten minutes of pretending not to watch me, Anthony moved on and disappeared. I waited for a minute and then went to check with the airline hostess. "Could you tell me if a Michael David Anthony is on this flight?"

"No sir."

"'No sir', he's not on the flight, or 'no sir' you can't tell me?" I gave her my warmest, most loving and—hopefully—charming smile, which didn't work.

"No, I can not tell you, sir."

"I understand, thank you." I went back to my chair and waited for boarding. If Anthony was on the flight, I'd know before the plane landed in Washington. I mean, where could he hide on a plane?

CHAPTER 24

The flights were pretty uneventful. After verifying that Michael David Anthony was not on the plane with me, I settled in and slept on the second flight from Washington to Florida. The sleep felt good, too. By the time we reached Orlando, I was ready to get up and stretch. I collected my suitcase off the luggage return and checked in at the car rental agency to obtain a set of keys. I stepped out of the terminal into an all-out assault of heat and humidity and wanted to go back in and hide in the air-conditioned airport.

I found my car in the lot of rentals and tossed my suitcase into its trunk. Having slept, I'd missed the box lunch. My stomach let me know as much as it rumbled and growled. I found a fast food place and went in for a quick bite.

I did not want to waste time. I took I4 toward Kissimmee, driving toward Disney World. The sky was blue and cloudless. Palm trees grew in Florida like maple trees in Rochester. I loved going out of state.

Jasmine was staying with an aunt. The aunt lived off U.S. 192, in a small residential area, behind an outlet mall geared at targeting tourists. After finding the aunt's street, I backtracked to the main road and pulled into the parking lot of the hotel closest to the aunt's home. Its sign advertised: Disney World: 5 Miles.

I checked in, paying for one night, and found my room on the third floor. I set my bag on the bed and switched on the room air-conditioning unit. The thing rattled to life and, surprisingly, blew out ice-cold air. The hotel, shaped like a "U," had a large in-ground pool tucked in the crevice of the "U." My room had a balcony that overlooked the pool. Families sat by the poolside and splashed in the water. I spent a few minutes leaning on the railing admiring some of the women in skimpy bathing suits and bikinis before getting back to work.

When I went back into the room, I closed and locked the balcony door. I unzipped my suitcase and stared in disbelief at what I found.

I stared in disbelief at what I had not found made more sense. The box from the Magic Circle was missing. I grabbed at my clothing and tossed everything out of the suitcase. "Where is it? Just where is it?"

My memory did flips. I saw myself at my house putting the box into the suitcase. I left the suitcase in my office, brought it with me to Safehouse, picked it up when I got off the plane, locked it in the trunk when I received the rental. For the most part the bag has not been out of my sight.

Somewhere, at some point, someone went into my suitcase and stole the box.

As my old friend the owl might say, Who?

***

I pulled into Jasmine's aunt's driveway and parked behind a well-used pick-up truck. I regretted that I would have to leave the climate-controlled atmosphere of the car and step into the sweltering early evening heat, but forced myself out of the car and walked casually up to the front door, immediately too hot to move any faster. Grass in Florida looked different than grass in Rochester: the blades looked thicker, wider and bluer than green. I could not get over seeing tiny lizards running all over the place, either.

I rang the doorbell. From somewhere inside, a dog—and by the sound of it—a large dog, began barking. Instinctively I stepped off the front step and looked around the front yard. The dog's barking became louder and I turned to see the front door slowly swinging open. "I'm here to see Jasmine," I said to the heavy, shirtless man answering the door.

"Yeah? Why?" The dog was at the screen, growling between barks, pressing its snout against the door.

"Because I came all the way from New York to talk to her," I said.

"Seems to me like you wasted a trip," the man said and closed the door.

This was crazy. I rang the doorbell again. The dog that never stopped barking barked more fiercely now. I rang the bell yet another time. The man, appearing irritated and angry, seemed to throw the door open. "You got a problem, buddy?"

"I didn't," I said. "Look, at least tell Jasmine that I'm here. I'm not bringing trouble and I'm not looking for it. There is a man back in New York who could spend a lot of time in jail for a crime he might not have committed."

"And Jasmine knows about this?"

"Not the crime, but she may have information that will help me figure out what happened," I said. "Bottom line, your niece is in no way connected to the crime, or to the alleged criminal. She knows some things about a special kind of book . . . and that's all I am looking to extract from her; information about that book."

"That's it, huh? What, are you an attorney?"

I laughed. "Now do I look like an attorney?"

Without missing a beat the man said, "Yeah, you do." And I don't think he meant that as a compliment.

We stood in the family room with the air on, but not set very high. The vicious dog, a large Black Lab, had somehow transformed into a gentle, crotch sniffing pain in the neck. I kept taking it by the face and pushing it away from my privates, but as if drawn to me by some magnetic force—as if I had a doggie bone in my shorts—the dog kept resisting my friendly attempts to get it the Hell away from me!

"I'm Nick, Nicholas. You can call me Nick," I said.

"Want a beer or something, Nick?"

"Yeah, you know, that sounds great. And maybe a place to sit." I decided sitting might be the easiest way to get the dog's nose away from my genitalia.

"Sure. Let's go in the kitchen. Jasmine and her aunt went out, but they should be back," the man said. I followed him into the kitchen and saw on the center of one of the windows a lizard. Without much thought the man slapped the back of his hand against the glass and the tiny green creature made his way across the window and disappeared. He took a beer out of his fridge and handed it to me.

"Thank you."

"Sure." He must have been cooking when I first rang the doorbell. He tossed a white hand towel over his shoulder and picked up a wooden spoon. He had spaghetti sauce simmering on a flame on the stove, next to a pot of boiling water. He opened a box of noodles and poured them into the water. "Like pasta, Nick?"

"Last name's Tartaglia," I said with a smile, accenting my Italian descent.

"Didn't ask ya what your name was, I asked if you liked pasta," the man said. He stared at me with an odd expression that seemed to ask, what is wrong with this strange man sitting at my table?

"Ah, yeah. I've been known to eat it once in a while," I said.

The dog had been standing at the threshold between the kitchen and the family room. It just stared at me. When it made up its mind, it came over and sat next to me, dying, I'm sure, to get back to its task of sniffing. I smiled a smile of pure satisfaction and took a healthy sip of cold refreshing beer. I felt my privates were safe as long as I sat in the chair.

The dog, perhaps attracted to the salt of my sweat began to lick my arm. "That's a nice doggie," I said, pulling my arm away. It craned its neck to reach me. It's long, pink tongue darted out of its mouth and continued to reach my arm. I pushed back in my chair. "This thing house broken? I think he wants to go outside."

"Bruce? Nah. He's fine," the man said, looking at me for an odd second before he went back to cooking. The dog had me backed into a corner. Bruce set his front paws on my lap. His head was like a rocking chair, rocking back and forth as his tongue swabbed every exposed area of flesh on my arms. I strained my head and stretched my neck to keep that salvia dripping tongue away from my face.

The door opened and I heard, "Bruce, get away from the nice man!"

Bruce, happy to see the rest of his family, left my lap and ran to great Jasmine and Jasmine's aunt by barking loudly and standing on two legs while his front paws mauled them—lovingly though, of course.

CHAPTER 25

We sat out on the front step sipping beer out of cans. Jasmine smoked a cigarette. She offered me one and though I declined the offer quickly enough, I spent a good amount of time in my mind debating whether or not to have just one.

"That's will power," she said. "Sounds like a classic line but, I have will power, but truth is, I don't want to quit."

I laughed. I understood what she was saying. Perhaps seventy-five percent of the statement was true. I had to guess the remaining percentage would be the nicotine addiction that kept a smoker feeling content.

"So, where's my box? When my brother called and told me you might show up down here, he said you had my box." Jasmine sounded slightly annoyed with me. To punctuate her sentence she cruelly exhaled a cloud of smoke in my face.

I fanned the smoke and pursed my lips, then said, "Gone."

She laughed. "Gone." She laughed again. The idea that I might not be kidding suddenly registered in her facial expression. The smile and giggle disappeared. "What's that mean, gone?"

"It means I had it, now I don't. It was in my suitcase . . . all day it was in my suitcase. I get down to Florida, I open the thing up in the hotel room and the lock box is gone."

"Well, then he has it." With her beer on the floor, she set her elbows on her knees and buried her face in the palms of her hands. "I was stupid to think I could hide it anyway."

"Believe it or not, I'm not really sure what you're talking about," I said.

We walked the sidewalk of the outlet mall. Jasmine kept her hands in the back pockets of her blue-jean shorts and chewed on her lower lip while I attempted to recite back to her the explanation she had just given to me.

"So you stumble across a book . . . the one you call earth," I said.

"Right. The middle, or the second ring. I mean, and this thing was old with yellow pages and everything, but it didn't feel, I don't know, it didn't feel right."

"How'd you find it?"

"It was in the wall. I was having some friends knock down a wall so we could put up a small coffee bar. People like that kind of thing . . . I mean it does well in those big chain bookstores, right? So when they knock down the wall, between the plaster or beams or whatever is in there that makes a wall . . . studs? Anyway, I find this book. It had to have been in there for decades, or longer. The building is old, we're talking eighteen hundreds old."

"And you ready it?"

"Started to, but I stopped. The book clearly had power. It was written in sixteen ninety-two," she said. She waited.

"And?" I asked.

"Doesn't that date mean anything to you?"

"Date? What date? It's a year."

"Well, my esteemed one, in the year sixteen ninety-two in Salem there were symbolic trials taking place."

"The witch trials?" I asked.

"Bingo. Anyway, when I started reading the thing I felt a surge inside me. It felt like an electrical current growing in my belly. That freaked me out," Jasmine said. "So I locked it away and stuck it in my safe."

"This is where I start to lose the story, so let me run through this part again. So after you lock this book away, maybe a few days later, a man shows up asking questions about an old exotic book that he called Earth?"

"Right."

"I mean he knows the title and everything."

"That's right."

"How long ago was this?"

"Not that long ago . . . last month maybe, maybe a little longer?"

"But you never advertised the fact that you had this book, right? So what did you tell him?" I asked.

"I told him I had no idea what he was talking about. I'd never even heard of a book like that before," she said.

"He buy it?"

"He accepted it. I mean, he gave me this odd look like he didn't believe me, but he wasn't going to make a big deal out of it. Besides, I didn't want to sell it. I might have been scared of it by what I felt, but I knew it was a book I was not going to get rid of. I've read a lot of books on witchcraft but never have I come across something like this. Authors write books on witchcraft. Some of the writers might be, or think they are witches because they have read other books about witchcraft, you know what I mean? Whitley Strieber . . . wrote that book Communion? He wrote books about witches, too . . . but he's no more a warlock than you are."

"Would you recognize the man if you saw him again?" I asked.

"Yes. No question about it."

"Jasmine, are you a witch?"

"Yes."

"I mean for real?"

"Yes." She picked up her beer and took a long swallow. "Being a witch is like being a homosexual. Some people are gay because it is the in thing to be, or because it is taboo . . . and people like to do things simply for the effect of shocking others . . . or because they are confused. You know? But then there are those who are gay because they are born that way . . . a man trapped in a woman's body, or the other way around. No matter how you look at it, they are gay because they were born gay. That's what I am. I'm a witch because I was born one. I didn't chose to be one, I didn't follow my friends and join . . . most people don't even know that I am one."

"I've got to ask: Are you a good witch, or a bad witch?" I said, trying to sound like Glinda from the Wizard of Oz. Jasmine stopped walking and just stared at me, then smiled, then laughed. "Was that insensitive?"

She pushed me. "I like you Nick. You're all right."

***

We sat on a rock by the stream that ran through Jasmine's aunt's backyard. Bruce was tied to a leash that was not long enough to let him come anywhere near us. This bothered the Lab, and he let us know by barking in a high-pitched whine.

Ignoring the dog's insistent pleas to be included, I asked, "Why'd you come to Florida?"

"Needed a break," Jasmine said, and I think we both knew she wasn't exactly telling the truth. "After that night you were in the store some strange things happened and the truth is I'd rather not discuss it." She stood up.

I was worn out. I remained sitting, but watched Jasmine squat and splash the palm of her hand in the water. "There's been many times where my aunt has been in the kitchen washing dishes and she looks outside the window over the sink and she sees a crocodile perched on the bank. Can you imagine that?"

"Jasmine, what happened? You can tell me . . . because you may not believe this . . . but when it comes to the bizarre I've actually got a much more open mind than most people can imagine."

"You might think so, but you have no clue what it is I'm not telling you," she said.

"You're right. I don't." I stayed quiet after that and watched her float the palm of her hand in the water. She had nice long, although ghost white, legs. The Florida sun would be good for her complexion.

After four or five minutes of silence and without turning to look at me, Jasmine said, "Ever talk to the dead?"

When I did not immediately respond—or react—Jasmine turned and studied my expression. She stood up and came closer. She gave me a quizzical look. "My goodness you have, haven't you?"

"I told you. I have a very open mind."

"Yeah? Well I'm hungry. How about dinner? There has got to be some of that pasta left over."

I pictured her big, fat and sweaty uncle cooking sauce with no shirt on. I thought of Bruce whose shed his hair floated all around the kitchen and uniformly covered the linoleum in patches of patterns. "I am hungry, but I'll take you out. There's a place out here I've always wanted to see."

CHAPTER 26

Relatively new to Florida, I impressed myself by finding the Planet Hollywood next to Disney World. It was a large globe-shaped restaurant started by some of Hollywood's legends of the silver screen. The line to get in looked long, but the wait went quickly. An employee of the restaurant walked up and down the line with a microphone and asked the "audience" movie trivia. If you answered correctly he gave you a movie pin. If you asked him a question and he was stumped, or gave an incorrect answer, you won a pin. By the time we were lead up to the hostess, I had four movie pins—and being a gentleman, I let Jasmine pick one to keep (but only one).

We sat in the science fiction section of the restaurant and we sat side-by-side so we could see the giant movie screen showing movie clips from movies by the owners of the business. I had seen them all, while Jasmine had recognized a few and finally admitted to something I'd already surmised: she rarely watched movies.

After the waiter took our order, I decided it was time to get down to business. Up until this point, the trip felt a little surreal. I felt as if I was on vacation—and it felt wonderful—except I wasn't on vacation. Sure, Jasmine needed some finessing to coax the answers out of her, but I was also enjoying the time we spent together.

"When do you head back?"

"My flight leaves late tomorrow morning," I said. "Want to come with me? I can get you a ticket."

She lowered her head. "I'm not going back . . . not yet, and maybe never."

"Tell me what happened," I said. She was hesitant. Her eyes stared into my eyes. When she looked away, down at her hands on the table, I knew she was going to open up.

"That night you were in and that guy ran out and you chased after him? Well, around midnight the store is empty except for me. I figure it's a slow night, but I've got this feeling in my fingertips . . . like an itchy feeling? The lights go out and I don't just mean in the store . . . but out on the cobblestone, too. So I think it's a black out, right? So I step out of the store onto the walk and I can't see anything. It had been raining, remember, earlier? So there must have been clouds in the sky blocking the moon and stars . . . so we're talking pitch black," she said. She was into the rendition and talked with her hands, which moved about with action-packed animation. "You ever drive through West Virginia?"

"No."

"Well, at night when you're driving through the mountains . . . sometimes it is so dark you can't see the mountains, but let me tell you something . . . you can sure feel them. They are like giants standing all around you as you try to maneuver your way past them. Man, can you feel them, and I don't think that has anything to do with me being, you know, a witch," Jasmine explained. "Anyway, that's what I felt when I stepped out of my store. I felt like a mountain was standing next to me, only I couldn't see it."

"Did it talk?"

"The mountain?" Jasmine asked.

"The mountain, the whatever it was masked by the darkness?"

"It talked . . . but not with a voice," she said.

"Of course not. A voice would have been expected, too simple . . . we're looking for the obscure here, the un-obvious," I said, shrugging my shoulders.

"Hey," Jasmine said, suddenly offended. "Nick you're supposed to have an open mind. You're supposed to . . . "

"I'm sorry. I'm sorry and you're right." I apologized some more. I put my hand on hers. "Please," I finally said, "go on."

"It was in the wind," she told me. "The voice was like a low howl . . . then like a tortured scream. It whipped around in a high-pitch. Let me tell you this though, it was clear . . . what the shadow told me

. . . I understood every word as if someone were standing in front of me whispering directly into both of my ears. It told me, it said, I'm coming for the book, Jasmine. I'm coming for the book."

"And you think it, the whisper, might belong to the man that first showed up for the book?"

"Without a doubt. I know it was him. No one else knew I had the book. I mean no one . . . except the guys that smashed down the wall for me. Trust me . . . I'd be surprised if any of them knew how to read. My friends aren't the brightest—but they're still my friends."

"How loyal of you," I said. Our food arrived. I ate what was on my plate while I mentally chewed on all I had learned.

"And you want to know what else, Nick?"

"Sure I do," I said.

"You know how one gay guy can always spot another gay guy? Well the man, the one that wanted the book, he was a warlock."

"And so this is why you left?"

"I was scared, Nick."

"And you didn't take the book with you?"

"No. I didn't want it with me. I was going to just leave it. Then when I got here, I knew I needed to keep the book. It came into my possession by some odd fate. Having been entrusted to guard it . . . I would be acting as a coward to give it up so easily," Jasmine said, lowering her head.

The book was gone. She had failed. "Hey," I said, "we'll get it back."

CHAPTER 27

Wednesday, May 22

Yesterday seemed like one of the longest days of my life. So much had happened—and yet I was no closer to any answers than before. When I arrived at the airport, a half-hour before my flight, I felt physically and mentally drained. Gordon Birdie's trial would be coming up in a few weeks and I did not want to let him down.

I had some ideas floating around in my head—obvious places to pick up my search once I got back home, but I did not feel too confident.

At the gift shop I bought a Thom Racina novel. I went to my gate and sat down to wait for boarding when it hit me. Michael David Anthony was behind all of this. Had to be. "That dirty little . . . "

"Nick," Jasmine said. She was standing in front of me with a handbag.

I stood up. "What are you doing here?"

"I'm coming home with you."

I must have looked as surprised as I felt. "But I thought you were scared?"

"I am. I'm petrified, but I realized something. I'm a good witch, Nick. That warlock, he's a bad one. I guess that makes you Dorothy." She laughed. "I don't really know why you are involved in all of this, but when I first met you . . . and all of yesterday while we talked, I knew there was something special about you, inside of you. If you were a witch, Nick . . . you'd be a good witch, too."

"Gee. Thanks," I said, unenthusiastically, while clearly touched by the compliment.

"I didn't tell you this yesterday, Nick . . . mainly because you didn't ask . . . but when I read the first few sections of Earth it was like a preamble . . . and I can only speculate that it is the same inside all three books. What it said was, you know . . . basically, the power of the spell is enhanced if you are in possession of all three books. Last night I was thinking . . . I had the second book and I'll bet you anything that the warlock has one of the other two," Jasmine said, trying her theory out on me.

I confirmed it. "I know that a man in Rochester has one of the books."

"I'll bet it's him, then."

"What's worse . . . I know where the third book is . . . and I'll bet, so does he. Do you need a ticket?"

She held up a boarding pass. "I booked my flight last night after you left."

I pulled out my cell phone. They called for Jasmine and me to board the plane. No one was answering at my agency. If Jasmine was right and the person in possession of the three books can cast more powerful spells—or even if he thinks he can—then I had to worry about the Baptist church. "Karis where are you?"

"Karis?"

"My secretary," I said. Jasmine smiled. "How do you think this, the warlock, knew you had the book?"

"I think he knew when I opened it and began reading. I think he sensed the book," Jasmine said while I rolled my eyes. "You don't believe me?"

"It's not that I don't believe you, it's that I can't believe the messes I get caught up in." I thought of Gordon Birdie sitting in jail, afraid to be released. Now I understood the reasoning behind his fear. He thought the big bad warlock might cast an evil spell over him, turn him into a toad or something. In jail he must think if he's out of sight, he is out of mind. I wondered if he was right, or was Philip Edwards planning revenge?

Damn. Could Philip Edwards have revenge in mind? Did he want to gather up the three books to go after Gordon Birdie?

We got on the plane and when we landed in Atlanta I tried calling the agency again. Karis answered the telephone. "Oh hey, Nick," she said. "How was the trip?"

"Hot. Productive, but hot."

"Not surprised. Eleanor's going to pick you up at the airport. She just called a little while ago to confirm your flight. I really like her," Karis said.

"I'm glad. Look, she say anything about her post?"

"She reported that nothing much was going on, that Lydia had not left the apartment building all night, but that this morning she went on a bus with some other tenants. The bus took them to the grocery store. Eleanor stayed right behind her while she shopped . . . the tenants got back on the bus and went home."

"Good. Perfect. Look, how busy are you?"

"Just working on an article, pretty slow. Why?"

"Call Father Paul for me . . . my plane's going to be boarding again soon . . . tell him to get over to the First Baptist Church and make sure everything is all right. Tell Father Paul to talk to the Pastor . . . man's name is Pastor Brown . . . have . . . "

"Whoa, Nick. You're rambling," Karis said.

"I'm sorry. Okay, let me slow down. Pastor Brown has a book that he is hiding, and supposedly no one knows about it," I said.

"Except you?"

"Wise guy," I said. "Tell Father Paul to explain to the Pastor that someone will be coming for that book. It is very, very important that Pastor Brown, one . . . not read it, and two, hide it good."

"Why?"

"Long story. I'll tell you when I get back."

"Anything else?"

"Right now? I'm sure there is, but for the life of me I can't figure out what," I said, feeling discombobulated.

During the rest of the trip, I felt lost in thought. I was putting a lot of faith in Jasmine and her concept of the three books. Did I believe in spells? Did I believe in foreboding shadows that used the wind as a means of communicating? Did I believe that someone in possession of three books, the complete Talisman, would have more power? Did I believe there was any power associated with a book of magic spells?

Was Lydia in danger? Was Whine? Was Pastor brown? Was sending Father Paul to see Pastor Brown such a good idea?

Was Philip Edwards, Sr., planning to get revenge?

And I also thought, Why in the Hell did I quit smoking?

***

The airplane dropped out of a slate gray sky and landed in a dreary Rochester. I was getting tired of the rain and gloom, especially after leaving a sunny state like Florida. Maybe after this case was put to rest, Karis and I could wind down with a little vacation. I would not mind heading back to Florida—not at all.

"There's no place like home," Jasmine said, staring out the plane window.

"At least it's not snowing, right?" I said, trying to make the best of it.

***

Eleanor greeted us when we came off the plane. "Look at the tan," she said to me, smiling. She liked mocking me openly.

"I was there on business," I said. "Besides, I don't sit out in the sun."

She shook her head and touched my cheek. "No kidding, Casper."

Choosing to ignore the insult, I said, "Eleanor, this is Jasmine."

"Wow. You don't stop, do you," Eleanor said. "Karis know?"

"His secretary?" Jasmine asked. "Does she know what?"

"Secretary, huh?" Eleanor said.

"Eleanor . . . Jasmine is the reason I went down to Florida," I explained.

"Yeah, well no wonder you don't have a tan," Eleanor said.

"What's up with your surveillance?" I asked since the subject needed to be changed.

Eleanor removed a memo pad from her back pocket, getting down to business. We all walked together and both Jasmine and I listened while Eleanor briefed me. It seemed like nothing much of anything had happened. Which was exactly what I wanted. We stopped at a car rental booth. And I rented a compact sized car for a week and tucked the receipt into my wallet, then handed the keys to Eleanor. "This is yours for a week. After that, you're on your own," I said as she returned my keys.

"So what, you want me to keep watching Lydia Henson?"

"Not this time. I just wanted you to keep an eye on her while I was gone. Now I want you to watch the First Baptist Church, on Lake and Stutson Streets. The church mostly has black people that attend," I said.

"So we're on the look out for a white guy," Eleanor added.

"Exactly. If we meet back at the office, I'll show you specifically the white guy we're looking out for," I said, then turned to talk to Jasmine. "And you can tell me if this is the same guy who came in to inquire about the book."

If Philip Edwards, Sr. was behind the book thefts, I had an idea where Jasmine's book of Earth might be.

CHAPTER 28

Karis ordered a pizza for our late lunch and we all ate slices while we talked about the case. Jasmine was very intelligent when it came to the topic of witches, warlocks, spells and magic, and Eleanor was full of questions.

"How about a long time ago when they used to persecute women because they thought they were witches," Eleanor asked, removing a piece of pepperoni off her slice. She was a vegetarian.

"The truth is, most of those women were not witches at all—some were, but most weren't. In fact, if a bat was near your home, then you were a witch. Can you imagine that?"

"Why?" Eleanor asked.

"Well, people would walk somewhere at night . . . through the grass, you know . . . and bats would dive bomb them. And that's got to be a pretty freaky experience, right? So then they would tell everyone what happened to them, because even back then bats were considered like, I don't know, devil creatures. So if a bat was near a house, or lived in your barn, then you were a witch and you had cast a spell and sicced the bats on those people. It wasn't until over a century later, when people started studying bats that they realized what really was happening," Jasmine said.

"And what was really happening?" Eleanor asked.

"Well, insects hang out on blades of grass. When you walk through the grass, you disturb them and they take off. So the bats start swooping in to eat the insects. They weren't after the people at all," Jasmine said, solemnly. "So a lot of women died needlessly."

"But you said some were witches," Eleanor pointed out.

"I did, but most witches are not evil like Hollywood makes them out to be. We don't . . ."

"You said 'we?'" Karis asked.

"I'm a witch," Jasmine said softly.

"A good witch," I added.

"You cast spells?"

"Not like you're thinking. I love the earth, and I worship it."

"What about God?" Karis asked. "Don't you believe in Him?"

"Actually, I do. Who else could have made such a beautiful world and everything?"

"But you're not supposed to worship anyone, or anything except Him," Karis argued. "It's in the Bible and part of the Ten Commandments."

"I understand that, but I didn't say I was religious. I just said I believed in God."

I shook my head. We were venturing into deep waters, deeper than I wanted to go. "Look. The pizza was great, but I have to run. Eleanor, before you head out, will you give Jasmine a lift to wherever she wants to go?"

"Sure Nick," Eleanor said.

As Eleanor and Jasmine got ready to leave, I told Jasmine I'd be in touch.

Karis told me she had been unable to get a hold of Father Paul. Before I left the agency I tried calling one more time. He answered the phone. "Busy?" I asked.

"Not right now. Just got back from the hospital. An elder woman in the parish needed Last Rites." Father Paul sounded deeply troubled.

"You all right?"

"Yes. I suppose. She was a wonderful woman, and this sickness seems so all-of-a-sudden."

Father Paul talked for a few minutes about the dying woman. "It's part of life, though Nick. And anyway, what can I do for you?"

"I've got to take a ride, and I think it would be beneficial for you to come with me, if you can spare some time," I said. Father Paul agreed and was anxious to talk to me about some things he had learned about the united book of The Talisman.

I drove to St. Anthony's rectory where Father Paul was waiting outside for me. "How are you?" Father Paul asked as he climbed into my car with a moan. "I think I need to lose some weight. And you need a maid. Nick, this car is a mess."

I laughed. I'm a slob, why defend it.

"Where are we headed exactly?" Father Paul asked, and I told him. "And you want me there to help you talk to Pastor Brown. I'll be kind of like your father?"

"In a matter if speaking, yes. I think the things we are going to be discussing will have more weight if a man of the cloth is there for my side of the conversation. Not to mention, you may also be able to help shed some light on what is going on," I said. "And I showed a picture of Philip Edwards to this lady who owns that bookstore I was telling you about."

"That magic bookstore?" Father Paul asked. He looked uneasy. "I'm not real comfortable with this, you know. Magic forces and evil spells, all of those things do exist . . . they always have. The powers of evil are very, very, well, powerful."

"I don't doubt that in the least. At one time, Father, I might have. Not anymore," I said. "Not anymore."

"So what did she have to say about the photo?"

"Well apparently Philip Edwards came to her store one day . . . not so long ago. He knew she had a book somehow and . . ."

"Somehow. What's that mean, somehow? The girl owns a bookstore, I'm not seeing the importance . . ."

"Jasmine, the girl, found the book in her wall. She was doing some renovating. The book was behind the plaster, or drywall. Anyway . . . it was old. Written in sixteen ninety-two. So she starts reading the first part of the book, like the prologue to the three books. You see there are three books that make up The Talisman. Heaven, Earth and Hell . . . and Earth, the one Jasmine had contained like a generic introduction. I don't know, maybe an identical chapter is in each of the three books. The segment she read was like a warning, but I don't want to make it sound all Curse of the Mummy's Tomb, but that's exactly what she took it to mean. Then next thing she knows there's Philip Edwards wanting to buy the book from her," I said. "Jasmine thinks that when she opened and read part of the book a signal was somehow sent to the other books . . . or their owners, or whatever."

Father Paul sat thoughtfully silent for a moment. "And Philip Edwards has one of the books?"

"Pretty sure he does . . . or did, yeah." He may now have two.

"And you think the Pastor at this church we're going to has the other?"

"I've been told that he does and that he's protecting it. More than that, he's also trying to gather up the other two volumes. He wants to protect The Talisman from getting into the wrong hands . . . if you can find it in yourself to ignore the cliché," I said.

"I can't, but I will try to overlook it for now."

"Jasmine said that whoever was in possession of the three titles, or the complete Talisman, would have magical strength and power . . . good or evil . . . that could prove to be, well . . . like nothing the world has ever seen before."

"A little dramatic, don't you think?"

"Completely. Here's where I get worried. Philip Edwards lost his son, okay? He's distraught. A man is in prison for the death of his son. So there is some justice being served, but maybe not in Edwards' eyes. He's still without his son. Maybe he's afraid that Gordon Birdie is going to get out of jail . . . get off at the trial. Maybe he doesn't care if Gordon is going to stay in jail for the rest of his life. The way I see it, Edwards wants his own revenge. Maybe he thinks if he can get the three books, he can cook up a spell and cast it on Gordon."

Father Paul screwed his face up. "Interesting."

"But you don't think so?"

"Let's say you're right, why are you in panic mode then? Let me play devil's advocate, here . . . if you'll forgive me the use of the cliché."

"Forgiven."

"Ah, a greater man than I," Father Paul said. "Look at it this way, Edwards' son is murdered, and Edwards also owns one of the three books that make up The Talisman. The man responsible for his son's death is in jail . . . ."

"Or has been murdered. It may be Anthony, the other man with Gordon, who was responsible for shooting junior."

"To grieving parents I've got to think that's of little consequence."

"I agree," I agreed.

"So with his one book, Edwards senior can concoct spells . . . small ones, but spells just the same. The spell he wants, should revenge be his forte, is more powerful than he can, how did you say it? Cook up? So he needs the other two books, am I right so far?"

"For the most part," I said, "except I think Edwards may now have two of the three books. I think he managed to get his hands on Earth, the book Jasmine had."

"She sold it to him?"

"She didn't . . . but that's another thing I've got to deal with later. Get back to playing devil's advocate."

Father Paul cleared his throat and smiled. "Why do we believe these three books, on their own or combined, will possess any real magical power in the first place?"

The question dropped from the priest's lips like an anvil.

"Well, I'm in panic mode for a variety of reasons. First, I have a job to do . . . for Gordon's attorney . . . to dig up as much background information as I can. This guy is set to go to trial soon and I'm not sure I'm getting all I need to help him. After talking with Gordon in prison a few times I got the same reaction from him. He's afraid. I mean, Father, he's terrified of getting out of jail. He thinks Edwards will get him. And he may be right."

"But right now Gordon is in jail . . . and he is safe. So why the panic?"

"Gordon's got a girlfriend . . . "

"Ah-hah," Father Paul said. "Now the plot thickens."

"It gets more complicated. I was jumped the other night," I said. "I got roughed up some. They told me to back off my investigation and they told me to leave Whine in jail."

"How terrible. Are you all right? What did the police have to say?"

"I'm fine, and I didn't call the police. I was roughed up, sure, but not hurt. They didn't want to hurt me. They just wanted to make a point. They made their point, but in doing so, they made a mistake."

"Which is?"

"We may get to talk about that at the church," I said. "But let me get something straight. You don't think someone in possession of one of these books can cast spells?"

"I never said that," Father Paul said.

"Then you think they can cast spells?"

"I never said that either. Just because someone has something, it doesn't mean they know how to use it. I had a friend, a nun I knew, owned a vintage Les Paul guitar . . . once owned by a famous musician. I've seen my friend hold that guitar and stare at that guitar, and at times I've heard her attempt to strum it. When she played . . . not knowing the first thing about chords, or even how to tune an instrument . . . it sounded awful," Father Paul said.

"Great parable, Father," I said.

"You get my point. The books themselves may hold magical secrets and have a certain power to them . . . but someone would have to know how to use the books to make them a threat, I would imagine."

I could not help but think about what Jasmine had told me, about how Edwards had been like the wind, like the shadow of a foreboding mountain. "So then if the right person had one book and was collecting up the other two . . . "

"If it were the right . . . and I hate to use this term, magician . . . yes. There might be a threat."

I retold Jasmine's story to Father Paul. "I believed her . . . with a grain of salt, you know. I mean, you and I, we've been through a lot. My mind is open to the supernatural . . . "

"Hopefully not your soul," Father Paul added. "I've not met Jasmine yet, but I do trust you and your judgment Nick. As I've told you, I too have been doing some researching," Father Paul said.

"Yeah, and what have you come up with?" I asked. The last I had heard, Father Paul's searching had been bone dry compared to all that I've dug up.

"To be honest, I'd like a little time to think about some things. Since all of this, everything you've just told me, I have some theories that I'd like to go over in my mind . . . and I'd like to pray about the possible meaning of it all," Father Paul said.

Respecting the priest's request, I backed out of the driveway and drove toward the First Baptist Church. I kept my mouth shut. There were things I could be thinking about, too, but mostly I did not want to bother the priest—especially if he was talking to the Big Cheese.

CHAPTER 29

Gray skies, gray skies, gray skies. It wasn't raining when we arrived at the church, but the sky seemed to be a constant threat. When we got out of my car, the smell from the river—the stench, to be more accurate—seemed overwhelming. If it wasn't plumes of smoke billowing from the factories in the area, it was the wafting odors of the river. Perhaps the two were loosely related?

"Always cars back here," I commented while locking my doors.

"Churches are like that," Father Paul said. "People need so much that sometimes they think the only way to find God and Heaven is to be at church as much as possible."

We climbed the steps and went in. "How come I don't remember cars always being at your church before it burned down?"

"Because sometimes you just have to send everybody home," the priest said, laughing.

I heard grunting and turned to my left in the vestibule. Marlow Henson was plowing his way up stairs and through a door with three folded folding chairs in each arm. I said, "Man, you rent a room here or what?"

Marlow set the chairs down and came at me. "This won't be like last time," he said threatening me with large hands rolling into bowling ball-sized fists.

"Oh, why not? Gonna throw a punch this time?" I teased as Father Paul stepped in between us.

"Boys, boys." He held up his hands and it quieted the both of us.

I felt like saying, well he started it, but kept silent. "Is Pastor Brown around?"

Marlow regarded Father Paul with complete respect. "He's downstairs in the basement, Father."

I felt my stomach churn. I was not big on church basements, and though I could not read Father Paul's expression, I had the feeling that he did not want to venture downstairs anymore than I did. "Would you be so kind as to inform him that he has visitors, and that we'll be waiting for him in a pew near the altar?"

"I can do that," Marlow said and Father Paul thanked him.

"What was that about?" Father Paul asked as he and I slid into a pew near the front of the church. "A scuffle?"

"You might call it that. He lunged and I knocked him on his keister," I said, smirking. "I didn't hurt him as much as his pride. Truth is, I don't think the boy has been in many fights before."

"With his size, probably doesn't have to," Father Paul said. "What a shame that you should be the one to land the first punch."

Father Paul made it clear by his tone that he was disappointed in me. His opinion counted. It bothered me to have him upset with my actions. "Well, I mean, he started it."

"Nick, Nick. I didn't say a word."

"No, but you implied it. You implied that I didn't turn the other cheek," I said.

"Did you?"

"Well . . . no."

"Then I didn't imply anything. You did not turn the other cheek and you took advantage of a man you knew you could beat. You are a skilled fighter . . . more streetwise than he is. What was the fight about exactly?"

I shut up. There seemed no point in pointing out the obvious fact that had I let that grizzly punch me in the cheek, my teeth would have been strewn across the parking lot at the bowling center.

"Nick? What was the fight about?"

"He didn't want me involving his sister in this mess," I admitted reluctantly.

"How noble of him," Father Paul said. Just then Lydia entered the church. She used her white cane to walk while she carried a folding chair with her. "I wonder who that might be," Father Paul said, standing up, ready to help the young blind woman.

"The guy's sister."

Father Paul turned to glare at me. He did not need to say a word. His point was made by the intense look. Marlow was protecting his blind sister. "I'll apologize as soon as he comes back up here," I said.

"Nick? Is that you?" Lydia called out, as she was halfway down the aisle of pews.

Thankful for the distraction, I rushed over to greet her. "I got that for you," I said, relieving her of the chair. "How are you?"

"I'm okay. Have you seen Gordon anymore?"

"Not since last time," I said. "But I would like to introduce you to a good friend of mine. Lydia, this is Father Paul."

"Hello, Father," Lydia said.

"Hello," Father Paul said while carefully reaching out to shake her hand. "How are you?"

"Lydia!" said Marlow from behind us. It came out like a bark.

Both Father Paul and I stared at Marlow as Lydia politely took back the folding chair and excused herself

"Let me," I said, trying to take the chair back, again.

"No. That's all right. I've got it," she said, and as if a timid animal, and nearly cowering, Lydia made her way down the rest of the aisle, but stopped before reaching the altar. "It was a pleasure to meet you, Father."

"The pleasure was mine," said the charming priest.

I watched as Marlow whispered intently into his sister's ear while holding onto her arm. I did not like the way he held her. From here I could see that his grip was too tight. Lydia did not deserve to have her arm squeezed. When Marlow was apparently done with his lecture, he released her. With her head bowed, she left through a door at the side of the altar.

Father Paul leaned over. "I'm starting to understand about the little dispute between you and Lurch over there."

I snickered. "That's exactly what I call him."

"Pastor Brown will be right with you," Marlow said. He stared at me. The look clearly signaled the final warning to leave his sister alone. I gave him a two-finger Boy Scout salute. Visibly agitated, his hands clenched into fists and a loud sigh escaping him, he turned and disappeared through the same doorway his sister had recently used.

"Gentlemen!" said Pastor Brown emerging from the back of the church, catching Father Paul and I by surprise by the sound of his voice. "I didn't mean to startle either of you, I'm sorry."

"Remember me, Pastor?"

"I'm very good with faces," Pastor Brown said, holding out his hand. "Terrible with names."

"Nick. Nicholas Tartaglia," I said as we shook hands.

"Ah yes. You're working for the attorney representing Gordon Birdie."

"Bingo," I told him. "And this is . . . "

"Father Paul of St. Anthony's Church," said the priest, shaking hands with the Baptist Minister.

"I'm Pastor Jacob Brown," he replied. "And your name I know. I remember reading about your church in the paper last year. Very unusual, very troubling," the Pastor said in an almost accusatory tone.

"What happened at my church, you are right, was very unusual and very troubling," Father Paul said, agreeing. "Luckily Nick and I were able to find resolve the situation."

"Yes. I remember. I remember. Something like 30 children burned with the church, though? Hmm." He smacked his lips together.

I wanted to punch his lips. "They were not children. They were adults . . . members of a satanic cult. The cult sacrificed people in the bowels of . . . "

Father Paul put his hand on my forearm and squeezed.

"We can sit here and play into your little battle plan . . ."

"Battle plan? I'm sorry if you think I'm trying to start trouble. All I did was comment on your past situation. If you are harboring any guilt . . ."

"Pastor," Father Paul said sternly. "We know all about The Talisman, all about it."

For only a microsecond, Pastor Brown's calm expression rocked. "Talisman?"

"The three books: Heaven, Earth and Hell. The three rings. The Talisman," I said. "Father Paul and I know where all three books are. And we think right now that one person is in possession of two of the books. We strongly believe that you have the third."

Pastor Brown while shaking his head and smiling, said, "I have no clue what the two of you are up to, nor do I have any idea what you are talking about. I have a Bible class for tonight and as you can see we are busy trying to get things organized."

I turned to look around. Marlow and another man stood near the Vestibule, arms crossed. Both men stared at the priest and me. "Let me tell you this, as a warning. I think that if you read the book, the one you have hidden away . . . then you send off a signal, a beacon, that can lead those in possession of the other books right to you."

"Thanks for the warning," Pastor Brown said with a hearty laugh. "An now I believe it is time for the two of you to leave." Pastor Brown placed a hand on my and father Paul's shoulder and turned us around and led us back down the aisle to the church's exit. We warned the Pastor about his ring. Hopefully he would consider our words heavily before dismissing them.

Outside Marlow and his friend stood near my car.

"I'll handle this, Nick," Father Paul said.

As we walked to the car, Marlow came forward. "I told you to stay away from my sister!"

"Sir," Father Paul said.

"Please Father, I don't mean to disrespect you . . . but stay out of this. Nick knew the rules and he broke them and we need to teach him a lesson," Marlow said, which in my eyes, was mistake number one. Why tell someone that you plan to beat them up?

Marlow's friend walked over and stood facing me on my right side. "Guys," I said while bringing my hands up and together, almost as if in prayer. Then I planted my right fist into the palm of my left hand and used the strength of my left hand to hammer my right elbow into the friend's face and heard the distinct sound of crunching bone. The nose, I felt confidant was broken.

"Oh, Nicholas," I heard Father Paul moan.

Stepping forward with my left foot, I faked a jabbed at Marlow's face and as he tensed his body and went to block the punch, I kicked his feet out from under him. He went down hard on the loose gravel. I kneeled with all my weight on his chest, less than an inch away from crushing his throat with my knee. "I'll tell you what. We're even. You ever, ever, think about jumping me in my own front yard again and I will beat you and your friend over there senseless. Do we understand each other?"

Marlow nodded and I stood up. The other guy was on his feet. He stood silently staring at me holding his nose as blood oozed out from between his fingers and ran down his wrist and forearm.

In the car, Father Paul said, "How did you know they were the one's to jump you?"

"Well, I'm pretty sure I recognized Marlow's voice . . . the other guy I'm not positive was there. But the two seem chummy enough. Besides, it was the warning they'd given me that night. They called Gordon Birdie, Whine. Whine is Gordon's church nickname," I said.

Father Paul smiled. "Elementary my dear Watson."

"Exactly."

CHAPTER 30

Thursday, May 23

I left two messages with Betty, my old secretary at Safehouse Investigations, to have Ned call me back. Each time she let my call roll over into his voice mail. She wasn't sure when he'd be in, but knew he'd be checking his voice mail periodically. I was about to call a third time when my telephone rang. "Tartaglia Agency," I said. It was my sister, the homicide detective's wife. "Arline, how are you?"

"Good, Nick," she said, but didn't sound it.

"And my niece? How's Madeline?"

"Eating every two seconds, and forcing me to change a diaper ever four," said my sister laughing. The laugh sounded forced. My sister never called me at work. Something was up.

"So what's up?" I asked.

"I was thinking it would be nice to have you and Karis over for dinner tonight. Capollini?" She asked, knowing full and well that Capollini was my favorite pasta.

Hungry or not, I would go to dinner. I heard a tone in my sister's voice that I did not like. "I think it sounds wonderful. I'll bring some of Uncle Tony's red wine?" He made his own. He loved his beer and though he had set my tap up in the refrigerator in my garage, he also loved making wine in his basement—which was one giant percolating grape festival waiting to explode.

"None for me, I'm breast feeding, but Tom loves it," said Arline.

"How about six, six-thirty?"

"Perfect," I said. I didn't ask her what was wrong. I didn't want to upset her any more than she apparently already was. If she did not express her feelings at dinner tonight, I would most certainly, and with care, probe for the cause of her distress.

We hung up and I told Karis about my plans for the evening and asked if she'd like to join me.

***

Karis and I parked in the driveway behind my sister's car. I took the bottle of wine and bag with two loaves of fresh Italian bread out of the car with me as we walked up to the front step. Even before I rang the doorbell, I could hear the sound of the baby crying.

"Suppose it's okay to ring the doorbell," I said, laughing.

"Suppose so," Karis agreed with a smile.

When the door opened, Arline looked worn out (a more polite term than saying terrible—which was how she really looked). She had some make-up on, her hair was done, and she wore nice jeans with a French blue blouse. Her eyes rested on top of dark and drooping bags. The eyes looked red and puffy as if she had been crying.

She unlocked and pushed open the screen door. "Hi guys," Arline said. She and Karis kissed on the cheeks. Karis took Madeline out of Arline's hands and began bouncing the baby up and down around the living room. I could just hear the soft lullaby Karis sang, in a whisper, into the baby's ear.

I gave my sister a big hug. "Where's Tommy?"

Taking the bottle of wine and bag of bread out of my hands, Arline said, "He called a little while ago. He's not going to be able to make it for dinner." She turned away from me and went into the kitchen. I stayed on her heals, flashing a look at Karis.

"What's going on, Arline?" I asked.

"Nothing. And dinner is just about ready," she said, picking up a wooden spoon. She stirred the noodles sitting in a pot of boiling water. The kitchen table was set for four, with a high chair pushed up to the end of the table.

"Arline," I said. She knew my tone. I was telling her, come on, it's me . . . talk!

Arline continued to stir the noodles, then she set the spoon down, all the while standing with her back to me. I saw her shoulders shake and knew she was crying. I went over and touched her back with my fingertips. She stepped away from my hand. "This is silly, Nick. My stupid hormones are just out of whack after having the baby," she said.

"Tell me about it," I said. First thought that popped into my mind was that Tommy was cheating on my little sister—and when I saw him next, I'd beat the piss out of him. Then I thought better of my brother-in-law. Tommy wouldn't cheat on my little sister. Arline was the perfect wife. They just had a baby together.

"It's Tom," she said.

That bastard! I'll beat the piss out of him.

"You read the paper today, right?" Arline asked.

"Actually, no. Why?"

She took the paper off the top of the refrigerator and handed it to me. There was a picture of Tommy and an article about the serial killer loose in Rochester. A fourth victim had been murdered. The body was found today floating in the Erie Canal, in Greece, under the bridge on Long Pond Road.

I knew then what this was about. Tommy was not having an affair with another woman—so I wouldn't have to beat the piss out of him. In a way, though, he was cheating on his wife. He was spending long days and, I would guess, late nights at the office. "He's working hard, huh?"

"He's never home, Nick. Never!" Arline looked angry. She was done crying. "I mean, when I married him I knew then that his job was going to be demanding. I knew his job was going to be dangerous. Those two facts alone almost kept me from marrying him. Almost. The entire time we were dating I would wonder what I might say if he ever asked me to marry him. And when he did ask, you would have thought I'd have known the answer. But I didn't. When he proposed I didn't just say, yes, and jump into his arms. I took two weeks to think it over. Two weeks, Nick. So I knew when we got married that there would be long, lonely nights and spending every day worrying about his safety. But lately, Nick, lately I just don't see him. When he's home he's asleep, or on the computer, or eating. We haven't said more than a few words to each other, and he's barely spent any time with Madeline," Arline finished, and was crying again. "I thought I could get him home for dinner if he knew we were having company," she said, then frowned. "That's not what I mean. I want you and Karis over for dinner. I . . ."

"That's all right, Arline. I know exactly what you mean," I said. I also knew I would need to stop by and see Tommy. He needed to know just how badly he was upsetting his wife. If I knew Arline, she would hide her feelings from him. It was a Tartaglia trait. She might be a Cerio now—but that was only by name. Her blood was like mine, mysterious, secretive and, well, stubborn.

"Damn," Arline said while stirring the noodles. "I left them in too long. Their soft."

"The way I like them best," I said as Karis came into the kitchen, a sleeping Madeline on her shoulders.

"Want to lay her down," Arline asked, "and we'll eat?"

"I haven't done this . . . " Karis started to say, but stopped. "I haven't done this in a long time."

I knew Karis was thinking of Darla, who had been Karis' daughter. Darla had died at the hands of the satanic high priest of the Tenth House as a sacrificial offering.

"You know what? I'm starving . . . and before those noodles get any softer, I think we should eat," Arline said. And we all sat down to a wonderful meal. All the while I knew Arline was thinking about Tommy, while Karis was thinking about Darla, and I was in turmoil thinking about the four of them, plus wondering what in the Hell Philip Edwards might be up to.

CHAPTER 31

Friday, May 24

Eleanor arrived at the office a little after nine, holding up a bag of bagels. "Hungry anyone?"

As we all got situated, Karis started a pot of coffee while I spread jalapeno cream cheese onto my wheat bagel. I asked, "Anything going on with your surveillance?"

"Nothing," Eleanor answered. "I'm bored out of my mind out there. I did see you and Father Paul, though. You're not a bad fighter," she said.

"You got in a fight?" Karis asked while digging through the bag for a bagel.

"I wouldn't call it a fight," Eleanor said. "Nick laid them out in maybe two seconds."

"Them?" Karis asked.

"Them," Eleanor confirmed. "And one of them was built like Frankenstein's monster!"

I just listened and ate. The telephone rang. Eleanor answered it. "It's for you, Nick. Your old boss."

"Ned?" I said after taking the phone from Eleanor.

"Hey Nick, by the time I got your messages last night I thought it might be too late to call. I was at the Red Wings game. Good game. They had one of the players run against a derby horse that has never won a race. The horse was something like zero and eighty-five.

Guess what? Guy won. This horse is zero and eighty-six. I don't know, though, the stretch they had to run was pretty short. If there had been even ten more feet to run, I think the horse might have broken his losing streak," Ned said. "Anyway, what can I do for you? Not more trouble with Anthony?"

"Trouble? I'm not sure. Why is he still tailing me, Ned? I don't like it. I want to know who his client is and I want to know what's going on. Your new hotshot detective stole an item out of my suitcase the other day and I want it back," I said. I was trying my hardest to talk calmly. Both Karis and Eleanor stood staring at me.

"What did the kid steal, Nick?"

"A book," I said, flatly. "He stole a book out of my suitcase and I want it back."

"He stole a book?" Ned said unconvincingly.

"Ned, I worked for you . . . Hell I've been with you since the beginning. You have your hand in every case going on up there. If Michael David Anthony's client wanted a book and Ned got it for him, you'd know. So don't tell me you don't have any idea what I'm talking about, don't do that to me," I said, nearly yelling now—talking between clenched teeth. I had put extra emphasis on the client being a him to let Ned know I had a pretty good idea who Anthony might be working for.

"Nick . . ."

"I want the book back, Ned. I want it back. If Anthony isn't going to give it to me, I'll be coming for it. You can tell the little piss-ant, too. Tell him I'll be coming for the book." I slammed the phone down.

"Everything all right?" Eleanor asked.

I looked at the bagel, my appetite gone. I ran the palms of my hands over my face, left them covering my eyes and took a long, cleansing, deep breath. "You know what? No. It's not. It's not all right. I have no clue, no freaking clue what's going on." I swiped my keys off the desk. "I'm gonna find out, though."

I've known for a while now that Philip Edwards needed looking into. It seemed highly probable that Michael David Anthony was Edwards' private investigator. Anthony, who I'd seen at the airport on my way down to Florida, had to have been the one to take Jasmine's book out of my suitcase. It only made too much sense now.

I had to assume Anthony already delivered the book to his client.

Pastor Jacob Brown had the last book. It didn't seem like too big a secret. If Edwards was after all three books, he should know where the third book was even if Pastor Brown never opened and read any of it. All Edwards would need to know is where Gordon Birdie and Anthony James came from. All roads would, with a little digging, lead to the First Baptist Church no matter how secretive their underground movement against evil and witchcraft might be.

There was one thing I felt good about. Pastor Brown seemed to understand our warning. If he didn't know before, he knew now not to open or read any of the book. If he kept the book safe and well hidden, then Edwards might have a much tougher time of finding it.

There was a mystery here—and the questions were spinning around my head. Just what in the Hell do I do next?

***

I drove out to Pittsford. I knew where the Edwards home was. When I arrived, a car sat in the wide driveway and I saw someone in the house, through a curtain silhouette. I assumed Mrs. Edwards was home. She stood by the picture window in the front room and appeared to be talking on the telephone. I drove slowly by the house. Back up on the main road, I parked on the shoulder and waited. From where my car was, I could just see the Edwards' driveway. When Mr. Edwards got home, I'd know.

When a car drove past me, turned down the street and pulled into the Edwards's driveway, I followed. As I got down the street I was just in time to see Mr. Edwards walk to the mailbox. He carried a briefcase in one hand with his dark suit coat draped over that arm. He wore a blue dress shirt with a yellow and dark striped tie. He looked good for an older man. Fit. He was losing his hair, but didn't try to hide his scalp and so he looked fine and confident despite the baldness, an admirable approach.

As I drove past the house I pretended to look distracted as if I was searching for a house number. When I looked back, Philip Edwards was halfway up his driveway busy shuffling through the mail. I turned the car around in a resident's driveway and left the private tract.

He looked like an ordinary man. I knew that Gordon Birdie sounded as if he was frightened of Edwards, but I wondered where the fear stemmed from? So often someone will tell a story and whoever hears the story takes the content of the tale at face value. If I were to wager a guess, I would assume the good Pastor Jacob Brown was the storyteller. I doubt very much that Gordon ever witnessed the dark side of Philip Edwards. The more I thought about it, the more I knew I was right. Gordon Birdie—and others, perhaps—were afraid of Philip Edwards because someone had told them, more or less, to be afraid of Philip Edwards. Did this mean Edwards was someone to be afraid of? Did it mean he was not someone to be afraid of? At this point, I didn't know what to think. I did know one thing. One way or the other I was going to find out what kind of a man Edwards is.

CHAPTER 32

"Hello?" I said, answering my cell phone. I was on my way downtown, headed toward Safehouse Investigations. I had looked in the telephone book and could not find a listing for a Michael David Anthony.

"Nick? It's Lynn," said the attorney, and my current client. "Where are you?"

"In the car, why?"

"Can you meet me at the courthouse?"

I wasn't far from the courthouse. "I can be there in ten minutes," I said. "Everything all right?"

"I have some time before a small trial, and we haven't talked since the beginning of the week. I thought we could touch base before the weekend?" By the calm tone in her voice, I imagined her casually leaning against a marble pillar glancing at her watch with her briefcase at her feet.

"Sounds good."

***

"That's it?" Lynn said. We were outside on the courthouse steps. People in business suits, and people not in business suits, but in casual clothes, or jeans, or rags, passed us going up and down the stairs.

"What do you mean, that's it?" I asked. "I've been working this case with everything I've got. I have a college co-op out there doing surveillance, and another working research on the web."

Lynn shook her head. She looked like she might be biting back words. "Nick, Whine is on trial for murder. He's been charged with counts of burglary. He was caught carrying a bag with explosives and a gun—a gun that just so happens to be the murder weapon, covered with his prints. The judge, Nick, the judge is not going to care about the book Whine planned on stealing," she said. Her Italian heritage seemed most prominent when she was angry. She yelled with her hands as well as her voice.

"The book is very important, Lynn. It's hard to explain . . . "

"Hard to explain? Nick it is so much more than just hard to explain. It is irrelevant. Let's pretend we're in court, Nick. Okay . . . do this with me. Picture Whine's trial and the judge, the honorable judge . . . he's sitting up behind the bench with his gavel and I stand up . . . what do you think I might say for an opening argument? 'Your Honor, Gordon Birdie did break into the home of the Edwards. He did try to blow up the safe in the Edwards basement. In the course of his burglary young Philip Edwards, Jr., came home unexpectedly and was killed . . . but your Honor, Whine was merely trying to recover a book on witchcraft to save the earth from the realms of black magic and evil sorcery?" She laughed a wicked laugh. "When everyone stops laughing at me, Nick, what do you think the judge will do?"

"Wait for you to enter your insanity plea?"

"Nick, I'm not joking around here. I can't tell the judge that everything here has to do with a book on witchcraft." Lynn sighed and stared at me, longing for me to say the right thing. I had no idea what the right thing to say might be.

"What did you expect me to do, Lynn? Why did you hire me?" I asked. I felt like I was being reprimanded unnecessarily. In my eyes The Talisman was the heart of the case. I saw Lynn's point. Finding the books and getting them locked away somewhere safe would not get Gordon Birdie off the murder charge . . . but I thought that was Lynn's job. "You hired me to find out what was going on that night, why Gordon and Anthony broke into the Edwards Home. You couldn't have hired me to find information to prove he's innocent. Hell, we both know perfectly well that he is not innocent—except for the fact that he may not have been the one to pull the trigger. I have no way of finding out that truth since the only two people who know for sure what happened that night . . . other than Gordon, who, at this point, would not be credible as a witness . . . are both dead."

"So that's it?"

I stared at her for a long, hard moment. "No. That's not it."

She waited. I let her wait until she asked, "Well?"

"Well, it's just possible that we can prove both Gordon and Anthony did what they did because they were instructed to."

"I'm not concerned with Anthony, just Whine," Lynn said. I had her attention and could tell she was anxious to hear what I had to say. "But what are you talking about, a Charles Manson thing?"

"More or less, well, less. I would hardly compare Pastor Brown to Charles Manson. There's a secret movement at Gordon's church. So far, I can't prove the Pastor runs it, but I'm like ninety-five percent positive it's operated under his control. I know I never met Gordon's partner, but I met Gordon and he does not seem like he could have been the mastermind behind the plan. Right?" I asked.

"I agree. It's possible Anthony was the brains . . . all right, highly probable," Lynn agreed.

"Right. Brains, definitely, but mastermind? I still don't think so. Unless this Anthony was a wizard or something, why would he want the book in Edwards' safe? Why would he or Gordon want it, for that matter?" I asked. "On the other hand I can figure out exactly why Pastor Brown wanted it. I can even imagine him coordinating the entire burglary . . . maybe not the fine details of the crime . . .but I can see him giving the command."

"Well, introducing that will . . . in a way . . . make Gordon's case better, but even Manson's girls went to prison," Lynn pointed out.

"And rightly so. Again, I'm not saying Gordon's innocent, all I'm doing now is trying to find out as much information as I can. Hey . . . there's nothing wrong with an insanity plea," I said.

"Yeah, except for the fact that he's not insane," Lynn said.

"Says you," I said. "Let a doctor decide. Let the doctor ask him about witches and witchcraft and spells and shit."

She took a thoughtful moment to consider my point. She neither accepted nor dismissed the idea. "We're running out of time. His trial is only a few weeks away."

"I'm trying," I told her. "I'm doing everything I can and trying to go in as many directions as possible."

Lynn reached out and touched me, her fingertips lingering on my shoulder. "I know you are. I'm sorry I got so excited. I've just got a heavy caseload and I haven't had much time off to relax," she said. She looked at her watch. "You know, this case I have isn't going to take long. Want to go out for a few drinks after?"

If Lynn weren't a knockout, I'd have said yes in a minute. Because she was beautiful, the seemingly innocent offer to go out after work played a different tune in my mind. Maybe the offer was more than an innocent plea for casual company?

Before I could answer, Lynn said, "Shit. They just brought in my waitress in cuffs. Excuse me, Nick. Maybe some other time?"

"Yes. Definitely," I said, sounding all sure of myself and confident. I watched her jog up the steps after two policemen escorting a young lady dressed in black slacks, a purple shirt and a white apron. There was no denying an animal-like attraction to Lynn's long legs.

While continuing to watch Lynn stop and talk with the policemen, I answered my ringing cell phone. "Hello?"

"Nick? It's Father Paul," said the priest. "I just got a call from Pastor Brown . . . he's all shaken up."

"Why? What's going on?" I asked, walking down the courthouse steps. I was headed for my car. It was parked in a garage ramp just down a block. "Father? What's happened?"

"There was a break-in at the church. The third book is missing," Father Paul said, sounding devastated. "I have got to tell you, this scares me. I'm more than a little scared Nick. Whoever took the book desecrated the room the book was kept in, apparently. Pastor brown says there are rings painted in blood on the walls."

"Has Pastor Brown called the police?" I asked, walking more briskly to my car. My mind gears were working, churning. I felt like I was getting nowhere.

"No and he doesn't plan to. He wants for you and me to meet with him tonight . . . after eight at the church," Father Paul said. "I told him I'd get in touch with you and set things up. Nick . . . black magic is nothing to take lightly. Even if these people can't cast spells, they are evil . . . they worship Satan."

"We know the type," I said.

"Yes. We do. They have proven, time and time again, to be dangerous people with no regard for anyone else's welfare. But what's worse, Nick, is that I think whoever took this last book can cast black magic spells. I honestly think we're dealing with a dark sorcerer," said the priest.

"You know something? So do I. Want me to come see you?"

"Not now. I have some obligations that need taking care of. You can swing by the rectory around seven if you'd like. We can ride down to Charlotte together?"

"Sounds good. Hey . . . wait. When did it happen?"

"That's the funny thing. It had to have just happened."

"Not last night?"

"No. Pastor Brown was certain the book was safe last night, and this morning. I think we gave him a little bit of a scare. He told me he checks on the book several times a day. He's pretty sure it happened some time in the last two hours, or so."

"Okay. All right. I'll see you around seven." I found my car, got in, and took off.

CHAPTER 33

Eleanor did not have a cell phone. She was going to need one. Riding around looking for her would get old, fast. I drove down Lake Avenue. As always, lately, the sky resembled one giant sized gray cotton ball. What's worse, the humidity was becoming a factor. I was perspiring, felt sticky and uncomfortable. A good cold rain would cool down the temperature and put a damper on the humidity levels.

I saw the rental car parked in the gas station on the corner and pulled in alongside it. Eleanor was not in the car. I got out of mine and looked around the street. I did not see her standing or walking around. Staring at the church across the road I couldn't help but wonder what might have happened to her. Had she seen Philip Edwards and tried to stop him? Who's blood painted the walls in the room where Pastor Brown kept the book hidden?

Again, somehow again, I had involved Eleanor in my business and because of it, I have put her life in danger. A wave of sudden and deeply sullen depression overcame my mood. I found it hard to breathe normally. I knew, with or without Father Paul, I needed to investigate the church and find Eleanor.

I started toward the crosswalk.

"Hey Nick," I heard. I turned and faced Eleanor. She carried a big red slushy drink with a clear dome-shaped lid. She used the end of her straw like a spoon to feed the contents of her refreshment into her mouth.

"Where've you been?" I asked. My heart did a leap inside my

chest. I felt like a parent; I was relieved to see her, but at the same time wanted to yell and punish her.

"In there," she said, waving her hand to indicate the mini-mart that coexisted with the gas station. "I needed something to drink. I'm dying in this heat."

"It's not hot, it's humid," I said.

"Are you sweating and sticky?"

"Yes," I said.

"Then it's hot. I hate that. I hate when people say they like Nevada because it's dry heat there. Ever been there, to Nevada? I went once. It was one hundred and seven degrees. Everyone kept telling me that it was dry heat and not like back in New York. Know what I said? I told them, 'Are you out of your mind? It's one hundred and seven degrees. Who cares if it's dry heat or not? I had to wear gloves driving my mother's car around because the steering wheel was so hot, it was burning the skin off my hands!'"

I watched Eleanor laugh, enjoying her own sense of humor. "Done?"

"What? You don't think that's funny?"

"Oh it's funny," I said. "You been watching the church?"

"Only every minute," she said, looking down at her drink. "Except when I'm thirsty."

"How about two hours ago? Were you thirsty then, because someone went into the church and stole the third book. They used blood to paint devil signs on the walls in the room where the book was kept," I said.

"When, two hours ago? Nick, I was here. I've been watching the place. If Edwards came anywhere near the church, I'd have known," she said. She looked at the church. "The front doors facing Lake Avenue don't open. People have to go into the church from the back and the north side door. Sure, I can't see that door from here, but all the parking is in the rear. Unless Edwards walked there . . . I'd have known."

"Any white guys at all?"

"Yes. There were some white people, but not Edwards. He's distinguished looking. I know exactly what he looks like," said Eleanor.

"Even from here, you think you would know Edwards if you saw him?" I asked.

"I know I would," she said.

"From here . . . "

"Nicholas!"

"All right, all right." I thought of Michael David Anthony. "Let's take a ride. I want to show someone to you. You think you could remember a particular white guy if you saw him again?"

"I guess . . . yes. I'm pretty sure I could," she said. She locked up the rental and climbed into my car. I wanted to make two stops. First, I drove us out to the home of the Edwards. I figured after stealing the book, Mr. Anthony, P.I., would want to deliver it as soon as possible and I was nearly one hundred percent positive that Philip Edwards was his client.

When we arrived at the house there were no cars in the driveway. We waited up the road for a few minutes before I decided to move on to the second stop. We drove to Safehouse. Whenever I had information for a client, especially if it wrapped up the case, or the job, I had the client meet me at the office and this way Betty would be there to handle the fees and any final paperwork.

Eleanor and I entered the office and caught Betty reading. She closed the book when she saw us, so for a moment the three of us stood there smiling at each other before Betty said playfully, "I see more of you now than when you worked here. What can I do for you?"

First off I introduced Eleanor to Betty, then I asked, "Ned in?"

"He's not." Betty stared at Eleanor. She was clearly trying to assess the situation. She had no idea what I was up to, and she had no idea how Eleanor fit into the scheme. I could tell she wanted to ask questions. Betty always had her nose buried in a detective novel. I knew in her heart she wanted to be like Lawrence Block's Matthew Scudder—only as a woman.

"How about the guy with three first names?" I asked. Betty made a funny face at me, as if trying to tell me that I wasn't being nice. "He in?"

"He's in," she said, sounding hesitant. She gave herself away when her eyes looked to the right, toward my old office.

"My old office?" I asked and Betty answered my question with a nod.

"But he's with a client right now. If you want to wait until he's finished?"

"Actually the client he's with is part of the reason why we're here," I said.

"Really?" asked Betty. This news seemed to puzzle her.

"Really," I said. "May we go in?"

"I don't know . . . I don't think that's such a good idea. You know rules, Nick, client confidentiality and everything. Even if you do know who the client is, I can't just let you walk in there. Understand what I'm saying?" Betty asked.

"Sure I do. How about you tell him I'm here and that I need to speak with him and that it is urgent, very urgent. How's that?" I asked, pointing at her telephone that also worked as an intercom system.

Betty reached for a button on her telephone. "Mr. Anthony, I hate to bother you, but Mr. Tartaglia is here and he needs to speak with you about an urgent matter."

"Thank you, Betty. Please explain to Mr. Tartaglia that I am in with a client and that as soon as I have concluded my business here, I will be out to discuss Mr. Tartaglia's problem," said a cool sounding voice. Cool sounding, except to a trained ear, and though I have never received any formal ear training, I could hear the annoyed tone in Michael David Anthony's voice.

We ended up waiting another ten minutes before the door to my old office opened and a well-dressed Michael David Anthony stepped out. His smile looked forced while his handshake was limp and without conviction. "Mr. Tartaglia, how are you? And who might this be?"

"Eleanor Kasap," said Eleanor, shaking hands with the newest hotshot Safehouse investigator.

"Russian?"

"Yes, some, and Ukrainian."

"No accent," Anthony said. "Maybe a faint one."

I never picked up on any accent. "Look, Mikey, you and I have many, many issues to resolve, and we will. But right now I need to know what in the Hell you think you're doing?"

"Well, if you must know, I was talking with a client," he said.

"I don't mean right now—I'm talking about what you did at the church," I said. I was trying to keep my tone of voice even and steady. I did not want to yell and lose my cool. I did not want this joker to think he was getting the better of me. I had already established a sense of dominance and I wanted to keep it.

"Nick . . . I swear I don't know what you're talking about," Anthony said.

"Look, we both know you stole a book out of my suitcase at the airport." I gave him a look that said, Don't even try to deny it, buddy!

"It was a box," Anthony said, radiating a smug smile "I have no idea what was inside the box."

"And we both know you did the same thing at The First Baptist Church," I added. I wanted to knock the smugness out of that irritating facial expression. He thought he was clever and cute and creative. A good, hard punch in the mouth might teach him otherwise.

"I know nothing about this church."

"You don't, huh?"

"Not a thing," he said. He looked back at my old office door. "Now if you're through I have an important client in there. We have some more business to discuss." Anthony smiled at me and gave me a slight bow. He turned and did the same to Eleanor. "It was a pleasure meeting you."

"Wish the feeling was mutual," Eleanor retorted, smiling.

I wasn't through. "Well let's just see what your client has to say about the book."

"Nick . . . that's my client and you can't just go in there," he said.

I pushed past him, an easy shove, and opened the office door. I stared in surprise at the woman who sat next to the young boy in a wheelchair. The mother had been crying and still held a crumbled wad of tissues in her hand. I swallowed and tried to smile.

I felt a hand pat me on the back and heard Anthony speak. "Mr. Tartaglia, this is Gloria Wiseman, a single mother of four. Her youngest son here, Todd, was struck by a hit and run in the fall. The police have been unable to find the person responsible. Ms. Wiseman has asked our agency to do a little pro-bono work since her insurance was not very helpful and the hospital bills have eaten away at her savings.

"How we doing Todd?" Anthony asked. The boy, maybe six years old, smiled.

"Ms. Wiseman . . . Mr. Tartaglia is also a private investigator and used to work for this agency. Mr. Tartaglia, if we're through here?" Anthony asked.

"We are," I said. I gave a sympathetic nod to the family and backed as quickly as possible out of the room. When I shut the door I said to Eleanor, "That bastard wanted me to walk into his office. He wanted to embarrass me."

"It's not him," Eleanor said, ignoring my whine.

"Him, who?"

"I didn't see him anywhere around the church," she said. She sounded confident, but I had to ask her why she was so sure. "Because. The guy's a doll. I'd have remembered seeing him."

As we left I realized we were no closer to finding out what happened at the church than we had been a few hours ago.

CHAPTER 34

I picked up Father Paul at seven, just as we had planned. Father Paul set up a meeting with the Pastor of The First Baptist Church. Pastor Jacob Brown was finally ready to talk, and I had questions that needed answering. I wanted to bring Jasmine with us. She seemed to be somewhat of an authority on all of this magic stuff. I knew little about magic and haven't had much time to do any research. I had no idea how this meeting would go tonight, so I decided to leave Jasmine out of it, for now anyway, and instead, choose to rely on the research Father Paul had conducted.

When we arrived, the parking lot was empty. Pastor Brown stood on the steps at the back door. We all said Hello and went inside.

"I suppose you'd like to see the room first," said Pastor Brown. Without waiting for a reply, he led us to the door on the right of the vestibule. The light on the other side of the door was already on. We took steps down into a completely amazing looking basement. It resembled a party hall with white linoleum, light wood colored paneling, ceiling fans with lights, tables folded and stacked against each other at one wall and chairs in rolling racks against another. "We renovated the basement about, I'd say, ten years ago. We went neutral with everything. Neutral never seems to go out of style, and it costs a heck of a lot less than getting things custom made."

Pastor Brown walked up to a wall and stopped by a portrait of Jesus. He looked at Father Paul and myself and smiled as he unlatched a concealed hook behind the frame of the portrait. The frame swung out about six inches—but enough so to reveal a recessed door handle hidden behind it. Pastor Brown pushed open the secret door to a long dark passageway.

Before following along after the Pastor, Father Paul and I examined the doorway. Since the door pushed open the hinges would not be visible to anyone in the party room. The creases in the paneling aligned to keep the doorway from being easily noticed. Clever. I felt like I just stumbled into a Sherlock Holmes novel—or a Scooby Doo episode. Jeepers.

The secret passageway was narrow. The damp, jagged rock walls smelled moldy. Naked bulbs dangled from the ceiling, the wires led back toward the church. We slopped downward, and to the east. We were walking toward the river.

After nearly thirty yards, we came to an abrupt right turn and then the narrow passageway exploded into a large round finished off room. The rocks were hidden behind drywall. The dry wall looked as if it had been sprayed with red paint. Aside from recognizing the three rings drawn in blood in different areas on the wall, the rest of the blood just looked as if it had been splattered at random. I took in the scene for a moment before I took the camera I was carrying out of my back pocket.

"What's that?" Pastor Brown asked.

"This? A camera."

"What are you going to do with it?" he asked.

"Take pictures," I said, tentatively wondering what else he thought I might do with a camera. I thought the answer would have been obvious to someone with his intelligence. The smell of mold, masked behind the scent of burning incense, was not missed. Standing in the center of the room was a lone pillar that stood waist high. On top of the pillar was an empty glass box. Why did Pastor Brown have a shrine constructed for a book on magic?

"What are you going to do after you take the pictures?" Pastor Brown continued.

I wanted to say, Get the film developed. "I'm not exactly sure, but I think it is a good idea to preserve this room as much as possible before anything gets too disturbed. If anything happens, at least we'll have something to document the way this room looks," I explained.

"That's a good idea," Father Paul said, dishing a small helping of support.

"Was that where the book was kept?" I asked, pointing to the empty glass box after snapping off some shots of the room. I looked closely at the glass. "Did you wash the glass?"

"No," Pastor Brown said. "Why?"

"It looks too clean. Look at this room . . . it's a bloody mess." I walked closer to the walls. The blood was everywhere. The more I looked at it, the more it resembled the paintings I had seen in Ned's office, where the artist had basically dipped the bristles of his brush into the paint and then waved his brush at the canvas letting the paint fling and land where ever it may.

I looked closely at a set of three rings. The rings were linked together, one on top of the other. The bloody rings had been painted onto the wall. It did not look like a finger had done the artwork. "Whoever was in here used a paint brush, or something. Maybe they had a bucket of blood with them?" I said.

"That's sick," Father Paul said. "I think we should call the police right away. They're going to need to take blood samples and determine if this is animal blood or, God forbid, human blood."

"I agree," I said. I looked at Pastor Brown. "When we get out of this tunnel, you call the police, and while we wait for them to arrive you can fill us in on everything you know."

"The police are going to want to know why you didn't call them right away," Father Paul pointed out. "They may even be curious to know why you have a room like this down here."

"That's easy enough," Pastor Brown said. "Ever heard of the Underground Railroad? This church was one of the stops slaves made. It's not a very big room, but I'll bet those people were thankful for the sanctuary provided."

"And why you didn't call the police right away?" I asked.

"Simple. I only just found this mess now. I will call and tell them so," Pastor Brown said, perhaps lying a bit too easily for my taste. "Will that do?"

"It will do," I said.

Pastor Brown just nodded his head solemnly as he walked around the corner and back down the dank passageway toward the church. Father Paul and I looked around the room for a few minutes longer.

"What do you think is going on?" I asked.

"I'm not sure what's going on, but I can tell you this, I don't think any of us will like what is about to happen." Father Paul followed after Pastor Brown and I was left alone in the room where I continued to take photographs from as many different angles as possible. I felt fairly confident that my theory was right. No person had been killed here—at this point in time. The blood on the walls was, more or less, a prop. It had been done to scare whoever saw it, but it had been done with careful consideration—the artist had used a paintbrush. It was possible that whoever found this hidden room and stole the book was not a raving lunatic. They might be, but I didn't think so. It all had a calculated feel to it. One word came to mind. Ritual.

**

It could turn out to be a long night. When we got back to the church it still took some doing to convince Pastor Brown to call the police. Once he made the call, however, he no longer seemed interested in talking to us. While we all sat in church pews waiting for the police to arrive, I tried my hardest to get some answers.

"Bottom line, Pastor Brown, you knew what Gordon Birdie and Anthony James had planned on doing, didn't you?" I said, trying not to sound accusatory. I stared at Pastor Brown, but he avoided eye contact and seemed to find it safest just looking at the floor. "Pastor Brown . . . "

"Brown," Father Paul interjected, "let's talk, please. There is a man in jail and two people are dead. Nick and I are just trying to get to the bottom of this—in no way are we trying to suggest that you are guilty of something . . ."

"Guilty? Guilty? Why, how dare you," Pastor Brown said, getting to his feet. I stood up too, ready to hold the feisty preacher back if necessary. "I've done absolutely nothing wrong. Absolutely nothing!"

"That's not true," a woman's voice said from behind us.

Lydia held a Bible in her hand and pressed it close to her chest. Her brother Marlow stood by her side and walked her down the center aisle. Pastor Brown had fallen silent, and his skin color paled a few shades. Lydia had something important to say and I was anxious to hear what it was.

A defeated Pastor Brown sat back down. "Lydia, you don't know what you're talking about," said the preacher in a tired whisper.

"She might not, but I do," Marlow said, while looking at me. "This isn't right. Everything that's been going on isn't right."

"Keep still," Pastor Brown ordered Marlow. "You just keep still."

"I can't do that, Pastor, and I mean no disrespect. These guys here, they're not bad guys . . . they're not evil. They are on the same side of God as we are. Same side. I believe everything that has been going on around us is bad, and I am afraid of all that is yet to come. If we can join forces . . . strength in numbers and all that . . . then why not? Right? Why try to do this alone? No where in the Bible does it say that we have to fight evil alone . . . we shouldn't fight it alone, not when there are others who share our beliefs and want to help," said Marlow. He was pleading with the Pastor. He wanted the Pastor's blessing before he revealed whatever secret plan or plot the church had been up to. "Pastor Brown?"

CHAPTER 35

"I guess you would call it a movement," Pastor Brown said. "Though I hate the way that sounds: Movement. But that's what it is . . . or was. A movement." He stared at Marlow while he spoke. I watched the expression on Marlow's face. The young man looked thankful and perhaps relieved to see that his Pastor—a clearly evident inspiration in Marlow's life—was going to do the right thing.

"When did it start?" I asked. I didn't want to interrupt the man, but I knew the police would be arriving shortly. I had some specific questions and I wanted specific answers. I could get the entire story when there was more time.

"When? Oh, since before I was the Pastor of this church. Most churches have a movement of some sort, or many different kinds of group efforts. You know missionaries and all. Get a group of teenagers and some supervising adults together and plan a trip down to Mexico to build houses for the poor. Churches do that kind of thing all the time. What we have here at The First Baptist isn't all that different," Pastor Brown said. He let out a loud sigh and leaned back in the pew. "The trouble with our movement is that we can't publicize the kinds of things we do. It really isn't all that different than the Catholic Church and the Inquisition. They thought that as a religion they were doing the right thing. It wasn't long after it started that people began to wonder what was really going on, but that's neither here nor there."

He was rambling. I wasn't going to stop him. I now knew that he did not talk much about this movement. This was the first time he has ever had to verbalize his thoughts and qualify his actions. It looked hard on him, opening up to all of us this way. I had to give the man credit.

"We, as a group, were responsible for many things. Some . . . before my time . . . I am not so sure I agreed with. In a sense, I guess, what I'm trying to say is . . . we have acted as vigilantes," he said. "And as I have said, a lot of what was done in the past I was not a part of, nor do I think I would have been a part of it. But recently, the . . . the activities this church has chosen to get involved in have been worthwhile. And right up to protecting that book . . . I know in my heart and in my soul that I have been doing God's work."

Coming from anyone else I would have considered his last statement corny. Hearing Pastor Jacob Brown recite it, I knew the man sounded genuine. "The book, what do you know about it?"

Pastor Brown sat forward and stared into my eyes with a vibrant intensity. "The book was called Hell. That was the title on the front cover, anyway. Hell. It was written during the end of the witch trials in Salem. One all-powerful sorcerer wrote all three of the books, I assure you all. But it was the book of Hell that tied the evil trinity together.

"The Salem Witch Trials came to be because of a man named Reverend Samuel Parris. Parris had an Indian slave named Tituba and Tituba was married to a slave named John. John was an African American slave. Well one night, Parris' daughter became ill and Tituba tried to help the child by preparing what is known as a witch cake. The cake is a mixture of rye and urine . . . the sick girl's urine. Tituba fed this pastry to the dog, believing it would then tell them who the witch was that had made the child ill.

"Well, when Parris found out what Tituba had done, that she was practicing witchcraft, he naturally believed her to be the witch . . . and ultimately responsible for his daughter's fits and illness. And he beat her. He beat out a confession. Tituba confessed to a town ring of witchcraft, and spouted off names of other witches in Salem. And on March first, sixteen ninety-two, Tituba was the first woman arrested for witchcraft in Salem.

"When it came time to go bring these other accused and afflicted to trial, Tituba took back everything she'd confessed. She was then thrown in jail. She spent thirteen months behind bars before some unknown person paid her bail and then bought both Tituba and her husband.

"Neither of them was seen from again. I told you that the room downstairs was a part of the Underground Railroad, and that's a fact. That's true . . . and the room was used in the seventeen and eighteen hundreds all the time to help black slaves make it to freedom. However, during the end of the century . . . the end of the sixteen hundreds . . . an Indian woman and her black husband showed up on these church steps looking for sanctuary.

"See, what Tituba told the priest at the time was that an evil sorcerer freed her. This new master proceeded to watch and document the Salem Witch Trials, all the while writing these three books. Once Tituba realized how dangerous this man was, and even more so, how dangerous his books were, she decided to steal them. She and her husband made it to Rochester, and their owner was not far behind. What the couple did was, discard two of the books. They hid one in a building that was just being constructed, and the other, apparently, they entrusted to a friend. The third book, they left with the church.

"I have no idea what happened after that. No one passed down any stories about Tituba or her husband. How long did they stay? Where did they go? Did their master ever find them? Who knows? I don't.

"But you see, the third book, the book stolen today, had been here for centuries. Seemingly always being a part of this church. Each Pastor that has been here over the years and decades and centuries, has been the keeper of that book, until me. I have been with this church for twenty-five years. In twenty-five years, every morning when I woke up and every night before I went to bed, I would check on that book. There were so many times, so many nights and mornings, when I said to myself, Jacob what in God's name are you doing? No one has ever tried to get that book. No one has ever asked about that book. Boy, no one even knows you have that book. Day after day and night after night I saw that book sitting on that pillar, under that box of glass and not once did I ever even think of reading it. Do you know why?"

His question brought me out of it. I was hooked listening to this man talk. He had my attention. He spoke like a leader with a message. He spoke with conviction. "Why?" I asked.

"Because I was told not to. And the Pastor before me, who told me not to, also told me if I ever thought I wanted to, to just remember Adam and Eve. They had an entire garden to enjoy . . . and all they had to do was stay away from one tree. I have all the world and can read any book I want . . . as long as I stayed away from that one book," Pastor Brown said. "And so I stayed away from it. There were many occasions where I wondered what the book might be about. I began to think that because I was told I shouldn't read it that I wanted to read it all the more. It must have been the same for Eve. I know it's the same for children. You tell a child not to touch the knobs on a television set and those knobs are the first things he touches. And we are all God's children. He tells us to stay away from a tree and that tree is where we will all wind up at one point, or another."

"So you read the book?" I asked.

Pastor Brown fell silent. He looked around his church. "You would think I could remember, but I can't. It was some time ago the first time it happened. I went down into the tunnel there and checked on the book, just as I have always done. This time, when I reached the room, the book had a glowing red aura around it." He let out a nervous laugh and was staring blankly at nothing. I knew he was replaying the memory like a video in his mind. "I didn't touch it. I was too afraid. I knew something was wrong somewhere, but I had no idea what to do about it, or even if I should do something about it. It was scary, one of the scariest things I'd ever seen. Doesn't sound that scary, does it? Let me tell you, when you see a book . . . just some dumb old book . . . and it's glowing red like fire or blood, that can freak you out."

He had me convinced. "So what happened?"

"Nothing. I didn't have anyone I could call. I didn't have anyone I could tell . . . I didn't think. But a few nights later I got to thinking about that book while I was lying in bed trying to fall asleep. It wasn't that I wanted to read it, but I wanted to know why it had been glowing. I had to keep saying to myself, over and over, Adam and Eve," Pastor Brown said.

"And that worked?" Father Paul asked.

"It worked that night. About a week later, in the morning, I went down to check the book and it was doing it again," said the Pastor, laughing. "A possessed book. I was guarding a possessed book. In a way it made sense. For twenty-five years I had been watching over a book I knew nothing about. I was getting a little closure. All these years and just then I was finding some purpose behind them. I was guarding a demonic book."

The title would have tipped it off for me—but that's, as Pastor Brown might say, neither here nor there.

"So I knew something was going on and I knew there were members of the church who were part of the past movements. For many years the movement had been, I guess you'd say, on hold. So what I did was, I called up some of those members and though I didn't show them the secret room . . . like I just showed you . . . I did tell them what was going on. I swore them to secrecy, which has always been kind of a code of the movement, but I swore them to secrecy again," Pastor Brown explained. "And then I did something stupid."

"You read the book," Father Paul said. I looked at Lydia to watch her expression change into a cringe.

"I went down there, all sneaky and everything, like I was afraid I'd get caught walking through my own church. That right there should have told me that what I was about to do was wrong, but it didn't stop me. I went into that room and I lifted the glass box, and I opened the book. I didn't read much, but I read enough to learn that there were three such books. Heaven, Earth and the one I had, Hell. Hell is the third ring. And I learned that when someone reads the book . . . the other books respond. I knew then what had happened. My book had been turning red and glowing because somewhere out there, someone else was reading one of the other books. So I waited. And when my book started to glow, I picked it up and . . . I don't know what happened."

"I think the books work like a honing device, too," I added.

"A honing device?" Lydia asked.

"Yeah. So if Pastor Brown was reading his book, one of the other people could find him as long as he was reading," I said. "Like RADAR."

"That's exactly right. It wasn't long after I first read the book that I found myself in an out of body experience," Pastor Brown said, cautiously. "I was soaring through the city. I found myself inside the home of Philip Edwards. Edwards had a book open in front of him. He was in his basement, kneeling by a safe. I tell you it was like I was there. Then, all at once, Edwards turned and stared directly at me. Panicked, I closed my copy of the book . . . and the experience shattered. It felt like an explosion in my head. I was not in the Edwards home anymore, I was here . . . alone and scared. A strange man . . . I say man, but really he was like a spirit . . . he appeared and whispered in my ear. He wanted that book. He knew I had it, and he wanted it," said Pastor Brown. "See, but I knew immediately that I needed to get that book away from him."

I knew the story. It was very similar to the one Jasmine had told me. "So you think the image you saw, was Philip Edwards, Sr.?"

"I know so."

"So what happened next?" Father Paul asked, attempting to dismiss the ghost-theory.

"Then I did bring the members of the movement down to see the book, because I wanted to monitor it. I set up a guard post and instructed everyone to stay away from the book, but to call me if the book started to glow." Pastor Brown stood up and paced back and forth in the aisle. "It was Anthony James who came to see me the next time the book was glowing. He was a black man, and when I say that, I mean he had skin nearly the color of night . . . but not that day he came to get me. He was as white skinned as you, Nick. He didn't have to tell me. I knew what he had seen and I ran with him back into the basement and I took the book out from under the glass box and held it in my hands while it was glowing, and knowing . . . "

We waited. "Knowing what?" I finally had to ask.

"Knowing where one of the other books was, I knew I had to do something to get it. I wanted to have all three books locked up and safe. From the small amount of reading I had done I knew that any person in possession of one of the books could possess magical powers. I knew with two books the powers of the possessor would be increased. If a person had possession of all three books, the limit to their powers might be without end," said Pastor Brown.

"So it was your calling, you think? You were to gather up the three books and keep them locked up and safe?" I asked.

"That's exactly right," Pastor Brown said. I didn't believe him—

at least not completely. The book he was in possession of offered power, perhaps more power than he had ever known. While owning two books would increase that power . . . one had to wonder about the motivation behind burglary. To question him at this time felt irrelevant. The damage was done.

"So you set it up to have Anthony James and Gordon Birdie burglarize the home of Philip Edwards," I said. I sounded cold and harsh, maybe because that was how I felt. I knew I was grinding my teeth.

"Nick," Father Paul said to calm me down.

Choosing to ignore Father Paul, I persisted. "Well?"

"Yes. That's what I did. But I did not force anyone to do anything," Pastor Brown yelled. "I did not make either one of them do any of this!"

We all knew differently. "So it just so happens that the two orphans of the church volunteered on their own?"

"Nick, please," Father Paul said, trying once again to calm me.

"Gordon and Anthony James came to you on their own? You didn't point them in the direction you wanted them facing? They asked you if they could break the law and steal a book out of a man's basement and risk their lives . . . they asked all of this without you mentioning it to them first?" I was yelling now, too. I was standing up and in Pastor Brown's face, but hadn't realized it, until I stopped yelling and looked around. Marlow was standing next to me, ready to hold me back.

I turned away and walked down the aisle. I only turned around when I heard sobbing. Maybe I expected to see Lydia crying, but she wasn't. She stood next to Pastor Brown with her hand on his back. The Pastor had his face cradled in his hands and was crying. At this point, I should have let it go, but I couldn't. Speaking softly, I said, "And for the last few months, months," I said, "Gordon Birdie has been alone in a jail cell, alone and without any visitors except for me and his attorney. How about that," I said. "How about that."

I walked out of the church, through the vestibule and out into the fresh night air. In the near distance, I heard sirens approaching. The sky was black and filled with stars and a crescent shaped moon. The clouds had moved on, and hopefully the rain would stop for a while. We, the good people of Rochester, have had our fair share of rain. I did not want it to rain ever again.

CHAPTER 36

Saturday, May 25

When Karis woke me up, I had been in the middle of a bizarre dream. I was standing on a stair in the middle of a pitch-black room. I was standing in the center of a staircase in the middle of a pitch-black room. I could only see two stairs going up, and two going down. Nothing else. All around me I could hear bats screeching. I could swear that the darkness around me was throbbing in time with the beating of my heart. I knew I was not alone in the dark because sometimes I could see glowing, blood red eyes watching me, but if I tried too hard to see them, the eyes would disappear, or close. I climbed up the two steps and turned all around only to find that above the darkness was another room, and directly above me, was another me, looking down on me. Only the other me was dead with rotting flesh and maggots squirming in and out of my mouth and nostrils. I wanted to look away, but couldn't seem to move my neck. When finally I did gather the strength to look away, the dead-me was standing right next to me, face-to-face, and I was giving myself a menacing maggot-filled smile. Then the head on the dead-me began ringing and ringing, and it exploded sending brain chunks all over, but the ringing didn't stop. It didn't stop.

"Come on Nick . . . the phone is for you," Karis said. She had the cordless phone in her hand, and was already rolling back over to go to sleep. I sat up and took the phone out of her hands.

"Hello," I said.

"Nick? It's Lynn. I just got a phone call from the prison. Gordon Birdie was transferred to Strong Memorial Hospital early this morning," said Scannella. She sounded tired and winded. I looked at the clock. It was eight.

"So what are you going to do?"

"At this point, nothing, but I wanted you to know," she said.

"First thing on a Saturday morning?" I asked.

"Why, were you asleep?" She said, laughing. Her revenge served. I hung up the telephone.

The telephone rang again. "Nick," Karis moaned. "If you're going to talk to your little girlfriend, go do it in another room." She pulled the pillow over her head. I sat up in bed. I was wide-awake now. I picked up the telephone.

"What Lynn?" I said, only it wasn't Lynn.

" I'm sorry. This isn't Lynn. It's Lydia. Nick, I just got a phone call from a doctor at Strong. Something's happened to Gordon," she said. She was crying. "Nick, they wouldn't tell me what was going on. I kept asking them what he had, but they wouldn't tell me. All they said, all they would tell me, was that Gordon wanted them to contact me . . . me and his attorney."

I stood up.

"Nick, what's wrong?" Karis asked. She sat up in bed.

"Lydia, would you like a ride down to the hospital?" I asked.

"Please. I called my brother, but he wasn't home. I've got other people I could call, but I would prefer it if you could take me," Lydia said. "Can you, Nick?"

"Give me a half hour and I'll pick you up. Wait inside that security area in the lobby and I'll come in for you," I said. We hung up. I told Karis what was going on before I jumped into the shower.

***

When I pulled up to the apartment building, the security guard was at the door holding it open for Lydia. He escorted her out to my car. She thanked him and he told her it was no problem. I thanked him and received a nod before the guard went back inside to his post.

In my mind, I tried over and over again to find the right way to strike up a conversation. We had been driving in silence for nearly three minutes and it was making me crazy. Nothing I could come up with seemed appropriate—or it all just sounded like senseless small talk. I didn't know anything more about Gordon's condition than Lydia did. I wasn't about to lie to her and say that everything would be all right because truthfully, I had no clue what was going on.

For the most part, the entire ride had been ridden in silence. Parking at Strong used to be terrible, and not what I would have called "visitor friendly." Recently, they completed a parking garage attached to the large hospital. And though the new high-rise lot seemed full, I thankfully found a spot on the roof of the garage.

Lydia and I took the elevators to the main lobby floor and walked up to the information desk. "We're here to see Gordon Birdie. He was brought in some time early this morning," I said. I watched as the young lady typed the name into her computer.

"He's in a secure room," she said.

"I understand. Could you tell me where?"

"Intensive Care. He's not allowed visitors, just family," she said.

"I'm his brother," I said. Lydia and I walked away. I knew the woman behind the counter would have Gordon's race in front of her. I couldn't help but smile.

I led Lydia as I followed signs, and color stripes on the linoleum floor to another bank of elevators and took them to the Intensive Care Unit. When we walked in, I knew immediately what room was Gordon's. It was the room with the policeman sitting in a chair outside of a closed door, flipping through a magazine.

"Follow my lead," I whispered to Lydia as we approached the policeman.

He must have felt us coming. As we got closer, he casually closed the magazine and set it on the floor. He stood up. We stopped right in front of him. "Is this where Gordon Birdie is?" I asked.

"This patient isn't seeing visitors right now," the policeman said. "Just family."

"That's why we're here," I said. "We're his family. I'm Gordon's big brother, and this is Lydia, our sister."

The policeman looked me over. I had him—almost. "Can I see some I.D."

"I don't carry a wallet," I said.

The policeman sighed. He looked at Lydia. "How about you ma'am? Do you carry a wallet in that purse?"

"She does officer, but she's married so her last name is different," I said, hopefully not too quickly.

"Yeah. Gordon's big brother and baby sister," the policeman said. He stood on his tiptoes and looked over my head. "Look, you go in, see your friend," he said to me, "and your boyfriend," he said to Lydia, "and then you get the Hell out of here and don't come back anymore. Understand?"

Lydia's face brightened. "Oh thank you, officer," she said. She reached out her hand to touch his face.

The police officer gave me an uncomfortable smile. He had not realized that Lydia was blind. He let Lydia caress his cheek, then became too embarrassed to let it continue. "All right. Get in there before I have to throw the two of you out," he said, and sat back down in his chair.

As we entered the room, I patted the officer on the shoulder. "Thank you," I said. "I'll put in a good word with Detective Cerio."

"Ah, God. Not you. I knew you looked familiar, geesh! You're not Cerio's brother-in-law? Man . . . get in that room and get out or I will change my mind. Get . . . hey, wait! If Detective Cerio ever hears you mention my name, I'll deny ever having seen you before. Got that? Don't even think about telling Cerio anything," the policeman said.

"Mum's the word," I told him with a smile.

"Nick?" Lydia asked as I closed the door to Gordon's private room in the Intensive Care Unit.

I knew what she wanted, without her asking. "He looks like he's asleep," I told her. I watched as she made her way to the foot of the bed. Her hands touched his blanket while she made her way toward him. Standing back, I saw Lydia's fingers reach for his face. Her fingertips gently touched him, and Gordon stirred.

"Oh Nick, he's so hot. He's burning up," Lydia said, resting her palm on his forehead. She leaned over and kissed him where her hand had been. I knew she was crying even before I saw her wipe away tears.

Thankful Lydia had not yet asked me to describe to her how Gordon looked; I silently assessed his appearance. The Gordon I saw lying in front of me looked nothing like the man I had talked to in the prison a few days ago. His skin looked clammy and pale, resembling wet clay. His lips were dry and cracked and looked as if they had been bleeding. The man's eyelids were swollen and black, like bruises, reminding me of the make-up design worn by the odd rock star, Alice Cooper. The one other thing I noticed, that Lydia was bound to feel, were the handcuffs securing him to the bed's rail.

I had to think that Gordon wasn't contagious, or he'd be quarantined. Still, I did not want to get too close to him until I found out what his illness was exactly. I cringed as I watched Lydia as she kept on touching him.

"What do you think is wrong with him?" Lydia asked me. She now held Gordon's hand in her own, choosing to completely ignore the cuff on his wrist.

"I'm not sure. We're going to find out though," I said. She had been looking in my general direction, waiting for me to speak. She then targeted the sound of my voice and stared directly at me. So I said, "We'll find a doctor and ask him."

The door opened. I was sure it would be the police officer from the hallway telling us our time was up. It wasn't. "Hello, doctor," I said.

The doctor gave us a smile, and closed the door silently behind her. She was a tall lanky looking doctor with straight brown, stringy-looking hair. Her complexion was pitted with acne scars. She did not look older than twenty and the hospital blues she wore looked too big and baggy for her build. "I'm Doctor Conroy," said the doctor as she held out her hand. I shook it and introduced myself. When Dr. Conroy went to shake hands with Lydia, she pulled her hand back in. She seemed to notice right away that Lydia was blind.

"This is Lydia," I said, and watched as the two women exchanged Hellos.

"Are the two of you family?" Dr. Conroy asked.

It seemed all right lying to the police. I felt funny about lying to the doctor. "We're not," I said. Dr. Conroy pursed her lips together in a sympathetic smile. "We told the policeman out there that we were . . . but we're not."

"I'm in love with him," Lydia said. "Please don't make us leave. I just want to be by his bed . . . so when he wakes up I'm the first one he sees."

"If you want, doctor, I'll leave," I said. "Just let her stay for a little while."

Dr. Conroy held up a hand. "That's not necessary. Unfortunately, in Mr. Birdie's condition, he isn't posing a real security threat to anyone."

I didn't like the way that sounded, and I could tell that Lydia was upset by the doctor's words, too. "Can you tell us what's wrong with him?" Lydia asked. She still held on tight to her boyfriend's hand.

"To be completely honest, we have run dozens of tests in the last few hours, and though all of the results have not come back yet . . . we can't find a thing wrong with him . . . other than his fever and the discoloration of his skin. The fever is posing the most serious threat at this time. It's been at a steady one-oh-five since he's arrived and nothing we seem to try brings it down any. We have him scheduled for a spinal tap later this afternoon, and as I've said, right now we're waiting for results on some of his blood work." She looked right at me while she was talking, but kept moving closer to Lydia. Finally she touched Lydia and gently started to massage her back. "I wish I could tell you more. I know this must be difficult. I assure you as soon as I know something, I'll let you know."

Lydia was crying, so I said thank you to the doctor.

"I just need to check his vitals, and then I'll leave you alone," Dr. Conroy said. She went to work, so I moved to stand next to Lydia and wrapped my arm around her shoulder. She pulled herself in to my chest so that I could hug her, so I hugged her tightly while she cried.

There was a lump caught in my throat and I couldn't seem to swallow it.

***

Two hours later and we were still in Gordon's room. The police officer guarding the room brought two cups of coffee with a handful of half-and-half and sugar packets. I sat in a chair in the back corner of the room sipping coffee while I watched Lydia sit in a chair by Gordon's bed. She ignored her coffee, leaving it on the nightstand, while she continually talked to Gordon in a whisper so soft I could not hear a word of what she was saying. While she talked, sometimes she smiled and sometimes she seemed to pause in reflection. I found the musical rhythm of her whispers to be soothing and for a moment I forgot about all the things I still needed to do with the rest of the day.

Outside the room I glimpsed Dr. Conroy. She was standing at the nurse's station. I excused myself and left the room. The police officer was not at the folding chair, but was two doors down talking to a nurse. He stood with his thumbs hooked in his belt. The nurse reminded me of a schoolgirl, only instead of holding books up close to her chest while she talked, she held a patient's clipboard.

"Dr. Conroy, can I have a minute?" I asked when the doctor stopped writing. She had been busy scrawling something into a journal. I didn't want to interrupt her.

She tucked the journal over the counter onto the nurse's desk, then turned and gave me a smile. "Yes?"

"Is Gordon Birdie in a coma or something?" I asked. I found it odd that Lydia could talk to him for two hours and Gordon remained asleep, no matter how soothing her voice.

"He appears to be in a heavy sleep, perhaps caused by the fever. He is not, however, in a coma." She folded her arms. "I'm going to be honest. I've received back more test results and I can't find a thing wrong with him. He'll be going down for that spinal tap in about another twenty minutes, but truthfully, I don't know that we'll find anything from that test, either. It's baffling. I've called on a few other doctors for advice. They plan to stop by sometime before the end of the day. What's weird is the way his skin is continuing to lose color, almost as if the pigment is evaporating. When I did an examination and checked his vitals last time, when I had you help me exercise his legs and his arms, it was because his body was developing bedsores. Now he's only been sick since this morning. From what I understand, according to the prison's doctor, this man was completely healthy yesterday. He should not have bedsores, but he does and I don't know what to make of that," said the doctor.

Her expression told me that she did not like being this uncertain. Gordon's unknown disease was a blank void that this particular doctor was not used to facing. Maybe she thought she was too smart, or too good a doctor to be stumped and kept from delivering the diagnosis of a patient with nothing more than an unwavering fever, swollen and blackened eyelids, and bizarre skin color loss. In a way, the doctor's feelings made me feel better. I knew she was going to do everything possible to find out what was wrong with Gordon Birdie because he presented a challenge. Of course, that did not mean she'd be able to cure him.

"How about pain?"

"He's in it. We got morphine running through one of the lines in his arm. He wasn't unconscious when he was brought in. He was awake and screaming. Part of the reason he's cuffed isn't just for police security . . . but also because he was trying to hurt himself. He was throwing punches at his own face and stomach. We tested for drugs and came up with nothing. It's like nothing I have ever seen."

Somehow I convinced Lydia to take a walk with me to the hospital's cafeteria. Gordon remained motionless in his bed, and I did not think he looked like he might wake up anytime soon. My stomach told me it was noon, and I obeyed. I ordered a burger with fries while Lydia, who insisted she didn't want anything, settled for a salad and chocolate milk.

The dining area was large with windows all around and full of people. I found the most secluded area and we sat there. While Lydia only stabbed at her lunch, I ate my burger with relish.

"I just keep thinking," Lydia said. "And these thoughts I have make me feel so guilty. I keep blaming Pastor Brown and at times I hate him for what he's done. I was there the other night, and I heard everything he told you about those evil books. So I've been using that these last few hours to try and calm my inner anger. I tell myself that what Gordon and Anthony did was noble. And it was, but still . . . Why did Pastor Brown have to pick Gordon to do his work? Why didn't he sneak into the guy's house and try to steal the book himself? I know Gordon. He would never have done such a thing. He was pressured into it. You heard Pastor Brown. He's a motivational speaker. He could get anybody to do anything, I'd bet."

I stared at and into Lydia's eyes. She looked right at me while she spoke. The eyes looked so vibrant and alive the way the lower eyelid swelled up with tears before they rolled down her cheek. Why can't she see me? Why don't those beautiful eyes work? "Lydia . . . this might not be easy, but the best thing to do is let what has happened in the past . . . stay in the past. If you keep asking yourself the 'why' and 'what if' questions, you'll only drive yourself crazy," I said. I felt like a mean person, but I know in my heart that what I just told her was some solid advice. "We have enough to think and worry about right here, right now."

"I know. You're right," she said, dropping her fork and bringing her hand to her forehead. Her shoulders shook as she sobbed. "I don't want him to die, Nick. Please God, don't let him die."

I went to her side of the table and got down on one knee. I took her hands in mine and let her hug me, and again, I hugged her just as tight—if not, tighter.

CHAPTER 37

Marlow Henson, Lydia's big and burly brother, answered the phone around four in the afternoon. I told him what had happened and where Lydia was. He made it from Lydia's apartment to the hospital, in what I would like to refer to as, record time. Though I believed I had done well comforting Lydia, she was happy to have her brother there with her. After they hugged and talked for a moment, I said my good-byes and received my thank you's and set out in search of Jasmine.

It didn't take a brilliant mind to make the link. With Gordon Birdie's sudden attack of an odd and compelling illness only hours after the theft of the third book of The Talisman . . . well, draw your own conclusions. Mine was drawn the moment I saw Gordon in bed looking the way he looked, and right now, though I was concerned about finding Philip Edwards and finishing the job, I was more concerned about Birdie's health. It seemed pretty clear that traditional medicine might not cure the man, while perhaps—and I am hoping—Jasmine might know of a non-conventional way to help him before he becomes sicker, or dies.

I called the office and talked with Karis. I told her to have Eleanor waiting for me outside. She knew where Jasmine lived. The two of them seemed to have hit it off. After she climbed into the car and strapped the seatbelt across her chest, she asked, "So what's going on?"

I told her.

"Damn, Nick. I knew it would turn out to be interesting working with you, but voodoo shit? Come on. I'm not too sure I'm buying all of this," she said. "I mean, I'm not saying I don't, but . . . voodoo?" She looked straight ahead, her hands sat folded in her lap. "And you buy it?"

"I'm not positive what's going on, Eleanor," I said. I still found it odd calling her by her given name and not Scar. What made it a little easier was that she no longer resembled the girl I'd known as Scar, thankfully. She clearly looked like a woman who could quite possibly be named Eleanor.

"But you buy it?" Now she looked at me. She needed an answer.

Though I was driving, I looked away from the road and right into Eleanor's eyes. "I buy it."

I made a left, and heard Eleanor sigh. "If you buy it, I buy it. I know what happened last time with Darla," she said. She'd known Karis' daughter at college. "And though I never saw some of the things you saw, I don't think I ever doubted your story. I mean . . . look at what ended up happening. I have no reason to doubt you now."

"Or Father Paul."

She laughed. "I'd doubt him before I doubted you," she said. "Having the two of you agree that something weird is going on, well, that just makes your case all the more strong."

"So glad I could convince you," I said sarcastically.

"It's right here," Eleanor said.

We were in Chili, pronounced with two long "i"'s, like cheye-lie. The brick apartment complex was just west of the I390 exit on Chili Avenue, and on the right. We pulled into the lot and followed the road like a maze weaving its way between the buildings that resembled Monopoly Game pieces. Eleanor directed me toward a parking space and as we walked up to the main door of Jasmine's building, Eleanor asked if I'd called first.

"Couldn't find a number," I said.

"It's unlisted," Eleanor said, "but I had Karis put it on file at the office."

"Good thinking," I said. Five doorbells had five names under them on the outer wall of the building. I rang Jasmine's. I saw an apartment door open through the windowpane and then watched as

Jasmine came down the stairs. She did not open the door, as I thought she would have. Instead she yelled through it, asking us what we wanted.

"We need to talk," I said. "Eleanor's here, too."

Eleanor stood right next to me so that Jasmine would be able to see her as well. I watched Jasmine flash a small, wimpy smile. "What do you need to talk about?"

"About you . . . about your magic," I said, trying to talk as softly as possible. I didn't want everyone in Jasmine's building knowing her business. I was sure the walls would be as paper-thin in these apartments as in any. "Jasmine, someone is in serious trouble and I need your help," I added. Jasmine was supposed to be a good witch. She loved the Earth and its creatures. How could she turn her back on someone suffering?

And she couldn't. The front door opened. I let Eleanor step in first. "Thank you," I said to Jasmine. I knew something had to be up—something had to be going on. Why else would she try to leave us stranded out on the front step? Before I could say another word, Jasmine turned and ran back up the stairs to her door and went through it.

Eleanor looked at me.

"Don't ask me," I said, answering the puzzled look on my summer co-op's face.

We went up the stairs and into Jasmine's apartment. I closed and locked her door, then took a moment to look around. I think I expected to see black painted walls with glowing moons and stars all over the place—and beaded doorways instead of doors leading to the other rooms. Maybe I was confusing the witch with the gypsy. Either way, it wasn't what I expected. Jasmine's apartment was tastefully decorated with little, enforcing the statement that less is sometimes more. I noted some art on some walls, a tan living room set. There was a twenty-seven inch television in a cabinet in the entertainment center.

"Beer?" Jasmine asked, popping her head out from around the kitchenette.

"Love one," Eleanor said.

"Nick?"

"Neither of us will have one," I said, "but water would be good."

207

Eleanor shot me a look. "You twenty-one?" I asked. I knew she was not. "Are you working for me? Are we on the clock right now?"

"Are you trying to sound like Robert Dinero?"

"Are you talking to me?" I asked.

Eleanor gave me a grunting sigh and turned away. I went back to looking around the room—and sniffing the mixed smells of two familiar scents.

When she gave us our drinks, I asked, "Smoking pot and hiding the scent with incense?"

"Smoking pot? Yes," Jasmine said. "Hiding the scent? No. I do this every Saturday. It's my 'alone time.' I like to meditate and get in touch with myself. I usually spend so much time doing this and that that there is rarely enough time for me."

"Is that why you were reluctant to let Eleanor and myself in just now?" I asked.

"Partly. But also because I think seeing you again is a bad omen." She stood up and went over to the television set. It was on the set that the incense bowl sat. She took a lighter and lit the end of an incense stick. From the bowl she picked up a small white wrapped joint and lit the end. I watched her as she took a long drag. She held the smoke in her mouth and continued to suck it into her lungs without breathing for nearly a minute. Most people began coughing when they did this—even most experienced drug smokers. Jasmine stayed calm, stayed focused and in control. She exhaled and very little smoke came out of her mouth. "You know that freak that wanted my book . . . and whatever else he was . . . he knew I had the book. He knew, but he didn't come for it. Maybe he would have eventually, but up until I met you, I felt somewhat safe, you know? I felt in control. I had the book. There was some control. But man, you show up and my book disappears." She went and sat Indian style on her recliner. "You guys can sit if you'd like."

I wanted to lecture Jasmine about her drug usage, but kept quiet. Inside, my own body craved a cigarette. The craving nearly felt physically painful. We sat on the love seat across from Jasmine.

"So what's going on?" Jasmine asked.

"There is a man who is sick in the hospital," I said. "Very sick. The doctors there have no idea what's wrong with him."

"And you think . . .?"

"And I think this man's illness is part of a spell," I said.

"A spell? Suddenly you are a major believer in witchcraft?" Jasmine asked. She looked from me to Eleanor while taking another long drag off the end of her joint, as the white rolling paper burned a bright orange and crackled and shrank.

"This man got sick a few hours after the third ring of The Talisman was stolen," I said.

Jasmine shot forward. Her swollen and puffy looking eyes could not open any more than they were. But through those tiny slits I saw a genuine look of fear. "When was it stolen?"

"Last night . . . or yesterday during the day, really."

Jasmine put out her joint and licked her fingertips. She touched the wet tips to the incense stick, extinguishing the burning end. "I told you that you were an omen, Nick. Did I tell you? Man, I knew you were an omen . . . a bad omen!"

"Is it the drug making you so paranoid?" I asked.

"It's the calming effect of the drug that's keeping me from punching the shit out of you!"

"Why are you so mad at me?" I asked.

Jasmine took a step at me. I watched Eleanor getting ready for a fight. Her hands rolled into anxious fists. "Haven't you been listening to me? My life is like up in arms because I don't know what I'm supposed to do next. I have no clue what my role is in your little plan. I mean, Nick, this is for real shit. Ever since we got back from Florida I've had a bad feeling inside. I knew something was going to happen. I knew something bad might happen. I got to tell you, I never, never thought that one person would wind up with all three rings. Man, this guy already knows how to use black magic. We know that. I know it first hand. I saw him as the wind. I heard him and felt him whispering in my ear. With all three books in his possession . . . I can't even begin to imagine what we might all be in store for." She stayed silent for a moment, and both Eleanor and I let her. She was highly emotional. I kept telling myself that, like it or not, witchcraft was her religion. I needed to respect that. Her beliefs seemed strong. "I can't believe The Talisman is complete." She kneeled down in front of me, placing her hand on my leg. "Who's sick and what do you need me to do?"

Before I explained anything to Jasmine about Gordon Birdie, she told me I needed to tell her everything. She explained, the more information she had, the better she could assess the situation and decide what might need to be done. Whereas I might think a piece of information is irrelevant; the impact of my neglected communication might have serious impact on her course of action. She wanted me to let her decide what might and might not be important.

She did not sound surprised to hear the way I described Gordon Birdie's appearance in the hospital. In fact, while I described him, she got up and went to one of her bookcases and removed a title. She began flipping through the yellow and crisp looking pages with great care, so I stopped talking.

"Go on," she insisted. "I'm listening."

When I finished, she sighed and sat back in the recliner. She held onto the old book and used her finger as a bookmark. "Let me ask you, is he in pain?"

"I asked the doctor," I said. "She told me, yes. He's in a lot of pain. They were giving him drugs to take the pain away. And I guess ever since he's been asleep. Not in a coma though, just asleep."

Jasmine frowned. "Only thing is, in his sleep, he's still in pain."

"No. The doctor assured me . . . "

"It don't matter what the doctor assured you of, Nick," Jasmine said. "He's not sick like they're thinking. You know that, or you wouldn't be here." She opened the book she had been holding and laid it down on the coffee table in front of me. "Does your friend look like this lady?"

I didn't need to pick up the book, hold it close to my eyes and study it, to know right away that the condition of the woman in the drawing looked identical to the way Gordon Birdie looked in the hospital.

Eleanor picked up the book. "Freaky," she said.

"Yeah. That's how this guy looks. Dark rings, pale skin . . . bed sores."

"Not bed sores," Jasmine said. "They look like bed sores, but they're not."

"What are they?" Eleanor asked, setting the book down. I thought I could see the color drain from her cheeks, while her hand massaged her belly, perhaps unnerved and upset by the drawing.

"It's an ulceration of the skin, but not induced from being in bed for long periods of time," Jasmine said.

"That's true. The doctor I spoke to found it extremely odd that Gordon was already suffering from bedsores when he'd only just been brought in to the hospital," I added.

"The spell that was placed on your friend is ancient. Your friend is dying and his death is painful. Very painful, both physically and mentally," Jasmine said, picking up her book. She flipped through it and stopped on the page with the drawing again. "The sores are caused by minions inside his body. These little beings are eating him alive inside," Jasmine explained.

"Minions?" Eleanor asked. She was staring at me, I could tell, to see if I was still 'buying this.' I did not turn to look at her. I had to admit I felt overwhelmed. It seemed hard to accept the fact that tiny followers of The Talisman were inside Gordon's body feasting on his organs and muscles and chewing their way through his skin.

"These minions hatch by the thousands and reproduce every so many hours."

"And it was a spell that placed these minions inside him?" I asked.

"A very powerful spell," Jasmine said.

"And you think Philip Edwards, because he now has all three books, concocted this spell?" I asked.

"Sounds like it to me," said Jasmine.

I felt a cloud of doom quickly covering my body and soul. I pictured Lydia back at the hospital close to her lover's side, hoping and praying Gordon would wake up and get well. I had no intention of predicting the future—nor did I have any intention of sharing this information with Lydia.

"And what can you do about it?" Eleanor asked.

I thought I knew the answer.

"Nothing," she said, confirming my feelings. "Maybe if I had one, or two of those rings, or all three, I could reverse the spell. Without those books, I don't think any witch or wizard is going to have much power. Especially not against a man with all three rings," Jasmine said.

"So what, like, this guy is going to just have to stay in the hospital and wait to be eaten alive . . . from the inside out?" Eleanor asked.

"How long has he got?" I managed. I thought I might be sick. My stomach fluids felt like they might be boiling inside and popping and splashing around the wall lining. The acid burned . . . instant indigestion.

"It doesn't say in this book. It says swiftly. I have no idea what swiftly might mean. They might not have put a time in this thing because each person's death may have occurred after different duration's, you know?" Jasmine said. "But Nick . . . "

"What?"

"Nothing," she said, her facial expression resembled a look of dire doom. I didn't press her because maybe I didn't want to know what she had to say.

CHAPTER 38

Sunday, May 26

My sleep was fitful. My stomach ached. At three in the morning I went down to the basement with a glass of ice water and worked on my manuscript. At seven I stopped. I had accomplished a lot of writing. I printed the pages I wrote and put them on the other stacks of pages to be read through for the purpose of editing. If I had my way, I would write every morning, and edit every evening. Life interfered with that plan. Still, I felt good. The book was coming along and, for the most part, I was impressed with what I had accomplished to date. I had sixty-five thousand words down and more than half of that edited—for the first draft, anyway. After I finished writing the entire thing I would let Karis read it, rough edges and all, but not until I completed the first draft.

Last night Marlow convinced Lydia to go home for the night. He promised to take her back to the hospital first thing in the morning. I told Marlow to stall the return visit until after nine. I wanted to bring Jasmine down to visit with Gordon so she could see him in person. She agreed readily. She had never seen a person with Gordon's ailment in person; she only knew of the signs and symptoms from the books she had read.

My mental list of things-to-do felt full. There were so many things to do that I had no idea what kind of time frame might be involved if I expected to complete each item. Aside from taking

Jasmine to the hospital to look in on Gordon, I also wanted to catch Father Paul up on events happening, and I wanted to talk to Lynn. Since it was Sunday, I figured talking with the attorney could wait until tomorrow. My kid sister floated around in my mind—and I did not want to let that evaporate. I needed to find an hour where I could track down and talk to my brother-in-law. I knew the case he was working on demanded his attention, but his wife and new baby needed him home occasionally, as well.

Before jumping into the shower, I called Jasmine to make sure she was up and getting ready. When I pulled up in front of her place, she was outside waiting for me. She stood holding a travel mug of coffee in one hand, while a giant black purse dangled off her shoulder. She waved, came over, and climbed into my car.

"You look chipper," I said. I pulled out onto the main road and drove toward the expressway.

"I'm a morning person," she said. "With the store, I have to be there late, and it drives me crazy. Business is business though, and when I was open normal hours, the place was dead. One of the customers, a witch from Gates, suggested to me that I change the store hours. I thought about it, and realized she was right. Being open from some unstable time like dusk and closing after the witching hour did a lot for my business."

I nodded. "Uh-huh. You're chipper and talkative."

We arrived at the hospital, and were greeted in the Intensive Care Unit by a police officer I knew. Mandi Dorsey was a tall woman with long, curly, dark hair. Today she wore it pulled back and rolled in a bun. She and my sister Julia were best friends all through high school. So for four years, Mandi hung out at our house regularly. At the time she'd been not much more than a pain in the ass, one of my kid sister's annoying little friends. She grew up and I still found it hard to think of her as a police officer. Looking at her, in uniform anyway, you could tell she was a cop. She had ice-blue eyes and an intimidating stance—not to be confused with a challenging stance. She had nothing to prove like some female police officers. Mandi had worked in the jails after high school before becoming an officer, so she had already proven herself.

We kissed on the cheeks. "How have you been, Mandi?"

"Good, great. You?" She smiled while she talked, genuinely happy to see me. Her stance softened. Now she was my sister's friend talking to me, and not Officer Dorsey. I liked that.

"Been better. See my brother-in-law much?"

"Not usually. He's good though. Whenever I do, he always talks about you," she said. "And good, too."

"Get out of here," I said.

"No. I'm serious."

Jasmine cleared her throat, so I introduced the two women to one another. "We need to get in there and see Gordon, all right?"

Mandi cringed. "Not supposed to let anyone in," she said.

"And I don't want you to go against any orders, I don't, but . . . "

I explained that Jasmine just wanted to bless him, that she was a Native American Medicine woman, and that Gordon Birdie was part Native American.

"Medicine Woman, huh?"

"More or less," I said. I felt funny lying, not because Mandi was a police officer, but because she was a good friend of the family's. I knew in a way that I was not actually lying though. I was stretching the truth. Jasmine might not be a Native American Medicine Woman, but she was a witch—a good witch—who wanted to try to help Gordon. Okay, okay. I was lying.

"Two minutes," Mandi said.

"All I need," Jasmine assured Mandi.

The lights were off in the room and the curtains were still drawn closed. I walked to the end of the room and pulled a string to open them. As sunlight filled the room it revealed the most horrific sight I'd ever seen and I nearly screamed out of sheer shock and surprise.

Gordon Birdie's body looked withered. He looked as if he had lost thirty pounds overnight. The rings around his eyes appeared larger, darker. Sores covered his arms, each bubbling with a bloody mucus-like body fluid. My stomach churned and I thought I might vomit. I turned away.

"This is bad," I heard Jasmine say. She sounded excited, like an archeologist discovering the remains of a dinosaur. "He looks ten time worse than the lady in the drawing."

"And he might be able to hear you," I said, whispering. "You might want to watch what you say."

"You're right. You're absolutely right. He can hear me. There's no reason why he can't."

I stayed near the window, but turned around to watch as Jasmine went to Gordon's side. She looked hesitant about touching him. Still, she took his hand into hers and closed her eyes, tilting her head back as far as it would go. She held her other hand out, palms up and began to hum. She began to sway to the slow rhythm of her wordless song.

I looked at Gordon's face and he was staring at me. His head was lifted off the pillow, and he was staring at me. My heart caught in my throat. The whites of his eyes—or what should have been the whites of his eyes—looked Coke can red, with miniature craters of sores, like the ones on his arms and face, bubbling in those pain-filled eyeballs. Then Gordon opened his mouth. A jagged half eaten tongue protruded, flickering all about his lips. A small black cloud escaped in a puff as he exhaled in a gasp. The cloud hovered over his face before being sucked back up through the dying man's nostrils. When this cloud happened a second time, I knew it was not a cloud, but a swarm of minions.

The minions had taken over his body and were eating him alive, just as Jasmine had explained. They were inside his head, chewing on his eyes and perhaps eating away at his brain. It explained the tongue; the tiny creatures had eaten off the tip of his tongue.

I had to close my eyes. I shook my head. I couldn't actually be seeing these things. Minions. It couldn't be real, none of it, any of it. When I opened my eyes, Gordon's eyes were closed and his head was resting, almost peacefully on the pillow.

"Jasmine," I said. "Jas?"

She looked to be out of it. She still held onto Gordon's hand. Her thumb rested next to a large, percolating sore. I did not venture anywhere near the bed. I debated having Jasmine call for a ride home. If she were infected with the minions now—I didn't want her anywhere near me or in my car.

What about the nurses and doctors, had they all been infected?

How come those inspecting every orifice in Gordon's body haven't noticed minion gnats flying around in his body?

"Jasmine," I said, more loudly this time. She broke from her trance and stared at me with a look that could kill. "Can we go?"

"I'm trying to ease this man's suffering," she said. "What is wrong with you?"

I shook my head, no, feeling like I couldn't speak. Swallowing, I managed, "Minions."

"I felt them," she said.

"Well, damn it, Jasmine. You were touching him. Those tiny bastards are all over his insides! How in the Hell can you touch him?" I was losing my cool. I knew I was shouting. I felt freaked out and itchy. Every part of my body itched. I kept rolling my fingernails into the palms of my hands. I wanted to leave the room, I felt like I needed to leave the room. Breathing seemed suddenly difficult.

"Nick," Jasmine said, speaking softly. "They can't leave their host. The infection is his and it is not contagious."

"So you say," I said. At this point, I didn't care what Gordon overheard.

"So says the law of spells," Jasmine said firmly.

I closed my eyes and pressed the heels of my palms into the lids and rubbed. "How is he?"

"Dying."

"Anything you can do?"

"Nothing."

"So what were you just doing?"

"Listening to him die." Jasmine was crying. She caressed Gordon's face. I felt ill just watching. I kept imaging a bloody tongue darting out of his mouth, licking her hand and leaving a wet trail of minions and blood along her wrist. "I tried to place a peaceful spell on him, but couldn't. The spell that encompasses his soul is complete, powerful and seemingly impregnable. I can't get in at all to leave a spell that might do some good. I tried, but I just can't. He is suffering, God, the pain he must be feeling . . . with no way of showing just how much he's going through."

We left the room and I said to Mandi, "Please, please, don't let any other visitors in that room."

"That bad?" Mandi asked.

"I've never seen anyone look that sick. His girlfriend will be by to visit. Her name is Lydia. She's blind, but her brother Marlow isn't. If just Lydia went in, she might not realize the seriousness of his appearance. She might touch his face. She has good hands and touching him might reveal to her just how bad off he is. But if Marlow goes in with her, then I know for sure she'll find out," I said.

"Protecting her, Nick?"

"I've got to. She doesn't need to know about his appearance."

"I'll keep them out, and Nick, you're a good person." Mandi smiled. Warmth filled those big blue eyes. We kissed goodbye.

When we left the hospital, and while driving Jasmine back to her place, I said, "Jasmine . . . "

"How come no one else sees the minions?"

"Yeah," I said.

"I'm surprised you could. I never once sensed anything about you," she said.

"Sensed about me? What?"

"You have something in you, a gift," she said.

"You saying I'm a witch?"

"No. I said you have a gift. You are a link. I bet you see ghosts," she said. She wasn't asking me. I had no intentions of telling her about Darla, Karis' daughter. "You can see the minions because you have the gift."

"Did you see them?" I asked.

"No."

But her eyes had been closed when Gordon opened his mouth. She had been in a trance. I wish I had been in a trance. I didn't want this gift. "I don't want this gift."

"You don't get to pick and choose your gift, Nick. Don't be silly."

I decided I needed a breather. I was being quickly overwhelmed and thought I might be drowning as I tried to swim against this supernatural tide. I dropped Jasmine off.

I knew where I needed to go to calm myself and to collect my thoughts, and I knew I did not want to go alone. I called Karis at the office and asked her to meet me at the pier.

CHAPTER 39

We were at the end of May, but it felt like the beginning of March. The gray clouds in the sky had persisted, as if trying to convince people that the blue skies above them were no more. I still had faith, albeit wavering, that one day I would see the sun and blue sky again. Despite the aggressive gloomy cloud coverage, people flocked to the beach, and would continue to do so every Sunday, and Saturday, and on any day they could get away from the office—and as soon as school let out. The beach was a place where things were always happening, while the water, despite its unnatural color of brown and pungent odor, soothed the soul and the mind with its rhythmic rolling.

The only way into the parking lot was off Lake Avenue, a curling roadway that led past a boat dock, then ran along the Genesee River for a tenth of a mile. Parking was on the left, nearer the restaurants and clubs, and larger than the stamp-shaped lot on the right, which sat along the river and nearer the pier.

Because of the volume of people, I had to park on the left. I got out of my car immediately noticing the acrimonious smell of the air. Still I inhaled it willfully because it beat the Hell out of smelling the wafting odors billowing from the factory stacks polluting the rest of Rochester (and which were primarily responsible for the stench in the river and lake).

I watched for Karis' car, and when it pulled up, I walked over to where she parked. She got out of the car, and I could immediately tell by the look on her face that I must have looked like shit. "What's wrong?" She asked. She slid her purse strap onto her shoulder and locked her car door before closing it. She held my hand. "Nick? What's the matter?"

Words escaped me. Fearing I might cry if I tried to speak, I opted for just shaking my head and leading Karis toward the sidewalk that led to the pier. "You're scaring me, Nick. This scares me."

Then Karis fell silent while we walked. I think she understood. I needed a minute to collect myself. She was here in the middle of the day because I needed someone to talk to. If she had called me, I would have dropped everything to be there for her. It felt good knowing she would do the same.

I paid no attention to the kids on the playground on my left, or to the people cooking on the park grills. I ignored the parties going on under the pavilions. What I found most delightfully distracting was the merry-go-round. The thing looked beautiful, though ancient. It had been at the beach for as long as I could remember. They used to have bumper cars here, too. Those closed, but the merry-go-round stayed up and running. Kids loved it. As Karis and I walked by, I watched the laughing and smiling children as they rode the diverse mixture of wood carved animals.

"I used to love riding that," I said to Karis. "How about you?"

"Only every time we were down here. My father loved coming to Charlotte. He'd have my mother pack a lunch and nearly every weekend, all summer long, we'd be down here," Karis said.

"Yeah. I remember you telling me that before," I said. "Back when we were dating in high school."

"You don't remember anything I ever told you," Karis said, slapping at my arm playfully. "I used to talk to you and I don't think you ever listened."

"I listened."

"I remember times I'd be talking and you'd say nothing."

"Yeah, and I remember then you'd ask me if I was listening to you, and I would repeat back to you . . . nearly verbatim . . . everything you had said," I noted. "Nearly verbatim, mind you."

"Yeah, but you didn't say anything while I was talking, or even after I'd finished," she said. "I hated that. I never knew if you were listening, or not."

"I just am not big on talking, I suppose. Or I wasn't, anyway."

"No. You were never big on sharing your feelings, you still aren't. You're terrible about keeping things in. You hold everything inside of you. I have no idea why you do that. I'm here, and Eleanor's here . . . you have a handful of people you could talk to where you shouldn't feel uncomfortable. How about Father Paul?" Karis asked.

"If I was going to talk to anyone, Karis, it would be you."

"Is that why you called me here? Do you want to talk?"

I stuffed my hands into my pockets. In the back of my mind I caught the tail end of a fleeting, or passing, thought. Get a cigarette right now you loser . . . was all I could recall. "No."

"Nick?"

"Look, I was just having a bad and busy day," I said.

"You can't do this forever. Keeping everything inside is going to cause you to explode. I'll tell you one thing Nick, and I mean it, don't ever think about exploding while I'm around. I'm here for you and I love you with all my heart, but I don't want any part of an explosion . . . especially one that could have been diffused time and time again. You hear me?" asked Karis.

"Loud and clear," I said. I took my hands out of my pockets and held her gently by the shoulders.

"Want to kiss me?"

"And hug you," I said.

"It's going to cost you," said Karis.

"Yeah? How much?" I asked. At this point I'd have sawed off my legs for a hug and a kiss.

"A ride on the merry-go-round," she said. I let go of her shoulders and put my hands back into my pockets. Slowly I walked away. She called out, "Hey. Where are you going?"

"I've got to think about it. We're talking about shelling out a buck. That's a lot of dough, and baby, I know how you kiss." Before I could even smile, she was chasing me.

"Why you," Karis called out. She balled her hand into a fist and was taking swings as I stepped this way and that to keep from being playfully punched. Finally I lost my footing, though did not fall. Karis caught me. Laughing and out of breath, Karis kissed me hard on the lips.

The plan was to talk to Karis. I wanted to open up and share myself with her. Some force always seemed to keep me from doing so. When I called her, I wanted to talk to her about my feelings. Gordon Birdie had monsters inside him—gnawing away at the strings of his life—and the poor bastard knew exactly what was happening. Seeing Gordon upset me more so than anything I had ever been through and because of that fact, everything else bad in the past stepped forward to benchmark itself against the experience.

Then when I saw Karis I asked myself, why do I need to tell her all of this? Why upset her? There was no need for the both of us to feel the strength of this consuming depression. She had enough on her mind and in her past that she didn't need me forcing her to exhume old skeletons.

I did decide one thing. If I ever planned to open up, as they say, the only person I would do it with would be Karis. One day for sure I planned to tell Karis everything.

CHAPTER 40

I met Lynn Scannella at the hospital, after dinner, around six that evening. She was waiting for me in the lobby. When she saw me walking toward her, she started walking toward me. "You seen him?"

"Yeah," I said. "I saw him." In my mind I kept hearing Jasmine's voice. I was supposed to believe that no one else could see the gnat-like creatures inside Gordon Birdie's body. I could see them. Jasmine could not, or did not see them. The doctors at the hospital had no clue and could not detect the minions even after taking blood and urine samples.

"Bad?"

"I can honestly say I have never seen someone in his condition before," I said. We stood in the lobby. I could sense Lynn's hesitation. She did not want to go up and see her client. I couldn't blame her. I didn't want to go. "Something wrong?"

"I don't like hospitals. I try to avoid them. Last time I had to come to a hospital, it was for my father." Lynn sucked her lower lip into her mouth and held it in place with her top front teeth. I clearly remembered the story Lynn had told me about her father. It must have been awful for her. After the accident, the plant would have called first for an ambulance to rush both halves of Mr. Scannella to the hospital and then would have called Mrs. Scannella and Lynn. The last thing a factory is going to do is pronounce a person dead while the person is still on company property—double indemnity. Insurance companies hate to dish out those accidental work death payoffs.

I put out my hand, palm up, and smiled as warmly as I could smile. Lynn sighed, but placed her hand in mine. Her palm felt warm and wet, balmy. I closed my fingers around her hand and gave it a squeeze. While we walked toward the elevator banks, I pretended not to notice as Lynn wiped away shed tears.

When we reached the intensive care unit, Marlow Henson popped out of the waiting room. Waving a finger in my face, he said, "Damn Nick, what's going on? Who's this?"

I pushed Marlow's finger to the side. "This is Ms. Scannella. She's Gordon's attorney."

Lynn and Marlow said Hello. "Where's your sister?" I asked.

"On the sofa in there," Marlow said. He pointed over his shoulder at the waiting room. "She cried herself to sleep. Man, Nick, they won't let us in to see the guy. They won't even let us down the hall. Something's going on."

"Excuse me?" Dr. Conroy stood behind us. She looked at me and flashed a most unusual smile. I felt something churn in my stomach and wanted to turn and leave. Against my better judgment, I stayed.

Marlow Henson must have sensed the same thing. One hand clutched at his stomach. "You want me to wake my sister?"

Dr. Conroy simply shook her head. "That's up to you. I don't have good news, and if you need me to, I can tell her, but Mr. Birdie did not make it."

I swallowed. I remembered the scared man from the prison. I looked over the doctor's shoulder down toward Gordon's hospital room. The policeman at the post stood at the doorway looking into the hospital room with his fists planted on his hips. His facial expression looked contorted. The cop appeared to be disgusted by the sight of the withered and inwardly eaten corpse. I concentrated my attention on Marlow and went as far as to place my hand on his back—for support.

"There was nothing we could do," Dr. Conroy said.

A nurse called from down the hall. "Dr. Conroy?"

Conroy turned and told the nurse, "Just a minute." She then said to the three of us, "I am very sorry. Please know this, we are going to continue to test tissue samples. We're sending samples out to more scientifically equipped labs, too. We will find out what happened to

Mr. Birdie . . .if that's any consolation."

"Dr. Conroy?" the same nurse called.

Dr. Conroy ignored the nurse. Like myself, she was staring into the waiting room. We all must have been staring at Lydia, the small, lovable and fragile looking young woman curled up asleep on the sofa with a balled up wad of tear soaked tissue in her hand.

When I am asleep, I can tell when someone is staring at me. I know when I am being watched. Many nights I'll wake up. My eyes will just open and there will be Karis just looking at me. I was sound asleep—how on earth would I know I was being stared at?

With all of us looking at Lydia, many questions ran through my mind: Would Lydia feel us staring at her? Would she sense . . . something? Would us watching her cause a ripple in her sleep?

"I can't tell her, man," Marlow said. He looked at Dr. Conroy with a pleading expression. "She'll be crushed. I can't believe I never knew it before, before all of this, but she was in love with that guy."

Dr. Conroy looked at me. "I can tell her," she said. "As long as she's sleeping, let me talk to this nurse and I'll come back."

As soon as Dr. Conroy walked away, Lydia stirred. Curiosity overcame me. Waking up is an interesting enough phenomenon for someone with sight. You open your eyes and see where you are. This visual information must immediately register in your brain, keeping you from becoming disoriented and panicked. Imagine waking up and all you can see is the pitch black that you always see?

Lynn looped her arm around mine. "Nick," she whispered. Marlow was gone. I looked behind me, to no avail. The little bastard. He'd chickened out. He saw his sister waking and took off.

"Marlow?" Lydia said, while sitting up and stretching. "Marlow?"

"Marlow just stepped out," I said, walking into the room. I sat on the love seat next to Lydia.

"Nicholas," she said. "When did you get here?"

"Just," I said.

"Why didn't you wake me?"

"How could I disturb a sleeping angel?" I asked. I could not help it. I let my knuckles softly brush along her cheek.

"Where did my brother go?" Lydia asked. Her tone had suddenly changed. Her voice had a shaky edge to it. "You know they won't let me in to see Gordie? I told them I'd been in there many times. All of a sudden, though, me and Marlow get here today and they say no. We can't go into Gordon's room. Nick, you've got to sneak me in. I have to see him."

Lynn started to cry.

"Who else is in here?" Lydia asked. "Nicholas?"

"Ms. Scannella's in here with us. She's Gordon's attorney," I managed to say.

"Why is she crying?"

I wanted to push Lynn the Hell out of the room. Dr. Conroy promised to come right back. Damn it. This was the doctor's job. It wasn't mine. "Lydia," I said while watching Lynn sit in a chair at the opposite end of the small 14 by 16 room. The strong and stubborn lawyer rested her elbows on her knees, cradled her face in her palms and sobbed.

"Nick . . ." Lydia said, knowingly. Her hands looked liked claws as they reached for my arms, and then latched on. "Nick, Gordon's all right, isn't he?"

This hurt, was tearing my heart in two. "Lydia, Gordon just passed away."

"When? When, Nick? How long have I been asleep?" Lydia used me to help her stand up. Her legs looked unsteady as she wobbled and attempted to gain balance. "He's not dead, though. No he's not. He's not dead for a lot of reasons," Lydia said. Tears streamed down her cheeks, but she did not sound like she was crying when she talked. She sounded strong. She sounded angry. "He can't be dead because I didn't get to say good-bye to him. He's not dead because I didn't have a chance to tell him how much I love him. I didn't get to tell him how much I'd miss him." Lydia bit her lower lip and used the back of her hand to wipe her nose. She ignored the tears as she laid her head against my chest.

"Lydia," I said.

She pulled away and punched my chest while she shook her head almost violently back and forth. "No. No. No. No! He's not dead. He's not dead." Then she seemed to magically calm herself down. "I'm going into his room now, and I'm going to tell him what's going on out here, and I don't think he's going to like it. Gordon is not going to like what's being said out here."

Lydia tentatively held out her hand. She was feeling for the wall.

She was trying to leave the room. At the threshold, I stopped her. "Lydia . . ."

She turned on me with teeth bared, and through those clenched teeth she warned me. "Back off, Nick. Just back off."

I saw Dr. Conroy. She was just walking away from the nurse, but didn't seem to notice Lydia awake. "Lydia . . ."

She slapped my chest. "Leave me alone, Nick . . . my God, can't you just leave me alone?"

I stayed quiet as Lydia walked out of the waiting room. She was crying now, releasing loud sobs. She stumbled and fell to her knees, but did not try to get up. Instead she stayed down on all fours and cried, body trembling.

Lydia felt me kneeling down next to her and collapsed into my arms. "Oh my God Nick, oh my God. I didn't tell him good-bye. He doesn't know how much I loved him. I didn't get to tell him good-bye . . ."

CHAPTER 41

Tuesday, May 28

Since Gordon Birdie did not have a family, there seemed no valid reason to hold calling hours. Karis and I drove to the church for the funeral together. The back parking lot at the First Bible Baptist was packed full. We decided to leave the car on Lake Avenue with the hazards flashing. Walking hand in hand did not ease the tension that twisted my neck muscles into knots. Karis must have sensed my reserve. She squeezed my hand.

"Don't want to go in there?"

"Not really," I said. I did not like funerals. The reasons for not wanting to go into this particular church had to exceed any reasons that might be given by someone other than me. For starters, I thought about the book stolen out of the basement of the church—pure and simple fear kept me from thinking about what exactly that might mean. I knew what Gordon's body looked like while dying. I prayed as hard and as loudly in my mind as I could that God let this be a closed casket service. I did not even want to imagine the condition of Gordon's corpse—and did not think I could stand, or stomach, seeing the decaying flesh or flying gnat-like minions.

"How's Lydia going to take this?" Karis asked.

I just shrugged. I did not think she really wanted an answer. The answer would be obvious. "Know what I want?"

"To go home?"

"Well, yes, but more than that I want a cigarette."

"You've been doing so good, Nicholas. Don't give in," Karis said.

I stopped walking and stared at the white church. I noticed the images on the stained glass windows. I saw Christ on the cross in one of those windows. Our Sins. That's what he died for. Christ died for our sins. "I'm not going to give in."

As we walked closer to the back door entrance, I was surprised to hear such loud and joyful singing. Karis and I exchanged glances and walked up the steps. Standing room only. That's all that was left. So we stood and were completely overtaken by the rhythm of the gospel music surging forth like the river spewing over Niagara Falls.

At the altar leading the parishioners in song stood Pastor Jacob Brown dressed in a black suit and tie. He swayed back and forth like a swinging pendulum. When he saw Karis and I, he waved us forward using both hands. So we walked toward the front of the church.

Sitting in the middle of the front pew the only persons not standing or singing were Lydia and her brother Marlow. A middle-aged couple stood and sang on one side of Lydia so Karis and I sat next to Marlow.

Marlow leaned over and whispered, "She's not doing well. Those are our parents standing next to her. She's hasn't said much in the last two days. Nothing at all, really."

There would be time for talking later. I didn't say anything, but nodded. I patted Marlow on the knee—my show of support. He might not have cared as much that Gordon was dead, but I could tell his heart was breaking. The man was helplessly watching his sister suffer.

As the song ended, attention was not directed at the Pastor, but turned to watch at the back doorway where four men guided a casket on a cart with wheels down the center aisle. The seemingly joyful expressions on the people who had been singing only moments ago disappeared without a trace. I felt my own stomach wall painfully twisting, as if shriveling—my solemn expression matching the faces of those around me.

The sound of Lydia sobbing filled my ears and I turned to look at her. She had her eyes closed and held a tissue to her wet lips while holding on tightly to her brother's arm. I looked back at the aisle in time to see the men stop in front of me. Pastor Brown dismissed them to the pew across from where I sat before he began to bless the casket.

I heard the prayer as it was recited by the Pastor from the pages of his well-used Bible, but could not focus on the words. It all sounded like a murmur with the volume turned up loud. Pastor Brown seemed to dance around the casket, a performance any evangelist would envy. But again the movements were blurred, matching the rhythm of the murmur of prayer.

I could not take my eyes off the casket. I felt myself being drawn toward it. I actually felt like my legs were moving, as if I was taking steps out of the pew and into the aisle. When a hand touched my shoulder, I could not react. Having no idea who might be touching me, I simply chose to ignore the sensation.

The beckoning casket seemed all that mattered.

And I heard the whispers. Murmurs. Slightly shaking my head from side to side, I tried to stop the susurration buzzing in my ears, to no avail. Karis was calling me, calling my name. It had to be her hand on my shoulder, now tugging at my arm.

Standing next to the casket I saw a sickening stream of minions, like a haunted swarm, escaping the airtight sealed seams of the casket. In horror I watched as billions and billions of minions, free of their confinement, hovered over the casket. Suddenly filled with anger, an overwhelming anger, I swatted at the creatures. "You bastards," I screamed. "You . . . bastards!" My arms flailed back and forth over the casket and through the minions, but the tiny beings did not disperse. They remained, tauntingly so, buzzing their sinister sound . . . screaming whispers.

Arms grabbed me and I struggled against the attack. My head felt light and my body disoriented. Still I fought, trying to shrug the hands off my arms. My footing got tripped up and I fell forward, sprawling on top of the casket. My head now in the center of the swarm, I thought I might go instantly mad. I felt the tiny bastards flying up my nostrils and in my ears.

The itch. It was in my head, behind my tongue and I could do nothing to scratch at it. "Let go of me," I yelled. I started coughing and felt like I couldn't breathe, as if I were unable to catch my breath. They had my arms pinned behind my back. They had me restrained against the top of the casket. They had no idea that my head was trapped in a swarm of parasites. "Get the Hell off me!" I managed to say.

Someone kept calling my name.

In all this time, I did not see one other person in the church. I could see the casket. I could see the minions. I could feel the tugging and pulling on my body. Everything else seemed to be swimming—a fuzzy cloud spinning around me.

I heard the crunch and thought my bones were breaking. I felt no pain, but knew I was falling.

I heard it, a gasp. The table the casket was on had broken. I fell onto the casket as the cart crashed to the floor. The minions were suddenly gone, the cloud suddenly cleared. Although I was aware of all that happened I could not get over the feeling inside me. I had had the feeling before after a long night of drinking. Habitual drunks called it black out.

Though I had not blacked out, it was exactly how I felt. Slowly I stood up and looked around. Most of the women in the church were crying, turned away and hiding their faces. I had made a terrible scene and did not know how to acknowledge this mistake.

The mistake was bigger than I imagined as I noticed the casket on the ground. The lock had broken and the front lid was open. Lying in white satin Gordon Birdie looked like a zombie. The closed casket was for a reason. No cosmetologist and no Hollywood make-up artist could have made Gordon look human. His death had devoured any sign of life. His skin looked like Play-Dough after a child mixes the colors together and winds up with a swirling charcoal-gray and pea-green glob of putty. Gray meat, rotten and spoiled, that's what Gordon's complexion looked most like to me. The masses of sores resembled tiny volcanoes that erupted on the moon.

All around me people stood statute-still. No one knew what to do.

I saw Marlow. He quickly closed the casket's lid. I closed my eyes. I couldn't see, but I heard people moving. When I opened my eyes, six men were carrying the casket out of the church.

Turning toward the altar I was confronted by Pastor Brown. He stood motionless silently staring down at me. I said, "I'm sorry. I have no idea . . . "

Before Pastor Brown could say anything, and given the situation I can't imagine what he might say, I turned and followed the pallbearers out of the church. Once I was outside, I realized I'd been holding my breath. I exhaled at the moment just before my lungs exploded.

I leaned onto the closest car in the parking lot and gasped in and out trying to catch my breath. What happened in there? What in the Hell just happened? The questions like shots fired out of an automatic weapon sprayed inside my brain.

"Nick are you all right?"

Startled by Karis' sudden appearance and at the sound of her voice, I spun around.

"My God, you look terrible," she said. I knew I was perspiring. I could feel the sweat dripping down my forehead.

"I need to see Jasmine," I said. "You've got to get me to Jasmine!"

CHAPTER 42

I didn't want to have to miss the funeral. I know Lydia wanted me there. Seeing Jasmine seemed more important. Those minions had been all over the place, everywhere like a giant storm cloud. Then they were gone. Either they vanished, or every one of those damned creatures is inside me right now.

I did not feel itchy inside my body, but kept scratching at my head and arms and legs. "How much further?"

"We're almost there. Hang on."

Karis drove. I rode in the backseat. I did not want to risk any of those bastards getting out of my body and entering Karis'. I laid on the backseat curled up in a fetal position. I felt sick and nauseated. There was a space vampire movie playing in my head. I had seen the film long ago. Somehow I suddenly felt like a part of the sequel.

Vampires. Minions. Witches. Warlocks. Philip Edwards was going to pay for this. The man was a beast; out of his mind.

When the car came to a screeching stop, I sat up. In a way, I expected to be unconscious by now. I imagined the tiny creatures rapidly multiplying in my body. The thought alone made me sick— made me think of people with lice. "We're there?" It was a dumb question, and Karis didn't answer it. She looked panicked and frantic.

"What is Jasmine going to do? What can Jasmine do? What happened, Nick?" Karis said over and over. I didn't feel ready to talk. As she helped me out of the car, I saw Jasmine at the door.

"Oh my goodness, Nick . . . what's going on?"

I was able to walk, and despite feeling strong, I used Karis as a crutch and leaned on her as she walked me quickly toward Jasmine. "The minions," I managed. "Jasmine, they were everywhere."

Karis stopped walking. She only looked terrified now. "Minions. Jesus, Nick, what the Hell are minions?"

Inside Jasmine's place the smell of incense dominated. Lilac incense. Karis sat on one of Jasmine's sofas while I recanted my rendition of what took place at Gordon Birdie's service while Jasmine paced back and forth.

"They didn't enter you Nick," Jasmine said matter-of-factly. "What you saw was the creatures departing the body. My guess is, just because Marlow was dead, did not mean that the minions were done feasting. During the service, the minions were leaving their host, and you saw what was happening. But they had no reason to enter you."

I swallowed and looked at Karis. I knew she understood enough now to realize Gordon was eaten alive by these creature-ettes. She looked like she might cry. I wanted to reach for her hand, but refrained. I was worried she might pull away. Just because Jasmine said the minions hadn't entered my body did not mean I was not contagious.

"How can you tell?" I asked. "I mean . . . you didn't grab my wrist and do that mumbo jumbo stuff you did in the hospital."

"There was no saving that man, Nick," Jasmine explained. "I saw the minions as we entered the room."

"I thought you didn't . . . "

"But I did, and I don't see them on or around you. Open your mouth," she instructed. So I opened my mouth slowly feeling more self-conscious and vulnerable than I might at a doctor's visit. "Nothing Nick. You're clean."

"And you're sure about this," I continued.

"Sure. Absolutely positive."

"So I have one question. Where did the tiny gnat-bastards go?"

"I wish I could say. Perhaps on to their next victim?"

I let out a loud, long sigh. Relief flooded through my body like a raging river, and I welcomed the charge. It was only when I looked over at Karis did I notice she was crying and trying to hide her face in her hands.

CHAPTER 43

Friday, May 30

Lynn Scannella took me for lunch downtown. We sat outside on the patio. I sipped a beer while she worked on a glass of Chardonnay. While we waited for our food we moved some small talk back and forth across the table. The attorney was upset and I couldn't blame her.

"I couldn't bring myself to go the funeral. I wanted to, though," Lynn said raising the glass to her lips. She closed her eyes while she took a sip.

I was thankful that Lynn did not go to the funeral, it had been bad enough having Karis with me. "I'm sure everyone understands," I said. I had no idea who "everyone" might be. Gordon had no family—and the parishioners at the church wouldn't know Lynn from Karis, for that matter.

Our food came. The waitress set a Rueben with chips in front of me. Lynn had ordered a tuna on toasted white bread, in place of the chips, she had asked for a side salad. Both of our sandwich halves were staked together with toothpicks. Before taking a first bite I said, "You know, I don't expect anything for this job."

"Don't be an asshole, Nick," Lynn said, stabbing at her salad with a fork. "You've put a lot of time and effort into this case. I have no idea where it was all headed," she said just before eating the salad off her fork.

"I'm not so sure I'm going to stop digging, either," I said.

"What?"

"There are still at least one hundred questions in my head . . . and man, Lynn, I haven't got the slightest idea what any of the answers might be," I said.

"Do you know all one hundred questions?"

Sliding a chip into my mouth, I said, "No. And that's part of it. See, I don't think this thing is over."

"What thing?"

"The books, the magic."

"The witchcraft crap."

"It's not crap, Lynn. I don't think it's crap." I was not about to tell her of my experiences with minions. "One person went through a lot of trouble to get their hands on three books. With the three rings now complete, The Talisman is complete. I think who ever has those three books cast a spell over Gordon."

The minute I said it, I wished I could take it back. I couldn't. The words were out. The impact they held over Lynn was obvious when she dropped her sandwich back into the plate. "It sounds bizarre, I know," I said.

"No it doesn't sound bizarre, Nick. It sounds crazy. You just told me that witches killed my client. Witches, Nick. That's not bizarre, that's crazy," she said. She stared at me with the most intense look I had ever seen. It was sexy, though I was trying to concentrate on the topic at hand.

"I don't expect you to understand," I said.

"Good, because I don't."

I thought she might leave. "Let's eat."

She looked uncertain. I touched her hand. "Please. Let's just eat."

To change the subject I reminded Lynn that I could get in touch with the paralegal I knew.

"Yeah that sounds good. Why don't you give me her number and I'll give her a call on Monday."

I continued to eat, but Lynn was not. "Witchcraft," she said. She'd been chewing on that, it appeared.

"I think so. Yes."

"How can that be? I mean really, how can that be? We all know about Salem and all the terrible things that went on there. We know there are witches today . . . but it's a form of religion, isn't it? It's just their own way of worshipping . . . what? I don't even know. The Earth?"

"For the most part, I agree. But there is a difference between white and black magic. When you start getting into black magic your religion is focused on Satan, the way Christianity is focused on God.

"You hear of miracles, right? Where God has done something miraculous? Think about it. Satan wants to prove himself, too. His followers call upon him . . . and he answers. God answers too, just in a different tone of voice most times. But Satan . . . he loves the attention." It was making more sense to me as I explained it to Lynn.

"God and Satan."

"Don't tell me you're an Atheist?"

"No. I'm not. I'm a born and raised Catholic . . . and anything having to do with the devil scares me," Lynn admitted.

"I guess it should. And that's why I can't ignore what's been happening. I have to find out what Philip Edwards plans to do with these books now that he has all three," I said, still noting the odd way Lynn stared at me. "I know how all of this sounds."

"I'm trying Nick. Really I am," Lynn said.

When my cell phone started ringing, I debated not answering it, but Lynn flashed me a look. "Hello," I said. It was Eleanor. She was at the office and was asking if I'd seen the news. "I'm eating lunch. Why? What's going on?"

"You're brother-in-law's on television. They just found another murdered victim," Eleanor said.

That made five in the serial killer's rampage. There was nothing I could do about it. I wondered why Eleanor had called to tell me. So I asked. "Why are you calling to tell me?"

"Because, Nick, where the body was found, at the base of the Genesee River Falls . . . a symbol was painted in blood on the rocks. The camera people for the news weren't allowed to cross the river, so they filmed from a . . . "

"Eleanor, Eleanor, why are you telling me this?"

"Because, Nick, the symbol is the three rings . . . like the ones on the books. One ring looping into the next. All three rings standing on top of one another," she said, finally making her point.

I told Eleanor where I was and asked her to come around and

pick me up.

"What's going on?" Lynn asked, swirling the wine around in her glass.

"Something came up and I'm going to have to run," I said.

"Still has to do with this case?"

"Yes."

"Want me to help?" Lynn asked, sounding slightly less than sincere. I let her off the hook gently.

"I tell you what . . . if I need your help, I'll call," I said.

"Sounds good. And if I come up with anymore work . . . you still want me to call you?" she asked.

"I wish you would," I said, standing up and tossing some bills onto the table.

"This was on me," Lynn said, protesting.

"I know, but I got the tip."

"So now what?" Lynn said.

I shrugged. I had the odd feeling that Lynn expected a kiss or something. I gave her a hug. Her arms wrapped tightly around my neck and back. She whispered in my ear, "You know what? I'm kind of scared still."

"Don't be," I said. She was out of it. She had no reason to be scared. Me? I was scared out of my mind. I could feel my heart beating wildly behind my ribcage. All that seemed to be standing before me was a void, the unknown . . . and I had no choice but to cross into the pagan world of the supernatural. Damn.

"Be careful, Nick. Be careful and tell me when it's over, okay?"

Lynn, the strong attorney, seemed more like a woman at this point than she had in the last few weeks and I liked it. I wasn't being chauvinistic. Women can have careers and do whatever in the Hell they want. It won't change the way I feel about them, except for the fact that I like a woman who is soft, caring, gentle and open. It's this list of characteristics, in my opinion, that make women the stronger gender, the better gender.

I decided to kiss Lynn on her forehead before walking from the patio back into the restaurant and out the front door. I waited for nearly five minutes before Eleanor drove up.

As I opened the door, I heard Eleanor say, "Sorry I took so long. I stopped to pick up Father Paul."

Father Paul said from the back seat, "Hello Nick."

"Father," I said as a greeting. "Eleanor, let's go."

"Aye, aye captain," she said while saluting me, and pulling away from the curb.

CHAPTER 44

"Okay," Eleanor said, "you know where the river goes over the falls there, under those old railroad tracks? Well, there is like a doorway in the face of the cliff . . . across from the R. G. and E. building." RG&E. Rochester Gas and Electric.

"I've seen that tunnel cut in the rock," I said. "I always wondered what was through that passage-way."

"I suppose you're about to find out," Father Paul said. He did not have his seatbelt on. He propped his head on his arms, which were crossed and resting on the front seat. He reminded me of a child. I wanted to tell him to sit back.

"And the rings were painted in blood over the tunnel's entrance?" I asked.

"That's what I saw on the news," Eleanor said.

"You know, I remember Tommy telling me something about each victim's body. It was a marking on them that let the police know a serial killer was at work. Tommy didn't tell me what the marks were. If I had to guess . . . "

"I think you'd be guessing correctly," Eleanor added.

"I wonder if we should have called Jasmine," I said.

"I tried. She wasn't home. I even called the shop—but I got a recorded message. No way to leave a message either."

Eleanor got off the expressway at the State Street exit. "Where should I park?"

"Try the garage," Father Paul said. Since it was lunchtime, there was likely to be vacancies in the multi-tiered lot. Eleanor pulled in, and parked near the top.

The three of us noticed the crowd of people gathered on the High Falls Bridge. "We'll never get close that way," Father Paul commented.

"I want to get down there . . . across the river," I said, thinking out loud.

"How are we supposed to do that?" Eleanor asked without sounding negative. She had her hands on her hips and was looking around for an answer while chewing on her lower lip. "How about the fence?" She asked, pointing at the RG&E fence across from Kodak's visitor's parking lot.

"Genius," I said, clapping her on the back.

"I'm not climbing any fences," Father Paul said, panting. He jogged a few paces behind Eleanor and myself. We all cut through the parking lot and crossed the street. The tall fence looked old and flimsy, but scalable.

"You first, padre," I said, lacing my fingers and cupping my hands together.

"Oh no," Father Paul said, laughing. "Nick, I'm an old and out-of-shape man. I can't climb a ten-foot high fence."

"Father Paul," Eleanor said, feigning shock.

"Don't tease dear. One day you too will be old," Father Paul lectured.

"Never. I won't let it happen."

"Climb, Father. We haven't got time," I urged. I squatted and braced my arms for the weight they were about to endure by resting my forearms on my thighs.

As father Paul placed his foot into my make-shift step he mumbled, "Next time you get yourself into some bizarre and stupid situation, don't expect me to help . . . and climb fences and fight killers and go on witch hunts . . ."

"Concentrate on climbing, old man," I said, boosting him up as high as I could. He was heavy and I suspected my lower back muscles would pay me back for this later. It took every bit of effort to keep Father Paul on the fence while he climbed. Once he slung a leg over the top, I thought we'd be home free. It appeared that the priest was like the proverbial egg at the tip of a pointed rooftop. Which way might he roll?

"Hang on," Eleanor called out. She quickly, but carefully climbed the fence to keep from rattling the links. I watched as the top bar of the fence post bowed. The entire structure did not look stable anymore.

"Eleanor," I said, in a warning tone.

She guided Father Paul's other leg over the post and he managed to climb down.

I looked around. I figured we had to be drawing attention—a man, a woman and a priest climb a fence (sounds like the beginning of a good joke). My stomach was a ball of nerves. I didn't have it in me to laugh.

Eleanor went over the top of the fence headfirst, swinging her legs over and then quickly climbed down. She took Father Paul by the hand and led him over to stand near a bush, more concealed and less obvious than standing and watching as I climbed over the fence.

We moved like snakes, slithering between the two pale and drab and dreary sunflower-yellow buildings. Then we stood at the top of a small loose gravel mountain. "We've got to get down there," I said. The cliff looked steep. The gravel would not be reliable and we were bound to slide down its face.

"Nick," Father Paul gasped.

"Exercise," I said. "It's good for you. Look. Let's all hold hands."

Holding hands turned out to be a bad idea. I needed mine to keep my balance. The face had to be twenty feet high, and it dropped like a ski slope. Twice I actually found myself skiing. When I reached the bottom I looked back up just in time to catch Eleanor as she came sprinting at me.

"Now that was fun," she said, laughing.

"Glad you thought so," I said, pointing halfway up the hill. Father Paul was sitting down in the loose gravel and was slowly scooting down. There was no way to suppress a smile. Here we were a few hundred yards away from Kodak and we didn't have a camera handy to capture this special moment.

"I'm glad the two of you find this so amusing," Father Paul said nearing the bottom of the hill. As he slid his butt kicked up a cloud of dust that followed him. It presented the illusion that Father Paul was moving quickly instead of at a snail's pace.

Eleanor held a hand over her mouth and hid her face in my chest while she giggled. "I'm not laughing," I called out. "Just enjoying the view."

"Yeah, well, you'll get yours, mind you. You will," Father Paul said, slapping his hands on his knees to get the dirt off his palms. I helped him stand up.

"I don't doubt it," I said.

"Good. Because you will," Father Paul said, and walked off toward the river.

Eleanor and I watched him go. We both laughed so hard. Father Paul caught on right away. His hands came around and slapped at the seat of his pants. The black slacks were covered in gray soot-like dirt from sliding down the hill.

CHAPTER 45

From where we stood we could see the ambulance and a few police cars parked along a loose gravel road that led to a small aluminum-sided hut that RG&E owned along the side of the river. I wasn't sure exactly where the road was that led down here, but even if I did, I knew access would be restricted.

On the river was a small outboard motor boat. A police officer played captain and attempted docking while two paramedic passengers waited patiently. Several people on the small pier off the RG&E hut grabbed the ropes the officer threw out, and secured the tiny craft to the pier. The paramedics stood up slowly. Police persons on the pier helped as the paramedics hoisted a full body bag out of the boat.

"Damn," I muttered.

"You're not supposed to be here," a voice said. I turned a little to the left.

I pulled out my wallet and showed the officer my ID.

"You might be a licensed private investigator, but this is a homicide scene and you are not allowed down here," the officer explained.

"I understand what you're saying officer," I said. "But this is a case I'm working on."

"Doesn't matter, see what I'm saying now? Now turn around and go back the way you came," the officer said.

"I should say we will not," Father Paul said, obviously opposed to the idea of climbing a hill that took him five minutes to crawl down.

Eleanor smirked.

"Excuse me, Father?" the officer asked, annoyed.

"I am not going back out the way I came. If you have a road or something, I'll leave that way," he said.

The police officer looked at me. "What's he talking about?"

"Nothing. Look, officer, is Detective Cerio over there," I asked.

"He is."

"Can you just tell him I'm here?"

The officer shook his head, thinking. He wouldn't want to interrupt the investigating detective if he didn't have to. I had told the officer I was working on the case, so he wouldn't want to obstruct my involvement if Cerio was expecting me, a tough dilemma for a not-too-bright cop.

"Just hold on here a minute, all right?" the officer said.

"Whatever you say," I said.

He took a few steps away and turned his back to us. His radio was on the shoulder of his uniform. He craned his neck and talked into the mouthpiece. When he came back, he shrugged. "Sorry Mr. Tartaglia. The Detective said to send you down."

I looked over at the hut. Tommy was standing out on the pier looking at us. I waved. Tommy did not wave back, but instead balled his hands into fists and planted them squarely on his hips. "He in a good mood?" I asked as we all began to walk over toward the hut.

"You kiddin' me, or what, pal?" the officer asked. "We been bustin' our asses for weeks. Wife and kids don't know who I am when I come home at night . . . and that's if I come home at night. What's the detective got to be in a good mood about, huh? What's any of us got to be in a good mood about?"

"I meant because his brother-in-law was here to see him," I said.

"Oh man, I should have recognized the name. Tartaglia," the officer said. "You're the Nicholas Tartaglia?"

"The one and only," I said. "The one and only."

***

Tommy and I shook hands, but Tommy never stopped looking at

Father Paul and Eleanor. "You remember Father Paul?" I asked. I had to talk loudly. The din of the river felt deafening.

As they all shook hands, Tommy said, "St. Anthony's Church. How have you been, father?"

"Busy," the priest said. "We're rebuilding the church. It should look wonderful when it's done."

"Are you going to do like the rest of the churches and make it modern and contemporary looking?" Tommy asked.

"It will not resemble the church it once was, but for obvious reasons. No. We're going to keep it simple. I'm not real happy with the way the churches look nowadays. Gaudy, if you ask me. A church is supposed to be simple. It's not supposed to spend a million dollars renovating. That money spent is money that should be used helping the community, the poor and the hungry. I must add, however, we will be installing central air," Father Paul said with a smile.

"And you," the detective said staring at Eleanor. "I know I've seen you before, but I can't place it. We have met, right?"

"I used to go by the name Scar. I was at St. Anthony's the night it burned down," Eleanor said. "You can call me Eleanor," she said.

"Scar." Tommy smiled. "Of course. Well, Eleanor, it's nice to see you again." With the pleasantries over, Tommy turned and wrapped his arm around my shoulder. "Will you excuse us for a moment?"

Tommy led me closer to the hut. "What the Hell are you doing here? You might not get it, Nick, this might not be sinking in, Nick, but I'm in the middle of investigating a murder. The city of Rochester has a sadistic serial killer on the loose and you bring your friends from school out to the scene of a crime on a field trip . . . "

"That's not how it is," I said.

"Oh? Then how is it, Nick? Enlighten me."

"You know, my sister's not very happy," I said.

He removed his arm and turned away as if I'd pushed him. "Nick, I don't have time for this. I love your sister, you know that . . . and she should know that. I'm not out here screwing around and having fun. Damn it! Doesn't anyone understand what I'm doing? Am I the only one with any clue about what's going on?"

"Actually, I have a clue, too," I said in a whisper.

"What?"

"I think I can help," I said, pointing across the river. I felt as if we were screaming at each other, but it was necessary to talk this loud. I could not believe just how loud raging water could be. It was loud. And there was always the possibility that Tommy just might be screaming at me.

"I don't have time for this," Detective Cerio said as he stared at the paramedics wheeling the gurney toward us. The back doors on the ambulance were open. The body bag was zipped up. The victim didn't need paramedics or an ambulance. "Where's the coroner?" Tommy suddenly shouted. He stopped the paramedics, and asked one of them again where the coroner was.

"He said he was done with the body and that we could take her to the morgue," was the paramedic's reply.

Tommy accepted the answer with a bobbing head.

"The circles in blood on the rocks," I said. "I know what they mean."

Tommy stared at me. "You do? How?"

"Can we go?" the other paramedic asked.

"One minute," Tommy instructed. He looked at me. "Same mark is on the bodies you know."

"I figured as much," I said. "I remember you saying that the bodies were all marked, that's how you knew you had a serial killer to contend with."

"Hearts are missing from the bodies, too."

"I didn't know that," I said.

"We're keeping those little tidbits silent. We get a hundred phone calls a day from loonies confessing to the killings. But none of them know about the hearts, or these marks," Tommy said and stood next to the gurney as he unzipped the bag.

Something punched me in the stomach and I could not breathe. Everything went dark, but I hadn't passed out. I had shut my eyes tightly. I felt the color drain from my face like a curtain being lowered.

"Nick?" Tommy said.

I thought about what I had seen. The girl was naked and three circular incisions had been made into her flesh. The first was where the left breast would have been. The breast and the heart were missing. The second and third incisions were just below each other, and slightly looped into one another.

I had one hope—one prayer to make before I opened my eyes again.

I hoped and prayed Jasmine was already dead when the killer had done this to her.

CHAPTER 46

Eleanor and Father Paul stood with me downstream from the falls. They both spent thirty minutes trying to console me. I let them, but I wasn't really listening, and once they caught on, they stopped trying and respected my need for silence.

My heart felt crushed, as if a gorilla had ripped it out from between my ribs and squashed it in his hand. Crushed. It seemed trite to say that my mind worked on a plan for revenge, but it was. Revenge, vengeance—it didn't matter at this point. I felt angry and solace might only be achievable after I destroyed the sick bastard responsible for Jasmine's death.

After most everyone had left the scene, Tommy strolled over. He had his hands in his pockets. He looked at the sky. "Might rain some more," he said.

No one commented. Father Paul and Eleanor walked away to give the detective and myself some privacy.

"You all right," Tommy asked. "I never thought in a million years that you might know the young lady."

I nodded. I didn't trust myself to speak. A lump sat in my throat.

"You know, but we didn't know who she was—don't know who she is. There was no ID on her. Maybe when you feel better, you know, you can tell me some things about her?"

Tommy wanted a name, so I gave it to him. "Not now," he said. "Later."

"Was she dead when that was done to her?" I asked. When

Tommy looked away without replying, I knew the answer. "Ah, Jesus," I said.

He put his hand on my shoulder. "You said you knew about the marks, the rings, what about them?"

The dark sky seemed to get much, much darker. I felt a chill race down my spine. I felt as if I was being watched, millions of eyes from nowhere in particular staring at me. "Jasmine was the one who told me about the rings and what they meant," I said.

"Was she involved, do you think? Did she know the killer?"

"She wasn't involved. She was working with me. It's a long story, Tommy," I said. I thought I knew who the killer was. No. I did know. I also knew I should share the information with Tommy. The killer could be caught and the city's nightmare over. Where would my vengeance fall into that plan? How would I get my revenge? "Can I come down to your office tomorrow . . . I'm not feeling right?"

"First thing tomorrow?" Tommy said. He looked disappointed.

"I think we can figure this out, Tommy, I do . . . but you have to do something for me," I said.

"What?"

"It's still pretty early, right? Go home. Go and be with your wife and kid. They need you," I said. "Tomorrow morning I'll give you enough information to catch the killer."

"You know who the killer is," Tommy asked.

"No," I lied. "But if we put our facts together, I think we'll be able to figure it out. This is like a life-sized version of the board game Clue. Together we'll be unstoppable," I said.

CHAPTER 47

I killed time downtown, wandering aimlessly up and down State Street after forcing Eleanor to take Father Paul home. I stopped at a small how-can-it-survive-downtown hardware store and bought a canvas bag, a pair of chain cutters, a flashlight with batteries, and extra batteries. I also picked out a pair of leather garden gloves and a single-use camera that was located near the register, on the impulse rack.

The days kept getting longer as summer continued to get closer. By nine-thirty it was dark, but I waited another hour before walking back toward the river. Earlier the police escorted us up a service road and out onto the city streets. The fence blocking the service road had been well intact, and laced with barbed wire along the top. I decided to jump the other fence again. It worked wonderfully the first time, so I had no reason to think it wouldn't work again.

I found the descent much easier this time, mainly because I didn't have the priest around to slow me down. Except for the crunching sound my shoes made on the loose gravel, I was quiet as a mouse—and it didn't matter because the roar of the river appeared even louder at nighttime.

I stayed along the wall of the bank and moved swiftly toward the hut. I did not dare use the flashlight. RG&E had, for the most part, their facility well lit, and the hut was lit.

The sight where Jasmine's body had been found was inside the tunnel across the river. I needed to see the place where Jasmine was

251

killed—or where she was dropped off after being brutally murdered.

Jasmine had been my friend. PI or not I'd be going across that river to see if there was anything left to see. I was sure the police would have collected it all. It didn't matter. I wanted to see the spot. I wanted to look around for myself. My mind was different than other peoples' minds, which I considered good. The more people looking at a scene, each from a unique perspective, the better. Throw all the ideas on the table, and watch a picture emerge.

When I reached the hut I saw that the boat was docked inside it, as I imagined it would be. The door was secured with a chain. I put on the gloves, stuck the camera in my front pocket and pulled the cutters out of the bag to cut a link. The chain clattered to the floor. I pushed open the door and walked carefully to the boat. Once inside, I untied it from the dock and pushed off on the dock to get the boat out of the hut.

The mighty river looked big, it looked strong, it raged and was loud. I never expected it to sweep the boat so quickly downstream. I pulled on the motor cord, over and over until it finally kicked on. I steered the boat back up the river. In order to get from the west to the east side, I needed to steer directly into the falls. The current then fought the direction enough so that I went from west to east, instead of south and directly into the waterfall. I was soaked immediately. The spray and mist was all consuming, raining on me as if I was in a shower. The water felt freezing.

I rode the boat right up onto the small, rocky shore. There was no dock on this side. In fact, the water levels often rose over this bit of land.

It was far too dark to see the red rings painted in blood above this tunnel entrance. (The more I looked at it now, the more I thought it resembled a cave entrance). I clicked on the flashlight and aimed the beam into the heart of the cave. The walls looked damp and wet, while parts dripped water like tears down a cheek.

I was maybe twenty yards into the cave when immediately the passageway split into different paths. I stayed straight on, figuring the less turns I made, the less likely it would be to become lost.

The darkness felt overwhelming. The flashlight beam penetrated the darkness to a point . . . but only so many feet in front of me. When I looked back, nothing but complete darkness, like a wall, stood behind me. I aimed the beam of light back the way I'd come, and could not see the exiting mouth of the cave.

I pressed on and stopped when I heard the moaning.

My imagination, wild and crazy, was teasing me. Perhaps it did not know that I was not in the mood to be teased. Just the thought of being teased made my heart rate accelerate. I knew I was sweating, despite being wet. I stood absolutely still and switched off the flashlight. Waiting for nearly three minutes, I was certain I'd not hear the moaning sounds again. As I switched back on the flashlight, the beam caught the shadowy-tail end of a white gown as someone ten—maybe fifteen feet away rounded a corner.

Then I heard the moaning again. It echoed and reverberated off the wet stone walls. I couldn't breathe and felt my breath catch in my throat. Switching off the flashlight, I opted for darkness and silence as I slowly started to back away. I headed back toward the mouth of the cave. Anticipation and intense anxiety racked my body and my muscles. My knees shook.

Whoever was in here knew their way around the cave. The darkness did not bother them. Obviously. I was an intruder. The person in the cave with me might be the serial killer. All I wanted now was out.

Who's lair had I entered?

Who's there, I wanted to call out. That would be dumb. It was a dumb move in the movies, it would be a dumb move in a book, and it's a dumb move now. Did it matter who was in the cave with me?

Another moan came and echoed to my left. I felt something strike my head. I heard it hit the floor. It didn't hurt as much as scare the Hell out of me and it's one thing to be angry at someone for entering your home—even if you live in a cave at the mouth of the Genesee River—but it is another thing all together to moan. What the Hell is with the moaning? I felt freaked out.

Feeling like screaming, feeling like I should turn and run and jump into the river, I switched on the flashlight. As fast as I could I swept the area with the beam. At the very last trace of light, eight feet away, I saw a person's shadow. Then I heard it. "Who's there?"

It was me asking the question. I had gone ahead and done it, asked the dumb question. The shadow moved so I could no longer see it. "I saw you, man," I said. I had said man, but I was certain the person hiding down one of the passageways was a woman in a white gown. I knew nothing else. I did not see hair color, or body type. All I had seen was a shadow and a gown. A white gown?

"I'm not going to hurt you," I called out. I kneeled down slowly. I kept my eyes forward, trying to keep the beam from wavering. I felt blindly around the ground for whatever it was that had struck me in the head.

Before I found anything, I stopped moving when the laugh started. I pictured a monster-woman with a deep throaty voice. She was back there laughing at me. What had I said that could have been so funny?

I'd only told her that I wasn't going to hurt her.

Swallowing, I felt more quickly around for some unknown object.

I looked down at the ground, but the point was useless. It was too dark. I lowered the flashlight some to give me more light and there it was. It was a five-pointed star inside a circle. The charm was on a black leather shoelace, as if to be warn like a necklace. As I picked it up, I raised the flashlight beam and followed its light.

"Shit!"

She was standing right there, not four feet away.

Her face was completely hidden under long brown curly hair covering her features.

She was in a gown. A white lacy gown—and she was wet, too. The gown clung to her body, was completely see through and revealing an older, though oddly erotic shape. She laughed, throwing her head back. When she was done laughing, despite the hair over her eyes, I knew she was staring at me.

I could see her breath. She exhaled like a taunted bull ready to charge, and through a slight part in her hair, I saw an ice blue eye . . . and I had been right. She was staring at me. Intense. Ice blue. Mad—mad like crazy, not so much angry.

Without warning she howled and her hands flew out straight—arms extended, fingers wiggling slowly, reaching for me.

I knew where this was going. When she ran at me full speed, I was already standing up and turning, trying to escape.

The sound of her feet pounding on the rocks behind me told me she was almost on me. I was unsure of the dark corridor. If I hit a rock, or tripped, she'd be on me, but if I slowed down, she'd get me for sure.

The sound of the river was like a refuge.

Like a madman I charged toward the water as fast as I could. Before my eyes could adjust to any sense of light, I felt the ground disappear beneath my feet. I felt my body receive a wild shock as the frigid Genesse River water swallowed me up whole.

When I was able to swim back to the surface, I stared at the cave and waited to see the crazy woman again. She did not emerge and stand at the mouth of the cave. But I knew she was just in the shadows watching me, moaning perhaps, or even laughing, but definitely watching.

It had to be all the rain coupled with the early-April melted snow that made the river water so cold, so frigid, so wild, so rough. The current, amazingly strong, kept me moving swiftly east and north toward Lake Ontario—though I was miles away from the lake. I shrugged out of my coat as quickly as possible, and kicked off my shoes under the water. The extra weight was amazingly heavy and I knew it would pull me under.

I feared hypothermia, and knew it could set in immediately. I needed to get out of the water before I drowned.

I kicked and used my arms, but until the rapids slowed, the effort proved useless, so I concentrated on keeping from going under, trying to tell myself I was warm. My leg slammed into a rock, though it didn't hurt too terribly, the unexpected jar caught me off guard and I swallowed a large mouthful of the murky, brown water.

Being geographically challenged, I was not even familiar enough with the river's flow to know what I might expect ahead. I did know I could not float all night long until the current stopped. I had to think I'd get tired sooner or later, and for all I know there are more waterfalls ahead.

Before passing completely by the RG&E building along the river, I managed to swim to the left and with the current and made it to the shore swiftly.

I had the charm in my hand still. Lying on my back, I put it in my pocket. Shivering, my teeth chattered uncontrollably. I could not feel my fingers, or feet. My ears burned, my chin even hurt.

I needed to get away from here. Though I had been wearing

gloves when I borrowed the utility company's boat, it wasn't going to take a homicide detective long to figure where I had been . . .

CHAPTER 48

Saturday, May 31

When I got home last night, I ignored the light flashing on my answering machine and took a fast, cleansing shower, before going directly to bed. This morning when the doorbell started ringing I almost gave it the same consideration as the telephone. It became clear after ten minutes that whoever was at the door was not going to go away until I told them to and maybe broke their little door ringing finger while at it.

Annoyance forced me out of bed, while vanity made me reach for my turquoise and white striped Miami Dolphins bathrobe, with a small emblem, like a crest, on the left side. I wasn't about to answer the door in my plaid boxer shorts.

Pulling open my front door, ready to shout, I contained myself, not because of my own self control, but because Karis was already yelling at me.

"Where have you been?" She asked. She stormed by me into my house, and went right to the answering machine. "See this light flashing? Means someone called you and left a message. I called you, Nick. I called you almost ten times last night before I gave up. I didn't go to sleep though. I couldn't sleep. Know why, Nick, huh? Know why? Because I knew as soon as you got in you'd hear your messages and call me back. I figured if I left any more messages, you'd think I was crazy," she said with a wicked laugh.

"As opposed to now?" I said with a please-forgive-me-smile.

"Not now, Nicholas. Now I'm angry. Eleanor came by the office and told me about what happened. She told me about Jasmine," Karis said. She held a wrist up to her lips and fought back crying. "I was so worried about you."

My cue. I hugged her. She held me tight, squeezing like a bear. "What's going on here, Nick? This whole thing is scaring me."

Me too. "Nothing," I said.

Karis pulled out of the hug and looked angry again. "Nothing? Do I look stupid?"

I tried to hug her again. She took a step back. "You don't look stupid," I said when I realized she wanted an answer.

"Then where the Hell do you come up with nothing? That was the dumbest thing you've ever said."

I sat down on the sofa, resting my elbows on my thighs near my knees. I intertwined my fingers, as if in prayer and stared at the floor. "Karis, I have no clue what's going on, but I knew this mess would not be over just Gordon Birdie died." I told her my theory—how Philip Edwards had the three books, how he had cast an evil spell over Gordon. Edwards had his revenge. He had avenged the death of his son. By all rights that means the nightmare should have ended.

Karis sat down in my recliner. "Maybe the books, once you use them, won't let you stop?"

"Could be. It could be some kind of mystic power. I don't know. I mean . . .makes no sense. I'm going to tell you, I'm in the middle of all of this and I don't believe it myself. Witches and evil spells? Come on. I'm a licensed private investigator. I do research, find missing persons, catch deadbeat parents who aren't paying child support. I follow people and catch them cheating on their spouse," I said. I had no intention of telling Karis about being at the river. She didn't need to know about me crossing it. There was no way I planned to tell her about being chased by a madwoman in the cave. At this point, it was easiest to keep silent. Mum's the word.

"Have you told the police about this?" Karis asked.

"I'm going down today to talk with Tommy," I said. "Want coffee?"

"I'll make it, you go get showered, I'll drive you down to the police station. Not my idea on how to spend a Saturday, but at least we'll be together." Karis came over and kissed me on the forehead. "Now go shower."

I watched her go into the kitchen. I picked up the telephone and called Eleanor. She answered on the seventh ring. "I wake you?"

"No," Eleanor said, "I was just playing a game of kill-whoever-calls-me-before-eight-in-the-morning!"

"You winning?"

"I will be," she said, yawning. "Nick, what's up?"

"I want you to shadow someone. All day."

"Lydia again?"

Good point. "No. I want you on Philip Edwards. If he's this serial killer . . ."

"He is?" She no longer sounded tired.

"I'm not positive, but I strongly suspect . . ."

"And you want me to shadow the serial killer, wild. Think I would have gained this kind of experience working as a security guard at Kodak for the summer? Not!"

And it hit me. "No Eleanor. I don't want you to shadow him."

"Huh? What are you talking about?"

"Let's forget I called . . . we'll talk later."

"Nick . . .I know what's going on," Eleanor said. "You don't have to worry about me."

"It's not just you. Here I am, jeopardizing everyone, and for what? A job? Does that make sense?"

"Nick, what you are doing far exceeds work in the traditional sense. Let me put it to you this way. I'm a big girl, and I'm in. If you tell me not to follow Edwards, guess what? I'm still going to follow him. Consider me his shadow."

"Eleanor . . . "

"No. No, Eleanor. Listen Nick, I'm with you. And though I can't speak for Karis, I'll bet she's with you too. I know Father Paul backs you. We all seem to be a part of something, Nick. Don't you feel it?"

I didn't feel it, but I got the point. Something else came to me. "Besides, Edwards won't be interested in Lydia and her big brother will be around more than likely. You'll be keeping her busy. Still, you have to promise you'll back out anytime you want. Got it?"

"I promise."

"Eleanor . . . listen," I said, giving her the run down. "And you

259

have my cell phone and pager number, right?"

"Got 'em."

"Good. Get dressed and get to work."

"Yes, boss," Eleanor said and hung up.

I took a shower, dressed and had a wonderful home cooked breakfast with Karis—who didn't seem angry with me anymore.

CHAPTER 49

Homicide Detective, Thomas Cerio—or for me, brother-in-law Tommy, had an interrogation room signed out and was ready and waiting for me as Karis and I entered the precinct. I could tell he was relieved to see me, sure I wouldn't show. I cupped my hand and patted his cheek. "O'Ye of little faith."

"Cut the crap," Tommy said, slapping my hand off his face. "Karis, how are you?"

"I'm okay Tommy. How's the baby?"

"Getting bigger every time I see her," the detective said, and I chose to let the comment slide without pointing blame. "Coffee before we get started?"

Karis said no. "I could use another cup," I said.

Tommy and I sat at the table with our coffee, and Karis sat by me keeping her hands folded in her lap. The room was not much different than the one I visited Gordon Birdie at when he was locked up. The walls were a soft blue. Calm, trusting colors. How nice.

I wondered how long it would be before Tommy brought up my little rendezvous at the cave. When he brought it up I knew Karis would get angry all over again because I didn't tell her about my little excursion.

"Okay, Nick. Let's talk. What have you got?"

I told him more about the job Lynn Scannella had hired me to do. "And it turns out that maybe Gordon Birdie and his partner there, the one who died, might not have been guilty as actual thieves."

"They broke into the home of Philip Edwards, right? They tried to blow apart a safe that was concealed in the Edwards' basement, okay? The son comes home early and tries to stop them . . . to protect his parents' home, with me so far? There is a gunfight. One of the thieves and Philip Edwards, Jr. die," Tommy said, throwing heavy, heavy emphasis on thieves. "So tell me again how they might not have been actually guilty?"

"You're missing the point, they . . ."

"Forget the point. We're not hear to argue the innocence or guilty verdict of two dead thieves," Tommy said.

Guilty until proven innocent. Maybe all police officers felt that way. I guess they might have to. They catch bag guys to have them put away, but the system—being fair like it is, truthful, and honest—turns the deemed 'innocent' ones back out onto the street. Hmm. Curious. "Legally they might be guilty, but morally . . ."

"Get to the point . . . the symbol," Tommy said, nearly drooling with anticipation.

I told my rendition of events, careful to include as much as possible about Jasmine. I did not want her death overlooked. She was an integral part of the story—and to its eventual conclusion. Without her we'd never have made it this far.

"And you don't think somehow she was involved?" Tommy asked.

"No. Not at all."

"Why?"

"Why? I just told you why. She was right there helping, all the time helping," I said.

"But she fled to Florida, right?"

"She was scared," I said.

"Scared, maybe, or she was hiding out?"

"What the Hell does that mean, hiding out?"

"You know, whoever she's working with tells her to take off for a few days, let things blow over."

I laughed.

"It could happen that way," Tommy said.

"It didn't."

"And you know this, how?"

"Because I knew Jasmine," I said. I was immediately offended.

"Don't try to make her out as bad."

"Don't you find it odd that the first magical bookstore you happen upon, you find exactly what you're looking for? And isn't it even more odd how Jasmine is then a part of this mysterious plot? Isn't it a little unrealistic to accept, or to expect me to accept that there are witches with magical powers casting spells?" Tommy asked.

"Oh my, God!" I exclaimed.

"What?" Tommy asked.

I stood up and walked over to the two-way mirror and leaned my back against it, crossing my arms over my chest. "You're actually questioning me." I banged my elbow into the glass. It wiggled and vibrated. I went forward and leaned on the table. "You bastard."

"Nick . . . "

"Go to Hell, Tommy. I was here to help you anyway. I was going to tell you everything I knew. Forget that we're family, I thought we were friends," I said.

"Nicholas . . . "

"Screw that, detective. Screw you, and screw this. This interrogation is over," I said, adding heavy, heavy emphasis on the word interrogation.

"I'm just trying to do everything by the book . . . I'm looking for answers and this is a serious, sick case!" Tommy said, getting to his feet. He slammed both palms onto the table. "And damn it, Nick, you can't just leave."

"Bullshit. By the book? If I'd a known this had been an interrogation I'd have asked to bring my lawyer down. You didn't give me that option," I said. I was winging it. Maybe he could stop me from leaving. I was betting he wouldn't.

"A lawyer? Nick, why would you need a lawyer if we're just talking?"

I pointed to the mirror. "Why do you need the assholes behind the glass?"

I opened the door. Karis was by my side.

"How about stomping through a murder scene, Nick. I can have charges made," Tommy threatened. It came out sounding lame and hollow.

"You pulled your men out. There was no police tape up," I said.

"It was on the other side of the river."

"You got nothing."

"Nick," Tommy said, pleading.

I took Karis by the hand and we left the police station.

When we walked outside I paid no attention to the rain. It seemed to bother Karis. She huddled close, held onto my arm and held her purse over her head. I wanted to punch something. "Is he nuts? Was that me? That was him, right? It sure as Hell wasn't me. Was it?"

"Can we get to the car first?" Karis asked. She ran ahead. I stopped and turned around. From the car I heard Karis yelling for me, her voice and the sound of the rain changed as the door behind me closed and I was back in the police station. Telephones rang and people were talking, but most of the people were looking at me. I stood in the lobby, soaking wet.

Tommy saw me and came over. "No umbrella?"

"Is that all you have to say?"

"Look, I'm sorry, all right? Maybe you're right and I shouldn't have had the other guys in that room. I'm not the boss here. I don't call the shots. Don't forget Delski," Tommy said, motioning over his shoulder.

"Delski was in the room?"

Tommy crossed his arms and nodded.

"So I made you look pretty bad in front of the boss?"

"Like a complete asshole."

"Good." I turned around to leave, but stopped when Tommy called my name.

"Last night, your sister and I did a lot of talking and things feel better all ready," he said.

"Good," I said, and couldn't help but fumble a small smile. "Good."

CHAPTER 50

Karis wanted to go back to her house, for us to spend the day together lounging. Jasmine's body was being flown down to Florida this afternoon. I hated missing the funeral, but at the same time felt thankful to be spared the obligation of attending. I had Eleanor working, shadowing Philip Edwards. How could I spend the day lounging when so much was happening?

"I want to swing by the office," I said. "I want to check some things on the computer. A while back I posted a question on a message board and book-marked some web sites . . . but never got around to seeing if anything came of it. Last time I'd checked, it was filled with replies from Stephen King and Peter Straub fans. Still, I think I should see if anything new is posted."

"What more do you need to know?"

"I just want to browse," I said. "You never know."

"I have my lap top in the trunk. I guess we could kill a little time at the office. But, Nick, it's Saturday, and if you think I'm spending my weekend fiddling around at the office, you're as crazy as your brother-in-law," Karis said.

"We'll do a little work and then go out for lunch and go back to your place," I said.

"Pick up a movie, or something?"

"I'll even let you choose the title," I added.

When we entered the building, I told Karis to go on up. "I'll be there in a second, I just want to have a word with Frieda."

Karis opened the door and went up the stairs and I entered Reliquus. It was something Tommy had said to me during the interrogation. He thought it odd that the first bookstore I visit happens to include and involve Jasmine and her copy of a magical book. What I had not included in the story I told to Tommy was that I stopped first to see Frieda VanValkenschmidt. Still, Frieda had pointed me directly at Jasmine and her store. Why? How?

I had a hunch. It felt strong, but it was still just a hunch.

"Be right with you," Frieda called out when she heard me enter the store.

"Take your time," I said.

"Hello, Nicholas," Frieda said, parting beads and stepping out of the back room.

I held up the charm that had been thrown at me in the cave. There was a look on her face. She knew something. I called her on it. "What's going on?"

"Jasmine's dead, isn't she?"

"How could you know that? The police haven't released a name to the newspapers yet. Frieda . . . how could you know that?" I asked.

"I felt it, yesterday. Something felt wrong in me all day long. Now, seeing you here, seeing you holding that, I just know in my heart what must have happened."

She didn't know the half of it. "You're one, too. Aren't you?"

"Yes," Frieda said. "I don't know why I keep it a secret. I am proud . . . or should be more proud of my beliefs. The world, Nicholas, it is not as understanding as you might think. People don't think of witches as being people. They perceive us as green-skinned, spell-casting, broom-flying demons." She laughed. She was nervous. Nothing about what she had just stated was funny.

"And you knew Jasmine?"

"I gave her that," Frieda said, pointing at the charm in my hand. "It was a gift. She was like a daughter. Her brother's a good kid, too. But the rest of her family was, how might you say, a little off."

"I've had the pleasure," I said.

"Then you know."

"Wish I didn't though," I said.

Frieda laughed a good laugh. "You know, all right."

"And what, so you turned Jasmine onto witchcraft?"

"Oh no, sweetie. It's the other way around. I stumbled across her store and the minute I stepped inside her shop I knew something. I felt something inside me. I had been touched. Jasmine helped explain aspects of witchcraft to me. She helped me explore my new religion and faith and I found the journey to be utterly amazing and mystical." Frieda closed her eyes. "And satisfying."

"I'm sorry for getting Jasmine involved," I said.

Frieda fought back crying, blinked away unshed tears. "It's not your fault. Let's go in back," she said.

I followed behind her counter and through the beads. Unlike Jasmine's bookstore, Frieda's back room resembled a traveling carnival's gypsy car. The walls had been painted black. Glowing stars and moons and planets had been affixed to the ceiling, a black light shinning on them. Black drapes hung, sectioning the room into quarters, or fifths, or more. I felt as if I just entered a dark maze. The room felt extremely bleak, except for the glowing astrology on the ceiling.

And then I realized I had no idea where Frieda was.

I stopped walking and thought of last night and the crazy woman in the cave. It could have been . . . "Frieda?" No reply.

The woman at the cave had been dressed in long white gown, had been barefoot and had scared the Hell of me. "Frieda!"

Both Crazy Woman and Frieda had long hair. "Frieda . . . this isn't funny!"

"What's not funny?" Frieda asked, appearing suddenly behind me.

I jumped. Felt my heart stop, and every muscle in my body tense.

Brown eyes. Frieda had brown eyes, not frigid ice blue. "Where'd you go?"

"Right here. I thought you were right behind me," Frieda said.

"Sorry. It was dark."

She led me behind the black curtain. Pay no attention to the man behind the curtain. Magic. Magic. Magician. Slight of hand.

On a small desk was a small desk lamp. We were standing in the center of a tiny library with books on shelves in cases. "I don't know much about The Talisman. That's the truth. When you brought it up that first time, I knew what you were talking about. I was at Jasmine's shop the day that book was found in her wall."

I watched Frieda proudly scan the titles in her collection as she talked.

"We were doing some renovating, painting. When we found the book, I reminded her about the evil of black magic. I mean, she didn't need me to remind her, she is the one who taught me. When she was holding that book, though, I thought I had better say something. A look changed in her expression, you know. The book has powers and I knew it immediately. But seeing Jasmine's eyes darken while she held the book . . . that was a little much," Frieda said.

"In a way, that's why I'm here," I said.

"I figured you had a question, and I'll do my best."

"It's all I can ask. Frieda, in your opinion, let's say someone uses a book of evil to cast a magic spell, all right? Then what?"

"What do you mean, then what?"

"Here's what I'm thinking. Someone kills your son, and having the bastard responsible going to jail just isn't enough punishment in the parents' eyes. So this parent casts a spell so the murderer suffers a long and torturous death, okay?" I asked.

"I'm with you, so far."

"Okay, so after the murderer dies . . . can the witch, or warlock, or whoever it was that cast this spell, just stop? I mean, can he put The Talisman away and not use it again?"

"I see what you're asking. You want to know if the book will have a hold over its user? Will the book begin to control the spell-caster and keep them active?" Frieda asked.

Clapping my hands together I said, "Exactly. Once you use it, the book forces, or beckons you to use it again." In for a pinch, in for a pound. Witches and warlocks and beckoning books.

"I really don't know," Frieda said, thoughtfully. "It's possible and sounds likely, but Nicholas, I can't tell you for sure one way or the other. It could depend on the book. The Talisman, being what it is . . . with all of its powers . . . very possible that it will control and overtake the spell-caster."

"Likely, but you're not sure?"

"Not positive, no," Frieda said. "Let me ask you a question. You think that someone used the evil power of the books and cast a spell already?"

"I am almost one hundred percent positive that that has happened, yes."

"And you think that the person who cast this spell would have no reason to continue using the books for the purpose of evil since they already achieved their purpose . . . revenge achieved?"

"Exactly," I said.

"Nick . . . in your life has only one person ever done anything wrong to you?"

The impact of her question was immediate. I set the charm down on the bookcase. "You hang onto this," I said.

Like a snake, Frieda's hand snatched up the five-pointed star enclosed in a circle and held it cupped close to her heart. The tears she'd been strong enough to blink away returned, and this time Frieda was defenseless against them. I touched her shoulder tenderly, and stared at the woman for a while. I missed Jasmine probably a fraction of how this woman felt, and yet my heart ached as if a dull knife were slicing through it.

CHAPTER 51

"Nick. Nick, wake up," I heard in my ear. Though I knew the voice was talking, it felt and sounded more like a fly buzzing around my head, so I tried to shoe away the annoying insect.

"Nick, someone's knocking on the door," Karis said.

I sat up. "What time is it?"

"Three in the morning, and someone is at my door," Karis said again.

I rubbed my face and got up. It took a moment for me to adjust. This was Karis' house, not mine. Furniture was arranged differently, and I didn't want, or need, to stub my toe.

As I walked down the hallway, Karis at my back trailing along, I heard the knock. Loud, hard knocks. I took my gun out of the shoulder holster, slung over the kitchen chair and yelled, "Coming." I looked at Karis, "Stay here."

Karis' door had a pane of clear glass. A flowery wreath hung over it. I parted it and looked out. Tommy Cerio stared at me with an agitated smile.

Opening the door I had to look a site. Tommy and his partner, Deanna, stood on Karis' front steps, snickering. I was in boxers holding a Glock. Some image, but it was three in the morning, so I had every right to be dressed this way.

"Nice shorts," Deanna said as I pushed open the screen door and allowed the officers into my girlfriend's house. I turned around, but Karis had disappeared. I'd bet my boxers she was getting dressed.

Great, I'd be the only person in the room standing around in his underwear.

"Glad you like them, Dee," I said. "Tommy what's up? What are you doing out so late. Thought you said you'd worked some things out around spending more time at home?"

Tommy shrugged. "Some things can't be helped."

"Heard you pissed of Chief Delski today," Deanna said. "Sorry I missed it."

"Maybe Tommy filmed it?" I said.

"Look," Tommy interjected, "something's happened."

"Another body?" I asked.

"Kind of," Deanna said.

Karis entered the room. She wore jeans and her nightshirt. She handed me my jeans and a shirt. While I dressed, I asked, "What do you mean . . . kind of?"

"No one new has been murdered, no new bodies found, anyway," Tommy said.

"But, a body has turned up missing," Deanna finished.

I could only think about Jasmine. Her body was going to be shipped to Florida. "Jasmine's body is missing?"

"No. The casket was shipped in the air to Florida," Tommy said.

"So who?"

"Philip Edwards, Jr.," Deanna said, delivering the punch line.

"Get the Hell out," I said. "What, you mean his grave was dug up?"

"No. Junior was in the mausoleum," Tommy said. "Only, the mausoleum was private . . . restricted vacancies for the Edwards family members."

I felt a tingle as if a cold wet worm were wiggling its way down my spine.

"So why are you here . . . want to search the house, detective?" I asked sarcastically.

"Quit the crap, Nick. Believe it or not, I think you know a bit more about what might be going on and . . . "

"And?" I wanted to hear it.

"And," Tommy said. "And I need your help."

I smiled. Three in the morning or not, I felt rejuvenated. "Both of you?" I swiveled my pointing finger from Tommy to Deanna to

Tommy to Deanna.

"Both of us," Deanna said. "Please be serious. You already know we're not getting much sleep here."

"All right. What have you got planned?" I asked.

"That's why we're here to see you. We have no idea what might be going on. None."

Trouble was stirring. It felt like something big might be about to happen. I wanted to work with the police, and help as much as I could, but I did not want them hanging around like shadows.

Deanna told me a crow bar had been used. The marble door had been chipped and shattered and smashed. The drawer was open when the police arrived. The entire theft could not have taken more than forty-five minutes. There was an alarm system on the mausoleum, but if activated, it reported to the cemetery office first where the night security would check out the situation. Apparently the guard on duty was not at his post when the alarm signaled. "He'd, allegedly, been on a road patrol securing the grounds. When he got back to his post, he saw the alarm, went to the mausoleum to investigate and then immediately contacted the police," she concluded.

"How'd he get in the gate, or out it? Aren't those things locked?"

"They are," Tommy said. "We think the person just jumped the wall to get in and out."

The stone wall around the cemetery stood maybe four feet tall, easy enough to climb. "And what? He ran through the cemetery with a stiff? It's not like the body would bend or anything. You can't sling a corpse over your shoulder, you know?"

"We know," Deanna said. "We don't think it could have been done by one person, but we don't know for sure."

"And the family?" I asked, as my cell phone rang. It sat on Karis' kitchen table. Everyone looked at me as I picked it up and said, "Hello?"

It was Eleanor. "Don't you ever sleep at home? I tried calling you there, but no one answered."

"Well, you got me. What's up?" I asked.

Karis asked everyone, "Coffee?"

We all nodded yes.

"Police car just pulled into the driveway," Eleanor said. It took me a moment before I realized what she was talking about.

"You're still . . . doing that job?" I asked. It was a break, a lead.

"Yeah, only I must have dozed off. I had the car windows open a crack. I was keeping down and out of site so no one would see a car parked on the road with a lady in it, you know?"

"Good thinking." Asleep. Figures.

"Yeah, and at least it's a nice looking car, so it doesn't attract attention. You didn't tell me it was a private tract. I found a house where no one was home and parked closer to their driveway than anyone else's," Eleanor said.

"Remind me to give you a raise."

"Don't tease," she said. "Anyway, the squawking of police radios woke me."

"And?"

"And, right, right now, two police officers are going to the front door. Hold on."

I smiled at Tommy and Deanna. They were more than intrigued by my middle of the night telephone call. I could see it in Tommy's eyes. He wanted to rip the phone out of my hand and see who was on the other line. Curiosity, I would warn, killed the cat—but I didn't have to say anything. Tommy kept his paws to himself.

"I hear them all mumbling, but I can't make out . . . oh man," Eleanor said.

"What?"

"The wife, Philip's wife . . . she's crying and punching the policeman on the chest. Her husband's trying to stop her."

"Just keep watching the house, all right? Stay there. After the police leave . . . don't fall asleep. If Mr. Edwards goes anywhere, follow him."

"Got it."

We hung up.

"What the Hell was that?" Deanna asked. "You got a spy watching Philip Edwards?"

"You could say that," I said.

"Tom?" Deana said, looking for support.

"What's your angle?" Tommy asked.

"Angle? I don't have an angle." I had to give them more. At this point there seemed no way around it. We all moved into the kitchen and while we sipped coffee I told Tommy and his partner, nearly everything, trying to leave out as much of the mumbo-jumbo as I could. From the looks on their faces, it didn't matter. They didn't believe a word of it.

"Nick, if I felt like playing games I'd have called and had everyone over to my place, see what I'm saying? But this," Tommy said, standing up, "this is nuts. You think I'm gonna let you just keep pulling my chain? A serial killer is on the loose, and a body has been stolen from the mausoleum, if you find these things amusing, then you are one sick and pathetic bastard. I don't have time for this. None. We came here tonight and confided in you. We need help. We do. I thought you'd be man enough to lend a hand. But you can't handle it. I didn't expect this from you, Tartaglia. I have no idea what's going through your mind right now . . . but I bet I could guess," Tommy said.

I shrugged. Guess. I wasn't going to stop him. He was making a total ass out of himself.

"You think you're better than the police. I don't know what's with you. We can solve the case together, you know. Deanna and I aren't proud like you, we would tell the press, or the news channels, or whoever it is you've got in your mind, that you helped," Tommy said.

"You know what," I said. "I think I'd like for you to leave."

"What makes you think we'd stay," Tommy said as he and his partner stood up.

"Why you holding out?" Deanna asked.

"Think what you want. What I just told you is the truth. It sounds hard to believe. Hell, I'm knee deep in it and I don't want to believe it," I said.

"It's not that I don't want to believe, Nick. No, it's that there's not a chance in Hell I will believe it," Tommy said as he opened Karis' front door. "You know, maybe your old boss at Safehouse was right, talking to ghosts and all, maybe you are a little off your rocker."

I pushed my brother-in-law. He may not have any way of knowing it, but he just insulted Karis. He was mocking the ghost—he was mocking Karis' dead daughter. Deanna grabbed me and held me back while Tommy straightened his tie.

"Stop it, just stop it!" Karis was upset and crying.

"Get out," I said. "Now."

Deanna let me go just as I was shrugging off her restraining hold. She took a defense step back, ready for anything. I laughed. "You two are pathetic. Get out."

"And Nick . . . better pull your spy out," Tommy warned.

"Hey Tommy," I said. I wanted to hit below the belt. I wanted to get mean and nasty, but I thought of my sister at home with my nephew. They were alone tonight, again. Tommy didn't need me to pick him apart. He was doing it to himself. "Drive safe."

I slammed the door, picked up my cell phone and ordered Eleanor to go home for the night.

CHAPTER 52

Sunday, June 1

Though Karis and I went back to bed last night or at four this morning, I barely slept. When I did manage to drift, the sleep was fitful. Unaccountable nightmares woke me. Karis confided that the rest of her night hadn't been much different. We went out for breakfast, to our favorite spot, and talked. There was much to talk about, too. News of the mausoleum break-in covered the front page of the Democrat & Chronicle and had been on the television since early this morning.

"I still can't believe the way your brother-in-law acted last night, my God he was like a raving lunatic," Karis said.

"Stress. Man doesn't know if he's coming or going. The more I think about it . . . what if someone told you the same story I told him last night. Would you be inclined to accept it?"

"I heard the same story and I accepted it," Karis said, smiling. I reached across the table and held her hand. "Let's forget about him and move on. What are we going to do?"

I had told Karis last night in bed about my phone call with Eleanor. "We're going to want to keep her around. I called her this morning while you were in the shower. I asked her to meet us here for breakfast. I have this feeling, but I don't want people panicking?" I hadn't revealed much, but I wasn't ready to start blabbing my theory. Things looked bad. I thought they might get a lot worse.

"What can I do?"

"Nothing."

"What the Hell's that supposed to mean? I'm helping, Nick."

"This is dangerous. Eleanor—she's training to become a police officer, or better."

"And what about me?" Karis asked.

What was I to say? You're a writer. "I want you safe."

"I'd rather be helping, than sitting home scared wondering what's going on," Karis said. She gave my hand a squeeze. "I'm helping, Nicholas. I'm in this all the way."

As the waitress set our breakfast plates down, Eleanor walked into the restaurant and slid into the booth next to me. "Can I get the same as her?" Eleanor asked. "And a coffee?"

After Eleanor got her coffee I gave the both of them a run down.

"So I go back to watching Lydia?" Eleanor asked.

"You might even want to make contact with her. Stay in the apartment with her . . . take her out, or something," I said.

"So I get an expense account?"

This had become a free-bee now that Scannella wasn't paying the tab. "Yeah, an expense account. Very small. Keep the receipts," I instructed.

"And I watch Edwards," Karis said confidently.

"Watch him. That's all. Don't get near him. If he's doing something wrong like, I don't know, killing someone? Don't go near him. Call for help, call the police . . . you have a cell phone in that purse. Keep it in your hand at all times. Dial the nine and the one and keep your thumb hovering over the one. Know what I mean?"

"Sure boss," Karis said.

"And what are you going to do?" Eleanor asked.

"Me? I've got a lot to do," I said. "The question is, where do I start?"

CHAPTER 53

When I arrived at the shop, Frieda VanValkenschmidt had been dusting. She was not expecting me, nor did she look happy to see me. Actually, she just did not look happy. I stood by the door until it closed. Frieda looked away and went back to the menial task. She did not greet me. Shoot the messenger!

"How are you holding up?" I asked softly. If I'd been wearing a hat, I'd have taken it off. It would be in my hands, and I'd be fidgeting with the brim. Since I wasn't wearing a hat, I had absolutely no idea what to do with my hands. "Frieda, I need to talk to you some more."

Frieda, without looking back, walked behind her counter and disappeared into her back room. I went after her. "Frieda, I think I might have an idea about what's going on. I think I might know what's going to happen next . . . and I'm scared on this one. I need help," I said. I was yelling in the dark back room. I did not know if she could hear me. I had no clue how large this room might be, or where it might snake around too. "Frieda, I need your help."

Again, from behind me, out popped Frieda. "Why? Why me?"

"Because you're a witch," I said.

"I saw the news this morning. I read the paper," she said. "I know why you're here, and I think yes. I think you're right. But what makes you think I can help? What makes you think I would help, even if I could? Damn it, Nicholas, you have no right to come in here and ask me to risk my life. None!"

I shook my head. "Frieda, I have no one else to ask." I didn't have to say more. We both knew what I meant when I didn't say it. Jasmine had helped—and would still be helping. She'd help from the grave, if she could. Jasmine was Jasmine. Frieda was Frieda.

"No."

"You're going to turn your back," I said.

"No. Now get out." She pointed at the darkness of her room.

"Don't do this. Don't say no. Think about it, at least, all right? Just think about it."

Frieda laughed. "Think about it? Since yesterday . . . since you walked in yesterday I've been thinking about it. It, and everything else. Jasmine was a wonderful girl . . . a woman. She's gone," Frieda said. Her teeth clenched and she nearly spat in my face when she continued, "Brutally murdered. Violently killed!"

"We need to stop the killer," I said.

"If we're right . . . then the killings will stop," Frieda said. She paused and looked down. I could barely see her. The room was far too dark. The dim black light shown on the ceiling stayed on the ceiling and did nothing for the rest of the room.

"What? What are you thinking?"

She took my hand and led me behind a black sheet into her library. The tiny desk lamp burned. "I've got to think about this. There might be one more death . . . a sacrificial death," Frieda said. She ran her hands through her hair in frustration. "But then who knows. If things go the way they could . . . the killing might never stop!"

"That's my point," I said. "Does this mean you'll help?"

Frieda closed her eyes. She clasped her hands together. I noted that around her neck she was wearing Jasmine's charm, black shoelace and all. When Frieda opened her eyes, she looked peaceful.

"Well?" I asked.

"Well, how can I not? Right? Right."

I nearly cheered. Instead she wrapped her arms around me and we hugged. "I am doing this for two reasons," Frieda whispered in my ear. "What we are going to do is right. And the right thing needs to get done."

She pulled out of the hug, but stood squarely with her hands planted on my shoulders.

"And the other reason?" I asked.

"Because I want to get the bastard that murdered my Jasmine."

CHAPTER 54

Frieda filled a suede bag with some herbs and charms and threw in a bunch of other stuff. "I'm going to need a few other things, but I don't have the stuff here. Want to take a ride to Jasmine's store?" She held up a key ring. "I've got a key."

For a lot of the ride we talked about nothing. The issue we wanted to discuss most was kept out of the conversation. A pinball of fear pinged and panged around in my belly, bouncing off this and ricocheting off that. I thought I might throw up.

I pulled the car down the road and stopped in front of Jasmine's store. A "Closed" sign hung on the front door. "I'll just be a minute," Frieda said. She climbed out of the car and using her key, let herself in the Magic Circle.

I got out of the car too. Casually I strolled down the empty street toward the High Falls Bridge. My nerves felt shot. The last few weeks had taken a toll on my body. The last year has been indescribable. I always knew evil existed in the world. I never once doubted the existence of Satan. If someone told me I'd be this close to Hell all of the time, I'd never believe it. But, now, being this close to Hell all of the time . . . I can't stand it.

As I reached the bridge, my cell phone rang. "Hello?"

"Nick," Eleanor's voice said. "Nick?"

"Yes? Eleanor, what is it?"

"Nick," Eleanor said, again. I realized now that she was crying. She sounded hysterical. "Nick."

"Sweetheart . . . take it easy. Are you all right? Eleanor, are you okay?"

I turned my back on the river. The roar was deafening. I held a finger in my ear so I could hear better. "Eleanor."

"Lydia's gone," Eleanor said. "Nick, Lydia's gone."

"Okay. Are you all right?"

"No. No. No. I'm . . . no," she said, sobbing.

"Do you need help, Eleanor, an ambulance?" I asked.

"I'm bleeding. My head's bleeding. Nick, they hit me on the head and they killed Marlow and they took Lydia," Eleanor said in one breath. Then her voice got distant and I heard a thump. Either Eleanor fell, or she dropped the phone.

"Eleanor," I yelled. "Eleanor!"

I kept the telephone to my ear and ran back to the Magic Circle. Frieda was not in the car. I went into the store and saw her fishing through the shelves behind the register.

"See, this was where Jasmine kept all the good stuff," Frieda said, smiling. She must have seen my expression. "What's wrong?"

"We have to go," I said.

"I don't have everything . . ."

"Grab it all, we have to move," I said. "Take my cell phone."

"Why?"

"Call nine-one-one, now. Come on, I'm driving!"

CHAPTER 55

I drove ten to fifteen miles over the speed limit, and only slowed down at red lights. I had Frieda explain to the police that I would meet them at Lydia Henson's apartment complex—and that I'd be making many moving violations in order to get there first. I also told Frieda to have the police dispatcher contact Homicide Detectives Cerio and O'Mara.

I wasn't first when I arrived. An ambulance, a fire truck and three police cars were parked all over the street in front of the complex. Traffic was congested. As soon as it was clear I could not advance any further, I left my car and ran the rest of the way.

After explaining my way through several police barriers, I made it up to Lydia's apartment. Whereas Lydia never had lamps, her room was now lit like a photo studio.

Eleanor was sitting on the sofa holding a compress on the back of her head. When I stepped into the room she saw me and started crying. I ran over and knelt beside her. "You all right?"

She nodded. "They got me from behind. They must have been in the house."

"They? More than one?"

"I don't know. I didn't get to see a thing. I was sitting, well, I was sitting right here, and Lydia was in the kitchen baking cookies. And her brother was sitting in the chair over there. He and I were talking, and then he looked over my shoulder, and started to say something as he stood up . . . it freaked me out. I mean, immediately the hairs on my arms and on the back of my neck stood up on end. It was so weird to be talking to someone, and have that happen. But then, before I could do anything, I felt a bang and saw the ground rush up to meet my face . . . and that's it," Eleanor said. "Marlow's dead."

"Did you already talk to police?" I asked.

"To one of them," she said. "He was just the first policeman here."

"What'd you tell him?"

"Same thing I just told you. And when I woke up, or got up, my head hurt so bad. I had to stay on all fours for a little while. I started calling out for Lydia and Marlow, but neither of them answered me. I forced myself up onto my feet and I went into the kitchen . . . and there was smoke. Lydia's cookies were burning," Eleanor explained. "I just switched off the stove and kept calling for her and for Marlow. So I checked down the hall, and found . . . ah, Nick, I found Marlow's body on the floor next to Lydia's bed."

I hugged Eleanor. She cried into my chest.

My brother-in-law and his partner walked in. I watched them as I comforted Eleanor. They were getting filled in. A policeman in uniform read to them out of his notebook. The cop used his pencil to point at Eleanor and then around the room. Tommy looked at Eleanor and me, and his eyes never looked elsewhere.

"Thank you officer," Tommy said. He and Deanna walked over. The three of us silently nodded to one another. Professional. Our fight was in the past—or pushed out of the way, for the time being. "Eleanor?"

Eleanor lifted up her head. She sniffled, wiping her eyes with the back of her wrist. Deanna pulled a tissue packet from her pocket, opened it and offered Eleanor a tissue.

"You know who we are, right Eleanor?" Tommy asked.

She nodded.

"We just need to ask you about what happened here, all right?"

She nodded, again.

The police officer came over. "Detectives, you want to see the body first?"

Insensitive little bastard, I thought.

"After, Delany. After," Deanna said.

I stood up. "Show me," I said.

Delany looked at Tommy. "Just don't let him touch anything," Tommy said. "Got it?"

The body of Marlow Henson was on the floor. The back of his blood soaked shirt looked shredded. "Stabbed?" I asked.

"Yeah, like a thousand times. Whoever done this, they was pretty mad," Officer Delany said. "Reason I says that is because . . . okay, from what I gather, and based on the lady's testimony, right? They is talkin' and what not, and then some freak comes out of the bedroom and stands behind the girl. Right? How the freak got in the place, I have no idea . . . and we may never know . . . but that's neither here nor there, because there's a freak in the house and at this point of the story, he's standing behind the girl, right?"

"I'm with you," I said.

"All right. So now this guy here jumps out of his chair, as if to stop the freak, only it's too late. The freak uses a blunt object and strikes our lady friend on the back of the head and she goes down. And she's out with a concussion," Officer Delany explained. "So then Marlow charges the freak and the two go stumbling into the bedroom. The freak gets the upper hand and winds up stabbing him in the back. Marlow goes down, and then the freak goes stab happy and just pulls a psycho and hacks away at the body."

Such poetic sensitivity. "That's your take."

"That's right."

I wanted to disagree with him, but the theory was plausible and made sense. "So the freak knocks out my friend, kills Marlow and steals Lydia Henson."

"Yep. We got assault and battery, murder and abduction. Damn."

I had to repeat it. It was the only thing that felt right and worth saying. "Damn."

***

Tommy and Deanna viewed Marlow's body with the coroner. I stayed with Eleanor on the sofa. She seemed to be doing better. A paramedic took care of her wound. The bleeding on the back of her head had stopped, but the bandage had a large blood-soaked circle.

"We're going to take you to the hospital," the paramedic explained. "It's possible you have a pretty severe concussion. The doctors there will want to look you over, all right?"

"I don't want to go," Eleanor said. The paramedic looked at me for help.

"I want you to go," I said.

"Will you ride with me?" Eleanor asked.

I couldn't. "I can't."

"Then I'm not going," she said.

"I need for you to go," I said. "Karis and I . . . "

Karis. Holy shit. I stood up.

"Nick?" Eleanor said. "What is it?"

I even had the paramedic's attention as I pulled out my cell phone.

The other end rang twice before Karis answered. "Hello?"

"Karis? Karis, everything all right?"

"Nick? Everything's fine. Edwards has been here all day, he hasn't moved."

That couldn't be possible. "All day?" I said.

"That's right. I've been watching the house," Karis said.

"You saw him?"

"At one point, yeah . . . maybe three hours ago. I haven't seen him since," she said. "And I haven't been sleeping, or daydreaming either. The man has not come out of his house."

No. That couldn't be right. "Hang tight," I said.

Tommy and Deanna came out of the bedroom. "You have any idea about this?" Tommy asked.

"I thought I did," I said. "I still have someone watching the Edwards house, and Philip's been there all day."

"You're still on that? I'm telling you, Philip Edwards is the victim. His son was murdered in his own house. He did not come here and kill that man . . . it doesn't even make sense. Show me motive? You can't because there isn't one," Tommy said. He wasn't screaming, but he had everyone's attention.

"I want you to leave all of this alone," Deanna said. "Understand?"

I just looked at her, too tired to argue anymore.

"Nick?" Eleanor said. "I don't want to go to the hospital."

I asked the paramedic, "Can I give her a lift to the hospital?"

"I really think she should ride in the van. She took a tremendous wallop."

"I realize this, but can she ride with me?"

"Of course she can," the paramedic said, giving up and closing up his medical bag.

"I know you know this Nick, but don't let her go anywhere," Tommy said.

"You mean like, Eleanor shouldn't leave town?" I laughed.

"Laugh all you want, but that's exactly what I mean," Tommy said.

Eleanor and I took the elevator down, made our way through the crowd of tenants and onlookers, and slid past the press and down the street to my car where Frieda sat on the hood.

"I know that lady, don't I?" Eleanor asked.

"She owns the business downstairs, I'll introduce you," I said.

CHAPTER 56

For the second time I listened as Eleanor retold her version of what just happened, only this time the telling was for Frieda's benefit. I could feel my blood boiling. Anger was filling me up. I had nowhere to direct the anger. "See," I said, "I would have sworn it was Philip Edwards."

"But?"

"But, I called Karis . . . she's staking out Mr. Edwards, and she swears he's not come out of the house," I said. It was murder getting out of the parking jam on the street. Cars were behind and in front of me. The emergency vehicles still blocked the road up ahead, and stalled traffic had me boxed in from behind. Eventually, with the help of an officer directing traffic, the congestion cleared. I hopped onto the expressway. We needed to get Eleanor to the hospital.

"You know what I think," Frieda said, suddenly. "I think we should go check on Mr. Edwards. Just because he didn't come out the front door, doesn't mean he didn't slip out a back door."

"What about his car. He didn't walk," I said.

"Still. One of us can go up and knock on his door. If he answers, we say 'sorry, wrong house.' If he doesn't answer, well, then we've made our point," Frieda said.

It was far from making a point—proving he was home or not—but it was a step in the right direction. I checked in the rear view mirror. Eleanor was not lying down. She was sitting up and attentive. "I say we go. I'll get to the hospital. I'm not worried about it."

So I got off the expressway and hopped back on, only going in the opposite direction this time.

We arrived at Edwards' street and parked behind Karis' car. I got out and went up to her window. "Anything?"

"Nothing, but this is going to look pretty suspicious," Karis said. We were blowing her cover.

"I'm going up to the door," I said.

"Why?"

"I don't think he's in there."

"There's his car," she said, pointing at the driveway.

"What about his wife's car?"

"She has it."

"I don't think he's in there," I said again. "Wait here."

I crossed the street and went up to the house and stopped before I rang the doorbell. I saw a trail of blood on plush white carpets. I cupped my hands and pressed my face into them up against the window. In the center of the hall was a body. I stepped back and kicked the door. I kicked again. I turned around. Karis, Eleanor and Frieda were out of their cars watching me. "Call the police," I said.

I pulled my gun out of the holster, stood back and shot the door handle off the door. I put another round a few inches up, splintering the wood around the dead bolt. I kicked the door and it gave, swinging open.

I recognized Philip Edwards immediately and raced over to him.

He was still alive. A dagger was sticking out of his chest. The blade curved, resembling a continuous "S." "Edwards," I said.

He looked at me. Blood oozed from his mouth, nose and ears. He was trying to talk. I knelt down, bent closer. "We've called for help," I said.

I heard people rushing forward and looked back. My entourage was standing in the doorway. "Keep people away," I said, certain neighbors would begin to emerge to fulfill their curiosities.

"My wife," he said. "My wife . . . "

"You want us to call her?"

"She did this. My wife did this," Edwards managed to say.

He coughed up blood. It sprayed into my face. Revolted, I tried wiping off my skin. "Edwards—your wife stabbed you?"

"She's crazy. She's crazy," Philip Edwards said. Like a vise,

Edwards suddenly grabbed my arm and squeezed. "I killed that Birdie guy. That's it. An eye for an eye. He killed my son, and I killed him. That's it. That is the entire killing I did. But my wife, Morgan . . . "

I sensed a bout of coughing about to emerge and leaned back. Edwards closed his mouth and coughed internally. Blood oozed from the corners of his mouth. His eyes were opened wide and bulging. "Stop my wife, all right? Stop her."

"How," I asked. I was taking it all in. I had no idea what to make of it.

"The subway," he said, coughing some more. Blood seeped out from between his lips and slid like tears down his cheek to his throat. "The subway, under the river."

The subway. "What subway?" I said. What did he mean by the subway? "Edwards? The old Rochester subway?"

He was dead. Philip Edwards was dead.

CHAPTER 57

Well before any emergency team arrived, Eleanor, Karis, Frieda and myself hopped into our cars and left with a plan to meet at the office.

Eleanor refused to go to the hospital. She kept telling me that time was of the essence. I wanted to drop her off so a doctor could look at her, but she'd have no part of it.

Once reassembled, I explained what I thought might be going on. Frieda backed my theory, though aside from the two of us— skepticism filled the room. I also realized now that Morgan had been the woman in the white nightgown in the cave.

"Before Philip Edwards died he told me how to find his wife. He told me the subway. Karis, can you go on line right now and see what you can find out about Rochester's subway," I said.

"Rochester has a subway?" Eleanor asked.

"Had a subway. It was shut down a long time ago," I said. "I remember hearing about it."

"You mean like a New York City subway?" Eleanor asked.

"Not exactly. It was more like an underground trolley," I said. "It closed way before I was even born." The telephone rang. "Don't answer it," I said. Eleanor gave me a quizzical look. "It'll be the police, my brother-in-law, to be more exact. I'm not ready to talk to him. Not yet, not now. He'll only slow us down. Morgan Edwards has Lydia and we don't have long."

"Midnight," Frieda said.

"Huh?" I said.

291

"We have until midnight to find her and stop her," Frieda said. Come on, everyone knows that midnight is the witching hour."

"Karis, anything?" I asked.

"Something," she said. "Okay, okay, the site gives some Rochester history, um, the Flour City to the Flower City."

"And?" I said.

"And . . . December, nineteen-twenty-seven. That's when the subway opened to the public. Here we go. It says here that for the most part the subway tunnels have been filled in," Karis said. "There were two stations, West Main Street and City Hall. It says that these stations have been hidden from the public."

"Filled in?" Eleanor asked.

"Doesn't say that. It just says hidden from the public. And it says that there is two miles of tunnel under Broad Street that is in need of repair, and will more than likely be filled in by the city," Karis added. "Broad Street was constructed on and ran along the roof of the subway."

"In need of repair? What might that mean? It's under ground," Frieda said. "Why wouldn't the city just fill it in?"

"Good place for the city to hide the homeless," Eleanor said. "Makes the streets look cleaner."

"The Broad Street tunnel would lead to the old City Hall," Karis pointed out.

"No. No, that's not it," I said. "Philip said the subway under the river. We need to find where the sub . . . My God I know how to get there." I felt a shudder spill through my body just thinking of the cave along the river. There had to be a passageway leading to the subway. "We need to find where the subway passed under the Genesee River. That in there anywhere, Karis?"

"The subway didn't go under the river. There was an aqueduct that crossed over the river somewhere between West Main and Court Street. That's near where the City Hall used to be on West Main and Broad. There was a subway station somewhere around there," Karis explained, reading from the web page.

"Filled in?" Eleanor asked.

"I really couldn't say," Karis said. "I guess they closed the subway on July first, nineteen fifty-six. At one-thirty-five a.m. to be exact."

"City Hall? My grandmother worked there for years . . . issuing licenses," I pointed out. "I could give her a call. She'd know about the subway."

I called Grandma and talked with her for a while. The group in the room with me waited impatiently, making faces and mouthing the word, Well?

When I hung up, I explained. "You don't rush your Grandma, people. It's bad enough I don't get to visit as often as I'd like."

"Sorry," Eleanor said first. She rubbed my back. "Well?"

"Well, Grandma . . . my own personal historian . . . says that the station wasn't right under city hall, not that she remembered. She remembered riding the subway with my aunts and my mother and her sisters, but couldn't remember much more," I said.

"Nick, dear, darling," Karis said. "You were on the phone with her for nearly a half hour. Was that all she had to say?"

"No. She also invited you and me over for pizza and wings for one day next week," I said, smiling. "Or she'd take us out for Chinese. She said it was your call."

"What about Father Paul?" Eleanor asked.

"Call him," I said. Eleanor punched in a number and waited. When she hung up she said she'd received an answering machine.

"Running out of time," Frieda said.

"Karis, can you keep trying to get a hold of Father Paul? Keep searching on the Internet, too. See if you can come up with anything else. Eleanor and Frieda, come with me. We'll take a quick ride downtown and explore Broad Street and the old City Hall," I said. "Karis, I'll have my phone on."

"Me too," Eleanor said.

"So will I," Frieda added, jotting her number down on a square of paper she tore off the edge of a notebook from Karis' desk.

CHAPTER 58

I drove. Eleanor sat in back, while Frieda sat next to me. Even though we took the expressway, it seemed like forever driving from Spencerport to downtown Rochester. I felt oblivious to the rain. It seemed standard springtime weather, as normal as urinating.

Though I enjoyed talking with Grandma, I had wasted a half-hour. Lydia Henson's life was at risk and though Frieda might be right—and we had until midnight—we still needed to locate exactly where Morgan was keeping her.

Parking was easy. It was a Sunday, early evening and no one was around. Downtown could be mistaken for a ghost town. It must be nothing was going on at the War Memorial—or the streets would be packed and parking would be a major hassle.

I pulled into a lot on Broad Street down near West Main and parked under a light pole. We got out of the car. The place looked deserted.

"So what are we looking for?" Eleanor asked.

I wasn't sure, exactly. "For an entrance down into the subway."

"And we should look, where?" Eleanor asked.

I looked all around. "Grates in the sidewalk, or in the road?"

"Sewer grates?" Frieda asked.

"No. There's got to be a difference between the two," I said.

"How could you tell the difference?" Eleanor asked.

"When you look down them," I said. We broke up and walked around the area.

Within moments, I heard Eleanor scream.

Standing in front of her was a bum. He wore a brown tattered coat, gloves with no fingers, jeans with holes and construction boats with no laces. He had long, stringy gray-white hair with a matching beard. Despite the thick beard, his face looked dirty. He had bags under bloodshot eyes.

"Got a dollar, man?" the bum asked Eleanor. She used both hands to shove him away. The man took a few stumbling steps backwards, but did not relent. "A dollar, man?"

"Eleanor," I said. "Wait." She was ready to slug the guy.

"What?" Eleanor said, disappointedly.

I went around to her side of the car. "Sir," I said, pulling my wallet out of my pocket. His eyes, which had been watching me with concern, now focused solely on the leather billfold in my hand. I removed a five-dollar bill, and held my hand out. "My name's Nick, what's yours?"

"Walter," he said, taking the bill and stuffing it down his shirt.

"Walter, it is very nice to meet you. Walter, can you tell me about the subway?"

Walter stamped his feet on the ground. "The one down here?"

Technically we were in a parking lot off of Broad Street, so I did not think the subway was directly underneath us. "Yes. The one down there," I said pointing at the ground.

"Depends. What do you want to know about it?" Walter asked.

I gave him another five. "Can you take us down there? Get us to the river?"

"Like a tour guide?" Walter said. He combed his fingers through the tangles in his beard, prideful. "I could do that, but it'll cost you."

I smiled. "How much?"

"How much you got?"

"Ten more now, ten when you get us to the other side of the river."

"Fifty now, fifty when I get you there," Walter said with the heart of a businessman and the breath of a dragon.

"I already gave you ten, Walter . . . so forty now, forty when you get us there."

"Deal." I paid the cash.

Walter walked away from us. We stood there watching him. We

were all getting soaked. No one had an umbrella. Walter stopped and turned. "You coming?"

I told Eleanor and Frieda to get back in the car and wait for me.

"No way," Eleanor said. "I'm with you."

"Frieda . . . wait here. You have a cell phone? Take it out, give me the number," I said. I called her on my phone. "We can keep in constant contact."

"I haven't got all day," Walter shouted. I nearly laughed wondering what pressing engagements might be on his calendar for this evening.

I gave Frieda the keys, had her pop open the trunk and removed two flashlights. Eleanor and I jogged to catch up to Walter.

Walter led us down Broad Street and stopped over a sewer grate at the far right of the road. He stood over it and looked at me.

"You're not serious?" Eleanor asked. "We have to climb down that?"

"Or walk another few blocks to a different entrance, what ever suits you," he said. "This is an easy way down, plus, no one is around to see us going in this way." Walter looked over his shoulder. "Place is dead, you know, man?"

I shrugged. What difference did it make? I handed Eleanor my phone and squatted over the grate. I stuck my fingers in holes in the grate and pulled. The thing was wedged in tightly and I did not think it budged.

When I looked up at Walter, I nearly fell over. He had a crowbar in his hand. "I'm not going to hurt anyone," he said calmly. Eleanor looked ready to deliver a karate kick. "Relax."

Walter knelt beside me and inserted the bar under the grate and leveraged it up. I removed the lid enough so we could climb down. I shown a flashlight beam into the darkness and saw a ladder going down the wall. I looked up at Walter. "You want to go first?"

He shrugged, sat on the street and slid his legs down the hole. "Kinda exciting, ain't it?" Walter said with a wide tooth-decay smile.

"We're climbing down a, like, a sewer hole on Broad Street," Eleanor said into the phone. She turned and looked down the street at my car and waved. Eleanor said to me, "She says she can see us."

I climbed down next. I stood at the bottom and waited for Eleanor, who before climbing down carefully slid the lid back in place. When she reached the bottom rung, she took one of the flashlights from me, and together we explored the subway tunnel with our lights.

Homeless people were everywhere. It was raining out, damp. This was a perfect place to get away from the weather elements. Many large steel drum containers had fire burning in them while people gathered around for warmth and to get dry.

"Should shut them lights," Walter said. "You'll upset these people, and draw attention to yourselves, and I don't think either of you would want to attract attention. Especially not down here . . . especially not a pretty girl like you, ma'am."

We switched the lights off. I held mine like a weapon, like a Billy club, ready to deliver a skull-crushing blow if necessary. "Be ready to use the light like a bat if you have to," I whispered.

"Already doing so," Eleanor said.

I had my gun, but did not think I should have it out. Instead, I told Walter, "Let's get moving."

"Sure thing, boss," Walter said and started walking south.

The flickering fire from the barrels made shadows dance. Slowly my eyes adjusted to the dim darkness. I saw young mothers sitting along the subway walls holding infants and children. The homeless had no idea who we were, but knew enough to feel shame. My heart felt like it might be breaking. "How can so many people be homeless?" I whispered.

Eleanor touched my arm. I looked at her, but in mostly darkness, I could not make out her expression. "We're being followed," she said.

Walter was several steps ahead of us. "Walter," I called out. "Hey Walter, slow down."

The man did not slow down. Eleanor and I picked up the pace. The people behind us matched our speed, neither gaining on us, nor falling behind.

The smell of garbage, feces, and of body odor overwhelmed my nostrils.

The further we walked, the fewer people I noticed along the subway walls.

We walked down the middle of the tracks. Walter was so far ahead that I could barely make out his shape.

"And this tunnel will lead us to the river?" Eleanor asked.

"It's supposed to." We couldn't be that far from the river.

Eleanor put the phone to her ear. "Frieda? Frieda?"

"Anything?" I asked.

"Nothing. Reception must not be good from down here."

"I hope she's all right," I said.

The people behind us were becoming boisterous. Grunts and groans echoed off the subway walls. "I hope we're all right. I don't like this," Eleanor said. "Nick, I'm getting scared."

"I've got my gun," I said. "Just be ready."

"Ready for what?"

"For that," I said, stopping. In front of us Walter cowered behind an extremely large black man with biceps and triceps like tree stumps. His head was shaved bald, but he had a thick, curly, black and unruly beard, with no mustache.

Behind the man was a cement wall. We had reached the end of the tracks.

Behind us, the people that had been following began laughing.

"Oh shit," Eleanor said.

CHAPTER 59

"Frieda! Frieda!" Eleanor called into the cell phone, to no avail.

Walter, our well-paid tour guide, had led us into a trap. He stood next to the large man with giant muscles. Two barrels with dying fires stood on either side of the man.

"Big E, this man has a wallet filled with money," Walter said. Big E had his mammoth arms folded across his chest.

Big E smiled. "He has so much more than money, Walter."

"The girl, Big E. I knew you'd like the girl."

Big E had to be like King of the Sub-Level Scum, or some crazy thing like that. Aside from being scared, frightened and worried, I knew I did not have time to dawdle. "Listen, Big E . . . Big E is it? Look, my associate and I are kind of pressed for time," I said. I knew there was not an easy way out of this. I was ready to go for my gun. I had to assume the others down here were armed seeing that weapons were easier to come by than food—or a shower.

"Shut up," Big E shouted. His voice boomed like thunder.

Eleanor stood close to me. She was holding her flashlight like a sword. I should have forced her to stay at the car with Frieda. Damn it, why was she always so stubborn.

"Bring the girl to me," Big E said, pointing at Eleanor.

A man came up from behind and grabbed Eleanor's arm. I spun to the right, came around full speed swinging my flashlight like a baseball bat and connected squarely with the man's head. I saw blood spray as his body rocketed forward. The man sprawled face down on the old tracks. He did not even so much as twitch.

Big E did not look pleased with my reaction. He grunted, and waited, and I knew instinctively that the rest of the people behind us would be attacking. I pulled my gun and aimed it at them. Surprisingly, they stopped.

I handed Eleanor my flashlight, then pushed her behind me. "Stay close."

"I'm on your ass," she said, and was.

"Big E . . . great meeting you. Walter . . . I hope you share that sixty dollars I gave you with these people. You earned it," I said. I had given him less, but that would make his friends mad to think that good old Walter was skimming off the top.

We were far from clear and free—but Big E was not making a move to stop us. No one was tending to the man out cold on the tracks. Everyone was simply watching as Eleanor and I back tracked.

We did not go all the way back to the same exit. I found a ladder on the wall and sent Eleanor up it. I heard her grunt as she pushed on the street lid. It gave and she did not hesitate, but climbed right out.

I aimed my gun this way and that as a warning. No one was close, or trying to get close. Big E and Walter were at least two hundred yards away. I stuffed my gun away and climbed up the ladder as fast as I could, all the while envisioning hands reaching out and grabbing my ankles. When I reached the street—I nearly screamed. I felt like spiders had just crawled all over my body.

Eleanor stood, hugging herself.

We closed the street lid and ran back to the car.

Frieda was standing outside of the car. She held the cell phone in her hand. "What happened? I didn't know what to do. I was going to call the police!"

What would the police have done? Would they have ventured down into the dark subway tunnel looking for us? Did they ever go down there? What the Hell would they think of Big E?

"We made it to the end of the tunnel. It stops before the river," I said. "Let's get out of here."

"But now what?" Eleanor asked.

I told them about the cave—Frieda already knew of it. "I'll bet the caves lead to the subway on the east side of the river, near Court Street."

"Caves?" Eleanor said, shivering.

"You don't have to go. In fact, only I'm going," I said. My mind was a mess. Even if my friends had insisted, I was still the one placing them in danger. "Frieda, call Karis . . . see what's happening there."

CHAPTER 60

11:00 P.M.

Frieda had called Karis and handed the phone over to Eleanor who, in turn, talked to Karis while I drove. I wanted to stop at a sporting goods store—but most everything was closed this late on a Sunday. I settled for hardware store and bought some supplies and transferred them into the knapsack in my trunk. I went south on State Street and crossed over the river and drove down to the Genesee Brewery. I figured after the last few jumps over the RG&E fence, and after I broke into their boathouse and stole their boat, that avenue might be closed to a third attempt. On the east side, I didn't need to worry about a boat to cross the river. I just needed to worry about getting down the embankment.

"She wants you, Nick," Eleanor said, passing the phone up front.

"Yeah," I said.

"Nick, I told Eleanor that I couldn't get a hold of Father Paul, but Nick, the police were here," Karis said.

"And?"

"It was Tommy and Deanna," Karis said.

"And?"

"And what, Nick? I told them what was going on. They want to talk to you. I told them I had no idea how to get a hold of you," she said. "Tommy did not look happy. Remember all that blood found on the walls in that church basement? It was human blood, not animals'

302

blood. I get the feeling they're starting to think that you are a suspect somehow in these killings."

My jaw dropped. "What?"

"I think they want to bring you in for questioning," Karis said.

"Is that what they told you?"

"No, but it sounded that way. What can I do to help?"

"Stay put." I needed to think. In a way it made sense for Tommy and Deanna to draw such a conclusion. I felt like the lady on that old television show, Murder, She Wrote. Damn—in my eyes, anywhere this writer showed up, someone died. I'd have named the show, Murder, She Did. "Did you tell the police about the subway?"

"Yes, I couldn't lie to them."

"I wouldn't want you to," I said. It would have been nice, though.

"What are you going to do?"

"Frieda and I are going witch hunting," I said. "Keep trying to find Father Paul." I told her where we were going to be, more exactly and hung up.

"Witch hunting?" Frieda said, cringing.

"Sorry, bad expression."

I parked on the street near the High Falls Bridge. "Eleanor stay in the car. Keep the engine running. If you need to, drive around, but don't leave."

Frieda and I got out of the car and went to the trunk. Frieda was already holding the two flashlights Eleanor and I had used. She took her bag filled with magical supplies out of the trunk and dropped the flashlights in with the other stuff.

"That's a high bank," I said. I removed my knapsack and slung it over my shoulder.

"So how are we supposed to get down it?"

"I've got rope."

CHAPTER 61

"Are you out of your mind?" Frieda asked. "Rope? This looks like laundry rope . . . like you might string it up in the back yard and hang wet clothes on it."

"It's nylon," I said. "It's strong." I tugged on the ends to illustrate my point.

"I'm not shimmying down the river bank on a rope. I'm not Batman," she said. "Come up with something better."

I didn't have anything better. It was nearly eight o'clock. "Lydia's life may be at stake here," I said. I felt like yelling, so instead I just balled my hands into fists and muttered. "Look, I know it's a long way down . . ."

"What's this," Eleanor called out. She was out of the car and standing over a long slatted grate. "I can't see down it, but . . . Nick, we're standing directly over the cave, right?"

I glanced over the edge of the embankment. "We are, yeah."

"Maybe if we can get down here . . ."

It was worth looking into. The three of us squatted at one end of the grate and lifted. Surprisingly, the grate was easily removed. Frieda shown her flashlight beam into the abyss, exposing ladder rungs fastened into the rock with old, rusted bolts. "You know, Nick, going down this doesn't seem much better than shimmying down a clothesline rope."

"I need your help," I said.

Frieda stared at me for a long moment. "Ah, Hell, Nick. Damn it all to Hell. Let's go."

"Hey guys," said Eleanor. "There's no way I'm staying up here alone."

It was a crazy statement. Eleanor would be completely safe "up here." The evil lurked below. I knew she did not want to go into the cave. She was scared. I was scared and pretty sure Frieda felt the same way. Eleanor wanted to come with us because she was a part of the team. She didn't want to let anyone down. "You sure?"

She smiled. "I wouldn't want it any other way."

I started down the ladder first. Several rungs were missing, and I called up with warning. The rock was wet, damp and cold. It felt slimy, moldy. Parts of it jutted out from behind and I scraped my back working my way down. The hole we descended felt as if it might be getting narrower. Claustrophobia set in. I felt it first in my lungs. I could not breathe regularly. I stopped and Frieda's foot crunched my knuckles. I screamed.

"Sorry, Nick. What's wrong?" Frieda asked.

"What's wrong? Why'd we stop?" Eleanor asked.

"Nick?" Frieda asked.

"I'm all right. It's just a tight space." I could not see down. It was black. Above me I could only see the shadow of Frieda—and more than likely it was only her rear.

"You all right?" Eleanor called down.

I started to climb down the rungs again. "We're moving," I heard Frieda tell Eleanor.

I kept my eyes closed, because I couldn't see anything anyway. I concentrated on my actions. Left foot down. Right hand down. Right foot down. Left hand down. I tried to keep three points of contact at all times, only letting one limb search for a rung at a time. This made it less likely to fall, and I had shared this tip with my associates before we started.

When finally we reached the bottom of the climb, I felt immensely relieved.

"You all right, Nicholas?" Eleanor asked. She held the flashlight between us, the beam point at the cave's ceiling. She resembled a shadowy figure on the opposite side of the light.

"Fine. You?"

"As ready as I'll ever be," Eleanor said.

"Is that the river making all that noise?" Frieda asked, stepping close enough to Eleanor's light to be seen. "My goodness, isn't that just deafening."

"Just," I admitted. I extracted a large knife from my bag of goodies. "I'm going to use this to mark our path." I cut an X into the stone behind me.

"Aren't we going to stay together?" Frieda asked.

"That's the plan," I said. I switched on my flashlight.

"Things never seem to work out the way you plan them," Eleanor added.

"Ready? Frieda, stay behind me. Eleanor, take up the back," I said.

"We know where we're going?" Frieda asked.

I held up my hand. "I have a compass."

"Oh. Goodie, goodie Boy Scouts."

"I always wanted to be one," I commented.

The cave did not seem to have many passages. It did not resemble the maze I thought it might be. We came across plenty of cul-de-sacs, if you wanted to call them that, little areas that were dead ends leading off the main path, but we only encountered two routes that went east. Each time we came to a potential passageway, I'd halt the group and start down it for a few yards just to give it an initial exploration.

When I returned this last time, Eleanor asked, "Anything?"

"Another cul-de-sac," I said. "Come on. We've got to be getting closer."

We walked slowly. A dark street, a dark alley—all meant nothing to you after being in true darkness. Aside from the flashlight beams— there was nothing. No moon, no stars or anything.

I could hear the walls leaking water, dripping, and the sound echoed. It could prove maddening if I'd been trapped down here for any given amount of time. The actual din of the river was gone. I heard the ghost of it vibrating in my ears, but the cave's tunnel ran south, and not upwards, whereas the mouth of the cave had been at the bottom of a large falls. The tunnel still ran parallel with the river, but we were below river level at this point in the path.

"Nick?" Frieda asked. "How can you be so sure that this cave will lead us to the subway?"

"Actually, I can't. I'm playing a hunch, but it's a strong hunch," I said.

"A hunch," Frieda said. "I thought you said you knew this for sure."

"I mean, that's what I said," I said, pressing on, "so I trust my hunches enough to know for sure that I'm right."

"I see," Frieda said.

"He's good on the hunches," Eleanor chimed in.

Then I stopped, and turned and said, "Shhh."

"What is it?" Frieda asked. She stood directly behind me. I felt her body pressed against my back. It trembled. Her hand was on my shoulder and I could tell she was trying to peer around my head.

"I heard something," I said. Just when I thought my heart couldn't beat any faster, the damned little thing kicked into hyper-acceleration. I knelt down. They knelt down behind me. I had no idea why I was doing this. It just felt right.

Images of the crazy woman in the white nightgown flashed through my mind. She had scared me before, and because of that first encounter, I now felt terrified. The temptation revved a motor in me, wanting me to turn and leave.

"What is that?" Eleanor asked.

"Talking, or whispering," I said. I strained to hear more clearly. I could not tell where the sound was coming from.

"You think it's Morgan?" Eleanor asked. I knew what she was thinking. The homeless in the subway had been intimidating. "It sounds like a woman, but are we far enough along that we've reached the subway?"

"I think we are," I said. "Switch off the lights."

We all did so, but were not completely plunged into darkness. A faint flickering of light came from around a bend in the cave tunnel.

Someone tapped me on the shoulder. "I see it," I whispered. "Follow me . . . and move quietly."

CHAPTER 62

The cave tunnel widened and stopped and we were eight feet above the old subway. Below us was what was left of the subway, and just to the west I could see a wall. It resembled the wall at the end of the tunnel on the other side of the river, where Eleanor and I were almost attacked.

The subway tracks were missing, perhaps removed and reused as something else, on this side of the river.

"What the Hell is going on?" Eleanor whispered.

I studied everything and felt like vomiting. Lydia was down there—alive—but terrified. She was on a platform—the place where passengers got on and off the subway. The wood looked old and splintered. Lydia's hands and legs were tied together behind her, hog tied is the term. She was left on her belly, rocking back and forth. Her hair tangled and matted and caught in the cloth wrapped around her head and mouth, to keep her from screaming.

It took every bit of strength I had to refrain from calling out to her. I wanted her to know that we were here and that she was all right.

There was a large white painted circle in the center of the ground—where the tracks used to be. Nine large wrought iron candleholders encircled the white circle, with burning black candles. The flames bounced and danced with every sound and draft of wind.

Morgan stood just outside the circle, in front of a pulpit. On the pulpit were the three books of The Talisman. She had one of the books opened.

She was again dressed in that white gown. This time I saw it more clearly. It was lace and long, reaching down to her ankles. The fabric was fine, and see-through and clung tightly to her body. Her hair looked dirty, greasy. It was long and hung in front of her face, hiding her features. And I noticed, just under the pulpit at her feet, stood a medium sized tin bucket filled with something.

I could smell the strong, overpowering stench of incense, but did not see any burning. The candles had to be scented.

All of Morgan's attention was focused on the object lying in the center of the circle.

The body of Philip Edwards, Jr. was naked and slightly decomposed, lying in the center of the circle. His finger and toenails looked long like talons, and the way the candlelight played on the shadows of darkness, I would swear his body was moving.

We were all silent as Morgan started speaking:

"Crone! I summon thy presence here. Oh friend and companion of night, thou who rejoices in the baying of dogs and spilt blood, who wanders in the midst of shades among the tombs, who longs for blood and brings terror to mortals. Come to me!

"Come Crone! She comes on the wing of the biting blast of the winter wind. Now the mists of death form a thick cloud. From this chilling source, the excellence of North, I draw in my power," Morgan said. She clutched her hands into fists and had curled her arms up close to her chest. She threw her head back and gasped.

She made the sign of an inverted pentagram with her finger and aimed it at the dead body of her fallen son. She lifted a bucket, reached in and the flung droplets of what looked like blood on the ground.

Morgan continued, "By the mysteries of Leviathan, by the flame in the eyes of angels, by the power of the east and the silence of north, by the holy rites of the Crone, Powers of Darkness, and spirits of death, join me here in the dark of this night, for I am a keeper of the legend."

"Okay," I whispered, "what do we do?"

"You were right," Frieda said. "She wants to bring her son back from the dead. She's also the serial killer . . ."

Morgan took the bucket of blood and finger splashed some onto her son. She reached into the bucket and removed a large oblong shaped rock and set it down near her son's head. She had many of these things in the bucket, and placed them all around her boy's body.

"My God," I whispered. "The missing hearts."

Morgan climbed the stairs to the platform, stood over Lydia and said an inaudible chant. She lifted the bucket.

"Ah, God, no," I heard Eleanor say.

Her prayer went unanswered as Morgan poured the bucket of blood over Lydia.

Hog-tied, and frantic, Lydia's body rocked back and forth. I knew she wanted to scream, needed to scream, but couldn't because of the gag. Blind—she was left in complete darkness, unaware of the evil surrounding her.

"We have to do something," I said.

Frieda stood turned around, and before I knew what she was up to, she lowered herself out of the tunnel and dropped to the subway ground. She held the pentagram in her hand, and held her arm out at Morgan.

Morgan watched in amusement as Frieda edged closer and closer with each tiny step she took.

I heard Frieda say, over and over, and louder and louder, "By the dragons light on this June night, I call to thee to give me your might, by the power of three I conjure thee to protect all that surrounds me, so mote it be, so mote it be."

Frieda thrust that pentagram forward like a crucifix at a vampire. She did not seem to notice, or care, that Morgan could care less.

Morgan jumped down from the platform, ignoring Lydia's writhing body. From somewhere, seemingly out of thin air, Morgan produced a dagger. The blade was long and shaped like a petrified snake—very much like the one buried in her husband's chest.

I jumped down from the tunnel, and pulled out my gun. I had no idea how witches fought one another, but the dagger in Morgan's hand made the fight uneven. Eleanor jumped down and stood beside me.

"What does Frieda have in her hand?" Eleanor asked.

"It was Jasmine's pentagram, but I can't figure out why she's holding it that way . . . as if Morgan should be scared of it," I said. "Why would she be scared of it?"

"When I saw Jasmine's, she told me if you hold it with the point of the star aiming upwards, then it is good . . . in honor of God. If you hold it upside down so the star points downwards, then it's evil," Eleanor said.

Morgan and Frieda stopped advancing on each other. Frieda continued to recite her chant. Morgan seemed to be watching all of us at once. Eleanor and I stopped walking and stood on either side of Frieda.

I aimed my gun at Morgan's head. "Eleanor, go free Lydia."

Morgan screamed as if she were being tortured. Her mouth was open all the way and her tongue protruded from it. The ear-shattering cry throbbed as it resounded in my head. I nearly had to cover my ears for protection.

Eleanor moved slowly around us toward the platform.

Morgan ignored Eleanor and turned back to her son. She began chanting again and I had no idea what she was saying this time. The words were not in English.

"Stop her, Nick," Frieda said. She took a step closer to Morgan and held that arm out with the pentagram. This time I noticed something different, and so did Morgan. Frieda lost her edge.

Morgan stopped moving, but did not stop chanting. She turned her head suddenly to face Frieda. Morgan's hand shot out and wrapped around Frieda's.

This time Frieda screamed, and I watched for a split second as Morgan crushed Frieda's hand. Bones broke, and the pentagram fell to the ground. Morgan did not let go of Frieda's hand as Frieda crumpled to her knees.

I aimed the gun at Morgan's head. "Let her go, bitch! Let her go."

Morgan ignored me as if I was not a cause for alarm. She continued on. Her chanting grew more intense, the tempo quickening.

"Eleanor!" I wanted to know how she was making out. I did not want to take my eyes off of Morgan.

"I've almost got her freed," Eleanor called back.

Frieda was crying, as Morgan was now bending back her arm at an unnatural angle.

I wanted to fire my gun, but having never shot anyone before, couldn't. I grabbed it by the barrel and wielded it like a club, charging Morgan.

In what seemed like an eternity, I was caught off guard as I saw the woman's face. Her teeth were elongated like fangs; her eyes were yellow and orange like the sun with black diamond shaped pupils, encircled in blood. Her skin looked like old worn leather, brown and creased and cracking.

My hesitation was the difference between whacking her on the head and what happened next.

She caught my forearm in mid-swing and lifted me off the ground. With feet flailing, I kicked and screamed as a searing and burning sensation cooked my skin where her hand wrapped around my flesh. She held me close to her, her eyes studied me before she hissed and cast me away.

I went down hard on my back, knocking the wind from my lungs.

I rolled myself into a ball and tried to sit up. I was in the center of the circle. I was sitting right next to the Philip Edwards, Jr. corpse.

And his eyes opened. I screamed and tried to scramble backwards. His hand shot out and with amazing strength, grabbed onto my ankle. My gun had fallen at some point, and was at Morgan's feet. I had the uncanny feeling that bullets might not help me at this point.

I raised my other leg in the air and brought the heel of my shoe down on the dead man's arm. His grip loosened for a fraction of a second and I took that advantage to pull free of his hold.

Frieda was cowering. Morgan stood over her, after bending Frieda's arm into an unlikely position, with her dagger raised in the air. The wicked witch was smiling—that much was clear. Her son was back from the dead.

She had raised the dead.

"He needs to sacrifice Lydia," Frieda screamed. "Keep that beast away from Lydia!"

Fearing I might be too far away to do anything, I picked up one of the wrought iron candleholders and lunged forward.

The candle fell out of the holder, the flame went out. The wrought iron slammed into Morgan's side and drove her off her feet. She went down hard and the dagger clattered to the rocky ground.

On her back, Morgan stared at me. I was keeping her at bay—and a few feet away—with the candleholder. Eleanor jumped off the platform and picked up the dagger. Frieda was trying to get to her feet.

Philip stayed in the circle, stayed lying down. Lydia looked safe on the platform. Scared and covered in blood, but safe.

"Everyone freeze!"

I looked up at the window to the tunnel. Tommy and Deanna and three unformed policemen were jumping down into the subway.

Though she no longer looked like a monster—Morgan was a creature. She grabbed onto the candleholder with both hands and yanked the wrought iron out of my grasp. She spun in a circle and whacked me in the arm, sending me reeling. I went down hard and banged my head on something sharp.

Ignoring the sensation of blood seeping down my neck, I got up just in time to see two police officers jump on Morgan as she was about to clobber me with the holder.

She went down, but did not stay down. Eleanor went back up onto the platform and hugged Lydia. I looked at Philip. He was sitting up in the center of the circle.

"Nick what the Hell is going on," Tommy was shouting.

I stood up as Morgan got to her feet. The two officers were down and not moving.

Morgan had blood on her face. It was on her hands and covered her gown. Some of the blood might have splashed when she poured the bucket over Lydia—but not all of it, and not the blood in her mouth.

Philip was walking, slowly making his way to the edge of the circle.

"Jesus," I heard Deanna say. She had her gun drawn and had it trained on Morgan, but she was looking at Philip. "Who the Hell is that?"

Morgan was looking at me. I fell to my knees and picked up Jasmine's pentagram. I held it so that the point of the star was on top, and mimicking Frieda, I thrust my arm at Morgan. "God help me," I commanded.

Morgan hissed like a panther, and shrank back.

"Nick," Eleanor shouted. I could see her with my peripheral vision. She was standing.

Morgan's eyes flickered. They turned from ice blue—to that of the beast, yellow and orange, with black and red pupils.

Deanna dropped her gun.

Morgan went for her. Tommy was ready. He fired two shots into Morgan. The shots sent Morgan forward onto her face at Deanna's feet. Deanna took two steps back.

"Check the men," Tommy said.

Deanna stepped around Morgan's body.

"Who's the naked guy," Tommy asked. It sounded like a casual question—but Tommy was tense and rigid, ready to fight. They were all in an abandoned subway tunnel. He'd just shot and killed a woman. Two of his men were down. Blood was everywhere. Black candles were burning around a white circle where a naked man was slowly walking toward Lydia and Eleanor, seemingly unfazed by everything taking place.

"Philip Edwards, Jr.," I said. I ran forward, holding the pentagram outward. Philip did not react to me charging him. He continued to walk toward Lydia. Eleanor was crying. She held Morgan's dagger in both hands.

I touched the pentagram to Philip's skin as I slammed into him. I heard decaying flesh sizzle and saw it begin to smoke. Now I had the dead man's attention. He turned around slowly.

Eleanor stood up and tossed me the dagger.

"Nick, he's not armed," Tommy yelled.

He was behind me. Somewhere back there was Deanna. They had guns. I was going against a walking-dead man with a dagger and a pentagram. I shouted, "I need help, here!"

Philip walked toward me, backing me up into the circle.

"Drop the dagger," Deanna said. "Now!"

She must have had her gun on me. I couldn't worry about her right now.

"Mister, stop walking. Stop right where you are," Tommy told Philip Edwards, Jr. The dead man did not heed the detective's warning. "I want you to stop, or I'll be forced to shoot."

"Nick . . . drop the dagger," Deanna said again.

"I can't do that."

"Nick . . ."

I turned around. Morgan had Deanna by the throat. The woman, covered in blood, had Deanna trapped in both hands and was violently

314

shaking her head. Gasping, Deanna lost her balance. Morgan pulled her backwards, to keep the detective from gaining any leverage.

"Tommy!" I called out.

Tommy turned and fired. He put a round in Morgan's head. Immediately Morgan's hands released Deanna as both women fell to the ground.

When I turned to see Philip, I was shocked to find him directly in front of me. The man looked dead. His eyes, glazed over and gray, looked lifeless—soulless. The skin was spotted with purplish bruises, especially along his throat and neck.

Philip opened his mouth and a thick, slimy substance drooled off the end of his tongue. His hands reached for my throat. Strong fingers locked around my neck. Thumbs pressed against my Adam's Apple. I felt my eyes rolling, and everything quickly growing fuzzy around me.

I had the dagger.

"Nick get down," I heard Tommy call. "Get down"

I had the pentagram.

"Nick . . . " I heard Eleanor cry out.

Despite the dark room, things got darker.

Somehow I used my left hand with the pentagram to grab Philip's back. I pressed my hand as hard as I could and felt the charm burn through the flesh. Holding him as tight as I could with the left hand, I raised my right hand shoulder high, and then with as much strength as I could muster I drove the jagged dagger into the dead man's heart.

At that moment the pentagram was gone—it had fallen into the burning hole in Philip's back and was now burning it's way through his insides. I hoped Junior did not feel anything—he did not ask to be brought back from the dead. He didn't ask for any of this.

Philip let go of my throat, and while I gasped for air, I watched as he collapsed to the ground before starting on fire. When I turned around, Tommy and Deanna were huddled over the fallen police officers. I jogged over the subway floor. "How are they?"

"Alive," Tommy said. "Barely." He called out for help into his police radio.

"How will they get down here in time?" I asked. Both the officers on the ground had throat wounds. Though I did not see it happen, I'd swear Morgan bit them. It explained the blood in her mouth and all

315

over her face.

Something inside me told me I needed to verify that Morgan was actually dead. Tentatively I walked over to the body and knelt beside it. The wound in her head did not bleed at all. Her body was covered in blood—a mixture of her own, and from others. Morgan's eyes remained open. Even in death they resembled frigid blue crystals of ice. No one could make me touch her wrist to feel for a pulse. My curiosity was satisfied. The wicked witch was dead. Ding. Dong.

I turned around. Frieda was collecting up the three books of The Talisman from the pulpit.

"What are you going to do with those?" I had to ask.

"Put them somewhere safe," she said. "That's what I'm going to do with these. They need to be hidden somewhere safe. If they fall into the wrong hands again . . . well, you know the rest."

A good witch, or not, I did not feel very trusting at this point. Besides, where exactly was safe?

"I'll take them," I said.

"Nick, do you know how powerful these are?" Frieda asked. I stared hard at her. The question was ridiculous. Reluctantly, Frieda handed them over. "That crone brought somebody back from the dead, Nick. She brought someone back from the dead! To the best of my knowledge, no one has done that since Jesus!"

Despite Frieda's continued protest, I went and stood by a burning black candle. "You're comparing a witch to Jesus?"

"No. Not at all. I was merely pointing out a fact, is all."

I held a book over the dancing flame.

"That's evidence," Deanna said.

I set the first book on fire. "So shoot me."

EPILOGUE

Friday, June 13

Pastor Jacob Brown was in the hospital. Attempted suicide. One of his neighbors found him parked in his garage at home. The doors were closed. The car was running.

I picked up a box of chocolates from the gift shop in the lobby before going to the emergency area to visit. When I entered his room, I knew the Pastor was not glad to see me. He looked deeply ashamed.

"Figured you'd be stopping by," he said, lowering his head.

I tossed the box of candy onto his bed. "I had this box of candy and have been waiting for someone to be in the hospital."

"I'm not worthy to receive this," Pastor Brown said, perhaps quoting scripture.

"You getting a room, or they going to keep you here in emergency?" I asked.

"I'm getting a room. A rubber room," he said. He tried to laugh. I knew he wasn't kidding. "I need a rest. I need a break."

"I'll come to visit," I promised.

"I'd rather you didn't. I want to start my life all over, maybe it sounds like I'm hiding. I don't know. But I do know that right now, I don't want to see anyone. But, Nick, thanks for the chocolate."

We shook hands. "Take care of yourself, Pastor. God bless. And, if it's any consolation, I don't think this is your fault. Everything that happened was bound to happen."

"I'm not so sure I agree with you, Nick."

And I wasn't so sure if I agreed with myself.

***

I tracked down Michael David Anthony. He was in the mall, hands in his pockets, perhaps window-shopping. I walked up behind him, tapped his shoulder.

"What are you doing?" I asked.

"Working," Anthony said.

"Working," I said, thoughtfully. "Look, I want to get one thing straight between us. You ever steal anything personal of mine again, and I'll beat the living shit out of you."

"But I didn't Nick," Anthony said.

"Don't play dumb with me, ass face," I said. "You followed me to the airport and managed to get at my bags before they were loaded onto the plane."

"I followed you to the airport, that's true. In no way did I tamper with your bags before they were loaded onto the plane," Anthony said smugly.

"I had that box in my suitcase, Michael David Anthony," I said, almost yelling.

"Now you sound like my mom."

"Your mom sounds like a man?"

He stopped walking. The muscles in his face were moving as he ground his teeth. "If you were any kind of detective, you'd know perfectly well who took the box from your bag."

"Oh yeah?"

"Yeah," Anthony said.

And it hit me. The one place I set my bag down and left it unattended. "Betty," I said out loud. My old secretary. Always reading the mystery novels. Always wanting to be in on the casework.

Anthony started walking away, and I let him go. I had been betrayed by someone I thought I could trust.

***

318

Lynn Scannella, though she did not want to hear anything about what wound up happening to her case, took her new paralegal and me out for lunch. Judy Swanson was working out perfectly—and lunch was Lynn's way of saying thank you. And though Karis was not too happy with my lunch dates, she held it together and stayed strong. I think she finally trusted me. Our relationship just keeps getting better and healthier.

I think the rain was finally done, too. Summer was nine days away and it felt like it might prove to be a hot and humid few months. Though I disliked the rain, I hated humidity. Today the temperature shot up to eight-nine degrees with an equal humidity level.

My sister Arline had invited Karis and me over for dinner.

Before Karis and I left the office for my sister's, I called Father Paul. He was getting ready to go on vacation. The church was going up nicely and he needed a break. He was glad he'd missed all the excitement, and told me, "Nick, you can come to me any time for help . . . and I'll help you, but I am much too old to be a field investigator, like yourself. Do you understand that?"

I told him I did. "And, Father . . . enjoy Arlington." He was headed to Virginia, wanted to see the famous cemetery and visit the Kennedy graves and witness the Changing of the Guard at the Tomb of the Unknown Soldier. He wanted to look up some old friends who died during several wars from his time.

Eleanor made plans to work with me for the rest of the summer and I was glad, and lucky, to have her help. Though this case received mixed reviews from the media—publicity is still publicity. People knew my name and were calling the agency. Even Ned from Safehouse called to congratulate me on helping the police crack the serial murder crimes. He also mentioned that his associate, Michael David Anthony, was duly impressed.

I just had one regret to go with the newfound fame. Everyone seemed to think that I only dealt with the supernatural. Most linked the deal with the Tenth House cult in their articles. A pattern was forming. I did not want to be known as a quack ghost-chaser. I was getting typecast.

When we got to my sister's house, Tommy offered me a beer. A peace offering, I imagined. I took it, but because I was thirsty—not because I was ready to let everything go. I kissed my sister Hello.

"Where is my niece?"

"Asleep," Arline said. "She should be up any minute."

Karis kissed Tommy and Arline Hello. "Can I help you get anything ready?" Karis asked.

"I've got everything under control, but if you want to keep me company in the kitchen," Arline said. She was looking at me. I was staring at Tommy. Tommy was staring at me. Karis picked up on this and nodded and the two women prodded off to leave us disgruntled men alone.

"Want to talk?" Tommy asked.

"I want to go outside and smoke a cigarette," I said.

"I thought I'd heard you quit?"

"I did."

"So why smoke now?"

"I didn't say I was going to, I said that's what I want to do." I smiled. "Let's still go outside," I said. I went out first, sipped my beer and then sat down on the front step. Tommy walked over and leaned against his car in the driveway. "I'd love to see the report from that night."

"You know I can't show you that," Tommy said. He pulled a few folded sheets of paper out of his pocket and set them on the roof of the car. "Reports, such as these, are not allowed to leave the precinct."

I smiled. He was getting close to having me forgive him.

"I'm still not sure I get it . . . or understand it," Tommy said. "Those books . . . "

"The Talisman . . . made up of three rings, heaven, earth and Hell."

"Right . . . they're evil?"

"Can be . . . or could be," I said, since I had destroyed them.

"Okay. That much is easy. So Mr. Edwards and his wife were both witches?"

"Yep," I said. Witch, warlock, sorcerer. Arguing semantics at this point was moot.

"And they had one of these books and that's why those two broke into their home . . . to take the book away, because they feared the Edwards family was full of black magic?"

"You're on the mark, so far," I said, sipping some beer.

"The father uses the books to kill Gordon Birdie, but the mother wants to bring their son back from the dead. To do this she has to kill people and take some of their blood and cut out their hearts. When the husband finds out and tries to stop her . . . she kills him?"

"Sick, but true. She kills him. She'd stolen her son's body out of the mausoleum. She must have dropped it off somewhere and rushed home. They were both home when the police arrived, if you remember correctly. So then she captures Lydia and saves her for her son to kill," I said. The sky was clear. Billions of stars were out. The moon was full, large—looking closer to the earth than I had ever noticed before.

"This is where I start getting confused. Why?"

"Frieda explained to me that the son would need to kill someone within hours of being brought back. We think Morgan chose Lydia since she believes Gordon Birdie was responsible for her son's death in the first place. A complete revenge. Gordon, Marlow and Lydia . . . saving Lydia for her son."

"Damn. That's all sick," Tommy said. "Sick. You'd think I'd seen and heard it all, but after the other night, I don't know what to think."

"If you boys have kissed and made up, dinner's on the table," Karis said from behind the storm door. "And I hear the baby crying. I'll get her!"

"You know what, Nick? I like her," Tommy said. He put out his hand, I took it, and he pulled me up onto my feet.

Still holding hands, I said, "You know what? I love her."

***

Lydia had moved back in with her parents. After the death of their son, they did not like the idea of their little girl being out on her own. I wasn't sure if this was a wise decision, but it was not my place to argue for Lydia's independence.

When I pulled into the Henson's driveway, I saw Lydia sitting out front on the porch swing. I saw her head turn in my direction. She had heard the car pull up, but didn't say anything as if she were waiting to hear the sound of the car door opening.

I sat and watched her for a full minute before getting out of the car.

"Hello?" Lydia said.

"Hello, Lydia," I said, walking up the lawn to the porch steps.

"Nicholas?"

Even though she could not see me, I nodded. "How are you?"

She shrugged, looking lost and lonely. "Want to sit with me for a little while?"

"I'd love to," I said, sitting on the swing next to her. She had a Braille copy of the Bible on her lap. "Reading?"

"A little, not really. I can't concentrate much. I'm finding it hard to focus," Lydia said. "My parents aren't doing so well either."

"I wouldn't think so," I said. "How is it being back home?"

"Different," Lydia said. "I couldn't be on my own though . . . I couldn't stay in that apartment, and I'm not up to moving." Her hands were folded in her lap. Her fingers fidgeted with one another. She had her head down, her chin resting on her chest.

"How are you handling it?" I asked, knowing the answer, but giving her an opening to talk about it.

"I loved my brother so much. Marlow took such good care of me, Nicholas. He was always there for me," she said, crying. "I can't take much more. I can't take anymore. I lost two men that I loved more than anything on this earth. My heart is broken. It has been crushed and shattered!"

I touched her shoulder. My fingers firmly massaged her skin. There were no comforting words to say. Everything I thought of saying would come out sounding like the lie it was. It will be all right. Time will heal your wounds. Your heart will mend. Everything happens for a reason . . . how about, bad things happen in threes and this isn't over yet . . .

"I have my parents, but really, Nicholas, really I'm all alone."

Marlow had been buried only last week. The gravesite was filled with fresh dirt and the headstone was not even in place yet. "I bought some really beautiful flowers," I said softly. "I have some gardening tools in my trunk. Would you like to go and visit your brother with me for a little while?"

Lydia looked up at me, at the sound of my voice, and I watched her expression as tears streamed down her cheeks as she nodded, yes, yes, yes.

We hugged, and while we held each other, I told her, "I will always be your friend, and I will always do my best to be there for you . . . whenever you need me."

The End

About the Author

Phillip Tomasso III is the author of the first Nicholas Tartaglia thriller, *Tenth House* (January 2001). Currently, he is talking with the producer of an independent film company. It is very likely that his novel will be made into a full-length movie. He is excited to have Barclay Books bring back P.I. Nicholas Tartaglia for the second book in the series, *Third Ring* (October 2001).

Tomasso's first novel, the critically acclaimed thriller, *Mind Play*, was released February 2000.

Chosen as the editor for an anthology of collected pieces, *Dry Bones Anthology*, was released in November 2000, and is filled with a wide variety of fiction and non-fiction stories, articles, essays and poetry.

Tomasso is also the author of more than 30 published short stories and articles. His work has appeared in an array of magazines ranging from *Crossroads*, *Ascending Shadows*, *Bathory House*, *Mausoleum*, *Lost Worlds*, *Lynx Eye*, *Eclipse*, *Rochester Shorts*, *Lite*, *Bay Forest*, *Dogwood Tales*, *The Legions of Light* and *Western Digest*, to *Byline*, *Modern Dad* and *Intellectual Property Today*.

Working full time as an Employment Law Paralegal for the Eastman Kodak Company, Tomasso also manages to write book reviews and conduct author interviews for BookBrowser.com, and work part-time as a freelance reporter for a small community newspaper. Phillip Tomasso III lives in Rochester, New York with his wife and their three children. Currently, he is tenaciously at work on his next novel.

The author welcomes you to contact him. To do so, please send e-mail messages to:

ptom3@hotmail.com

Feel free to take the time to visit his web site:

www.philliptomasso.go2click.com

A Spectral Visions Imprint

Riverwatch by Joseph Nassise

When his construction team finds the tunnel hidden beneath the cellar floor in the old Blake family mansion in Harrington Falls, Jake Caruso is excited by the possibility of what he might find hidden there. Exploring its depths, he discovers an even greater mystery: a sealed stone chamber at the end of that tunnel.

When the seal on that long forgotten chamber is broken, a reign of terror and death comes unbidden to the residents of the small mountain community. Something is stalking its citizens; something that comes in the dark of night on silent wings and strikes without warning, leaving a trail of blood in its wake. Something that should never have been released from the prison the Guardian had fashioned for it years before.

Now Jake, with the help of his friends Sam Travers and Katelynn Riley, will be forced to confront this ancient evil in an effort to stop the creature's rampage. The Nightshade, however, has other plans. **ISBN: 1-931402-19-1**

NOW AVAILABLE

* * *

A Spectral Visions Imprint

Night Terrors by Drew Williams

He came to them in summer, while everyone slept . . .

For Detective Steve Wyckoff, the summer brought four suicides and a grisly murder to his hometown. Deaths that would haunt his dreams and lead him to the brink of madness.

For David Cavanaugh, the summer brought back long forgotten dreams of childhood. Dreams that became nightmares for which there would be no escape.

For Nathan Espy, the summer brought freedom from a life of abuse. Freedom purchased at the cost of his own soul.

From an abyss of darkness, he came to their dreams and whispered his name.

"Dust" **ISBN: 1-931402-24-8**

NOW AVAILABLE

Published By Barclay Books, LLC
http://www.barclaybooks.com

A Spectral Visions Imprint

Island Life by William Meikle

On a small, sparsely populated island in the Scottish Outer Hebrides, a group of archeology students are opening what seems to be an early Neolithic burial mound. Marine biologist Duncan McKenzie is also working on the island, staying with the lighthouse caretakers, Dick and Tom, while he completes his studies of the local water supply.

One afternoon the three men are disturbed in their work by the appearance of a dazed female student from the excavation, who is badly traumatized. She tells of the slaughter of the rest of her party by something released from the mound.

Soon everyone Duncan knows is either missing or dead and there are things moving in the fog.

Large, hulking, unholy things.

Things with a taste for human flesh. **ISBN: 1-931402-20-5**

NOW AVAILABLE

* * *

A Spectral Visions Imprint

Dark Resurrection by John Karr

When Victor Galloway, a prominent surgeon and family man, suffers a heart attack while home alone, he claws his way to the phone and manages to dial 911. The paramedics arrive, smile down at him, and, to his horror, give him a lethal injection.

As Victor's life is ending, his nightmare begins. Rushed to the Holy Evangelical Lady of the Lake Medical Center, he is met in the emergency room by Randolph Tobias, CEO of H.E. L.L. "I need your skills as a surgeon to harvest the living and feed my people," says Tobias. "Join us and you may remain with your family. Join us and you will never die again."

Despite his refusal of Tobias' offer, Victor is pressed into the ranks of the undead. Like Tobias and his people, Victor begins to crave human flesh. His humanity, however, refuses to be vanquished. Risking the lives of his wife and son, Victor wages a battle against Tobias in an attempt to stop him and his people from preying further upon the living. **ISBN: 1-931402-23-X**

NOW AVAILABLE

Published By Barclay Books, LLC
http://www.barclaybooks.com

A Spectral Visions Imprint
Spirit Of Independence by Keith Rommel

Travis Winter, the Spirit of Independence, was viciously murdered in World War II. Soon after his untimely death, he discovers he is a chosen celestial knight—a new breed of Angel destined to fight the age-old war between Heaven and Hell. Yet, confusion reigns for Travis when he is pulled into Hell and is confronted by the Devil himself, somewhat disguised as a saddened creature who begs only to be heard.

Freed by a band of Angels sent to rescue him, Travis rejects the Devil's plea and begins a fifty-year-long odyssey to uncover the true reasons why Heaven and Hell war.

Now, in this, the present day, Travis comes to you, the reader, to share recent and extraordinary revelations that will no doubt change the way you view the Kingdom of Heaven and Hell. And what is revealed will change your own afterlife in ways you could never imagine! **ISBN: 1-931402-07-8**

NOW AVAILABLE

* * *

A Spectral Visions Imprint
Psyclone by Roger Sharp

Dr. David Brooks is a front-runner in the cloning realm and a renowned Geneticist. He is a highly successful scientist who seems to stumble into one discovery after another. However, Dr. Brooks cannot find anyone close to him that shares his views on the cloning of humans.

Therefore he works in secrecy on a cloning project and has hidden his most recent discovery, the ability to clone beyond infancy. It is a clone of himself that this successful and secret experiment has rendered. The goal he has in mind is to recreate, in this clone, his twin brother, who had been abducted over twenty years ago.

Though the clone grows rapidly and is identical to David in appearance, a major question remains: Can anyone really clone a soul? Or is the clone an open vessel to an opportunistic spirit . . . a demon? The answer comes to Dr. Brooks soon, and at a cost . . . that of material destruction and the slaughter of innocent lives. **ISBN: 1-931402-01-9**

NOW AVAILABLE
Published By Barclay Books, LLC
http://www.barclaybooks.com

Sci-Fi Suspense

Memory Bank by Sandi Marchetti

A planetary crisis has pulled the world's leaders together in a most deadly period in history. Virus after virus has attacked the earth leaving only a small remaining human population. Even those who have been working on a cure for these organisms have succumbed to them.

What can a planet do to survive? The answer, after careful consideration, came from a scientist in the Mid East. Regression. This theory had been proven in 2010. Now, all the great minds of the past could be brought back and have them forward the planet once again. Greats such as Einstein, Edison, Bell, and hundreds of thousands of others who were instrumental in promoting the prosperity of our earth could return.

Microchips were placed in every newborn child and were to be activated on the child's 18th birthday. Persons already living had these chips implanted behind their ears with activation set for one year after implant. Regression centers were set up in every large city with prominent leaders, expert hypnotherapists, and psychologists in attendance, all practicing a standard protocol. Except for one, in New York City; the August Webster Center wasn't playing by the rules. Unlike the other centers, Dr. Webster wasn't eradicating past memory after he regressed his subjects. They were left holding horrific memories of past lives. Soon, rapists, murderers, and villains of the past were on the streets again. The suicide rate increased astronomically in New York City, and those with new souls did not seem to live more than six months after their regression session.

Upon the initiation of the Webster Center psychologist in session, three professionals take on the task of investigating Webster. A frustrating road they travel, with death as a stumbling block along the way. It is not until they reach the very end that they discover an astonishing motivating past-life factor behind the demise of so many. **ISBN: 1-931402-12-4**

NOW AVAILABLE

* * *

Suspense

The Institut by John Warmus

LaRochelle, France: 1938: "Gently," Inspector Edmund Defont ordered the body to be cut down. Those who did not know him would suspect he feared he might hurt the dead girl—or wake her. The two policemen who worked silently under his command knew his sole intent was to preserve the crime scene. Thus, begins Edmond Defont's police investigation into the nightmares of David Proust, a young, affable priest who dreams and women die. When Defont's prime suspect and best friend both disappear in the middle of the night, his search takes him to the *Institut d'Infantiles*: an ancient Roman fortress in the middle of the Carpathian Mountains in the wilds of Poland: a place that conceals the mysteries of centuries. **ISBN: 1-931402-09-4**

NOW AVAILABLE

Published By Barclay Books, LLC
http://www.barclaybooks.com

Mystery\Suspense

Soft Case by John Misak

New York City homicide detective John Keegan wants nothing more than a dose of excitement. After nine years on the job and countless cases, his life has fallen into a series of routines. He no longer sees purpose in his job or his life, and with each day that passes, he tries to think of another way to break the monotony. It would take a miracle case to restore his faith and enthusiasm. A miracle case he wants, a disastrous one he receives. Excitement he gets in droves.

When software giant Ronald Mullins is apparently murdered, the case falls on his desk, thanks to his eager partner. At first reluctant to take on the high profile murder, Keegan dives in head first, only to find that there is a lot more to it than any one could have imagined. Along the way he will not only have to examine the clouded facts of the case, but the facts of his own life as well. To investigate the case of his life, he'll have to fend off the media, handle his over-zealous partner, and confront conspiracy and corruption which go to the top of the city government.

When the entire police organization turns against him, Keegan is forced to handle the case alone. Armed with a sardonic wit and a distrust of everyone around him, Keegan must risk his job, his friendships, and even his life to solve the biggest case the city has seen in decades.
ISBN: 1-931402-10-8

NOW AVAILABLE

* * *

Mystery\Fantasy

The House On The Bluff by

Elena Dorothy Bowman

A deserted house in New England contains a secret reaching back to the Crusades.

In a White Stone Abbey, situated in a dense English forest, a scroll, which held the secret to the present day Pierce House on the opposite side of the Atlantic, lay hidden in a chamber behind an alter, protected down thru the ages by brown robed monks until the 18th Century. On the quill scripted parchment were words that foretold the future of a dwelling, its surrounding properties, and, through the generations, to its final location in consecrated grounds to a distant land across the seas. It also foretold of the horrendous trials set before it, and who the true owner would ultimately be.

To the day she entered her ancestral home, with its promise of terror or fulfillment, The House On The Bluff maintained its enchantment and its ageless elegance, standing as a silent sentinel waiting for the one long destined to enter with her Consort, to claim ownership.

ISBN: 1-931402-00-0   ## NOW AVAILABLE

Published By Barclay Books, LLC
http://www.barclaybooks.com

Mystery

Death On The Hill by James R. Snedden

As a favor to an old friend, a vacationing Chicago investigative reporter is pressed into action to cover the story. Due to the nature of the killing, it soon becomes obvious that standard police investigative procedures won't be enough to solve the crime.

After the murdered woman's identity is established, it becomes apparent that things aren't what they appear to be. During a visit to the dead woman's office, the reporter notices a picture of the woman and two Chinese men. He recognizes one as the key figure in the Democratic National Committee fundraising scandal, and the other turns out to be a Triad leader wanted in Hong Kong.

Calling on his contacts in Washington, he is put in touch with three local Asian sources in the Los Angeles area to help him dig out information. Enlisting the help of influential members of the local Chinese community and two tenacious detectives from Hong Kong, the mystery is solved . . . but in the most bizarre way imaginable!

ISBN: 1-931402-05-1

NOW AVAILABLE

* * *

Nonfiction Health\Fitness

The Workout Notebook by Karen Madrid

Karen has always had an interest in staying in shape. After the latest fad diet on the market left her with acne and exhaustion, she decided to develop her own plan and devise easy methods that work for weight control. She decided that she didn't want any more suffering from diet plans that were concocted by people who were just plain CRAZY! Her goal is to have *The Workout Notebook* all medical doctors as a natural way to help their patients manage weight control and good health; it is already being used by many with positive results. **ISBN: 1-931402-06-X**

NOW AVAILABLE

Published By Barclay Books, LLC
http://www.barclaybooks.com

Action\Adventure
Vultures In The Sky by Shields McTavish

Lieutenant-Colonel Douglas Mark White, a fighter squadron commander stationed on Vancouver Island, analyzes evidence surrounding the crash of an Arcturus maritime patrol plane: he concludes that the aircraft was shot down by a hostile fighter. Aggressively, Doug pushes for authorities to investigate the incident. Subsequently, large-scale air activity in Canadian air space is detected involving unregistered jet transports and fighters. The armed aircraft are marked with the insignia of the United States Air Force.

Doug attempts to solve the mystery despite the resistance of the Wing Commander, the seeming disinterest of authorities at higher HQ, and a lack of resources. Accidental damage to his eyes, which places his position as a flyer and squadron commander in jeopardy, complicates his quest. Ultimately, he discovers that there is a large-scale drug-smuggling operation flying from Mexico and Columbia to a fake USAF air base in British Columbia.

Doug, despite eyesight difficulties and self-doubt related to the death of a squadron pilot, struggles to defeat the smugglers. His fight to destroy the 'Vultures' culminates in an air battle and personal clash for survival with their detestable leader.

ISBN: 1-931402-02-7
COMING JANUARY 2002

* * *

Action\Adventure\Suspense
Appointment In Samara by Clive Warner

A part time job with the CIA is fun. That's what Martin Conley thinks until one day a dying KGB agent gives him information that changes his life. Conley sets off for the Wadi Hadhramout to retrieve the codes to a biological weapon that can wipe out America. A beautiful Lebanese girl, Alia, acts as his guide. A storm wrecks their boat on the Yemen shore, leaving them to struggle on, and Alia is abducted by tribesmen. Realizing he has fallen in love with her, Conley rescues Alia, and is drawn into a civil war between North and South Yemen.

Conley delivers the codes to his masters but new evidence makes him wonder if the weapon will neutralized —or used against China?

There is only one thing to be done: destroy the weapon himself. Defying his CIA masters, Conley and Alia set off on a mission to find and destroy it—but time has run out. ISBN: 1-931402-25-6
COMING JANUARY 2002

Published By Barclay Books, LLC
http://www.barclaybooks.com

Drama

Do No Harm by James R. Snedden

Three young men with totally different aspirations meet in medical school where they form a lasting friendship. The author follows their lives, cleverly weaving their stories of intrigue and sex, probing the events influencing their lives, ambitions, and career:

Charles, poor boy from up state New York, whose goal is wealth and social status. He sets up practice in the City of New York; however, when legitimate means don't produce financial rewards quickly enough, he resorts to criminal activity, consorting with members of the underworld and making himself vulnerable to blackmail.

Abner, a farm boy from rural Illinois, inspired by the doctor who cared for his family. His altruistic motives turn to disappointment when reality replaces dreams. Returning to his hometown, he is met with resentment and hostility and must decide to leave or stay and fight.

David, the rich boy from San Francisco. The only son of a wealthy businessman, he chooses medical school to escape his parents and their plans for him to carry on the family business. An adventurer and ladies man, tragedy strikes just as he finds purpose in his life.

ISBN: 1-931402-27-2

COMING JANUARY 2002

* * *

Dark Drama

Silent Screams by Annette Gisby

Jessica is a troubled young girl whose life is full of secrets, dark secrets that she can't tell. She believes she would be better off dead than living in the hell in which she finds herself. She slashes her wrists.

Someone is calling her, calling her back from the darkness, the emptiness. The voice is faint but getting stronger. She struggles to open her eyes, but they rebel against the bright lights. Is this heaven?

He is stalking her. He says she has been a naughty girl; naughty girls have to be punished.

Footsteps. Footsteps on the stairs. She hears the last stair creaking. Any minute now. She jumps from the bed and dives underneath. It's useless to hide; she knows he will find her. As her bedroom door opens, she holds her breath and peeks out. First she sees the shiny black shoes and the bottoms of black trousers.

She has always wondered about the black. She has always assumed that the devil wears red. She tries to scream, but no sound escapes from her locked throat. Her screams, as always, are silent.
ISBN: 1-931402-23-X

COMING JANUARY 2002

Published By Barclay Books, LLC
http://www.barclaybooks.com

A Spectral Visions Imprint
Monstrosity by Paul Lonardo

A prominent New England university is slowly falling under the influence of an alien cult that promises to deliver an elixir of immortality to its followers. Jack McRae is the only person in town who suspects that the cult may not be delivering exactly what it has promised. But he is a young outcast whose only connection to Bister University is his girlfriend, Katie. However, after a string of disappearances, Katie falls prey to the Second Chance Cult and its charismatic leader, and it is now up to Jack to rescue her from its greedy clutches. His suspicions lead him on a perilous journey into the inner sanctum of one of the Nation's oldest private institutions. As Jack closes in on the truth behind the alien mystery, he witnesses cult members undergoing bizarre transformations, discovers grotesque insect/rodent creatures hiding in the walls and floors all around the university, and then uncovers the possible plotting of a mass suicide ritual. All the evidence leads Jack to affirm his belief that an alien intelligence may not exist. But Jack soon finds out that what's really going on involves something even more sinister, though very much terrestrial. **ISBN: 1-931402-14-0**

COMING JANUARY 2002

* * *

A Spectral Visions Imprint
The Burning Of Her Sin by Patty Henderson

Meet Brenda Strange. Wealthy. Dead Ringer for Princess Diana. Once a junior Partner in a thriving and prestigious New Jersey law firm, she had everything going for her. But something went wrong. When a disgruntled client goes on a killing spree in the offices, Brenda is counted among the dead. Except she came back.

After learning to cope with her near death experience and newfound psychic abilities, Brenda and her lover decide to move to Tampa, Florida and the house of their dreams. Malfour House is a very old Victorian located in The Tides of Palmetto, an exclusive community for the rich.

But after she and Tina move in, Brenda finds the dingy walls and empty rooms screaming their secrets in her mind. Brenda begins tracing a path filled with murder, betrayal, ghosts, and the deadly curses of Santeria, a dark and exotic religion. Realizing that Malfour House will not let her leave until she unravels the clues to the horrifying murders long buried in it's past, Brenda renews her career as a private investigator.

And if that isn't enough of a puzzle to solve, she must confront the mysterious intruder trying to chase her and Tina away. **ISBN: 1-931402-26-4**

COMING JANUARY 2002
Published By Barclay Books, LLC
http://www.barclaybooks.com

A Spectral Visions Imprint
Watchers Of The Wall by William Meikle

Since the time of the Bruce, dark shadows have ruled Scotland, and lusted after the rich pickings of the nation to the south. The Old Protector staked one King before the Tower of London, thus ending the previous bid for the throne. But now, in 1745, the ruler by blood, the Boy-King, is massing his vampire army and heading south. Only the ancient wall stands in their way, and the watchers who protect it. This is the story of two of them.
ISBN: 1-931402-28-0

COMING Winter 2002

* * *

A Spectral Visions Imprint
Spirit Of Independence Repentance by Keith Rommel

Travis Winter, the Spirit of Independence, has battled the Devil since his redemption. Travis seeks, by direct intervention, to change the evil men do. But every turn, at every intervention, he finds his efforts thwarted by the Devil. For it is the Devil's wish to prevent Travis from earning his way back into the Kingdom of Heaven.

Desperate to save his charges—and himself—from the unseen forces of temptation, Travis follows the Devil into his sadistic world of corruption. What he discovers along the way will either break his faith or bring him to salvation. That is, until an elder Spirit named Wallace comes to Travis and reveals hidden messages in the Bible that show Earth engulfed in fire and destruction. Without immediate change, the world is fated to this foretold ruination.

Now Travis must find a way to keep mankind from such a future. No matter what the Devil and the recently discovered hidden messages of the Bible have to say about it! **ISBN: 1-931402-08-6**

COMING Winter 2002

Published By Barclay Books, LLC
http://www.barclaybooks.com

Mystery\Suspense\Sci-Fi

Time Stand Still by John Misak

When private investigator Darren Camponi is hired to find an old classmate, he considers it a routine job with the opportunity to see a friend from the past. After locating him, Camponi learns that his classmate is working on a top-secret project: time travel. Torn between earning his pay and helping his classmate out, Camponi gets caught in the middle of a conspiracy and cover-up that appears to go to the top of the federal government, and down to his own family. With no other choices, Camponi enlists to help his classmate, and even volunteers to help finish the research, if only to get to the bottom of the trouble.

Along the way, Camponi follows a string of coincidental events, leading from the death of a fellow PI to a conspicuous medical malpractice suit brought against his father. When trouble comes to his family, Camponi will stop at nothing to end the problems, and clear his classmates' name. He volunteers to test the time machine, only to find out his past was better the first time around. **ISBN: 1-931402-18-3**

COMING Winter 2002

* * *

Drama

Angel With A Broken Wing by

Leslie Bremner

Mariah's world is torn apart with an announcement by her husband, Michael, that he is leaving to join a cult. Despite his having become increasingly distant during the past year, never in her wildest dreams would she have imagined this. Apparently love was not enough.

Oak Forest, a sleepy mountain community, beckons Mariah to return to the cabin where she was raised. Abandoned, she must now provide the financial and emotional support for herself and her eight-year-old daughter. Torn apart by Michaels desertion, the future now rests on her shoulders alone. **ISBN: 1-931402-17-5**

COMING Winter 2002

Published By Barclay Books, LLC
http://www.barclaybooks.com

Mystery\Fantasy\Sci-Fi

Time In A Rift by
Elena Dorothy Bowman

A young, beautiful, lonely girl, searching for ancient treasures off the shores of Hawaii, is caught in an undersea earthquake. This opens a "doorway" between the present and the past, and she quickly finds herself immersed in the political events of the islands. These circumstances lead to love, mystery, cataclysmic explosions, and an end to a way of life. She uses special technology to triumph and find her way back home. Most of all, she finds a new beginning when past becomes present as foretold by the legends. **ISBN: 1-931402-16-7**

COMING Winter 2002

* * *

Psychological Suspense
Off Pace by Brittan Barclay

Meagan, a Registered Nurse with a Pre-Med degree, has always wanted to be a doctor. Yet, financial and personal issues have prevented her from going to medical school. So, when a major national pacemaker company offers her a job with promises of community prestige and significant financial rewards, she decides to accept this new career.

Although Meagan builds her assigned territory to a peak, she discovers that success comes with many prices and personal sacrifices.

As the sole female representative among male colleagues, not only does Meagan learn of the unethical and corrupt methods in which business is obtained by others, she begins to suspect that the apparently accidental deaths of certain people with ties to the pacemaker industry are not really accidents. No one takes her suspicions seriously, however. Not until she becomes the killer's obvious target. **ISBN: 1-931402-04-3**

COMING Winter 2002

Published By Barclay Books, LLC
http://www.barclaybooks.com